Praise for Steven Womack and his previous Harry James Denton mystery, WAY PAST DEAD

"As an exotic setting for a regional mystery series, Nashville's got it all. . . . For the local color alone, Steven Womack's WAY PAST DEAD is a real hoot."
—*The New York Times Book Review*

"The third Denton mystery is a little jewel. . . . Toss him into the colorful Nashville musical milieu, and you get a mystery in which the mournful wail of a pedal steel guitar represents death as well as heartbreak."
—*Booklist*

"Womack really outdoes himself in WAY PAST DEAD. . . . An honest approach to detection through the first-person eyes of a lifelike P.I."
—*The Armchair Detective*

"WAY PAST DEAD has action and mystery enough to keep the reader eagerly turning pages all night. . . . Brilliantly crafted."
—*Southern Book Trade*

"Irresistible."
—*Nashville Business Journal*

By Steven Womack:

The Harry James Denton Books
DEAD FOLKS' BLUES*
TORCH TOWN BOOGIE*
WAY PAST DEAD*
CHAIN OF FOOLS*
MURDER MANUAL*

The Jack Lynch Trilogy
MURPHY'S FAULT
SMASH CUT
THE SOFTWARE BOMB

*Published by Ballantine Books

CHAIN OF FOOLS

Steven Womack

BALLANTINE BOOKS • NEW YORK

A Ballantine Book
Published by The Ballantine Publishing Group
Copyright © 1996 by Steven Womack

All rights reserved under International and Pan-American Copyright Conventions. Published in the United States by The Ballantine Publishing Group, a division of Random House, Inc., New York, and simultaneously in Canada by Random House of Canada Limited, Toronto.

Ballantine and colophon are registered trademarks of Random House, Inc.

www.randomhouse.com/BB/

Library of Congress Catalog Card Number: 95-96255

Printed in the United States of America

ISBN 0-345-46188-6

BVG 01

Bed is dangerous country.
                    —John D. MacDonald
                    A Deadly Shade of Gold

Acknowledgments

I am deeply grateful to a number of people who aided me in the research and the gathering of information that was necessary to write this book.

Detective Officer Joseph Ladnier, of the Metropolitan Nashville Police Department's Vice Control/Narcotics Division, was instrumental in acquainting me with the sex industry in Nashville. His years of experience and insight were invaluable. Any mistakes contained herein are mine, not his.

On the other side of the equation were the women I interviewed who work in "show bars" or "gentleman's clubs," which is what we call strip joints now that the term *strip joints* has fallen out of favor. I'm grateful to all the women who took the time and patience to talk to a very nervous novelist about what it's like to dance naked for a living. A few even did so without compensation. Especially helpful was Ally, who worked at Bob's Gold Club in Nashville.

Many thanks as well to Bill Stewart—known affectionately as Mr. Bill—for accompanying me on these research excursions and encouraging me to complete my tasks when I went into shock. Also thanks to Brenda Stewart for being so understanding.

As always, my thanks to Joe Blades for his continued patience, support, guidance, and friendship.

Once again, I am grateful for the critical eyes and sharp blue pencils of my friends and colleagues in the Nashville Writers Alliance and Dr. James Veatch of Nashville State Technical Institute.

Finally, my wife, Cathryn, has provided the most support, patience, and trust of all. Not many wives would calmly understand their husbands' spending an afternoon interviewing a naked nineteen-year-old.

Chapter 1

Don't get me wrong; I like sex.

Really.

It's just that I never—well, I never thought, how do I say this? Never thought *that there'd be so much of it.*

But wait, let me backtrack just a bit. When I was a reporter, before I got fired from the newspaper and entered the glamorous world of private investigating, I got to be friends with an inmate out at The Walls, the old Tennessee State Penitentiary. Many convicts are compulsive letter writers, and the victims of their correspondence are usually either women or reporters.

This particular jailbird was a fellow named William "Baby Face" Yeager, and I finally answered his letters out of curiosity more than anything else. Baby Face—so nicknamed because he was still getting carded buying beer at forty—was a real party animal in his younger days, but one night he passed out half on and half off a railroad track outside Memphis. The Panama Limited came along and whacked off both his legs just above the knee as neatly as if he'd paid a surgeon to do it for him.

His nurse in the rehab home was an African American dwarf named Darnelle. Given that they were now about the same height—and that they considered this a sufficient emotional connection to sustain a relationship—Baby Face and Darnelle soon fell in love. When Baby Face was released with a new pair of artificial legs and a guaranteed four hundred dollars a month for life from Social Security disability, he and Darnelle set up shop in a trailer outside a little town just east of Nashville called Lebanon.

One night, Darnelle and Baby Face got to drinking, and the next thing you know, there was a big fight. Darnelle had a mouth on her far out of proportion to her diminutive size, and she apparently wasn't afraid to use it. Baby Face, who was as intellectually challenged as he was physically, was an unarmed man in this battle of verbal wit. He finally felt he had no recourse but to go after her. No one's ever been able to figure out the exact logistics, but somehow Baby Face got Darnelle pinned in a corner, and then proceeded to beat her to death with one of his prosthetic limbs.

Baby Face pulled "The Bitch" out of it—a life sentence at The Walls—with his earliest parole date set for June, 2047. One has to wonder if the nickname will still apply by then.

I used to go visit Baby Face whenever I felt in need of a good laugh. We'd sit on the picnic grounds, away from the open copulating that took place on the picnic tables nearest the far corner of the chain-link fence, and he'd babble away about the system.

One day we got to talking about how weird life gets without women. I hadn't yet met the woman who would become my first ex-wife, so I was familiar with long dry spells. And he started talking about the ways you handle it in prison, and the hierarchy of sexual release. There were the standard, mostly solitary, ways of course. Then there were the ones more unique to prison: ritual gang rape, girlfriends, and the guys who were, he maintained, the most dangerous men in prison—sissies.

Sissies, he explained, were the men who wore makeup, tight pants, walked with an exaggerated swish, and would cut your heart out if you said the wrong thing to them.

"But how could you, I mean—how could you *do* it with them?" I asked.

"Hey, man." He laughed. "Nobody's chain lays straight."

Okay, so it's not grammatically correct. But it pretty well sums up the human condition. Nobody's chain lays straight. We've all got kinks in our links, little dark corners in the psyche that we'd just as soon not have anyone illuminate. Desires, obsessions, urges, predilections, tastes. Things we'd like to try, even if just once. Secrets.

Only thing is, until Betty Jameson called my office a few weeks ago and asked me to drop by her home in Belle Meade that afternoon, I thought my chain lay about as straight as anyone's. The closest I've ever come to pushing the sexual envelope was dating two women at the same time when I was a Boston College undergraduate in the early Seventies. That was before AIDS, though, and before a whole laundry list of STDs brought the sexual revolution to a grinding—if you'll pardon the expression—halt. Dating two women, and frankly only intermittently sleeping with either of them, was about as risqué as I ever got.

Not only that, it was about as risqué as I ever wanted to get. All my life—with that one exception—I've been a practitioner of serial monogamy, never getting into one relationship without severing another. It was never an ethical issue; I'm just a lousy juggler.

And while that wasn't a pain-free way to handle one's affairs, it was much simpler. I clung to that policy through the frustration of a deteriorating marriage and the frontier of divorce. Even now, I'm deeply involved with only one woman—Dr. Marsha Helms, the assistant medical examiner for Metropolitan Nashville and Davidson County. We've been seeing each other nearly three years now, and in that time, never a thought of straying.

Well, okay, maybe a thought or two now and then. After all, I'm in what is referred to in the Nineties as a "committed relationship." But hell, I'm not dead. At least not today. That could change any minute, though. One of the things I've learned in the past few weeks is just how quickly that can change.

And it all started when Betty Jameson called my office one afternoon and said: "Mr. Denton, I have a problem. . . ."

Every time I drive in Belle Meade, the wealthiest and most exclusive of Nashville enclaves, I get tangled up. The streets wind around, change names, are more confusing than even the normal Nashville maze. The other source of discomfort, though, is that I've never been particularly fond of rich people; they have too much money, and it skews their perspective. Come to think of it, it doesn't do mine any good.

I had an address on Tyne Boulevard and instructions to turn left off Harding Road onto Belle Meade Boulevard, then head toward the Belle Meade Country Club and Percy Warner Park. In theory, I'd find Tyne tucked in there somewhere.

I caught a glimpse of the black-and-gold street sign announcing Tyne Boulevard just as I passed it. I growled under my breath, then made a U-turn at the next break in the median. I made my turn, then fumbled with the note in my jacket pocket to find the house number.

The Jamesons' black, ornate wrought-iron gate caught my attention first. It hung between two redbrick pillars the size of small silos. In the middle of the gate, woven into the iron, was a circle with a cursive *J* in the center.

I pulled onto the parqueted brick drive and nosed up to the fence. A silver box mounted on a curved pole protruded into the driveway. I pressed a green button below a speaker grille and waited.

"Yes?" an older woman's voice asked, nearly drowned out by the buzzing of the speaker.

"I'm Harry James Denton," I called. "I have an appointment with Betty Jameson."

I waited for some response, but got none. Then I heard the clicking of relays and the grind of an electric motor. The gate swung open slowly. I eased the car past as soon as the opening was wide enough, then headed up a long, circular drive that swung lazily around the front of a two-story Colonial mansion.

I whistled softly. So this is how the other half lives. I hadn't had a chance to check out the Jamesons before the appointment. Wonder where it all came from.

I took the brick steps up to the veranda that ran the width of the house. Tall Doric columns supported the wide, two-story-high roof. Oak double doors twelve-feet high slowly opened in front of me, eased inward by an elderly black woman in a gray maid's uniform.

"Hi," I said, stepping forward. "I'm Harry Ja—"

"Come in, Mr. Denton," she said in weary tones. "Miss Betty's waiting for you."

Her voice had been the one on the gate speaker. Her hair was conked—in the Forties and Fifties tradition of fried, dyed, and laid to the side—and laced with silver. She had the proud yet burdened carriage of a woman who'd spent her life in service to wealth, walking the several blocks from Tyne to Belle Meade Boulevard each evening to catch the bus that would carry her home to North Nashville, where she would securely lock her doors and close the shutters before the sun set.

She held the door for me, and I nodded in thanks as I entered. The entrance foyer was straight out of *Gone with the Wind*, with a circular staircase leading up to the second floor seemingly without support. An oversize

Oriental rug covered most of the hardwood floor. Opposite the front doors, a hallway led to the back of the house.

"Miss Betty's in the study," the maid said, motioning to the right. She opened the door and held it for me.

I stepped onto another Oriental rug that covered the floor of a large square room with floor-to-ceiling, built-in bookcases on opposite walls, left and right. On the wall facing the door, two portraits in baroque gold frames hung next to each other above an antique credenza. The one on the left was of a stern yet distinguished gentleman of middle age wearing a general's uniform. Next to it was a portrait of a young Southern belle in an evening gown with a bouquet of roses and a far-off look on her face.

I heard a voice say: "I've got to ring off now. I'll call you later."

A high-backed chair behind a desk that faced the portraits swiveled around. The woman in the chair stood up. Her face was chiseled, patrician; her hair a kind of auburn tinged with gold and more than a couple of strands of white. In the dim light, she was of indeterminate age. She wore a simple but elegant blue dress with a wide lace collar and a long string of pearls.

"Mr. Denton, would you care for something to drink? Coffee, iced tea, perhaps?"

"No, thanks," I said. "I'm fine."

She looked past me. "Thank you, Emily. That'll be all."

"Yes ma'am," the maid said, as she left the room and pulled the door closed behind her.

The woman motioned for me to sit. I took a seat in a leather wingback chair across the desk from her.

"Thank you for coming, Mr. Denton," she said. "I'll get right to the point. I called you because you had the smallest and least conspicuous ad in the yellow pages.

I took this to mean that you're a low-profile kind of investigator, one that can be trusted to remain absolutely discreet in all your clients' matters. Is that assumption correct?"

I didn't have the heart to tell her I had the smallest and least conspicuous ad in the yellow pages because it was all I could afford.

"Yes, ma'am," I said, "that's right."

"What I'm about to tell you has got to be kept in the strictest confidence. If word about this ever got out, then scandal of the worst sort could result."

She leaned back, propped her elbows on the arms of the chair, and made a tent with her hands, the fingertips barely touching. There was a weariness about her in addition to the formality, and when she relaxed, gravity tugged at her face.

"You have my assurance that any work I do for you and anything you tell me will be kept in complete confidence."

"My father is General Breckenridge Jameson," she said. "You've heard of him?"

Damn, I must be slipping. Suddenly it all came together. General Breckenridge "Wreckin' Brecken" Jameson had been one of George Patton's top tank commanders during the tail end of World War II, when Patton was coming up from the south to rescue all those guys in Bastogne the horrible Christmas of 1944. Wreckin' Brecken—so called because as a young captain in 1942, he'd once disabled a Nazi tank in North Africa by ramming it with his own tank when he ran out of shells—came home to Nashville in 1946 a hero, then went on to start his own insurance business. Forty-nine years later, he retired as chairman of the board of the Magna Capital Life & Health Insurance Company of America. Among his many honors was a permanent invitation to the annual Swan Ball and a firmly entrenched position on every local list that mattered.

"Yes, ma'am," I said. "I've heard of him. Only not much lately."

"He's been ill," she said. "In fact, both my parents are ill, and that's why it's so important that this matter be handled judiciously. I'm dreadfully afraid that if my father learns anything of this awful situation, it will kill him."

I leaned forward in the chair and slipped my notebook out of my coat pocket. "Why don't you tell me all about it?"

Betty Jameson stared off somewhere behind me, her gaze intense, unsettling.

"My father married late in life," she began. "And while his business judgments have always been superb, some of the decisions he made in his personal life were, well, not superb."

I made a note, then nodded. "I understand."

"My father is—or was, before he became ill—a demanding and . . ." She hesitated for a few moments, then cleared the tight catch in her throat. ". . . almost brutal man at times. My mother, on the other hand, is simply unavailable. When I was a child, times were different. Not so dangerous for young people. I ran around, sowed my wild oats, but eventually I grew up and managed to survive it all."

She sighed deeply and twisted uncomfortably in the chair. "My younger sister, though, is another matter."

"Younger sister?" I asked.

"I was in college when Stacey was born," she said. "She was a late and somewhat unwelcome surprise in my father's life."

I scribbled again. "That's Stacey with an *e*?"

"Yes. She's seventeen, and she's gone."

I looked up.

She nodded. "Run off, for about the fourth or fifth time. Only this time, I think she's gone too far."

"What do you mean? In what way?"

"She's run off with a man whom I fear may cause her more trouble than even she's used to handling. Stacey has always been a problem. She was kicked out of Harpeth Hall for getting drunk at a school party and running her Miata through a plate-glass window in one of the buildings.

"At which point," she added, "we took it away. Permanently."

Harpeth Hall was the local private, exclusive all-girls school. I'd briefly dated a Harpeth Hall girl back when I was in high school. I thought they all got drunk and drove their convertibles through plate-glass windows.

"That one cost us a pretty penny," she said. "And it was the last straw for the school. Mother nearly had a stroke."

"And your father?" I asked.

"We didn't tell him," she answered, then added, "it wouldn't have done any good anyway."

"Where's she going to school now?"

Betty Jameson mashed her lips together until they were a thin line surrounded by dimpled skin. "Nowhere. She's dropped out."

"Great," I said.

"I want you to find her and get her back here. Any way you have to."

"Well, there are certain legal limitations on what I can do in that regard, but there are ways."

"Don't worry about the legal limitations. I'll take care of that." Her voice tightened. The set of her jaw hardened.

"Okay, I'll need a recent photo, plus her full name, Social Security number, date of birth. Oh, and a list of her friends, if you've got them. Runaway teenage girls sometimes wind up hiding out at a buddy's house for a while."

"You don't understand, Mr. Denton. This is much more serious than that. First of all, Stacey turns eighteen next month."

I shrugged my shoulders. "Once she turns eighteen, she's an adult," I said. "I can locate her, but there's not much I can do to get her back."

"Which is why it's so important to get her back before then." With each word, she tapped her index finger on the desk.

I shook my head. "I don't get it. Stacey's about to be an adult anyway. She can make her own decisions, legally and every other way. I can understand your wanting to make sure she's healthy, but I don't understand why she has to physically be back here."

"That's something I don't wish to discuss."

I flipped my notebook shut, then uncocked my ballpoint. "Something's not right here, Ms. Jameson. It's going to be awfully difficult for me to work for you when you're not willing to work with me. If you're going to ask me to skirt the law, you've got to tell me why. I like to know what I'm up against."

Her voice grew even colder. "I'm afraid that's not possible."

I stood up. "Then you need yourself another boy. Sorry to have wasted your time."

I pushed the chair with the backs of my knees and started for the door.

"Wait a minute," she said. "Sit down."

I turned back to her and lifted an eyebrow. "Lady, you don't know me well enough to talk to me like that."

Her mouth formed a small O. She took a deep breath, held it for a second as the pressure built up. Then she exhaled and relaxed.

"Please?"

I stepped back and leaned against the chair, my arms

crossed, then wagged an index finger at her. "Only if you make nice with me," I said.

Betty Jameson almost cracked a smile, the first one I'd seen.

She stood up and eased over in front of the desk, then crossed her arms and leaned back with her hips over the lip of the desk. "Stacey's run off with a real scumbag," she said. The Belle Meade formality vanished. "A sleazeball of the worst sort. That wouldn't worry me so much, given that she probably deserves the guy. What worries me is that when Stacey turns eighteen, she becomes the beneficiary of an *irrevocable inter vivos* trust. Do you know what that is, Mr. Denton?"

"No, I played hooky that day."

"Well, I probably couldn't define one either, except that I know it means when Stacey turns forty-five, she inherits somewhere in the neighborhood of three million dollars, more or less. If she's not dead by then. Until that time, she receives the income from the trust. The trust officer at the bank tells me that will be somewhere in the region of twenty thousand dollars a month."

I whistled.

"Yes," she said. "Do you know how much trouble an eighteen-year-old, undisciplined, spoiled, self-indulgent, margarita-drinking, cocaine-snorting, bed-hopping little bitch can get into with twenty thousand dollars a month?"

It was my turn to grin. "Don't mince words. Tell me how you really feel."

"I think you can safely gather that my sister and I don't get along very well."

"Yeah, well, I'm a detective, you know. I pick up on these things pretty quick. Why don't you just cut her off?"

"My father, in his infinitely bad people judgment, made the trust irrevocable. No one can cut her off."

Once the stiffness went away, Betty was all right. She even seemed a few years younger. And beneath the expensive clothes and jewelry, she had a body and face that were very nice to look at.

"And that jerk she's run off with, that really worries me. I don't think he'd hurt her seriously; that would be like killing the Golden Goose. But God knows what he'll turn her into. There are worse things even than Stacey, and I'd hate to see her become one. For my father's sake, more than anything else."

"Know the guy's name?"

"No, but one of her friends told me he's called Red Dog. And here's the scary part. He works at one of those clubs, I believe."

"Clubs?" I asked.

She glanced down, embarrassed. "Yes, one of those clubs where women dance, you know, naked. . . . For all I know, he's recruited Stacey."

I rolled my eyes. Just freaking great. There were a ton of nude dance clubs in Nashville, with more opening all the time. It'd be a bitch to find her, not to mention getting her away from a guy who calls himself Red Dog.

"How long's she been gone?" I asked.

"Almost three weeks."

"A seventeen-year-old girl's gone for three weeks and you're just now getting around to calling somebody?"

"It's not like this is the first time," Betty said defensively. "She's always come back before, but usually after a few days. Never this long."

I scribbled a few more notes.

"Listen, Mr. Denton. I don't care what it costs. Send me a bill. If you need a retainer up front, just tell me. But find my sister and get her away from that awful man. And do it before she turns legal."

"And starts getting all that nasty, wicked money," I said. "Can I search her room?"

"Can we do it sometime when my mother's not awake and skulking around upstairs like a ghost?"

What kind of house is this? I wondered. "Sure. Just get me the other information I need. Then I'll send you a copy of my standard contract and you can write me a check for the retainer."

She wrote out everything I needed that she knew on less than half a sheet of paper. There was a lot of distance between Betty Jameson and her younger sister.

"Okay," I said, as I folded the paper and stuffed it in my pocket. "I get five hundred a day plus expenses. Case like this would usually involve just a few days' retainer. Let's say three days. I'll type up a contract and pop it in the mail to you."

"Drop it by first thing in the morning and you're hired."

I walked to the door of the study. "Deal. I'll be in touch."

"Oh, and Mr. Denton," she added. "There's another reason I called you. Not just the ad."

I turned. "Really?"

"I used to read you in the newspaper. You were the best political reporter in the state."

I smiled at her. "Yeah, I was, wasn't I? Why don't you call me Harry?"

She smiled at me from across the room. "Okay, Harry. And I'm Betty."

Emily was waiting in the entranceway and held the front door open for me. Suddenly, from above, I heard the rustling of clothes. I stepped back and craned my neck to look up the circular staircase to the second floor. A drawn, gray face with dark bags under its eyes stared down. When she saw me, she let loose with a muffled shriek and jerked back behind the railing. The padding of bare feet on hardwood floors disappeared down the upstairs hallway.

"Emily, this is a screwy house, isn't it?" I asked as I stepped outside.

The whites of her eyes were more yellow than white, and very bloodshot.

"Mister, you don't know the half of it...," she muttered.

Chapter 2

Nashville, Tennessee, prides itself on two things: country music and its reputation as the buckle of the Bible Belt. We've got more churches down here than a junkyard dog's got ticks. Only thing is, we've also got more "gentleman's clubs," massage parlors, escort services, swing clubs, peep shows, and adult bookstores per capita than any place I've ever seen. We've got one porn outlet down here that claims proudly, in a billboard that hovers over Interstate 40, to be the world's largest adult bookstore.

So it seems the old buckle gets undone every now and then, right? The churches fight like hell to get these places closed down, but they've never had any success. I'll let you draw your own conclusions as to the connection between a plethora of churches and an oversupply of massage parlors. My guess is the words *frustration, inhibition,* and perhaps even *repression* might come to mind. Personally, I've always thought that the reason the churches can't rid the city of the sex industry is that they share too much of the same customer base.

A year or so before I got fired from the newspaper, I got roped into a bachelor party at one of these joints, a place down off Demonbreun Street called Otra Vez. I'd never been in one before, didn't really know what to expect. But whatever it was, I was a full-grown adult male, so I figured I could handle it.

Yeah, right. My jaw dropped so far I damn near had

15

to get a tetanus shot. We walked into the place, and first of all the music's so loud you can't hear yourself think. The ambient light is low, much of it black light. Strobes burst and flash in time to the music, and the place is as crowded as I-40 at rush hour. It's a sensory overload—maybe *assault* is a better word—from the moment you saunter in.

Then it hits you: the place is full of naked women. Oh, there might be a flimsy scarf wrapped around a neck or two, and here and there a see-through baby-doll nightie. But mostly, uncovered female bodies stroll around like nothing's going on.

Well, some of them stroll. Others gyrate, spin, wrap themselves around brass fireman poles, jump, dance, boogie.

Weird. And I don't mean to sound like I'm pulling some kind of sensitive-Nineties-guy bullshit, but the truth is, it was no turn-on. Very, very weird.

Stacey Jameson, it seems, didn't have a lot of friends left at Harpeth Hall. I spent the better part of the afternoon in a conference room at the old mansion that served as an administration building talking to everyone on Betty Jameson's list. The headmistress was very cooperative, concerned about Stacey, even a bit overly solicitous. She was, however, clearly relieved that Stacey's fate at the school had been settled.

She rounded up the girls for interviews and sent them in one at a time. She warned them that the situation was quite serious and was to be kept absolutely confidential. Each of the students seemed earnest and solemn. None had heard from Stacey, either directly or secondhand.

The afternoon wasn't a total waste. The headmistress told me Stacey had once been a good student; not one of the best, but certainly second-fifth anyway. She'd tested better than her grades, reaching bottom of the first fifth on her SATs, and had been expected to get into a decent college. At the beginning of Stacey's senior year, however, it became clear that a change had come over her.

I interviewed two of Stacey's teachers as well, and they both described a volatile yet potentially impressive young woman who had suddenly and mysteriously taken a turn for the worse. No one knew why. She had always been a bit rebellious, but only in that superficial way that the more creative and unconventional students often were. Little things like pushing the envelope on the dress code, chronic tardiness, an occasional display of disrespect or bad attitude.

This most recent change had been far more than superficial. She began losing weight, wearing black any time she could get away with it, and her art class paintings had taken on a psychologically dark quality. She wrote poetry in an adolescent style that mimicked Sylvia Plath, and she read Virginia Woolf. A talented photographer, she became captivated with the work of Diane Arbus and her student projects reflected that obsession.

Then there was the substance abuse. It's not particularly perceptive to note that teenage kids often experiment with things better left alone. Fortunately, the resilience of youth is a built-in protector. Most kids survive the occasional bootlegged six-pack of beer or an evening spent in a cloud of dope smoke and loud music. But if Stacey's former classmates were being truthful, she had gone on to something more serious and, I thought, revealing: downers, coke, God knew what else. She especially enjoyed washing down pills with a big slug of either Scotch or tequila, depending on her mood and what was available.

Stacey Jameson had made the jump from sneaking cigarettes, buying beer with a fake ID, and partying with Belle Meade preppies to sharing Seconal margari-

tas with guys in shiny suits. And she was obsessed with
doomed women.

From that bit of gossip, I drew one more inference
that struck me as both odd and disturbing. Since Betty
Jameson didn't tell me that Stacey's serious emotional
and behavioral problems had all started in the past few
months, I reasoned that she either didn't know it herself
or chose to keep it hidden.

All in all, I figured, none of this was good news.

"Yeah, but you must have felt something," Marsha
said as she slid another carrot across the counter onto
the cutting board. The rat-a-tat-tat of the knife as she
sliced was as methodical and regular as an assembly
line.

"Well, yeah," I answered, stirring a foamy boiling pot
full of angel-hair pasta. I pulled the wooden spoon out
and set it down on the counter. "I mean, you can't help
but notice a room full of naked women. But it wasn't
anything I enjoyed."

She raised the cutting board and wiped the carrots
into a salad bowl full of greens. Then she turned and
pointed the knife at me like a scolding index finger.

"I don't believe you for a second."

"Hey," I said defensively, "it was pretty damn bi-
zarre." I raised my wineglass and tried not to slurp.
Marsha'd been to another wine tasting last week at a
gourmet restaurant in Germantown, The Mad Platter,
and had come away with yet another staggering list of
California wines. This one was a Chardonnay as crisp
and buttery and smooth as any I'd ever tasted. I was
definitely dating above my station.

"Look," I continued, turning back to the pot, which
was now threatening to boil over. "Here I am with a
bunch of sweaty, stressed-out, middle-aged newspaper
reporters and editors in a dark building full of naked
women young enough to be our daughters. And these

guys are yelling and hooting and slathering all over the place, and I'm thinking, *What am I doing here?*"

She came up from behind and wrapped her arms around me. Marsha's a couple inches taller than me, so her chin rested against the back of my neck.

"Good question," she murmured. "The fact that you would even ask it says a lot."

"You flatter me unjustly, darling," I said, reaching down and rubbing her leg with my free hand. "The truth is I was very nervous, maybe even scared. There was a certain, I don't know, hostility to it."

I turned with the wooden spoon in my hand like a teacher's pointer. "For instance, they do this thing where for a big enough tip, a woman gets up on a table in front of a sofa full of guys and does a little special show just for you. Up close and personal like."

"Yeah?" Marsha asked. "What's so special about it?"

"One of the guys tipped this woman a twenty, and she was a big woman, see? Not one of these dainty little wisps. I mean, this woman was solid, and older than most. She hops up on the table, spreads her legs till she's about to dislocate her hips, leans back in a kind of upside-down crab position, and then she—"

Marsha smirked, then turned back to the salad. "Yeah? She what?"

"I don't quite know how to describe it. She, well, *winked* at us. . . ."

"Winked? You mean like?"

I rolled my eyes upward and nodded my head.

She turned away. "Oh, dear."

"And apparently," I continued, "she was quite talented at it, because all the guys were cheering and yelling. Only I was so blown away by it all that I was kind of gazing around the room, my head lolling around like Forrest Gump or something. You know, *naked is as naked does.* . . ."

Marsha giggled and reached for a cucumber, then began expertly slicing it into thin slivers.

"So this woman looks over and sees me staring off at something else and, I don't know, hell, I guess it offended her. Because she pulled herself up into a squatting position and leaned across practically right into my face, and she screams loud enough to hear above this deafening rap music: *'Hey! You're not paying attention!'* "

Marsha's laugh became a cackle just as she swallowed a sip of wine, which then erupted back out through her nose. In a flash, she was choking and laughing and shaking all at the same time. I reached over and yanked off a two-foot section of paper towel and handed it to her. In a few moments, she had her esophageal functions back under control.

She cleared her throat with a deep rumble. "God, Harry, that's incredible."

"Tell me about it," I said, pouring the pasta into a colander. "I thought she was going to hit me. And it goes without saying that all the other guys ragged the stew out of me the rest of the night."

I was shoveling pasta onto two plates when I felt her arms entwine around my waist, followed by soft, hot breath on the back of my neck.

"You know, all this talk about naked bodies . . ."

I stopped midshovel. "Yeah?"

"How hungry are you?"

I set the colander back down in the sink, then swiveled around while still in her arms, wrapping mine around her waist. She bent her knees slightly, so we were nose to nose.

"I don't know," I said. "Depends on what you're hungry for."

"I'm losing my appetite for pasta," she said.

"Okay," I teased. "Let's go out for burgers."

"That's not what I had in mind." She pressed her

right leg between my thighs. I felt a pulse beating in my temples.

Marsha leaned over and gave me one of the softest, sweetest, and most lingering kisses I'd ever had while wearing an apron and holding a serving fork. Then she reached down to my waist, untied the strings with one hand, pulled the apron over my head and dropped it on the floor. I let the fork fall out of my hand; it clattered as it hit the bottom of the stainless-steel sink.

She took my hand, turned, and led me out of the kitchen, down the hallway to her bedroom.

"Let me guess," I said. "When you were a kid, you always wanted dessert first, right?"

"So what are you going to do?" she asked. She sat across from me at the small table in her breakfast nook. It was after eleven before we got back to the by-now cold angel hair. I swallowed a mouthful of salad and washed it down with another sip of lukewarm wine.

"What do you mean?" I was too sleepy and wrung out to segue seamlessly back into conversations we'd left hours ago. Sometimes this woman amazes me. She'd wrapped me in knots until we both passed out from exhaustion, then woke me up and did it all over again. We finally crawled back into the kitchen because we were starting to blood-sugar crash.

"You know," she said, swirling pasta neatly around her fork, "about the girl. The runaway."

I thought for a moment. "I guess the next thing is start looking for this Red Dog character. I didn't have any luck with her school friends."

She took a sip of wine and gazed at me over the top of the wineglass. "I guess that means you'll have to go into those . . . places again."

I paused with my fork halfway to my mouth. "That okay?"

She set down the wineglass. "If it has to be, it has to

be." She paused for a moment, then picked up the glass again. "You know, don't you dear, why you felt so weird about being in that place?"

"Why?" I mumbled, my mouth full of pasta.

"Because, sweetie, it's abuse. Every woman who's ever breathed air understands that. Not many men do."

"Wait a minute," I said. "These are grown women voluntarily making pretty good bucks, I'll bet, for work that ain't exactly heavy lifting."

"Doesn't matter," she said casually. "Doesn't matter if they're getting a million bucks a day. It's still abuse."

I shrugged. "I'll have to give that one some thought." I reached across the table and took her hand. Even late at night, exhausted, half-asleep, there was a spark.

"Look, I'd offer to give the case up, except for one small thing."

"What?"

"I need the money. Bad."

She pouted. "You always need the money. Bad."

"Well," I said, turning back to my pasta, "I can't help it. I have a high-maintenance girlfriend."

The next thing I felt was the cold, slimy impact of a strand of angel hair on my face.

Next morning, I locked myself in my office with a hot cup of Morning Thunder. Outside, the sky shifted slowly through its sunrise colors, with the traffic just beginning to clog Seventh Avenue. Ordinarily, I'd still be in bed at six-fifteen in the morning, but Marsha woke me when she got up at five. She has to be in the morgue by six. Nights I sleep over at her place, I usually dive back under the covers and let her go about her business, but this particular morning, I woke up thinking about Stacey Jameson and couldn't go back to sleep.

I stared out the window as I drank the tea. The sun glittered orange, silver, and black off the twin spires of

the South Central Bell building, which the folks in
Nashville had taken to calling the Bat Building since it
looked like a monstrous rendition of Michael Keaton's
headpiece when he played the Dark Knight.

Where to start? I reviewed my notes from yesterday's
meeting at Betty Jameson's house. Stacey's personal
data—her social, DOB, and driver's license numbers—
were all there along with a couple of pictures. She
looked so young in them. In one, she wore a pair of old
jeans and a Harpeth Hall sweatshirt and was down on
one knee with her arms wrapped around a proud, beam-
ing collie. In the second, she wore a prom dress of silver, blue, and pink, next to a private-school, geeky type
of guy in a tasteful tuxedo. Neither picture revealed
much beyond the stereotypical portrait of a well-off,
blonde, innocent, perky, wide-eyed, teenage girl.

I wondered what had gone wrong. Given all she had,
what made her run off with a guy who bore the nickname Red Dog?

And what about this Red Dog fellow? I pulled the
yellow pages down off a small bookcase I'd bought to
hold my growing collection of resource books. I flipped
through the index and couldn't find a heading for Exotic Dance Clubs, Nude Dance Clubs, Adult Entertain-
ment, or anything like that. But I was shocked to find
there were eight pages of listings in the Nashville yellow pages for Escort Services, and one full spread—to
coin a phrase—devoted to Massages.

Good heavens, I thought. Just for grins, I turned to
the section on churches and counted pages. There were
eleven pages of church listings, versus ten pages of sex
listings.

Yea, Jesus. Sinners down by one.

Back in the Escort section, I discovered that most of
the listings had phone numbers only. No addresses. And
I hadn't realized Nashville was such a cosmopolitan
kind of place. One ad proudly proclaimed SE HABLA

ESPAÑOL, while another declared FOREIGN LANGUAGES SPOKEN HERE.

And what a menu: one could order up blondes, brunettes, or redheads, males or females, chubbies or skinnies, blacks, whites, Asians—although I was surprised to find no mention of Native Americans—and they all took most major credit cards and assured complete discretion.

The only problem was, Betty Jameson didn't tell me Red Dog worked for an escort service. He worked in a gentleman's club. And there were no listings for gentleman's clubs in the yellow pages.

Wait, I thought, there's always the *Scene*. In addition to all our other attributes, Music City has one of the best alternative weeklies in the country, the *Nashville Scene*. Their political reporting was on par with anything the dailies did anywhere in the state—or better—and back when I worked at the newspaper, we regularly got our knickers in a twist because they'd scooped us once again on some saga of political corruption and intrigue. And since they didn't have to answer to staid, conservative advertisers—they don't have any staid, conservative advertisers—their feature stories had a lot more spark. They're irreverent and smart-assed, and I admired the hell out of them, although I never said that around the Legislative Plaza pressroom.

I left my office and walked around the corner onto Church Street. Halfway down the block, a bin on the sidewalk next to machines for the regular papers, plus the *New York Times* and the *Wall Street Journal*, held a stack of the freebie newspapers. I grabbed one and hoofed it back around the corner and up to my office. I spread the *Scene* out on my desk and flipped to the last few pages, where the classifieds and the adult display ads would be.

The classifieds were an interesting enough read in themselves. I never knew there were so many variations: straights wanting straights, gays wanting gays, maybe gays and maybe straights looking for others with a sexual-identity crisis. Leather freaks, vinyl freaks, rubber freaks. People into bodily functions—I'm not even going to speculate about that one. People who like to give pain looking for those who like to receive it. Dominants cruising for submissives; submissives begging for dominants.

I circled the ads for the show bars. The one for Club Exotique was the biggest, along with Otra Vez, Deja Vu, the Classic Cat, Autumn Dancers, the Double Platinum Club, and the XXX A-Go-Go.

I wrote the names, addresses, and phone numbers down on a legal pad. Only problem was, none of them were open this early. I typed up a contract for Betty Jameson, then slipped it into an envelope. I'd drop it by her house later. I had some other correspondence to take care of, a couple of bills to pay, a couple of follow-up invoices on money owed me that had somehow never made it to my mailbox. Just picky stuff, mostly, but by the time I got it all finished it was nearly ten.

I never eat much in the way of breakfast, and since I'd been up a few hours already, I was getting a little peckish. There was a sub shop down Church Street, so I rambled down the street slowly, soaking up the sun and enjoying the day. The summer heat had broken a few weeks earlier, but the dreary winter had yet to set in. It was the best weather of the year in Nashville, and I intended to enjoy every minute of it. Winters and summers are harsh in this part of the country, and when you get a break like this one, you owe it to yourself not to let it slip by unnoticed.

I sat on a concrete bench on the sidewalk and ate my sandwich, drank a soda, and read the early edition of the afternoon paper. Another gay man had been murdered in Cedar Hill Park. Police had descriptions of two suspects, whom they described as homophobic psychopaths. I wondered if they weren't just a couple of redneck idiots who wouldn't know what the word *homophobe* meant if you tattooed it on their butts.

I took another walk after snarfing down lunch and going through the paper, circling the area all the way down to Commerce Street, then along the Convention Center and the Stouffer Hotel, then back up Seventh to my office.

My legal pad was right where I left it. I took off my jacket, checked the answering machine, then sat down in front of the phone and dialed the first number on my list. It rang four times before a young woman answered.

"Double Platinum Club," she said.

I lowered my voice and laid on a Southern accent as thick as axle grease.

"Yeah, Red Dog in yet?"

"I'm sorry, who were you looking for?"

"Red Dog. You know 'at Red Dog, don'tcha?"

"Who is this?"

I mumbled something into the phone.

"I'm sorry, sir. You must have the wrong number."

Yeah, maybe and maybe not, I thought. I dialed the next.

A guy answered. "Deja Vu."

"Hey, has Red Dog come in yet?"

"Who?"

"Red Dog. You know, guy works there, right?"

There was a long silence on the line. "Naw, buddy. Nobody works here by that name."

I hung up, drew a line through the second number, dialed the third. Same deal; first hesitation, then denial. Then the fourth. Again, a voice demanded to know who I was, then dropped back and punted.

The fifth number on the list was for the biggest ad: Club Exotique. Three rings, then a high-pitched female voice, urban black, young, answered.

"Club Exotique."

I shifted gears, tried to throw on my best MTV voice.
"Hey, baby, is that rascal Red Dog working today?"
"Yeah," she said with a chuckle. "But he ain't usu-
ally in till fo'."
I smiled. "Great. Thank you, darlin'."
"Any time, baby." I hung up the phone, grinning.
Damn, I'm good.

Chapter 3

"Oh, Harry, can't it wait?" Marsha sounded tired, plaintive.

"I'm sorry, love, but this case I got involved in is kind of . . ."

"Hot, right?"

There was an edge to her voice that was just this side of ridicule. I couldn't gauge just exactly how steamed she was going to be at me. I'd promised her a month ago that I'd trudge along, but the thought of a private black-tie fund-raising party was about as exciting as filling out my income-tax forms.

"Sweetheart, it's a seventeen-year-old girl."

"A seventeen-year-old girl who works in a nude dance club," Marsha complained.

"If she does, then I've got her back easy. You've got to be eighteen to get paid for taking your clothes off."

"So let me get this straight," she said. "You're passing up a black-tie dinner at my boss's home in order to go to a nude dance club to look for a rich, seventeen-year-old runaway who may or may not be willing to go with you."

"Okay," I said. "I surrender. Just remember this the next time we have a date and you get called in to cut open a stiff."

Silence followed. My point was valid, but I'd probably pushed it too far. It was like my mouth drove off the showroom floor before my brain could issue a recall notice.

"You're right," she said sharply. "Work takes precedence. I should be more understanding."

"I didn't mean it like that. I'll pick you up at seven, dressed, groomed, and housebroken."

"Forget it, Harry. It wasn't going to be much fun, anyway. I'll make your excuses."

"No, wait, I—"

"Harry, I said forget it. Just drop it."

I shook my head in the silence of my office. "Marsha, I—"

"I've got to run. There's a ton of paper on my desk."

"Call you later?" I asked. "Maybe drop by?"

"I'm going to crash early. Just call me tomorrow. If you like . . ." Her voice trailed off.

"What do you mean, *if I like*? C'mon, you know I like."

"Fine, talk to you tomorrow."

"Yeah, okay."

"Bye."

"Yeah. Bye."

There was that awkward moment when nobody wants to let go. Then I heard a click and a dial tone. Damn, I thought as I set the handset back down on the phone, don't I feel like a jerk?

Betty Jameson wasn't home when I dropped by later that morning, so I left my invoice and contract with Emily. Then I headed downtown to do a little research in the few hours left before the Club Exotique opened.

When I started my career as a private investigator, back before you had to have any qualifications to get a license, I didn't have any idea what I was doing. For the first year or so, I skirted about as close to bankruptcy as I'd ever been. Then little by little, things started to break. An insurance-fraud case here, a few background checks there, a couple of cases that got kind of nasty and became public; next thing I knew, I was almost making a living.

A couple of months ago, I bought a computer for the office, then managed to buy my own cameras and VCR, which meant that I didn't have to borrow my friend Lonnie's equipment anymore. Then last week, just as my clunker Mazda was about to burn its last quart of oil, Lonnie repossessed a partially restored 1968 Mustang. The motor had been rebuilt; it had new tires and brakes, and an air conditioner that still blew cold after nearly three decades. The guy who owned it had borrowed three grand against it from your friendly neighborhood money store and never made the first payment.

"C'mon, man, it's a classic!" Lonnie yelled into the phone. "Don't let this one get away from you. Move!"

I had this vision of me as Robert Urich, you know, in a high-speed chase in a bad-ass car with a sexy blonde in the seat next to me squealing. So I rushed down to the finance company office on Gallatin Road two stores down from the big Wal-Mart, feeling the sap that rises when a middle-aged man confronts the notion of buying a really sexy classic car.

Only this really sexy '68 Mustang was a six-cylinder, three-speed, with a big ding on the side and rust on the left front fender. The passenger's seat was ripped down the middle and it needed a new headliner.

"But it's solid, man," Lonnie said. "I checked it out. It'll run forever. You can finish the restoration on your own. And they'll take twenty-five hundred."

I trotted down to the credit union and tried to borrow the cash. The credit union won't lend on cars that old, so I went for a signature loan and was promptly turned down. This hacked me off so bad I took the money as a cash advance off a credit card, which means I'm now paying nineteen percent for a car loan.

Ain't prosperity grand?

At least the damn thing starts every time I put the key in, which is something I haven't been able to say about my last few cars. And that unique faded lime green color frequently gets me eyeballed on the crowded streets of Music City.

I pulled into the parking lot of the Metro property tax assessor's office on Second Avenue just as the employee lunch rush hour was beginning. Inside the building, in an alcove off the reception area, was a long counter lined with computer terminals. From there, any citizen could pull up the tax assessment on any property in the county. I unfolded the *Scene* in front of me and pulled my small notebook out of my pocket.

I started with Club Exotique. When I plugged in the address, the property tax records came up on the screen. It was listed as commercial property, of course, with what struck me as a real high assessment. Historically, property tax assessments in this state had been low because it made the voters happy and got the assessors reelected. In appeals, the state Equalization Board usually sided with the property owner. But as the government got more strapped, with Tennessee voters time and time again maintaining they'd publicly hang anybody who supported a state income tax, the bureaucrats began to go after the landed gentry.

Club Exotique, I noted, was owned by something called K & K Enterprises, Ltd. I pushed a function key on the terminal and the printer to my right buzzed to life. By the time the record for the Club Exotique was printed, I had the records for Otra Vez up on the screen.

That club was owned by something called the Bluenote Corporation. Somebody, I figured, had a sense of humor. I spooled that record off to the printer, then brought up the club called Autumn Dancers.

Autumn Dancers was also owned by K & K. The next club, the XXX A-Go-Go, was K & K as well.

The Double Platinum Club was owned by Bluenote. Just for grins, I borrowed a phone book and looked up the address of the famous world's largest adult bookstore. When I typed in that address, the owner came up as K & K as well.

I whistled. Somebody had quite a little empire going. I typed in two other places; one owned by K & K, the other by a corporation called Camerotica, Inc.

"Camerotica," I whispered, studying the printout. "Sounds like somebody's making *dirty peectures....*"

The receptionist behind me had just finished taking a call when I rolled my chair around and caught her attention.

"Excuse me, ma'am. Can I do a search by owner? You know, plug in somebody's name and get a list of all the properties they own in the county."

"Yes," she answered. "But not through that menu. Hit the Escape key, back out to the main menu, then hit F4."

I did as she instructed and found myself at the top of the shell menu. I hit F4 and typed in K & K Enterprises, Ltd.

In a second, a list of properties rolled by and filled up the screen. Some I recognized; others I didn't. They all went off to the printer.

I did the same for Bluenote, then again for Camerotica. At a quarter apiece, I'd soon burned up the better part of a ten-dollar bill in printout charges. I paid the bill and stuck the pile of paper under my arm as I exited.

Next stop was the secretary of state's corporate service office in the Polk Office Building down near Legislative Plaza. I drove around for ten minutes hunting for a parking space, then gave up and went back to Seventh Avenue where I had contract parking. I left the Mustang in a slot on the top floor of the garage, then backtracked the six or seven blocks to where I'd just been.

I stepped off the elevator onto the eighteenth floor of the Polk Building, then wandered down to the Services Division.

"Hiya', Patsy," I said as I walked in. Patsy—last name unknown—had worked there since before I got old enough to go potty by myself. She'd been invaluable back in my newspaper days, but I hadn't seen her since I'd changed careers.

"Well I'll be sheep-dipped," she said. Her bouffant hair was still cemented into place with cheap hair spray, but it was tinged with a lot more gray then I remembered. "Harry Denton, you rascal, get over here and give me a hug."

I wrapped my arms around her and embraced her with genuine affection.

"A voice from your past, sweetheart," I said.

"Where'd you disappear to?"

"I left the paper, jeez, I guess it must be almost four years ago now. I'm a private detective."

"Oh my goodness," she squealed. "That must be a hoot 'n' a holler."

"It has its moments," I said. "Unfortunately, one of them is right now so this is more business than pleasure."

"It always was with you. What can I get you?"

"Trying to track down the ownership of three corporations," I said. "Can you get me the certifications?"

"Sure, what you got?"

I filled out a quick form and listed the three companies I'd found at the tax assessor's office. Patsy disappeared, then came back about ten minutes later with three printouts.

"Here you go, babe," she said. "Officers, directors, and addresses. They're all legit."

"Thanks, Patsy. What do I owe you?"

"No charge," she said. "Just drop by some time and buy me a cup of coffee."
"You're on, sweetie," I said. "Thanks."

I crossed the river and made my way to Gallatin Road, which is the main drag through East Nashville. It was usually clogged with traffic, with stoplights every block or so all timed so that no matter how fast or how slow you drove, every one seemed to catch you.

A break in the parade of cars opened and I shot into the gap. I headed toward Madison, but turned into the tiny parking lot of Mrs. Lee's restaurant, which served the best cheap Szechuan food I'd ever had. Over the past few years, I'd taken to eating most of my evening meals there because it was almost cheaper than cooking at home.

And given my cooking, it was a hell of a lot better.

I grabbed a copy of the morning paper out of a rack next to the entrance and walked in. My nostrils were assaulted by airborne chili oil and hot Szechuan peppers. It was just past the lunch hour rush; an hour before, there'd been a line out the door. Now, only a few tables were taken.

Mrs. Lee stood behind the counter, a thin sheen of sweat on her forehead. I worried about her, too. It was hard to tell how old she was, but I figured she had to be at least in her late forties. She and Mr. Lee worked six days a week, sixteen or eighteen hours a day, and just in the short couple of years I'd known her, it had taken its toll on both her body and her disposition. The lines in her face had deepened, and her hair had become increasingly streaked with gray. She had about her a weariness that came from shouldering a never-ending burden. There were days when she didn't even have the energy to give me a hard time. I found that most worrisome of all.

To top it off, Mrs. Lee's daughter, Mary, had gone off

to college. Brilliant and beautiful, Mary Lee had won full scholarships to a half-dozen major private universities, and was now in her first semester at Harvard. Mrs. Lee never mentioned it, but she missed Mary a lot. Mary was not only her daughter, she was her only relief at the restaurant.

"Hi, Mrs. Lee," I said. "Lunch rush over?"

"Tank God," she said. "What you want today, as if I did'un know?"

I smiled back at her. "Got any left?"

She turned and shouted something in Chinese back to her husband in the kitchen. He shouted something back, and all I recognized was my name greatly mispronounced.

"Yeah," she said. "Bottom of the pot."

"That's the best part," I answered.

"You learning. . . ."

I took the Styrofoam plate, cup of iced tea, and plastic fork over to a table and spread out the paper in front of me. As I dug into the Szechuan chicken and felt the roof of my mouth go off like a Fourth of July celebration, I flicked back and forth quickly through the sections of paper.

Mrs. Lee walked out from behind the counter and weaved her way in between the tables to where I sat scraping the plastic fork across the plate.

"You mind I sit down?" I looked up at her, surprised. She'd never joined me while I was eating before, and if I ever thought she would, I certainly wouldn't have expected her to ask permission first.

"Sure."

"How da' food, Harry?"

"You know the answer to that," I said. "Incredible. Like always."

She stared through me, almost as if I weren't there.

"Mrs. Lee, what's the matter?"

I wondered for a moment if she'd even heard me, but

decided to let it ride for a while and see what happened. Finally, she spoke as if she'd suddenly snapped back from an attack of narcolepsy and didn't know where she was.

"It's nothing. Nothing. Sorry bother you."

She stood up, the plastic chair scraping across the vinyl floor. I reached out and took her hand, which was probably an incredibly stupid and inappropriate gesture.

"What's going on?"

Mrs. Lee looked at my hand on top of hers, then into my eyes.

"It's Mary," she said.

My heart did one of those jumps that makes you think you're having a heart attack. You get real conscious of these things after forty.

"What's the matter with Mary?" There was urgency, even desperation, in my voice.

She sat back down and lowered her voice. "She okay foah now. But I worry bad foah her."

"Why? What's the matter? Is it school?"

"She meet a boy."

I sat back, shocked. A boy. If Mary'd ever had any interest in anything besides calculus and Greek tragedy, I'd never seen any evidence of it.

"So she met a boy," I said. "She's in college, Mrs. Lee. That happens."

She gave me a what-planet-are-you-from? look. "He odor than her."

"How much older?"

"Two, tree year. He graduate next May."

"From Harvard?"

"Of coahs Harvard. You tink she date UT boy?"

I snickered. "So what's the problem? She met an older boy. I'm sure he's very nice."

"I not want her meet boys," she said. "Very dangerous. Let her finish school, get odor, too."

"Is he Chinese?" I asked.

Her eyes fell. "No."

"Oh, I see. That's a problem, isn't it?"

She didn't answer.

"What does Mr. Lee think of all this?" I asked.

Fear tightened the lines on her face, made them deeper, more taut. "He not know."

"Well, dear, you know things can change. Mary's young, she's away from home for the first time. She's met somebody she likes. Happens all the time. She's a good girl, though."

Mrs. Lee shot me a look with more than a dose of fury in it. "You bettah believe she good girl."

I tried to soothe her. "And I'm sure she'll stay that way. Why don't you give her a little credit?"

"You nie-eve, Harry."

"No I'm not. I just have a little faith, that's all."

"I got faith, too," she said. "Faith that world is damn bad prace and people no damn good."

"C'mon," I said. "Trust her."

"She coming home next week foah midterm break. Maybe I not let her go back."

"That's kind of drastic, isn't it? Passing up a free ride to Harvard because you're afraid she might meet a boy?"

"Kids today. What we supposed to do wit' dem?"

"Talk to her," I said. "Let her know you're worried. Let her know you care, maybe. That's all. But she's a big girl, Mrs. Lee."

"Yeah, dat what I'm afraid of."

"You're worrying too much. . . ," I said, but by that time she'd walked off, disgusted with me, I guess, for not agreeing that the best thing to do would be to catch the next plane to Boston and shoot this daughter-corrupting Harvard senior in the kneecaps. I almost laughed at the thought of her worrying over a girl like Mary meeting someone.

Then I remembered Stacey Jameson and Red Dog

and none of it seemed very funny anymore. Suddenly, it occurred to me that if Mary were my daughter, I'd be worried, too.

I cut through the neighborhood over to Mrs. Hawkins's house, where I'd rented her attic apartment for going on four years now. Mrs. Hawkins had grown increasingly frail over the past year or so. She was somewhere in her seventies, hearing-impaired beyond repair, but until recently had remained nimble and busy.

I pulled into the driveway and braked to a stop. Mrs. Hawkins reclined in an aluminum folding chair in the backyard, her glasses nested in a mass of white hair that spilled down her forehead, her chin on her chest. She felt me slam the heavy car door and awoke with a start.

Mrs. Hawkins fumbled with her glasses and squinted at me. "Harry?"

"Hello, dear," I said loudly. Sometimes she turned off her hearing aids, which lately hadn't helped much anyway. "Enjoying the sunshine?"

She shook her head, trying to bring herself to. "Just resting. When are you going to get rid of that awful color?"

I laughed. Mrs. Hawkins had a way of saying whatever was on her mind regardless of consequence; a trait I admired greatly in old ladies.

I leaned down in front of her. "It's not something you can just wash off. I'll have the car repainted just as soon as I can afford it."

"If I had the money, I'd give it to you now."

"I couldn't take it anyway," I said. "I've got to go change. I might be working late tonight."

"Another late-night stakeout," she said. "You have such an exciting life."

Mrs. Hawkins watched a lot of television. I'd never had the heart to tell her most of my work was spent either on the phone interviewing accident victims or sitting in a car taking pictures of supposedly disabled people for so long my bladder threatened mutiny.

Although tonight, she might be right. This evening would not be like most. As I dressed down in a khaki shirt, pair of faded jeans, running shoes, and a cap with a Hester Battery logo on it, I thought how weird it was to be paid for patronizing the Club Exotique.

Chapter 4

Club Exotique was a square cinder-block building nestled on a side street between Third and Fourth Avenues south of the new convention center. The area was mostly warehouses, plumbing- and electrical-supply houses, and old buildings that had been converted into chic restaurants and dance clubs. The Ace of Clubs was just north of Club Exotique, and some grunge place called Punk Aeschylus filled part of a block a couple of minutes away. Punk Aeschylus was completely black, except for a stark white rendition of its name slashed across the painted bricks. What a fifth century B.C. Greek dramatist had to do with bodysurfing a mosh pit is beyond me. Maybe it's the universal nature of tragedy.

At four-thirty in the afternoon, the after-work suit-and-tie crowd was just beginning to filter into the parking lot of the Club Exotique. A little postwork stress release, I guess. I parked the Mustang over in a corner next to a large Dempster Dumpster and hoped no one would recognize me as I walked up to the windowless building.

A large, hunter green awning snaked its way over the asphalt and led up to an alcove that was dark and foreboding. Music—loud, frenetic, thumping—filtered through the door. It felt like entering a tunnel. It struck me that maybe this was done on purpose, to give one the sense of being transported back into the womb. Or perhaps given where I was headed, I was just hung up on whatever sexual imagery was available.

I walked up to the dark green door and pushed on it. Nothing, locked solid. There were guys who'd walked in ahead of me, couple more behind me. How did they—

Suddenly a wooden panel to my right slid back, and a thin guy with long black, greasy hair and a cheap tux stared out at me.

"Ten bucks cover," he said automatically. "Two drink minimum inside. We don't serve alcohol. You can bring in your own, but we can't serve it to you. Don't touch the babes and have a good time."

"Yes, sir," I said, pulling a ten out of my wallet. He punched a button on the wall next to him and I heard a release click in the door.

I pushed open the heavy door and a blast of sound came at me like a hurricane. I stepped inside and felt the vibration through the floor. Mrs. Hawkins would love this place; she could dance to the pulsing beneath her feet. It was so loud even thought was difficult. Ahead of me, a long bar with no bottles behind it stretched out the length of one wall to my right.

Club Exotique was square inside, with a circular stage against one wall and booths lining the other two. Crammed into the center of the room were dozens of small tables, like an airport cocktail lounge, and here and there, eight-sided platforms a few feet off the floor with shiny brass poles rising up from the center.

Mirrors glittered like sparks in the dimly lit room. Flashing strobes ricocheted off the glass; a thousand Tinker Bells danced against the ceiling.

I waded in through a throng of men in dark suits standing near the entrance. Farther in the main room, the crowd was thinner, but it was hard for me to notice because of what was on the spotlit center stage.

She was tall, blonde, leggy like someone out of a

Mickey Spillane novel. And she had just dropped her last article of clothing, a frilly wisp of cloth that floated to the floor. She grabbed the brass pole in the center of the stage, writhed around it like she was trying to smother it, then with one smooth motion, threw her legs up in the air above her head, grabbed the pole with her feet, and wrapped herself around the brass upside down.

I stared for a moment; hell, I couldn't help it. I'd never seen anything like it.

Now what had I come in here for? Oh, yeah, business.

She pumped herself up and down the pole for a few seconds, then threw her legs out to the side and stretched parallel to the floor maybe four feet up, a naked blonde flag proudly on display. She hung there fully fifteen seconds without a trace of strain. This undraped gymnast, I thought, was in remarkable shape.

And around me everywhere, women of every size, shape, and color in stages of undress: baby-doll nighties, lace bras and panties, vinyl bikinis, garter belts, sheer satin short robes untied at the waist. There was a kind of soporific headiness to it, as if walking into a room full of physically perfect, nearly naked women could stone one as hard as a pitcher of martinis or a thick round joint.

Then it occurred to me that this was precisely the point.

Again, I struggled to stay focused on the mission du jour. The music faded, followed by the grating voice of the DJ in his booth to the right of the stage.

"Give it up, gentlemen!" he yelled, his voice echoing through the PA system. "Put your hands together for Crystal!"

I took a seat at a small table near the back of the club, behind a crowd of cheering college-aged guys. A waitress wearing a white teddy and black seamed stockings walked up to the table and smiled.

"What can I get you?"

Before I could answer, the music—if you can call it that—exploded again. I vaguely recognized the song; some cut off a grunge album, but it was impossible to understand the words because of the volume-induced distortion. I leaned over to the waitress and mouthed the words, "Club soda." She scribbled down the order and wobbled off on a pair of hooker heels that had to be eight inches high.

To my left, in one of the booths, a naked redhead reclined on her back, her legs wide open in an obscene V toward the couch that was out of my line of sight. There was a small placard on my table that explained what I was seeing was a COUCH DANCE. The redhead swung her legs together, then wide again, then did a 180-degree swirl on the slick table, hopped onto all fours, and wagged her rear end toward the couch. I looked away as she lowered her head to the surface of the table, her bottom still high in the air, an alley cat in heat waiting for a mounting that would never come.

As the redhead finished her private couch dance and the latest dancer on the main stage was wrapping up her last naked split, a young brunette walked toward my table out of the shadows. My stomach knotted up.

She wore only a frilly purple bra and matching pair of panties, no stockings, and heels that were barely off the ground. She seemed younger than the rest. While the other women were almost anorexically thin, she was rounded and curvy, fresh-faced, innocent. Her hair was thick and long, parted off to one side, and fell down onto her shoulders in waves. A deep red lipstick outlined her mouth, its edges sharp, hard.

"Hi," she said cheerily as she approached. "Mind if I sit down?"

I swallowed. "Sure," I mouthed over the music, then nodded toward the chair.

She crossed the table in front of me and settled into

the chair. "I'm Ginger," she said, leaning toward me to talk over the music.

"Hi," I answered. "I'm Harry."

She giggled. "Oh, really?"

"Yeah." I grinned stupidly. "I get that a lot."

"Where you from, Harry?"

"Here. I live in Nashville."

"Great. You don't sound like it, though. Not much of an accent."

"I lived up north for a long time. Also I work at it."

"Where'd you live up north?"

Jesus, a lady in her underwear sits down next to me and the next thing you know, I'm telling her my life story.

"Boston. I went to college there, then stayed on a few years after."

She brightened. "Boston? You're kidding! I dropped out of Simmons last year."

My eyes widened. *A Simmons girl dancing at Club Exotique. Well take me Lord, I've seen it all now.*

The waitress approached the table and set my club soda down. "Five dollars," she said, then asked: "Like to buy the lady a drink?"

Ginger looked at me, the request on her face.

"Sure," I said.

Ginger turned to the waitress. "Apple juice."

"If you don't mind my asking," I ventured, as the waitress trotted off. "How'd you wind up in Nashville?"

"A girlfriend and I went to Daytona for spring break last year. When it was time to go back to school, we just weren't interested. We got a job dancing, kept it for a while. Then she started dating this guy from Vandy she met and we decided to move."

The song ended and the DJ went into his spiel, then another dancer sauntered onto the stage. This time, the DJ put on something a little slower and a lot less loud. We could talk without shouting.

"How long you been dancing here?"

"A month or so," she said. "Maybe a little longer. Not much, though."

"How you like Nashville?"

"It's okay. I'm getting used to it."

I tried not to stare at her, but it's tough to be matter-of-fact with a healthy young college dropout sitting next to you in her underwear.

"If you don't mind my asking," I said, then hesitated, "how is it—I mean, what's it like dancing here, you know, like this?"

She put her hand on my forearm and patted it. "You mean nude?"

"Yeah . . ."

"It's okay to say it, you know."

I smiled. "Yeah. So what's it like to dance nude?"

She smiled back at me, revealing a healthy set of brilliant white straight teeth. "It's a lot of fun. I never knew I was pretty before. I like it that these guys enjoy watching me.

"You, too, Harry," she added. "Otherwise, you wouldn't be here."

The DJ cut in again, screaming into the mike, urging the boys to clap and cheer. I slapped my hands together weakly. Then another song started, one I recognized. Sade's sweet jazzy voice filled the room, crooning "Your Love Is King," as a skinny woman with mousy brown hair and acne scars bad enough to spot across the room gyrated at the brass pole. I don't offend easily, but having that woman dance to Sade was damn near sacrilegious.

I turned back to Ginger as she swayed slowly back and forth to the music. She seemed sweet, unsullied. Part of me wondered what she was doing in a place like this. I leaned in to her and decided to take a chance.

"Actually, Ginger, that's not entirely true."

She'd been staring at the stage, but turned back to me with a quizzical look on her face.

"Well, I am having a good time, but that's not why I came here." I bent in closer to her. "I'm looking for someone. I was hoping you could help me."

She stiffened, almost imperceptibly. "You're not like kinky or anything, are you, Harry? We don't get into that here."

"No, that's not what I'm looking for. If you don't mind my asking Ginger, how old are you?"

She scrunched up her face for a moment, suspicious. "I'm twenty-one. Legal everywhere. What are you, a cop?"

"No, I'm just trying to help somebody. The girl I'm looking for is only seventeen. Her family thinks she may be working in a club like this. Or that maybe she's running around with a guy who works here."

"If she's seventeen, she's not supposed to be working here. She's not even supposed to be let in."

"I know that, but sometimes the rules don't get followed, right?"

"Yeah, I know."

"And her family's worried about her. If she was grown, like you, it wouldn't be anybody else's business. But she's still a kid."

I reached into my shirt pocket and discreetly pulled out a snapshot, then palmed it toward her. "Recognize her?"

Ginger looked around quickly, nervously, then stared down at the photo. "No, but the light's pretty bad. People look real different in pictures sometimes."

"I know. But if you could just think for me."

She studied the picture a few more moments. "Maybe. I'm just not sure. We get a lot of young blondes coming through here."

"Yeah, so I'm told. But she runs around with a guy

I think works here. I don't know his name, but people call him Red Dog."

She pulled away and sat straight up. "You sure you're not a cop?"

I shook my head. "Private investigator. I'm not trying to cause anybody trouble. I'm just trying to find a runaway before she gets hurt. You can understand that, can't you?"

The waitress brought a small glass full of amber and set it on the table in front of Ginger.

"Five dollars," she said. Jeez, I thought, I didn't come here to get screwed. I hope Betty Jameson thinks her sister's worth it.

I handed the lady a five and she rambled off. Ginger picked up the glass and sipped. I looked at my tall glass full of soda, then down at hers.

"You guys aren't allowed to have grown-up drinks?"

She grinned. "These are lady's drinks," she explained. "As long as one of these is on your table, the other girls leave you alone."

"Sort of like marking your territory," I commented.

Ginger handed me the picture back. "Harry, you seem like a nice guy."

I rolled my eyes and tucked the photo back in my shirt. "Yeah, women tell me that all the time. S'why I never get anywhere."

"Oh, like I really believe that," she teased. "But listen, you want to get hurt, then hassling Red Dog is a good way to do it. And I hate to see a nice guy get hurt."

"So who is this Red Dog character?"

"When I first started working here, I thought he owned the place. It's like the manager was afraid of him or something. He's not here every night. I later found out he works for Mr. Klinkenstein."

"Who?"

"Mr. Klinkenstein. He owns the club. But he owns a lot of other places, too."

I did a quick search of my mental database. Klinkenstein... Klinkenstein...

That's it! Klinkenstein had been the only name in common among all three sets of corporate papers I'd gotten at the Polk Building that afternoon. What was his first name? Blast, I'd lost it.

"So he works for Mr. Klinkenstein, but you don't know exactly what he does."

"Yeah. We just see him in here a lot. Bobby, the manager—that's him over there—" She pointed toward the bar, where the greasy-haired guy in the tux who'd taken my cover stood. "Bobby gets real cranky when Red Dog's around here a lot. He's bad-tempered enough as it is."

"But you don't know what Red Dog does?"

"No."

"You got a name for him? Surely Red Dog's not printed on his birth certificate."

She smiled again, sweetly. She had a pleasant smile, an attractive face, but without the hard edge she'd have after pursuing this career for another few years. I liked her instinctively.

"No, don't know his name. I could ask around. If I do, though, it'd be best for both of us if you don't ask the other girls. Word might get back to him."

"If you could do that for me, there'd be a little something in it for you. But be careful."

I reached into my pocket and slid out a twenty. "In fact, I appreciate your time now."

I palmed the twenty and slid it across the table to her.

"Thanks, Harry. That's sweet of you."

Then the music died down again, and the DJ was screaming at us to put our hands together or give it up or some such crap.

"Oh, I forgot," Ginger said quickly. "I'm up next."

She hopped up from the table and skipped away, the heavier parts of her bouncing as she walked. She was firm and young now, but gravity and time would take its toll.

"Okay, gentlemen," the idiot behind the mike yelled. "Let's welcome Ginger!"

Then some gangsta-rap audio assault commenced thumping and I watched as the sweet young girl I'd spent the last ten minutes talking to—at two dollars a minute—jumped on the stage and began undulating to the beat. She wrapped herself around the pole, rolled her head back, shook from side-to-side. Then she turned her back to the audience, grabbed a shiny brass handrail that ran the length of the stage, raised her rump in the air and bent over at the waist. By the time the chorus came around again, she was on her back in the middle of the stage, completely nude, her legs spread in a wide V, giving the room a view straight out of an ob-gyn textbook. The other guys in the audience loved it, especially the rowdy group over in the corner, next to the stage, wearing orange UT shirts.

As for me, I felt like I was watching my kid sister being violated.

Chapter 5

Ginger's turn on the stage came around a dozen more times before Red Dog finally showed up at the club. It was past ten o'clock by then. My stomach growled with hunger and my kidneys were threatening to resign after a succession of five-dollar Cokes.

If ever there was a guy with a fitting nickname, Red Dog was it. He was midtwenties, maybe, and thin, with a pinched face that looked hard and mean. His sharp nose slanted out too far and had a ridge midway up, like it'd been broken before. He glanced around nervously, and his eyes bulged slightly, giving him the aura of an agitated Chihuahua.

His flaming red hair gave him away. It was long, down to his shoulders, wavy, and badly in need of a good scrubbing. Maybe he'd piled on too much gel. Either way, the greasy hair and the shiny suit struck me as the textbook definition of redneck punk, although Red Dog probably preferred to think of himself as one cool made guy.

As soon as he entered the place, I noticed a subtle shift in the karma. The customers weren't aware, of course; they were too busy leering. But the manager at the door set his jaw and straightened a bit. The girls, who had sauntered around relaxed and cheerful beforehand, now became almost frenetic. Before, they would casually walk up to your table and ask "Like a dance?"

If your answer was no, then they'd smile, chat a moment or two.

Now it was, "Okay, how 'bout it? No? Fine. Next." The music boomed and echoed. Ginger walked over to my table and put herself directly in my line of sight, between me and Red Dog across the room.

"He's here," she said tightly.

"I figured that. Can you sit down? We need to talk."

"You can't sit and chat while Red Dog's here."

I thought for a moment. "If I buy a couch dance, do you actually have to *do* it?"

"No, I mean, sometimes guys just want to talk."

I stood up and motioned toward an empty booth behind me and to my right. "That's me. I'm lonely, my wife doesn't understand me, and I just need somebody to talk to."

"You also need twenty bucks," she said.

I fished in my pocket and pulled out my last twenty. "Christ," I said, "who says talk is cheap?"

She took the bill and nodded to a big guy in the corner, then led me away from the table. There were two carpeted steps leading up to the chrome-and-black booth. Ginger stepped aside to let me go in first, then nestled next to me. She turned and gave me a radiant yet plastic smile.

I leaned in close to her, but mainly to make myself heard without yelling. "Who was the guy over there?" I asked.

"The big guy in the tux? He's a floor man. He keeps track of the dances."

"Why?" I asked.

"Harry, we pay to work here."

I stared at her. "What?"

"Yeah, we hustle the dances and the house gets a cut. That's how it works. That and tips."

I let out a long breath. "What a racket."

She brought her right hand up to my cheek and lightly traced my jawline with a painted fingernail.

"You have to do that?" I asked.

"We have to look like we're having a good time."

"I can't touch you, but you—"

She nodded her head. "That's right. Those are the rules, big guy."

"How long have we got?"

"Five minutes or so. Maybe longer."

"Geez," I spewed. "Twenty bucks for five minutes. I could have heart surgery cheaper."

She gave me this little-girl-Lolita look that must have appeared lucrative to the suits across the room, but there was iron in her voice.

"Harry, you want to talk or you want to bitch? It's your money."

I stared at her for a second. "You get his name?"

"Not all of it. Kitten said she thought his last name was Turner."

"Red Dog Turner. Any idea where he lives?"

"You didn't ask me for that one, Harry. Get your shit straight next time."

"What's he drive?"

"That's easy. Some kind of Mercedes or something. You know, one of those nigger Mercedes."

I scowled at her. "Don't say that word. I hate that word." Then after a moment, "What's a—?"

"You know, it's one of those shiny black jobs with gold trim everywhere. The emblems, the tires, and the windows are smoked so thick you can barely see through 'em. Real gaudy. Cheap if you ask me. Why would anybody take a classy car like that and screw it up?"

"I wouldn't know. I've never had a car like that. I wonder where Red Dog gets that kind of scratch."

"No answer to that one either."

"Anybody ever seen anybody that looks like Stacey around here?"

"I asked a couple of the girls," Ginger said. "But, you know, I can't just ask everybody. But Tawny said there was a real young blonde dancing here a couple of months ago, off and on, and Red Dog really had the eye for her."

"A couple of months ago," I said. "Her sister told me she's only been gone for three weeks."

Ginger shrugged. "I don't know, baby. That's just what she told me."

My mind turned in circles as I attempted to think. Billy Idol screamed "White Wedding" in the background with the decibel level of a 747 on takeoff. On-stage, an ash-gray blonde spun her breasts in counter-rotating circles in time to the thumping.

"Can breasts get carpal tunnel syndrome?" I asked out loud.

Ginger leaned in close to me. "What?"

"Never mind."

"Harry, I gotta go. I get off at eleven. I do one more turn on the main stage, then I gotta cash out."

She stood up and ran her fingers through my hair. I looked up at her almost absentmindedly.

"Nice talking to you, sweetie," she said.

"Yeah, thanks, Ginger."

She leaned down and put her mouth close to my ear. I tried not to stare, but the purple lace of her bra was nearly in my face.

"My name's not Ginger," she said. "We all use stage names. I'm really Corey."

She patted me on the shoulder and stood back up. "Thanks, Corey," I said. "You watch yourself, you hear?"

As she walked away, I realized I didn't even get my five minutes.

* * *

I went through my wallet while sitting in the car in the far corner of the Club Exotique parking lot. I'd gone through ninety dollars since four that afternoon. The Club Exotique could more appropriately have been called the Club Expensif. I didn't even get dinner in the deal.

How, I wondered, was I going to list this on my expense report to Betty Jameson?

I had the radio on softly and the seat back far enough that I could relax and keep an eye on the front door of the Club in the rear-view mirror without being seen. The parking lot was crowded with cars. Two bouncers stood outside the club under the awning, just keeping an eye on things. I was half afraid they'd notice I'd walked to my car, then never left. If they did, it didn't bother them. I suspected they were mostly there to keep the underage kids out and to stop the homeless panhandlers from hassling the customers.

Red Dog's Mercedes was next to the awning in a reserved place. Despite Ginger's inappropriate description of the car, it was a slick Mercedes sedan redone tacky, with a vanity plate: REDDOG1. I adjusted the mirror to take some of the strain out of my neck.

I was hungry, tired, and bored. It was also a good thing Marsha hadn't wanted company after her fundraising dinner, given that I would have stood her up for that as well. I hoped she'd have time to cool off a bit by tomorrow. As we say down South, bidness is bidness.

And this, I thought, is the glamorous private-investigator bidness. . . .

The night was cool, the air clear and dry. Sometimes, you get some pretty funky smells blowing your way in Nashville, especially at night. The thermal plant burns a lot of stuff downtown, and then there's the rendering plant over near I-265. It's really foul sometimes. But a gentle, soft wind blew over Nashville this night. The distant horn of a tugboat on the river bellowed, and the white noise of traffic going over the Silliman Evans bridge could barely be heard. It made me wish I was sitting with Marsha in one of the padded lawn chairs on her balcony, looking out over the woods in back of her condo.

I reached down and adjusted the volume on the radio. The public radio station in Murfreesboro, a growing college town just southeast of Nashville, was playing an especially mellow jazz set this evening. It beat the snot out of that loud pounding crap inside the club. Only problem was the station was just far enough away to be tough to pick up sometimes. I fiddled with the tuning knob, trying to get a better fix on the station, and looked back up just as Red Dog was slapping one of the bouncers on the back and turning for his Mercedes.

I nearly wrenched my back yanking the seat up enough to drive. I reached for the key while simultaneously pumping the accelerator pedal like killing rats. The engine turned, sputtered, caught, then died.

Damn.

I ground the starter again, and this time when it caught, I gave it just the right amount of gas. I checked to see if the bouncers had noticed my starting the car. Red Dog's brake lights came on, then his back-up lights. I shifted the car into reverse, being careful not to touch my brakes. I wanted to slide out of the far side of the lot without lights if possible.

Suddenly, out of the corner of my eye, there was movement from behind the Dempster Dumpster that had partially shielded me from the entrance. Before I could do anything, the door opened, the dome light came on, and a figure slid into the car next to me.

I jumped like a scalded dog and cocked a fist. "Who the hell!" I yelped.

Then I saw the hair. Only this time it was pulled back and held in place with a thick ponytail tie.

"Ginger—" I sputtered. "Corey?"

She looked at me in the dim green glow of the dashboard lights. "What?" she said. "You don't recognize me with my clothes on?"

"Corey, have you lost your mind!" It was a decidedly rhetorical question. "Get out of this car!"

"I'm going with you," she said.

"Like hell!"

"Harry, I'm going with you. If Red Dog's messing around with a seventeen-year-old girl, I want to see him go down for it. I was seventeen myself once."

"Yeah," I said, "about a week ago!"

"Oh, shut up and drive."

"Not till you get out of this car."

"I am not getting out of this car."

"Corey, for the last time—"

She pointed over my shoulder. "Harry, you're losing him."

My heart raced. I rolled my head around just in time to see Red Dog Turner speed out of the parking lot, then go right toward the river. There was a stop sign a block ahead. If I wasn't with him by then, I'd lose him. Which meant another night hanging out at the Club Exotique.

"Oh, Jesus," I muttered, then raced the engine and popped the clutch. With a squeal and a puff of gray smoke from the tires, the Mustang roared out of the parking lot. Corey ducked down so the goons couldn't see her, and we took off up the street. Ahead of us, the brake lights of Red Dog's Mercedes dimmed, and he turned right onto Third Avenue headed toward Rutledge Hill.

"When I was fantasizing about Robert Urich in *Spenser: For Hire*, this isn't exactly what I had in mind," I said, exasperated.

Corey sat back up as we disappeared down the block and I turned the headlights on.

"I didn't know you fantasized about other men, Harry. Want to talk about it?"

I'd never done a whole lot of tailing before. I mostly practiced by following random cars when I didn't have anything else to do. You know, just pick a car in traffic and stay with it for a while, trying different methods to see which one gets you spotted first. I could usually tell when I'd been seen. The driver would start nervously looking in the mirror, then changing lanes without notice just to see if I mimicked the shift. The occasional paranoid would suddenly turn off on a sidestreet, usually by being right in the middle of the intersection without slowing down, then jerking into a turn without warning.

What I mostly found, though, was that people are pretty oblivious when they're driving. They're talking on the cell phone, putting on makeup, adjusting the radio, barely paying any attention to driving, let alone who's behind them. A common joke about Nashville drivers is that they all think a rear-view mirror is a grooming aid.

We followed him down Lafayette Street, skirting a housing project south of the interstate, to a liquor store. He pulled into the store and parked in front. I pulled off to the side and sat nervously; this wasn't the greatest neighborhood to be in at—I looked at my watch—eleven-fifteen at night.

"You know, if this wasn't such a crappy neighborhood, I'd put you out here and make you take a cab home."

"Yeah." She pouted. "Would you give me cab fare?"

"Cab fare?" I said. "Hell, you didn't leave me with gas money."

She rolled her lower lip out. "You want some of it back?"

I turned to her. In the subdued light, she looked even

younger, if that was possible. Maybe I was getting really crisp, but this whole scene was becoming just a tad
surrealistic.

"No, keep it. My client can afford it."

"Who is your client?" she asked.

"None of your business." I stared out the windshield,
watching the liquor store.

"You said earlier her family was looking for her."

"Wouldn't yours?"

She turned away. "No."

I looked back in her direction. "Sorry."

Red Dog was inside the brightly lit store talking to
the guy behind the cash register. It was getting pretty
late and there were only a few other customers. Most
liquor stores in Nashville, even in the seedy parts of
town, shut down by eleven or so on weeknights. The
guy behind the cash register took a pint of something
down off the shelf behind him and passed it across to
Red Dog. Then he rang open the cash register, reached
in, and handed Red Dog something.

"What the hell?" I whispered.

"What?" Corey asked.

"Funny. He just bought a pint." I reached behind the
driver's seat, to where I kept a small canvas bag. I
pulled the bag around and unzipped it, then fumbled
around for my cheap pair of binoculars.

"So he bought a pint," she said.

"Yeah, and he got back a fistful of bills as change.
Only I never saw him give the cashier any money."

"Weird."

"Yeah." I looked through the binoculars, but by then
it was too late. Red Dog pocketed the pint, turned, and
pushed his way through the double plate-glass doors.

I slipped the binoculars back inside the bag as Red
Dog fired up the Mercedes and jerked around in the
parking lot.

"Duck," I said, as we came into his line of sight.

Corey bent over, just below the high dashboard of the Mustang, and I leaned over her, mashing her down, hoping we were enough in the shadows.

If Red Dog saw us, it didn't register. With a squeal of tires, he pulled out onto Lafayette and headed back toward town.

I had my arm across Corey's back, draped over her to the armrest on the opposite side of the car, with her head almost nestled in my lap. We sat like that a moment, then I peeked up as the Mercedes pulled away. I held that position for a moment longer than I should have.

"Oh," I said, jerking myself upright. "Sorry."

She came up slowly and shook her shoulders, massaging the left one with her right hand. "Don't apologize."

Corey gave me this look. I don't know how to describe it, but it made me real uncomfortable.

"Let's go," I said.

About ten heartbeats later, she said: "Okay, what are you waiting for?" I twisted the key in the ignition and the car churned to life.

Man, I thought, I'm really tired. This is getting goofy.

I thought we'd lost him. Ahead of us, I couldn't see his taillights. I gunned the car through a yellow light on the edge of the housing project, then shot up Lafayette as fast as the car would accelerate. Ahead of me, just before the I-40 bridge, the light was about to change again. It went yellow on me, but in Nashville that means haul ass and you might make it.

I stomped the accelerator; the engine coughed a couple of times, then whined roughly toward redline. The light went red on me when I was about fifty feet away. I didn't even have time to check the cross streets for traffic or cops.

Next to me, Corey squealed, planted her feet on the floorboard and pushed back into the seat as if braking the car herself—which was more than I was doing.

We shot through the light without getting pulled over by blue lights or T-boned. Ahead of us, down the hill toward the old downtown Sears that closed a few years ago, Red Dog slowed his Mercedes to a stop at the next light.

"God, Harry." She sighed. "Are you crazy or what?"

My throat was so tight I could barely talk. "Sorry about that."

I braked quickly and geared down, then coasted the rest of the hill. I tried to time it so that the Mercedes would be pulling away just as I got there.

The light changed and Red Dog pulled left onto a sidestreet, then quickly right again to the light at Eighth Avenue. I turned left behind him, but passed the immediate right.

"Where you going?" she asked.

"He must be turning left onto Eighth," I said. "Otherwise, he'd have stayed on Lafayette. We'll catch him at the next block."

I pulled on up the hill, over the railroad tracks, then found myself turning right onto Division at yet another show bar/strip club called The Odyssey.

"Know anybody that works there?" I asked.

She turned to me and I felt her hard glare. "No, Harry. I don't. Remember, I just moved here a month or so ago."

I made the turn, then coasted down Division to the light at Eighth. Just as we pulled up to it, the black Mercedes went through a yellow light and our side changed to green. I jerked onto Eighth Avenue and maneuvered so that there was only one car between us and Red Dog.

He drove slowly, in no particular hurry. We made our way out Eighth in the thinning late-night traffic, past the old city reservoir. I wondered if he'd spotted us and was just meandering around to see what we'd do. My anxiety levels were rising by the block. Suddenly, he jerked into the right-hand lane, went through the parking lot of a BP Oil station, then roared onto Wedgewood heading toward Hillsboro Village.

If he'd spotted us, so be it. I'd gone too far to give up without a fight. I let him cut through the gas station as I went on to the intersection slowly, doing it by the book, making a legitimate right turn on red, then gunning the engine as he was out of sight. I pushed it up the hill through another light, then saw him again as he slowed down past Belmont University.

I cut another yellow kind of close, but close enough not to get nailed. As he turned left at the next light, I decided to set back a bit. Maybe he'd just been screwing around; maybe his medication finally took effect. Either way, he didn't seemed too concerned about us anymore.

He meandered around until he was on Belmont Avenue, down in front of this throwback-to-the-beat-era coffeehouse called Bongo Java, and past the International Market. He turned right on a sidestreet, with me and Corey a half block behind, then up a block.

He slowed and turned left into an alley behind a huge complex of old New York–style apartment buildings. The buildings were redbrick, several stories high, with metal fire escapes down the sides. The buildings were configured into a U-shape and surrounded three sides of a well-landscaped courtyard.

"You think he lives here?" Corey asked.

"Why don't we find out."

I cut the headlights and made the left turn. Down the alley, the Mercedes slid into a space in a small parking lot behind one of the buildings. Just ahead of me, there was a small cutoff in the alley next to a cinder-block garage. I pulled off to the side, into the shadows, and let the engine idle. I had a clear view up the alley by leaning my head out the window.

"See him?" she asked.

"Not yet," I said softly.

Out of the sulfurous yellow glow of the sodium lights in the parking lot, a lone figure strode across the alley and onto the back stairs that doubled as a fire escape. He climbed to the top floor of the building and entered through a heavy door.

A few seconds later, a light in a window to the left of the staircase flicked on.

I put the car in gear and backed out of the cutoff, then drove slowly up the alley until I was just past the spidery metal of the back stairs. The parking lot was crowded, not a space anywhere. Two rows over, Red Dog's Mercedes sat still and cooling in the night. Above us, another light flashed on next to the one we'd just seen.

I backed the car into the lot as noiselessly as I could and stopped in the middle between two rows. Then I killed the engine and set the parking brake.

"You gonna just leave it here?" Corey asked.

"Why not?"

"What do we do now?" she asked.

I turned to her. I could barely make out her face in the dim light, and what I could see was pale yellow and soft in focus.

"We wait."

Chapter 6

I looked down at my watch—twelve-thirty. Corey and I'd sat for an hour with no sign of movement. But the lights in the upstairs apartment had stayed on.

"How long we going to hang around?" she asked.

"I don't know. I keep thinking he'll come back out and have the girl with him. Maybe he won't. If those lights go out, then maybe they've crashed. We'll give it a few minutes and see."

"So we're just going to wing it?"

"That's about it."

I leaned back and fought off sleep. It had been a long day; I'd gotten up early at Marsha's and not stopped since. One of these days, I thought, I'd be able to afford a cell phone so I could check in with her on nights like this.

"I mean, it's not like I've ever seen anybody do it," Corey said, picking up the thread of a conversation we'd started a half hour earlier. "People think show girls do coke all the time."

"You're serious," I said. "You've never seen it?"

"Never in the clubs," she said. "I've been to parties and stuff where it's been, but I've never tried it myself. A few of the girls have talked about liking it, but never while we're working."

"That seems pretty weird to me. There's so much of the shit out there."

"Now, I'll tell you what you do see a lot of...," she said, her voice trailing off.

I turned to her. "What?"

"These over-the-counter diet pills. You know, like caffeine and that decongestant stuff. Same thing truckers take to stay awake. In fact, I've got some in my purse here somewhere. You want one?"

"No, thanks," I answered, turning my eyes back to the lit windows above us. "I don't indulge."

"C'mon, Harry. It just helps you stay awake. It's even legal."

"I'll pass."

I heard her pop the plastic cap off a pill bottle, then the shuffle of capsules as she sorted one into her hand. She popped it into her mouth and swallowed it dry with a kind of thunking sound.

"Most of the girls are married or in committed relationships," she continued. "None of us screw around, Harry. We really don't. We're not looking for anybody."

"Yeah, so where's your husband?"

"I don't have one, but I do have a steady boyfriend. He's in college. We're engaged, see?"

She held out her hand to show me a small diamond engagement ring.

I turned to her. "Yeah, but you've got to admit this is a pretty weird way to make a living."

"That's just it, it *is* a living. My last job before this was working in a mall. Six bucks an hour and all the assholes I could deal with."

"So you don't have to deal with assholes now?"

"Sure, but I get well paid for it."

I scooted around in the seat, trying to get comfortable. "You ever been scared?"

"You mean, dancing?"

"Yeah, like run into anybody weird or anything."

"No. The clubs do a pretty good job of protecting us. If you ask, one of the guys will escort you to your car.

At the end of the night, they don't let us leave until the security guys clear the parking lot."

"That's more concern than I would have thought."

"The customers know not to start anything that way. One night, I worked until closing time and they found a guy hiding under one of the girls' cars. He won't be back."

I turned to her. "What, they kill the guy?"

She laughed softly. "No, Harry. You watch too much TV. They roughed him up a little and took down his name and license number. They banned him from the club."

"Oh," I muttered, then turned my eyes back up to the building. Behind a curtain in the lit window to the right, a dark form moved.

"Mostly you just get grossed out," Corey went on. "Some of these guys are real pigs. Once, I was doing a coffee-table dance and this guy had his hands down his pants playing with himself. Yuk, I thought, so I turned around and faced away from him so I wouldn't have to watch."

The dark form stopped in front of the right window, then disappeared. A moment later, the shape appeared in the left window, and in the diffuse light filtering through the curtain, I saw the vague outline of an arm raise.

"A couple of minutes later, I turned back around and this guy—ugh, it was awful. He had it, like you know, *out*, and he was going to town. I thought I was going to hurl. I grabbed my clothes and got out of there."

I scrunched my eyes and tried to focus on the window. What was going on up there?

"I went over and told the manager," Corey said, "and they ran that guy out of there but quick. We don't need that kind of tacky—"

"*Stop!*" The garbled voice three floors up was barely intelligible. "*Don't—*"

Corey's voice broke midsentence. "What was that?" she whispered.

I shushed her and listened hard.

A thin, warbling scream trailed out of the window; then a thumping noise, followed by another thump. I'm no expert, but the raised hand and the muffled thump sounded like what I've always imagined was the hushed report of a silenced pistol.

The shadow dashed from left to right, passing each window, then disappeared.

I jumped out of the car and bolted for the metal fire escape. Out of the corner of my eye, I saw Corey climb out of the car.

"Stay there!" I ordered. She ignored me; I didn't have time to argue with her.

I hit the metal three steps up and pumped as hard as I could, past the landing into the first floor, then up to the second. The staircase was old, rusty, and swayed with every stomp. Flakes of rust came off in my hand and the smell of mildew filled my nostrils.

I hit the third-floor landing and pushed open a heavy white door with dirty windowpanes reflecting the red glow of an EXIT sign. In the hall, two ancient ceiling receptacles provided the only light. To my left, a dirty white door was cracked open, the harsh glare of a bare light bulb shining through the gap.

Corey's steps behind me clanged on the metal. From another direction, ahead of me and down, I heard softer footsteps running.

I ran over to the landing and stared down just as the front door opened and a shadowed form vanished through it. I knew I couldn't catch him, whoever it was, and wasn't sure I wanted to. Behind me, the fire-escape door opened and Corey hopped breathlessly through. Her huffing and puffing made me realize I was barely getting enough breath myself.

"What—" She gasped. "What are we going to do?"

I turned back to her, stretched an arm, and leaned against the damp wall. "Somebody just ran down the stairs." I wheezed. "But he was gone before I could get a look at him."

"Should we call the police?"

I looked around. No other apartment door had opened. No sign of any activity anywhere. Either these people were sound sleepers or they didn't want to get involved.

"C'mon," I said, pushing past her to the cracked door. "Stay behind me. I'm serious here, okay?"

She nodded. I pushed the door open slowly, my eyes scanning the room quickly. The first room was the kitchen. A grungy, half-century-old gas stove was tucked in one corner with a couple of filthy pots perched on top. The rotten, fecund, smell of garbage filled the air.

I saw no one, so tiptoed in carefully. A short hallway led to a square living room. A ratty sofa with the stuffing coming out sat in the middle of the room, with a huge TV facing it on a black stand. The thick, heavy aroma of marijuana hung in the fabric, the air, off the walls.

"Doobie," Corey whispered behind me. I waved my hand to quiet her.

Still no one, but ahead of me a partially opened door led into what I guessed was a bedroom. I approached it slowly, cautiously. The only sound I could hear was the pounding of blood in my ears. I stood against the wall, and waved Corey behind me. I gently pushed the door open a couple of inches, then jerked back quickly.

From inside the room, I heard a high-pitched giggle. I slowly pushed the bedroom door open and peered in.

Stacey Jameson sat cross-legged in the middle of a nasty, squalid water bed with yellow sheets that were once white bunched up around her. Behind her on the headboard cabinet, a half-empty bottle of tequila leaned precariously close to falling off. She was pale, thin, with great black circles under her eyes. Her blonde hair was spiked and splayed in all directions.

And she was stark, staring, buck-assed naked.

She put a hand on each hip, curved her arms, and grinned at me, her eyes glazed over. Then, slurring her words like a drunk, she sang:

"I'm a little teapot, short and stout."

She looked down at her left arm.

"This is my handle, this is my—"

She rolled her head over and sighted down her right arm.

"—is my ... is my ... Well, goddamn, I'm a sugar bowl."

She looked up at me with a dazed smile on her face. Then her eyes closed slowly and she fell straight back onto the water bed, rolling back and forth with the wave motion, unconscious.

I stepped over to her. Corey came in behind me. "Boy, is she laced."

I hovered over the bed. She may have been seventeen years old, but right now she had an extra couple of decades' worth of mileage on her. Her ribs showed through nearly translucent skin. Her breasts were small and sagged to either side of her sternum. She was strung-out, dissipated, probably malnourished. And from between her legs, a small trickle ran out to form the traditional post-coital wet spot.

But she was breathing.

"I'm going to get a washcloth," I said. "Cover her up, will you?"

She tightened. "I'm not touching those sheets."

"Damn it, Corey," I said as I turned for the bathroom, "you're the one who insisted on following—"

I stopped cold, sucked in a hard, quick breath.

"Oh shit," I muttered.

"What?" Corey asked. Then she stepped over, put her hands on my shoulder and looked around me.

She jerked, let out a squeal, then buried her face against my shirt. I brought my arms up around her and held her tight.

Red Dog Turner was sprawled half in and half out of the bathtub, nude and spread-eagled with the shower curtain partially covering his torso. He'd grabbed at it as he'd fallen backward.

A small dark hole in his throat lay open and ugly, with a thin trickle of blood dribbling down the side of his neck. A second hole, dead center in his chest, had a starburst pattern, like someone had hit him from only an inch or so away.

It looked neat and professional: one in the voice box to shut him up; the second one straight through the heart. There was very little blood.

Whoever'd killed him must have caught him right after the act. He was still half erect, his penis lying off to one side. A foul smell filled the bathroom. I glanced over the edge of the bathtub for confirmation.

Yeah, his guts had emptied at the moment of death. Red Dog Turner had died in his own excrement.

Corey pulled away from me and looked up into my face. "Is he—?"

I nodded my head.

"Aren't you even going to check?"

"No point," I said softly. "Besides, they can lift prints off bodies now."

She sniffed. "Oh, God, get me out of here." She went weak and I felt her knees start to buckle. I pulled her up hard, hugged her in close to me. Her thick flannel shirt felt damp with perspiration and seemed almost to glow with her heat.

I fought off my own nausea, hoping that shock would take over and I wouldn't really feel this for a few hours.

"Listen, sweetie," I said soothingly, "we've got a lot of trouble here. Don't go south on me, okay?"

She swallowed hard and nodded. We stepped back into the bedroom. As Corey leaned against the wall, I pulled my shirt cuff down over my hand and wrapped it around the doorknob, then pulled it closed. Stacey stirred on the bed, moaning as if in a bad dream.

I looked around. No weapon.

"Think she did it?" Corey asked.

I snorted. "Hell, she can't even sit up."

"Should we call the police?"

My mind ran in circles. *Think,* damn it, *think.*

"Why don't we assume somebody's already done that."

"How much time have we got?" she asked weakly.

"Five minutes, if we're lucky. Maybe more."

"God, Harry, what are we going to do?"

I looked around the room. The floor was cluttered with scrunched dirty clothes, crumpled fast-food sacks, and discarded beer bottles. Over in the corner, a scuffed leather purse had been offhandedly tossed.

"Get that purse; see if it's Stacey's."

Corey crossed around the bed and picked the purse up. As she leaned down, something caught her attention.

"Oh my God," she said.

"What?"

She came up with a small green ashtray in her right hand. In the ashtray, a tiny glass pipe lay on its side. A brown, foul-smelling wire screen was crunched inside the bowl.

"Crack," she said.

"Great," I said. "Just great."

My anxiety levels were rising faster than the yen against the dollar. So far, we had a dead body, a nude underage runaway zonked out on God knew what, pot, crack cocaine, and half a bottle of tequila, which was the only goddamn legal thing in the whole place.

What were we going to do about this?

I looked over at the passed-out, very sick young lady over on the bed and wondered what would happen to her if I left her here. She'd gone to the edge, was right at the line between salvageable and unsalvageable. Whatever life and her crazy family and Red Dog Turner and God only knew how many others had set out to do to her, they had just about finished the job. It was stupid and naive on my part, not to mention illegal and morally reprehensible and probably professional suicide, but in that instant I decided to take a shot at yanking her back.

"That her purse?"

Corey looked up. "Yeah."

"Okay, let's get her dressed. We're getting her out of here."

She looked at me like I'd lost my mind.

"I'm serious," I added. "Let's go." And in the next five minutes, I crossed a line myself.

I got behind Stacey, grabbed her by the head, and yanked her into a sitting position.

"Hand me her bra." I pointed.

"Are you crazy?" Corey snapped. "We don't have time for underwear. Just throw a T-shirt over her."

Stacey yelped and came awake for a moment, called me motherfucker, then began moaning in protest as we raised her skinny arms and fed them into the sleeves of a dingy T-shirt. Corey yanked the cloth down over her head as I knelt on the floor before her, guided her feet into a pair of jeans, then lifted her legs in the air. She rolled onto her back. I yanked the cloth down.

Stacey giggled an obscene, half-crazed chortle and tried to spread her legs. Obviously, she'd been in this position before.

Then I dropped her legs, grabbed her arms, yanked

her into a standing position, and before she could fall
back down, grabbed the jeans and wrenched them the
rest of the way up. She groaned in protest.

"Let me go," she grumbled.

"Stand up," I snapped. "Behave yourself."

"Fuck you," she slurred. "Who are you?"

"The man who's going to drag you out of here, in or
out of your clothes. It's your call."

"I'm not going anywhere," she mumbled. "Where's
Billy?"

"Who's Billy?" Corey asked.

"Who cares?" I turned to her. "Take her purse. Go to
the front door and make sure nobody's coming. Try not
to touch anything. I'll follow you with her."

"Harry, this is insane."

"Move, damn it." I grabbed Stacey's wrists and set
my legs to take her weight.

Corey nodded, fear in her eyes. At this point, she
wanted out as much as I did.

She walked softly ahead of me as I easily pulled
Stacey along. If she weighed ninety pounds, I'm a left-
handed Japanese pole-vaulter.

We trudged through the living room and into the
kitchen. Corey opened the door and stuck her head out,
then turned back to us. "Let's go," she whispered.

I half walked, half dragged Stacey through the door
into the hallway. As we turned toward the fire escape,
she rolled her head back and opened her eyes.

"Who are you?"

The last thing in the world Stacey Jameson needed to
know was my name.

"Ssshhh," I whispered. "My friends call me Riley.
Doghouse Riley."

"Well, you're a nice man, Mr. Riley. I'm sorry I
called you motherfucker."

I held the heavy door open with one hand, while

keeping the other around Stacey's waist, and hauled her out onto the fire escape.

"Think nothing of it," I said. It felt wonderful to be outside, in fresh air and the cool of the night. The steps clattered as we went down, but no lights flicked on, no windows opened.

We were on the second-floor landing when I heard it. Faint at first, barely noticeable. But then, by the second, louder.

Sirens.

"Corey, move," I stage-whispered.

Stacey rolled her head up off my shoulder. "I'm sleepy. Where we going?" she murmured.

That's when I screwed up, big time.

"Home," I whispered. "We're taking you home."

Suddenly the submissive, acquiescent young girl half-unconscious in my arms exploded. She screamed like a tomcat in a gang fight, then in a split second, slapped me so hard my ears rang.

She howled, flailed, fought like a tiger. I slapped back at her, more to protect myself than anything else. Below us a few steps, Corey whipped around, her eyes wide open and shimmering in the streetlights.

"Harry!" she yelled. "What's going—"

"Damn it, be quiet!" I sputtered as a buzz saw of arms and legs whirled around me. I still had one arm around her waist. I clapped a palm across her mouth to stop the screaming, but that left me nothing to hold the rest of her down.

"Stacey, hush," I growled into her ear as I fought. "Be still!"

Corey bounded up the stairs. "What are we going to do?"

The sirens grew louder. "Shit, we gotta get out of here," I said. "Hold her legs."

Corey grabbed at Stacey's legs and got a kick in the shoulder that nearly sent her flying off the second-story landing. I pushed the bundle of wildcat in front of me, holding my hand over her mouth. I could feel her jaw working back and forth, trying to get a grip.

"You bite me, you little bitch, and I'm going to throw you overboard," I snarled. I don't believe I'd ever talked to anyone like that before. It felt weird and I didn't like it.

That seemed to slow her a bit. Corey steadied herself and managed to grab hold of Stacey's ankles. Stacey tried to snatch a handful of Corey's hair, but I managed to let go of her waist, grab her right hand, fold it into her left hand, then wrap my arm back around her with her arms folded helplessly within.

She squirmed, fought, squealed with a fury and a terror that shocked me. What in the hell did I do to her? What caused her to go off like this?

"We're not going to hurt you, Stacey," I whispered. "Calm down. The cops are coming!"

The sirens grew louder. I figured they were down around Wedgewood, making the turn toward Belmont Avenue. If they stopped on Belmont and came in through the front, we had a chance. If they blocked the alley and came in the back way, we were screwed.

Stacey twisted and fought nonstop as we pummeled our way down the stairs and into the parking lot. We literally carried her across the asphalt to the Mustang. Corey opened the driver's-side door.

"You drive a straight shift?" I asked.

She nodded her head, frantically looking back and forth.

"Okay, throw the seat forward." I bent over at the waist, folding Stacey in half with me. As Corey held the seat forward, I dove into the back of the car headfirst with Stacey under me. She writhed and twisted, but I managed to throw my weight on top of her and hold her down. I freed a hand and dug in my pants pocket for my keyring, then handed it to Corey.

"Go right out of the parking lot. We'll take the alley to the next sidestreet. Then go up to Hillsboro Road and make our way to I-440."

Corey closed the door and adjusted the driver's seat. She stuck the key in the ignition and twisted. The Mustang lunged against itself and made a horrible grinding noise. I hung my head over Stacey's back and shut my eyes.

"Either push in the clutch or take it out of gear," I suggested.

"I'm sorry," Corey snapped. "I'm a little nervous."

The starter ground away, then caught. She put the car in gear, let out the clutch too fast, and with a terrible jolt, the engine coughed and died.

I wondered if I could bend around far enough to kiss my own ass goodbye.

"Try it again, Corey. And relax."

The starter whirred and churned. I could hear her foot stomping the pedal frenetically.

"Don't pump it too hard," I warned. "You'll flood it."

The car kicked over and started, the heavy cylinders pounding in a coarse rhythm. This time, she eased the clutch out and we rolled forward. Stacey had calmed down, but with the movement of the car, she went off again.

"What's going on back there?" Corey demanded as we bounced around in the backseat.

"Just drive," I said desperately.

She crept down the alley in first gear as the sirens crescendoed and faded away. Blue lights flickered off the neighboring houses as we turned right out of the alley, onto a sidestreet away from the scene.

Corey pressed in on the clutch and tried to shift gears. She briefly found reverse, with an expensive-sounding clatter, before slipping into second. She gave it some gas and drove us calmly up the hill toward Hillsboro Road, the freeway, and away from the police.

And beneath me, Stacey Jameson began quietly weeping.

Chapter 7

Corey claimed to know how to drive a straight shift, but I saw little.evidence of it. She did, however, manage to find Belle Meade without ripping the guts out of the car or getting stopped by the cops.

Beneath me, Stacey Jameson's sobs had finally ceased, and she drifted off into a fitful, uneasy sleep. I slid off of her, resting my weight on my knees between the floorboards and the transmission hump. She curled into a fetal position and tucked her folded hands under her chin.

"Turn left here," I instructed.

"Where are we going?" Corey asked as she strained to turn the wheel.

"I think it's the fourth house or so down. I'll recognize it."

As we approached the brick pillars and the iron gates, I told her to pull in close to the intercom box. Corey rolled the window down and reached over to hit the button. We sat there nervously for perhaps twenty seconds or so, with me poised to jump back on Stacey if she decided to repeat her imitation of Sheba the Leopard Woman.

"Hit it again," I said. "And this time, lay on it."

Corey leaned out the window and held the button down with her finger, the continuous buzzing crackling through the night air. After a few moments, a static-filled voice came through the cheap speaker.

"Who is it?" It was Betty Jameson's voice, and she was not a happy camper.

"Open up. Please," Corey pleaded, "we've got Stacey."

"Who is this?" The voice came through the speaker, louder this time.

"Please, just open the gate."

"I'm going to call the police if you don't tell me who this is."

"Oh, great," I muttered in frustration. Then louder: "Betty, open the goddamn gate! It's me, Harry Denton."

The speaker clicked off and the massive iron gates began to spread. As soon as we had enough clearance, Corey pulled through over the brick hump, coasted down the long circular driveway, and eased to a stop in front of the columns.

"Wow," she said. "Nice place."

"I don't think you'd want to live here," I said.

Corey turned and looked over her shoulder into the backseat. "Sure seems like she doesn't want to."

"Let's go. My knees are killing me."

Corey slid out of the car and pulled back the seat just as Betty Jameson opened the front door. She came down the steps quickly and was behind me as I climbed out of the car. I reached in, called Stacey's name as gently as I could, then pulled her arms until she was sitting up. Her head rolled from side to side, as if the muscles in her neck had gone slack. I maneuvered her as carefully as I could until I got her upper torso almost out of the car. Then I let her fall into my arms.

Betty stepped closer and gazed down at her sister. "How bad is it?"

"I don't know what she's on, but it's all pretty bad," I said as I carried Stacey like a baby, up the steps onto the portico.

Betty and Corey followed. "Who's she?" Betty asked, pointing behind her.

"I'm Co—"

"Doesn't matter," I interrupted. "She hasn't been here; you've never seen her."

I walked through the massive doors into the hallway, then turned to face Betty. "Where can I put her? She's not much, but I'm tired. It's been a long night."

"Can you make it upstairs?"

"Lead the way."

I trudged up the staircase behind Betty Jameson, with her sister deadweight in my arms and Corey behind me. The curved staircase up to the second floor was thickly carpeted, but our footsteps still thudded softly as we walked. At the top of the stairs, Betty went right, down a wide hallway with doors on either side. Behind us, a door cracked open, light spilling out. I glanced behind and got a glimpse of a face peeking through the gap. It was just a quick look, but my impression was that the face was a frightened one.

Betty went halfway down the hall, then opened a door on the left. I turned to get Stacey through the door, and entered a bedroom filled with antique furniture and a canopy bed with stuffed animals carefully arrayed on pillows. A bare student desk and bookcase rested in one corner.

It didn't look like what I'd imagined as a teenage girl's bedroom. No music posters on the wall, nothing personal, no clutter. If this was Stacey's room, there wasn't much trace of her in it.

Betty brushed the stuffed animals off with one swipe and pulled the quilt back. "Here," she said, "put her here."

I eased Stacey onto the bed. She moaned as I settled her into the thick covers and seemed not to want to let go of me. I pulled her arms from around my neck and backed away.

Betty Jameson sat on the bed and placed her hand on

the girl's forehead. She smoothed her hair back, then took her arm and felt for a pulse.

"Do I need to call a doctor?"

"I don't know," I answered. "When we found her, she was awake, but medicated out the wazoo. She's been drifting in and out ever since."

Corey slipped over and stood next to me, her arms folded, and studied the two women on the bed.

"She's so dirty," Betty muttered. Then she suddenly stiffened, jerked her head around and glared at me. "Did you have anything to do with this?"

My jaw went slack. "Get real. We found her like that."

Her shoulders drooped and she stood up in front of me. "I'm sorry. It's just that, well, seeing her like this. Where did you find her?"

"You don't want to know." I shook my head.

"Who was she with?"

I shook my head again.

"It's that bad?"

"You should've told me what kind of shape she was in," I said. "At least I'd have been prepared. That would have helped a lot."

Her eyes darkened. "You think I knew?"

"She isn't just a disturbed teenager," I said. "This kid's trying to kill herself. You ask me, she's on her way to succeeding."

Betty crossed her arms and jutted her chin at me. "Well, nobody asked you, Mr. Denton. You were hired to find her and you've done that. Send me your bill. Thank you. Good night."

I motioned with my head toward the hallway. "Where's her parents?"

"Mother's in bed," she said. "I'm not going to disturb her this time of night."

"And your father?"

"My father's not home right now."

"I thought you said he was—"

"This is none of your business, Mr. Denton," she snapped.

"They ought to know about this," I said. "Was that your mother peeking out the door at the other end?"

This time, her nostrils flared in anger. "Again, that's none of your business, Mr. Denton. I'm asking you to leave. Now."

I sighed in defeat. "Okay, you win. But one last bit of advice. Get her a shrink, a good one. And get her in rehab. And while you're at it, get her a lawyer. Unless Stacey's got a guardian angel we don't know about, she's going to need one."

I turned to Corey. "C'mon, let's get out of here."

As we stepped back into the hallway, the door at the other end of the hall slammed shut with the dull thunk of wood hitting wood.

Moments later, Corey and I were ushered out the front door. Corey stepped quickly down the steps to the car, eager to get as far from the Jamesons as possible. Off to the side of the house, I saw the black form of a long sedan.

"Get in and start the car," I said. "Then coast around and pick me up." Corey looked at me with a question on her face, but did what I told her. I walked quickly down the walk that bordered the driveway, around the edge of the gallery, and over to the car. I stepped around front, hidden by the full branches of a large magnolia tree, and placed my hand palm down on the hood of the car.

It was still warm.

As the gates protecting the Jameson home closed shut behind us, I wondered how far we'd get before being pulled over. I wondered how many laws I'd broken that night. I'm no lawyer, but I figured we could start with evidence tampering, leaving the scene of a crime, and

obstruction of justice. I didn't know how much trouble
that would buy you, but it was probably more than I
wanted.

"What a night," Corey mumbled next to me. She'd
scooted over into the passenger's seat as I got in and
was now leaning back, her hands to her face, rubbing
her eyes. I turned right onto Harding Road and headed
toward downtown Nashville, being extra careful to stay
right at the speed limit.

"I'm sorry you were there," I said, then added, "but
I'm glad you were there."

She stopped rubbing her face. "Thanks, I think. God,
I'm exhausted. What time is it?"

I glanced down at my watch. "Just past one-thirty."

She stared ahead as we passed under a traffic light, the
green glow filling the car for a couple of seconds, then
back to streetlights.

"That's the first dead body I've ever seen," she said.

"I know this is tough, but try not to think about it."

"Funny thing, Harry. He didn't look real anymore."

"He wasn't."

She wrapped her arms around her shoulders and
hugged herself tightly.

"You cold?" I asked. "I could turn on some heat."

"No," she said after a second or two. "But I am
starving."

I laughed. "I was just thinking the same thing. The
only thing I've had since lunchtime was a stack of five-
dollar Cokes at the Club Exotique."

"What's open this time of night?"

"Damn little." We approached a blinking light at
White Bridge Road. After eleven at night in Nashville,
a lot of the traffic lights go to blinking yellows and
reds, the last vestige of small-town mentality. It has the
effect of shutting down the city traffic-control system
just as the drunks are trying to find their way home.

"There's a Waffle House at I-40. How about breakfast?"

She grinned. "Let's do it."

I made a quick left onto White Bridge Road and drove down past the shopping centers and the Nashville Tech campus. We waded through the traffic at Charlotte Avenue, still thick even at this time of night. Finally, we pulled into the parking lot of the Waffle House, which was tucked in between a motel and the entrance ramp to I-40. The parking lot was crowded with pickup trucks and gas guzzlers. Through the plate-glass window, we could hear the strains of Lynyrd Skynyrd's "Free Bird."

"This place is rocking tonight," I said, opening the door and sliding out.

Corey hesitated by the side of the car. "I don't know, Harry. Some of those guys look pretty rough."

I leaned against the side of the car and rested my elbows on the roof. "Corey, you've just spent the evening shadowing someone in a dark parking lot, tampering with a murder scene, then skirting away a material witness under the very eyes of the cops," I said. "And you're worried about a greasy spoon full of trailer trash with the munchies?"

She put her hands on her hips. "You're a real smartass sometimes, aren't you?"

"I prefer to think of it as sardonic wit," I said, heading for the entrance.

"What kind of wit?"

"Never mind," I said.

The Waffle House waitress gave me a gap-toothed smile as she set a plate in front of me with enough food on it for a lumberjack. I dove into fried eggs, bacon, and toast dripping margarine with a passion bordering on the desperate. I was halfway through the plate when I noticed Corey picking at her waffle.

"What's the matter?" I asked. "You said you were starving."

"I keep seeing that man in the bathtub," she said after a moment.

I dropped the fork on the table next to my plate. "Well, that certainly played hell with my appetite."

"I'm sorry, Harry, really. But I'm afraid. How much trouble are we in?"

"You're not in any trouble. If the heat comes down, I'll take it."

"Oh," she said, "like you can control heat."

"Don't worry. We didn't kill Red Dog Turner. All we did was get a sick little girl—who wouldn't have been so sick if not for him—out of a very bad place."

"What if the person who killed him starts looking for us?" Her eyes got bigger and filled with tears.

"Why would he do that? We didn't get a look at him. He didn't see us."

"You're sure of that?"

I tried to rub the tension out of my forehead, with little success.

"The one thing I can't figure out is why Stacey's not dead, too."

"What a horrible thing to say," she said.

"It doesn't make sense. Say it was a drug killing or a contract killing, whatever. Why leave a witness? And if it wasn't a hit, then what was it? Why was Red Dog murdered?"

"I don't know," she said. "And I don't want to know. This has been the worst night of my life."

"It's been a rough one. But you'll feel better after a good night's sleep. Why don't you let me take you home?"

"No, I don't think so. I don't think I want you knowing where I live. I'll call a cab."

I stared at her for a few moments. "Yeah, maybe

you're right. It might be better for both of us if we forget this night ever happened."

She nodded her head, then looked down at her plate.

"Hey," I said. "It was a hell of a night, though, wasn't it?"

I expected the reality to hit, but I didn't know it would hit that hard. From the moment Corey stepped into the back of the blue-and-white cab, I could feel it setting in.

I pulled onto I-40, went north on I-265, then got off at Trinity Lane. East Nashville is dark and silent this time of night. On any other night, I would have welcomed the silent drive home. Not on this night, though. Even the rumbling of the motor wasn't enough to keep the demons away. I turned on the radio and scanned from one station to another, stopping only to listen to the sound of voices.

Only it wouldn't work. I'd seen one man through a curtain, from three stories below, raise his arm and cold-bloodedly shoot another man in the throat and the chest. Red Dog Turner didn't sound like much of a human being to me, but somebody, somewhere must have loved him. Don't ask me why.

I kept seeing him over and over, lying in the bathtub still warm, naked and exposed, invulnerable now only because of death.

Maybe Stacey Jameson loved him. Perhaps when she came to—whenever that might be—and remembered the gruesome death of the man she'd made love with the night before, her already damaged heart would permanently break.

And questions, so many questions. Who killed Red Dog Turner, and why? Why did the murderer let Stacey Jameson live? Why didn't he shoot me through the head rather than take off running down the steps? If it was a contract murder done by a professional, why leave any witnesses at all?

It was nearly three in the morning by the time I got home. I climbed the stairs to my apartment and locked myself in as quickly as I could. I stripped off my clothes and kicked them in a pile, then stepped into the shower and scoured every inch of my body to within a layer of bleeding. I wanted all traces of that apartment, of Stacey Jameson, of Club Exotique, of this whole bloody night washed off me.

I eased into bed and flicked the lights off, exhausted beyond belief, begging for sleep and getting none. I fought the urge to call Marsha, to wake her up and plead with her for the chance to crawl into bed next to her. I stared at the ceiling in the darkness, with only the shadows cast by the streetlight on the curb in front of Mrs. Hawkins's house keeping me out of total blackness.

Should I call a lawyer? Should I have everything ready for when the police came? When it all started coming down, how bad would it be?

I'd done some crazy shit off and on the last couple of years. My life had gone off in some weird directions. But nothing could match yanking a stoned, naked, sick seventeen-year-old girl out of a murder scene and sneaking her off under the nose of the police.

I squirmed and fidgeted, my mind running around in circles until it seemed like nothing would ever be calm on the inside again. But then, as the sun came up and the light filtering through the thin sheers over my windows changed in color and intensity, a thought occurred to me that gave me what little solace I'd ever get out of the past twenty-four hours.

I'd been asked to do a job and I'd done it.

Now it was over, I told myself.

Chapter 8

No, I thought, it can't be. But there it was, in backlit digital numbers—one-thirty. The clock only says that twice a day, and since bright sunlight was intruding into my space, I put two and two together and figured it was afternoon. Thursday afternoon, if memory served me.

I hadn't slept this late since I was in college and had to recover from an all-nighter.

Everything in me hurt. There's this muscle in your shoulder, kind of behind the collarbone but more toward the back. When I get tense, most of the tension settles there, on either side of my neck. When I rolled over to get out of bed, put my feet on the floor, and then tried to stand up, that part of my body hit me so hard I practically fell backward.

My head pounded like a ten-on-the-Richter-scale hangover, only I hadn't had anything to drink. My back ached. I was sick to my stomach.

Who poisoned me? I thought. Then I remembered. And I saw Red Dog Turner again, and Stacey Jameson.

I woke up thinking about Corey, wondering if she got home okay, remembering how she felt when she jumped into my arms when we found Red Dog. We'd wound up going through a lot together. Now if there's a God in heaven, I'll never see her again.

I wasn't sure how I felt about that. I could fix it so I never saw her again, but I'd have a hard time not thinking about her.

87

I loaded the coffeemaker with a fistful of grounds, then jumped into the shower again. I'd tried to wash it all off me the night before, but here I was again. Maybe what I had couldn't be washed off.

I shaved, then scrubbed my teeth until my gums hurt, yanked a comb through my hair, put on my bathrobe, and swilled down a couple of cups of thick, hot coffee. I was awake, almost, and starting to loosen up again.

This day was going to be a waste. I'd wander over to the office, type up my invoice for the Jamesons, then blow off the rest. This would be the first time I felt like I wasn't charging enough for a job. As rich as she was, Betty Jameson didn't have enough money to pay me for last night.

Around two-thirty I became curious to see what the newspapers had to say about Red Dog's death. I doubted the murder made the morning paper, but the early edition of the afternoon paper ought to have something.

I slid back into jeans and a loose cotton shirt, then locked the door behind me and casually walked down the stairs. As I'd come awake and fought off that heavy, sleep-logged weight that comes from having one's night completely disrupted, the night before had become less real. I thought again of Stacey Jameson passed out on the nasty water bed, Red Dog Turner sprawled in the bathtub, the look on Corey's face as she saw him. The images were becoming less focused by the second, less vivid; in time, the lines would be so soft they'd barely register.

That was a time I looked forward to.

Mrs. Hawkins was nowhere to be seen. She usually spent her afternoons gardening when the weather was pleasant, or busying herself inside in some visible way when it wasn't. She canned fruit and vegetables, cooked and baked far more than she could ever eat, or cleaned and polished her small house until it shone.

Lately, though, there had been more and more silence from her house. Increasingly, I'd spotted her shadow in the living room, sitting in front of the flickering light of a television she could barely hear. Her hearing, she'd once told me, had started to go in her late fifties. Gradually, that part of the world she could hear had diminished to just a speck, but it seemed never to have limited her. Now age and infirmity were shrinking her world. When, in my late thirties, I'd had a marriage and a career collapse on me almost simultaneously, she'd taken me in and helped me when I'd responded to her anonymous classified ad. I'd never met her, had no job, was starting over, but she'd sensed something in me that led her to trust I wouldn't abuse her or take advantage of her. I'd respected that, and even though I could probably afford a better place these days, I chose to stay in her attic apartment because she made it so easy.

She was a widow, though, and had no children. Most of her friends and contemporaries had begun the long, slow, and inexorable slide into what were euphemistically referred to as "the Golden Years," although at my age, I could see damn little about them that was golden. I had come to sense that the day would come when she needed me more than I needed her. I didn't know how I would feel about that.

Mrs. Lee was too busy with an unusually late rush hour to spend much time with me. She loaded my tray up and sent me on my way, which was fine. I was still too spent from the night before to have much to say to anyone.

There it was, in the local section, below the fold. It was a short, two-column box story with no picture and no jump. Red Dog's real name, it turned out, was William Ray Turner, and he was twenty-five years old. Death was attributed to multiple gunshot wounds. Police had been called to his apartment after neighbors

reported screams and a scuffle. There were no eyewit-
nesses, but a police spokesman reported that statements
and evidence indicated at least several other people
were present during or about the time of the murder.
Police were searching for an unidentified material witness, a young girl who was supposedly living with
Turner. Anyone with information leading to the arrest
and conviction of the perpetrators could call the anonymous Crimestoppers line and be eligible for a reward.

Turner, the story continued, had a string of arrests
and convictions. In his short and unremarkable life,
he'd been arrested for possession, possession with intent
to distribute, B & E, carrying a weapon for the purpose
of going armed, misdemeanor assault, and for abetting
prostitution. He was, in short, just what he appeared to
be: a small-time punk scumbag.

I read the story, then reread it twice more. Astound-
ingly enough, neither my name nor Stacey Jameson's
was there. I felt that with such a small amount of white
space devoted to the murder, it wouldn't be real high
priority with anyone. William Ray Red Dog Turner
didn't have enough juice for that.

I breathed a sigh of relief that echoed down to my
socks. Could we possibly, I wondered, have gotten
away with it?

I pumped a quarter in Mrs. Lee's pay phone before
leaving, and dialed the morgue. Kay Delacorte, who'd
been the administrative center of the morgue for the
past two decades, answered the phone on the second
ring.

"Simpkins Center," she said. Actually, shouted might
be a better word. Kay had a voice that was, diplomatically speaking, penetrating.

"Hi there," I said.

She cackled, a sharp, almost barking sound. "Well,
hello, Sam Spade. . . ."

I hated when she called me Sam Spade, but it would give her too much pleasure for me to ever let her know that.

"*Lisshen schweethart.*" I was known far and wide for my terrible Bogart imitation. "*I'm looking for the doc....*"

She broke out laughing again. "Hold on, she's in her office. Up to her bra straps in paperwork."

"Well, thanks for sharing that, Kay...," I said after I'd been put on hold. A few seconds later, Marsha picked up the phone.

"Dr. Helms," she said professionally.

"This is Dr. Kevorkian," I said. "You guys got any job openings down there?"

"Oh, Jesus, Harry," she said, suppressing a giggle. "She didn't tell me it was you."

"She never does. How are you?"

"I'm okay, I guess. Buried in paperwork today."

"Up to your bra straps, I hear."

"Did she say that?"

"Yep."

"God," Marsha said. "If a man said that, I'd have him up on charges."

"I miss you," I said. "Can I see you tonight?"

There was a long pause before she spoke. "I miss you, too. Sure, I mean, well ... I'm sorry about last night."

"Me, too," I said. "Kind of a rough time, huh?"

"Yeah, what's going on with us?"

"I wish I knew," I said, "Seems like we've been at cross-purposes lately. Is it work? Stress levels a bit too high?"

"Stress levels aren't any worse than they've always been," she commented.

"Maybe that's the problem."

"Yeah, maybe." Then there was one of those long moments of awkward silence.

"So," I said, clearing my throat. "Why don't we have dinner, maybe talk about it. You working late?"

"Sevenish or so," she answered. "How about you?"

"No," I said, suddenly uncomfortable at talking about my work, given that she probably had a part of my last night's work displayed on a steel table in the autopsy room waiting for her.

"This day's a waste for me," I said. "It was three this morning before I got home."

"Wow," she said quietly. "Must have been a busy night at the strip bars."

"The important thing is, it's over. I found the girl. Look, I'll tell you all about it tonight, okay? What I can of it anyway."

"Oh, got something to hide?"

Was she kidding, I wondered, or was this serious?

"Client confidentiality," I said. "Remember?"

"Oh, yeah. That."

By this time, I could feel some anger rising in the back of my throat. Either that or the Szechuan chicken was backfiring on me. Didn't matter; I stuffed it back down.

"Marsh, we'll talk tonight. I'll pick up some wine and some groceries and be over, say seven-thirty. How's that?"

"Fine," she said. "I'll be there."

"I hope the rest of your day goes okay."

"You, too, Harry. See you tonight."

I hung up feeling like there was some unspoken but keenly felt tension between us, as if some dark clouds in the distance were becoming bigger and more distinctively formed by the minute. The air pressure was shifting, and I was suddenly, uncomfortably nervous for the first time in all the time we'd been together.

My skills at figuring these things out were no better than most men's, which is to say they were practically nonexistent. And like most men, my response to storm warnings was to ride it out and hope for the best.

I got into my car and pulled back out onto Gallatin Road. The storm I feared in my love life was also taking shape for real, as to the north a line of purple and black clouds seemed to be moving straight toward me. I pulled into traffic and headed toward the squall line on Gallatin Road, through the line of body shops, garages, fast-food joints, strip malls, and funeral homes in the direction of Inglewood. On a sidestreet in Inglewood, one of my closest and strangest friends lived part-time behind the eight-foot-high chain-link fence of an urban junkyard in a dilapidated, ancient mobile home.

I say he lived there part-time, because sometimes he slept there and other times he slept somewhere else. Only nobody knew where.

At the old Inglewood Theatre, I turned left onto the sidestreet that curved in a quarter circle around the back of the movie house and connected Gallatin Road to Ben Allen Road. Besides Lonnie's junkyard, only a couple of other cinder-block buildings dotted the street. One was a garage that I secretly suspected was a chop shop; the other was the worldwide headquarters of the Death Rangers, the local East Nashville version of the Hell's Angels.

I pulled to a stop in front of the fence, got out of the Mustang and locked it. I whistled for Shadow, Lonnie's timber shepherd and queen of the junkyard.

There was no response. I whistled again, shook the chain-link fence, and rattled the gate. Nothing. I hesitated for a moment. I could just lift the latch and go on in, but one always risked having one's arms torn off if Shadow wasn't expecting company. On the other hand, where was she?

I gave it one more try, then lifted the latch on the gate and pushed it open, poised to jump back outside if

I heard the thunder of heavy paws on hard-baked, bare
Tennessee clay.

So far, so good. I eased slowly across the yard, between the carcasses of the cars, engine blocks, piles of
rusting parts, empty fifty-five-gallon oil drums, puddles
of grease, and made my way to the trailer door. I
knocked once against the metal, loudly, as the line of
thick clouds formed high over my right shoulder. I
looked up; the ugliest of the clouds was starting to boil
and coagulate.

I rapped on the door again, and heard from within the
deep rumbling of Shadow's bark, followed by footsteps.
In a second, the rusty green door squeaked open and
Lonnie stood there, barefoot, white T-shirt, and faded
jeans. He hadn't shaved in a day or two and his thin
face seemed to be all jawline.

"Hey, dude," he said, "c'mon in."

I followed him in and shut the door behind me.
Shadow was on the couch, spread out full-length, her
massive head resting just over the edge. I walked over
to her and leaned down.

"How's she doing?" I asked.

"Vet says the hip's about gone." Like a lot of shep-
herds, Shadow was afflicted with congenital hip dyspla-
sia. The last year or so had seen a steady decline. Now
she could barely get around.

"Nothing they can do?" I asked, rubbing her ears.
Her tail flopped back and forth on the vinyl sofa like a
drumbeat and her eyes seemed to come alive for a moment.

"Doc says make her comfortable. That's about it."

"I didn't bring her any chicken, like you said."

"Yeah, she's on a special diet. Hates it, too."

I nuzzled down in her fur, her hot breath strong, pun-
gent in my face. We rubbed each other back and forth.
I didn't see that he could let this go on much longer, al-

though she didn't seem to be in any obvious pain. I decided not to bring the question up.

"Hell of a storm brewing outside," I said, standing up.

"Yeah, c'mon back. I'm in the office."

Lonnie'd converted one of the back bedrooms of the trailer into an office that was filled from wall-to-wall and floor to ceiling with radios, computers, electronics equipment, and bookcases that held books you couldn't find just anyplace. I'd had a chance to thumb through some of them: volumes one and two of *The Poor Man's James Bond* and a three-chapbook set called *Homemade Bomb Making for Dummies*. I sincerely hoped the Feds never got a search warrant for Lonnie's trailer.

I followed him through the narrow, cluttered hallway to the back bedroom. In the cramped space, he'd wedged a small desk and chair.

"I just got Web access last week," he said. "I've been doing a lot of surfing."

I looked down at the computer, where a screen full of impressive graphics and text that meant nothing to me flickered in the room's dim light.

"That's very interesting," I said. "What are you talking about?"

"World Wide Web," he said. "Hottest thing on the Internet."

"I've heard about it," I said. "What I've read in the newspapers, but that's about all."

"It makes the Internet manageable," he said. "Now you don't have to memorize a bunch of commands and stuff. You just point and click, and it's all hypertext related."

"You want to speak English for me?"

"Look," he said, pointing. "See where that word is highlighted?"

"Yeah?"

"That's a key word that will take you somewhere else

on the Web. You're at a Web site reading about, say, something about the government. The Feds are really into Web sites. A lot of government agencies have their own Web pages. So you're at the FBI's Web site and they make a reference to some Department of Justice regulation. So you can double-click on the keyword and go to the Department of Justice's Web site.

"Cool, huh?" he said.

"Yeah. But shouldn't we be, like, I don't know, making a living or playing with our kids or something?"

He turned to me. "We don't have kids."

"I know that. But isn't this just another version of watching cable TV?"

"I think of it as a tool," he said. "And there's some pretty weird shit out there. Not all of it's a civics lesson, at least not the kind the government will appreciate."

I looked at him, questioning. "Okay," I said. "Something tells me you've been getting weird again."

He grinned. "Watch."

He turned to the keyboard and, using the mouse, put the cursor on a blank line near the top of the screen. Then he typed in a series of letters, slashes, and numbers, and hit the Enter button.

Lights flashed on the menu bar at the top of the screen, then it went blank for a moment. When an image came back on the screen, it was that of a large Confederate flag, with a hooded figure outlined in front of it, arm raised in a Nazi salute.

WELCOME TO THE EXALTED KNIGHTS OF THE KU KLUX KLAN the title across the top of the screen read, and below that: RESTORING OUR ARYAN HERITAGE!

"Give me a break," I whispered over Lonnie's shoulder.

"Yeah, this is some pretty crazy shit," he said.

"I thought the Klan was dead," I said. "When's the last time you even saw a Klucker?"

"They are dead, except in cyberspace one guy can

open up a Web page like this and get read by ten thousand people in an hour."

"The ultimate soapbox," I said.

"It's all anarchy, my man. Nobody can control it. Not even Uncle Sam."

"That's either good or bad, and I'm not sure which."

"Check this out," Lonnie said, and he began typing again. This time, the screen went blank for a longer time, then began filling in again. Only now instead of a robed Klucker, we were treated to an extremely graphic graphic of a young, slim, naked Caucasian woman being—I think the euphemism is "serviced"—by a muscular African American man of astounding proportions.

"Why does this not surprise me?" I asked.

"No shit," he said. "Political extremism and pornography; two of the five basic food groups."

"I'd hate to ask what the other three are," I said. "Say, speaking of sex, I've had an interesting couple of days."

That elicited a head-turning. "Okay," he said. "I'm listening."

"What do you know about the sex biz?"

"I'm not a regular patron, if that's what you mean."

"Not exactly. Let's just call it professional curiosity. Who runs these show-bar clubs, dirty books stores, private dancer places, and the like? Is it organized crime, or just further evidence of the enduring entrepreneurial spirit?"

He thought for a moment. "I don't know, but it wouldn't be that hard to find out. Why the sudden interest in the sex biz?"

I leaned against the wall and folded my arms. "I had a client with a runaway little sister. My client thought the girl may have gotten a job in one of these show-bar places."

"Paid you to snatch her, eh?"

"Something like that."

"Have any luck?" he asked, turning back to the keyboard.

"Some. I got the girl back. Got a little sticky, but I think it may be over."

He looked back at me. "Get paid yet?"

I shook my head.

"Well, buddy," he said, "it's never over till the check clears."

Traffic was blocked up Seventh Avenue all the way from Broadway, as it usually is when the weather's about to take a turn. I stepped out of the garage after parking the Mustang and skirted my way in between the fuming cars as, above me, the sky rumbled and shifted in huge, multicolored shapes. I took the steps onto the first floor of my building with more energy than I expected to have. The old building where I rent office space doesn't even have a lobby; it's just a plate-glass door into a dark hallway floored with scuffed, chipped linoleum and painted in a war-surplus puke green. But it is cheap and, for what it's worth, well located.

I took the stairs to the second floor and made a left down the short hallway to my office door. As I fished around in my jeans pocket for my keys, I suddenly heard breathing behind me, followed by the clicking of heels.

Betty Jameson stepped out of the shadows of a small alcove in front of the janitor's closet by the stairs. She stepped over quickly as I stared at her in a kind of shock.

"Where have you been?" she said, her voice hoarse, desperate, demanding. She wore a professional, stark business suit that consisted of a dark, tight skirt with a matching jacket. Her makeup was perfect, every line sharp, every tone blended skillfully, but it couldn't hide the dark circles under her eyes.

"Recovering from the night your sister put me

through," I said, twisting the key in the lock and pushing the door open. "That okay?"

She followed me into my one-room office and glanced around with a look on her face like she'd just come across something in the rodentia family.

"I didn't know you were into slumming," I said. The red light on my answering machine was blinking faster and more continuously than I'd ever seen before.

"Damn it," she said, almost spitting. "I've been trying to call you all day."

"Yeah?" I said, picking the mail up off the floor and jogging it into a neat stack on my desk. I wasn't in the mood to be talked to in that tone of voice, and didn't think I'd be inclined to take it too much longer. "How come?"

"It's Stacey," she said, her voice dropping, all the intensity dissipated at the mention of her sister's name.

"She's gone again."

Chapter 9

I couldn't have been more thunderstruck if she'd been Ed McMahon pulling up in front of my house with the Publisher's Clearinghouse check.

"She's *what*?"

"Gone. We can't find her."

"Betty," I said, my voice tightening, "last night she couldn't even walk."

Her hands fell to her side. "May I sit down? I don't feel well."

I pushed my visitor's chair toward her. She settled into it like she was never going to get up again. I stuffed my own anger back down, fighting off the urge to scream at her. I'd gotten pretty torqued at clients before; they can be their own worst enemies. But I'd never completely gone off on one.

I sat down in my desk chair and leaned back. "Okay, Ms. Jameson. What are we going to do about this?"

She raised her head and I saw in her eyes a stone weariness that made me feel guilty for being so hard on her. "Find her again," she said, pleading.

"Maybe this is one for the cops," I said.

"No," she insisted. "You don't understand. We can't go to the police."

"Why?" I demanded. "It's not like you're the only family with a teenager who's fixing to crash and burn."

"We cannot go to the police," she repeated. "If you don't want to do this, I'll find someone else."

I shook my head. "No, don't do that. Hell, at least I know where to start looking. I think I do, anyway."

Betty Jameson stared directly at me for a long moment of silence, studying my face in a way that she'd never done before. It made me uncomfortable. I fiddled with a stack of papers on my desk and came up with a notepad and pen.

"Now let's see," I said, "when did you last see her?"

She gazed at me for a while longer, then her lips parted slightly.

"I read the paper," she said in a monotone. "And it was on TV this morning."

I set the notepad down in my lap. "Okay. So you read the paper."

"Did you kill him?"

"Oh, Jesus," I said, sighing. "First you think I got Stacey blasted out of her gourd, then you think I killed her boyfriend. You don't have a very high opinion of me, do you Ms. Jameson?"

She reached out and put her hand on top of mine. Her touch was cool, dry.

"It would be okay if you did," she said softly. "In fact, I'd be grateful. That's one less thing we have to worry about."

"It may interest you to know that the 'one less thing' you're talking about used to be a living human being, albeit not a very nice one. And, lady, he died a pretty damn lousy death."

She spoke through gritted teeth. "I don't care. After what he did to my sister, he deserved it. I just want to know, did you do it?"

I shook my head. "No. I didn't kill Red Dog Turner. We were staking out the place when I heard a scream and a couple of thumps. I ran up the back stairs and got to the apartment just as the killer was headed out the front door. I never saw him. I don't carry a gun, so I was not inclined to go after him."

"We?" she asked. "You mean you and that—girl . . ."

"Yes, that girl."

"Does she work for you?"

"Objection, your honor. The question is irrelevant." I paused for a moment. "Objection sustained."

"Besides," I added. "It was more important to get Stacey. I didn't know for sure anyone had been killed until I got into the apartment. For all I knew, Stacey was the victim."

She squeezed my hand, then dragged hers across the back of mine as she pulled away.

"You're right. It was more important."

"And now she's gone again," I said. "This is a hell of a mess. What worries me is that Stacey's not the only one out there who's running loose."

"Who else?"

"Red Dog's killer is still out there, too. And Stacey's the only witness to the murder."

"Oh my God," she gasped, blanching. "You don't think he'd—?"

I shrugged. "Maybe that's all the more reason the police should be brought into this. Then again, maybe it's a good reason to keep them out."

"Yes," she said, nodding rapidly. "If the police look for Stacey, the murderer may think it's because they know she's a witness."

I reached for the notepad again. "You told me she turns eighteen next month. We're almost to next month now."

"Her birthday's the tenth," she said. I looked at my desk calendar and counted days.

"We've got twelve days to find her and get her put away somewhere. Once she turns eighteen, you'll have to go before a judge and file a petition to have her declared incompetent. Until then, you can sign her in someplace and maybe, just maybe, keep her there on a doctor's order. Not forever, but long enough to get her cleaned out."

"That's what we want to do," Betty said.

"You should have had her there first thing this morning."

"Don't lecture me, Harry. I know we've made mistakes."

"That's a diplomatic way to put it," I said, "but I'm willing to be a diplomat for the time being. Who was the last one to see her?"

"I guess that would be Emily," she answered. "I stayed by her bedside all night, until Emily came at six this morning. I went off to get some sleep. Emily said she checked on Stacey about eight and she was awake, sitting up in bed, hungry.

"So Emily took her breakfast. Then, maybe a half hour later, she heard Stacey in the shower. God knows she needed one. Emily said the shower ran for about forty minutes, and she got worried. She went to check on Stacey and the bedroom door was locked."

"Locked from the inside, with the shower still running?"

"Yes."

"What did Emily do when she found the door locked?"

"She knocked and yelled for her. Then she went down to the kitchen where the extra keys are kept. She came up and unlocked Stacey's bedroom door."

"And?"

"The breakfast was eaten, but Stacey was gone and the shower was still running."

I made a few notes. "Stacey was gone and the door was locked from her side. Hmmm, sneaky little rascal, isn't she? That running shower probably bought her a half-hour head start. So what happened next?"

"Well, Emily nearly had a heart attack. She ran all

through the house looking for her, then she and the gardener checked the grounds. No sign of her anywhere."

"And where were you while this was going on?"

"Dead-to-the-world asleep. I was exhausted. It was only when Emily and Jack couldn't find Stacey that she came and woke me up."

I thought for a few moments. "Where were your parents in the middle of all this hubbub?"

Her face darkened. "Let's leave them out of this."

I sat forward, angry at her once again. "It's their daughter who's missing. I'm not sure we can leave them out of this."

"I don't need you to tell me how to deal with my parents."

"Where were they?" I demanded. "You're not getting out of this one. Not this time."

She sighed; resigned, disgusted, whatever. "My mother never left her bedroom. She rarely does. My father was in his office."

"His office? The one downstairs?"

She nodded.

"I thought your father was an invalid."

"I never said he was an invalid," she protested. "I said he was ill."

"What's he got?" I asked.

"That's none of your business," she said, looking away.

I jumped to my feet and slammed the notepad down on my desk. She jerked in the chair but kept herself tight.

"I've had it!" I shouted. "That's it!"

"What difference does it make?"

"It might make all the difference in the world. Do you even know why Stacey's so screwed up?"

A thunderclap exploded outside, beyond the tops of the downtown buildings, from across the river. As it rolled over us, windows shook and great heavy drops of rain began hitting windows with audible slaps. Betty jumped slightly, but then calmed and averted her eyes again.

"No. Well, I mean, not really. . . . She's just a mess."

I stepped toward her and leaned against my desk, trying to ease my voice. "Why didn't you tell me Stacey's problems had gotten worse over the past few months?"

Betty looked back up at me. "How did you—"

"Her classmates, the headmistress, her teachers."

Her face went blank, a silent mask.

"Sometimes when somebody goes off the deep end like Stacey has," I continued, "it's all tied together. Don't you see? What's going on with you, your mother, the General; it's all working together to ruin Stacey's life. I'm not trying to be your therapist, Betty. But if I know what's going on, then I'll have some idea how to handle her."

"Alzheimer's," she whispered.

I drew in a deep breath. "How far along?"

She looked up at me. "He's past the initial stages. Most of the time, he's still with us, more or less. He has good days and bad, though."

"And the bad ones?"

"Are terrible."

"Last night, when we brought Stacey home, there was a car parked by the side of the house. The hood was still warm."

Betty wrung her hands in her lap. "We can't get him to stop. So far, he hasn't been pulled over or anything, but sometimes he takes off and he's gone for hours. He's not far enough along to have him declared incompetent. He's a very headstrong man. His independence means everything to him. Last night he wandered off. Jack Maples, our chauffeur and gardener, took the car and cruised the neighborhood for him. He must have found him around one or so, down near the entrance to Percy Warner Park."

Something about all this didn't sound right, but I let it go for the moment.

"What about your mother?"

Betty Jameson dipped her head and rubbed her eyes with her right hand. "They call it bipolar these days," she answered. "And alcoholic. Not exactly the Brady Bunch, are we?"

"There's no one else, right? No other brothers or sisters?"

She shook her head.

"So in this house full of secrets and sickness, you're the only healthy person."

She shook her head again, slowly, wearily. I don't know why, but I reached out and put my right hand on her shoulder and squeezed.

"Lot of weight to carry . . . ," I murmured.

And then she was on her feet, in my arms, sobbing against my chest. Her whole frame shook with weeping, her tears hot on my shirt. Outside, the storm moved in and the wind accelerated into a howl. The windows vibrated in their frames and rattled with the impact of the rain. Her arms were tucked in under her chin and she bent forward into me in a standing fetal position. As the squall line blew over us, I wrapped my arms around her tighter and patted her gently on the back.

I'll say one thing for these Jameson women: they sure know how to have a good cry.

The storm passed in minutes. Betty Jameson was embarrassed when her own whimpering stopped, but I told her I certainly wasn't going to hold it against her, and nobody else ever had to know. The truth was, I was glad to see her break down a bit. My first impression of the Jamesons was that when you looked up the word *dysfunctional* in your *Webster's Dictionary*, you'd find a Jameson family portrait.

So General Breckenridge "Wreckin' Brecken" Jameson had Alzheimer's disease. It would be a tragic and ignoble end to a heroic and adventurous life, but it certainly wasn't anything to be ashamed of. As for the General's wife; hell, these days you have to hunt to find somebody that's not either depressed or drunk. She was just unfortunate enough to be both.

I always wondered what it would be like to be rich. I grew up in an unfragmented, upper middle-class home with two parents who got along pretty well. My father had a solid, successful business career, and he and my mother are now enjoying the rewards on one of the smaller islands in the Hawaiian chain. My mother and father stayed together in a marriage that's now approaching a half century in length, and for the most part each one of them still lights up when the other enters the room.

The point of this is that while I've always been intrigued, curious, about great wealth, I didn't come from that background of dysfunction, misery, and poverty that sometimes drives people to actually achieve it. As a newspaper reporter, I was often exposed to wealth and power, especially political power. I always figured that the acquisition of wealth and power was usually the process of swapping one set of problems for another. That certainly seemed so in the Jamesons' case.

The immediate problem, though, was finding Stacey again. It was possible that she was so blitzed she wouldn't even remember Red Dog was dead. If she went back to the apartment on Belmont, she'd find the yellow tape that roped off the crime scene. Her best bet after that would be to latch on to somebody whom she met through Red Dog.

I guess she could have gone to hide out with a girlfriend, but that didn't seem likely given her physical and mental state. The other girls' parents would run her back home as soon as they took one look at her. All the same, I'd asked Betty Jameson to call around and poll all the Harpeth Hall girls again and she'd agreed.

I was sure nothing would come out of it. Stacey was too desperate and too wild to do anything that would make it easy for us. She'd rabbited for real this time, gone to ground somewhere where she'd be tough to find. Maybe she'd even left the city. If she'd hit the road, escaped to New York or LA, then she was gone. We could kiss her malnourished ass goodbye for good.

But, I thought, on the other hand, there was the trust fund. That's a lot of money to run away from; even Stacey with all her problems would understand that.

So I had a race on my hands. In twelve days, Stacey Jameson could walk into an attorney's office, sign a few papers, and flip off the rest of the world. Then what? Give it away to the next Red Dog Turner? Shoot it up? Toast it in a crack pipe? Slug it down with a slice of lime and a rimful of rock salt?

I stared out my office window, thinking, as the jazz station in Murfreesboro played a cut off a Tony Bennett album. If I peered around hard, I could get just a glimpse of the thinning rush-hour traffic on Seventh Avenue. The sun had just set below the office buildings. The sky glowed in soft oranges, purples, and streaks of white and blue; the last residue of the afternoon storm and the only appealing by-product of automobile exhaust.

I had dinner plans with Marsha, and I knew better than to cancel them. I'd have to call it an early night, though. Something told me I was going back to the Club Exotique.

"Oh, well," I said out loud as I turned off the radio and shut down my office. "It's a dirty job, but somebody's gotta do it."

On the way to Marsha's condo that evening, I stopped off at the International Market, a Thai place down the road from Red Dog's apartment. I parked the Mustang and walked to the apartment building, then casually entered it just like I belonged there. Up three flights of stairs, I found the door to Red Dog's apartment padlocked, with about a dozen strands of crime-scene tape stretched across the door frame. I checked it closely; if anyone had tried to get past it, they'd covered it up well.

I knocked on the other three apartments on Red Dog's floor. There was no answer at two, but at the one farthest from the crime scene, diagonally across the stairwell, an elderly woman furtively cracked her door.

"Excuse me, ma'am," I said, dipping into my most syrupy drawl. "My name's Harry Denton."

I produced my license. "I'm a private investigator looking into some of the trouble y'all had here the other night."

"I didn't see anything," she said, staring out from behind a cheap security chain.

"I understand that. It was late. I'm trying to track down the young girl who was staying there with Mr. Turner. She's seventeen, blonde, very thin. Ever see her?"

"I don't want any trouble."

"There won't be any trouble, ma'am. I'm just trying to help the girl."

"I didn't see her much," she whispered. "They mostly came and went really late."

"Yes, ma'am, but have you seen her since the shooting?"

She shook her head back and forth.

"Has there been anyone else up here since the shooting?"

"Police. Lots of police."

"Anyone else besides the police?"

"No."

I thought for a moment. "Did the man who lived here ever have visitors?"

Her eyes grew wider. In the background, I heard the mewing of a cat and the soft din of a television.

"Any visitors, ma'am?"

She glanced behind her, then turned back to the door crack. "No," she insisted, protesting a bit too much. "Nobody."

"Are you sure, ma'am? I certainly won't let anybody else know we've talked."

She thought for a moment. "Well, sometimes there were girls up there, you know. Cheap girls. Not ladies. Then there was this one young man. He had real short hair, looked like it was dyed blond to me, and he usually wore those pants that were different colors of green. Oh, and he was a Yankee. I heard him talk once. Definitely a Yankee."

I smiled. "Thank you, ma'am. You've been a great help." Although I couldn't exactly figure out how.

I made my way back to the car and fought the traffic over to Hillsboro Road, through Green Hills, then turned right at Abbott Martin Road and pulled into the parking lot of the Kroger's. I had something special in mind tonight, sort of a peace offering to Marsha, although I wasn't exactly sure why I needed to make one.

I picked up a couple of fresh salmon steaks, a handful of fresh dill, salad makings, asparagus, and a baguette of French bread. I also grabbed a bouquet of fresh flowers and some expensive designer ice cream for dessert. One meal, one bag of groceries, thirty bucks. Thank God I don't have a house full of hungry kids.

I picked up two bottles of an Australian Chardonnay I'd heard Marsha mention, then loaded it all in the car and pulled back out into traffic.

She was just walking up the steps as I pulled into the parking lot. I scooted in next to her black Porsche 911, the one with the vanity plate that read DEDFLKS.

"Need any help?" she called, fumbling with her keys and punching in the code on her burglar alarm.

"Got it," I said, struggling with the bags and the car door all at once.

I followed her through the front door and walked past her into the kitchen. Marsha walked down the hall to her home office and dumped her purse and a briefcase bulging with papers. She moseyed back into the kitchen as I was stowing groceries away and popping the wine bottles into the fridge.

"Hi," she said.

I turned. "You brought home a stack of work."

She stood in the doorway a second, then came over to me. "Yeah," she said, smiling. I took her in my arms and wrapped myself around her. She felt good, warm, like home and safety. We kissed, my head bent back slightly to compensate for her extra inches. It was a drawn-out kiss, slow, languorous, almost sleepy. It had been a long couple of days.

"I don't have to do it tonight," she said, when we'd eased apart.

"Do what?"

She chuckled. "The work I brought home."

"Oh yeah, that."

She backed away and opened a cabinet, then pulled down a couple of wineglasses. The wine bottles were already cold, so I pulled one out and went to work on it with a corkscrew.

"How was your day?" I asked.

"The usual. Autopsying sleazeballs . . . ," she said absentmindedly. Then her voice sharpened. "Including, by the way, one very dead sleazeball whose nickname was Red Dog."

I yanked the cork out of the bottle. "Why don't we have a little disrespect for the dead."

I poured a couple of glasses of wine and handed one to her. She took it and held it in midair.

"Is there anything you want to tell me, Harry?"

"Yes." I brought my glass up to hers and clinked it. "I brought you fresh salmon for dinner." I brushed the back of my free hand tenderly across her cheek.

"Sounds like you had a rough day," I said. "Hungry?"

"Yeah," she said, then smiled. "I don't mean to put you on the spot. It has been a long day."

Then she stared at the front of my shirt for a second and her eyes darkened. "Looks like you had a rough day, too."

I looked down and noticed for the first time a long, crimson red lipstick smudge just below the right collar point. I reached for the sink sponge.

"Teary client," I said, then began rubbing.

"Stop that," she said, "you'll only make it worse. You'll have to break down and have this one dry-cleaned, my darling."

I set the sponge back down. "Glad to hear you're still calling me darling."

She took her glass, left the kitchen, and crossed the open foyer into her living room, which was sunken a couple of steps and set off from the rest of the area.

"Of course I am, Harry. If you were screwing around," she said as she walked away, "you'd be smart enough to change clothes before you came over."

A cold wind blew over me. I followed her into the living room. She sat on her overstuffed sofa and let herself be swallowed by it. I sat down on the fireplace hearth across from her.

"That's not the first time you've made a crack like that lately," I said. "What's going on?"

She picked up the *TV Guide* and started flipping through it, then looked up. "I don't know. You tell me."

"Have I ever given you any reason to think there's anybody else?" I said, my voice tightening.

She tossed the magazine onto the glass-and-chrome

coffee table. It slid across the surface and fell off the other side at my feet.

"Just staying out all night in strip bars, coming over to my place with lipstick on your shirt. Little things like that."

"A client in trouble came into my office," I protested. "There's a runaway teenager involved, and she's going to be in a lot of trouble if I don't find her."

"Harrumph, Harry, if I remember correctly, you called my office this morning and told me you'd already found her. Don't you think you should get your story straight?"

"I did find her," I insisted. "She's run away again."

"Oh, great, so now you get to do the strip-bar crawl again. Maybe you should try the massage parlors. She might be working there, you know."

I gritted my teeth and set the wineglass carefully down on the bricks. I suddenly found myself incredibly angry with her, angrier than I'd ever been, angrier than I ever wanted to be.

"I haven't done anything wrong," I said slowly. "And I don't appreciate this one bit. I don't know where it's coming from. I don't know what caused it, but I can tell you this—it scares me and I don't like it."

Her eyes filmed over and the glass in her hand shook. "What do I mean to you?"

"What are you talking about? Marsha, I'm crazy about you. You know that," I said, my voice softening.

I got up and crossed behind the coffee table, then settled down on my knees in front of her. I reached out and put a hand on her knee.

She put her hand on top of mine and squeezed it. "Harry, it's just that I'm wondering where we are . . . where we're going."

"What brought this on?" I asked. "Where's this coming from?"

Marsha let her head fall back on the sofa, relaxing

into it. Her face seemed to fall. "You're going to think I'm crazy if I tell you."

"Honestly, dear, I think it's too late for that."

She raised her head back up. "Smartass," she said. And then, after a few moments: "I've got a birthday."

Ohmigod! I thought. *And I missed it!*

Then a little calculating gave me relief. "Yeah, in another three months," I said.

She stared into my eyes. "You don't get it, do you?"

I furiously scanned every brain cell I could get to. I'm missing something here, but what the hell could it be?

"Harry, I turn forty this year," she said, her eyes filling.

Bells went off in my head like a pinball jackpot. I thought carefully, keeping my jaw in neutral pending a careful check to make sure my brain was fully engaged and in gear. Somewhere in the innumerable combinations of the twenty-six letters that make up the English alphabet, there were the right words for just this moment.

Now if I could only find them.

"Okay," I said gingerly, "okay. I'm trying real hard to understand this. I mean, we went through this last year when I turned forty. Granted, it's not the easiest thing to get through. It's a definite passage. But Marsha, love, even when it was my turn, I never thought you'd run off with a younger man. I never thought you'd be messing around. That just wasn't in my vocabulary. So help me understand this."

She stood up and paced around the room as my head swiveled to keep up with her.

"Oh, it's so silly," she burst out. "It's so damned clichéd.

"All I've ever done is work," she continued after a moment. "My career has meant everything. There've been men, dates, relationships, all that. But until you came along, my dear, nothing that's ever lasted like this. It was all work. And now it's paying off. If my investments hold on, I can retire in ten years and travel the world. Or I could hang in there, and slide into Dr. Henry's job when he retires. Or I could teach, go back into academia."

I was trying real hard to follow this, but frankly, I didn't know what the hell she was talking about. And I certainly didn't know what she was complaining about.

"But none of it means a damn thing, Harry! It's empty. All of it. Worthless. Totally without value."

"How can you say that?" I asked. "There are people who'd give anything to be where you are."

"Oh, great, you know where I am, Harry? You know where I am? I'm forty years old, I'm alone, and damn it—"

She sat down on the brick hearth, crossed her arms on her knees, and laid her head down wearily, her energies spent.

"—damn it, damn it, damn it. I want a baby. . . ."

Chapter 10

Well, isn't life just *full* of little surprises.

It was as if Marsha had confessed some terrible, dark, and shameful secret. Her uterus and her heart had betrayed her. All her life she'd worked to prove something to herself and others, to seek fulfillment, and she had found herself ultimately unfulfilled. In being all that she could be, she had become less than what she didn't even know she wanted.

There was a full minute of silence after her announcement. Finally, she raised her head.

"You can go if you want to," she said.

Confused, I looked at her for a moment, trying to read her. "Is that what you want?"

"No," she answered slowly. "But isn't this where you start to feel smothered? Isn't this where you deliver the lines about not wanting to make a commitment, about being too old for parenthood, or too young for parenthood? Or just not ready for it?"

"How nice of you to write my script for me," I said. "Unfortunately, you don't have a grip on the character. You see, Dr. Helms, I thought I already had made a commitment."

"Get real, Harry. You don't want this."

My legs started to cramp. I stood up, stretched, and wandered around the coffee table, and stood facing the hearth with my back to her.

"This is a surprise," I said. "Not something I expected. Not because there's anything wrong with it. I just didn't see it coming."

"Neither did I."

"I mean, I always thought that we'd . . . well, I mean, that we would at least get serious one day." I turned and looked back at her, hoping I was saying the right thing. I was working blind here, still in shock. "At least I'd hoped we were heading in that direction. I don't want to be presumptuous or anything."

She gave me a weak, haggard smile. "You're not being presumptuous. We've been together long enough to assume we're serious."

I smiled back at her. "Well, I'm glad to hear that much, anyway. So what's all this got to do with the case I've been working on?"

"I'm forty years old, darling—"

"Not yet," I interrupted.

"As good as," she continued. "And you're very good at flattery, but nobody's good enough to make that go away."

"You're worried that I might get interested in somebody younger?"

"Of course. Or that I'm just getting old. The old life's-passing-me-by thing."

I sat back down on the hearth and shook my head slowly back and forth. "You know, you spend time with somebody, you sleep with somebody, you think you know them. . . ."

"What's that supposed to mean?"

"It means I've never seen this side of you. I've always thought of you as so self-confident, so sure of yourself; an intelligent, attractive, accomplished woman out there in a man's world, cutting up dead bodies with the best of them. Always quick with the comeback, always the 'That's Doctor Babe to you.' But now, this.

"Wow," I added after a moment. "What a shocker."

"Think less of me?"

I chuckled. "No, of course not. I just never realized."

She picked up her wineglass and took a hefty sip. "So what do we do about this?" she asked after swallowing the wine with a gulp.

I folded my arms. "You sure about this?" I asked.

She nodded. "I don't think it's going away."

"So," I said, "you want to get married or what?"

She laughed. "God, I'll give you this much: you're a silver-tongued devil."

"I'd get down on my knees and do it properly, but at my age the knees would give out."

"Great, I'm thinking about becoming a parent with somebody who can't bend down without creaking," she said, laughing. Then she turned somber. "You really shouldn't joke about something like that."

I stared her down. "I wasn't joking. I always hoped we'd get married someday. The ticking biological clock just moves the timetable up."

She pulled herself up out of the couch and stepped over to me. She was close in, her face only a few inches from mine. "You're serious, aren't you?"

"As a heart attack."

"What about this baby stuff?"

"It'll take me some time to get used to the idea," I said. Suddenly, a thought struck me. "You're not pregnant now, are you? Two surprises in one night?"

"No," she answered, embarrassed, "but I did throw away my pills."

"So you could be pregnant," I said.

Tears welled up in her eyes. "I took a pregnancy test as soon as I could. Negative. When you get to be my age, it's not that easy."

I didn't make it back to the Club Exotique that night. I found myself comforting her, and one thing led to another. Marsha and I made tentative love, then ate the grilled salmon and drank the better part of two bottles of wine.

We even slept late the next morning. Marsha, who was normally out of bed around five, rolled over and yanked the alarm clock plug out of the wall when it went off. She knocked the phone off the hook so nobody could call. As I heard it drop with a thud onto the carpet, I felt her rolling against me. I turned and we faced each other, rumpled, twisted in the covers, with morning breath like a couple of old lions who'd feasted the night before on something that had been dead for a bit too long.

No matter. She scooted toward me and let her lips fall into mine. We ground together for a while, then she rolled on top, her weight smooth and even, and slid onto me as easily as fitting together two pieces of a well-worn puzzle.

An odd shift for us. We're both fastidious in the morning, usually not even kissing until teeth were scrubbed and faces washed. This time, though, she put her hands on my chest and pushed herself into a sitting position, riding me like a steeplechase jockey, in rhythm with each other, momentum building, cantering, then galloping, then charging for the finish until finally we crossed the line together and collapsed. She fell on me sweaty and flushed, and we lay there panting until the call of nature drove us out of bed and into the bathrooms.

My professional, compulsive, overachieving lover wandered in to work at ten that morning, with no phone call and no explanation. She walked into her office and closed the door behind her, leaving Kay Delacorte and the rest of the help to speculate wildly on the whys and the how comes.

As for me, I wasn't ready to think about this baby thing in the unforgiving light of day. I checked the answering machine in my office from Marsha's apartment.

There were a few calls, nothing pressing. Lonnie had a couple of interesting cars he was picking up that weekend and wanted to know if I was available. Another call was from an insurance company I'd done some work for. Seems they had another workmen's comp fraud case brewing. There was a message from Betty Jameson, saying that she'd called all of Stacey's private-school friends with no results. She wanted me to call her back with a progress report, but she wouldn't be home until about two. She was taking her mother to the doctor and had some errands to run afterward.

So Betty Jameson wouldn't be home until two.

I drank coffee at Marsha's and ate a light breakfast, then got as cleaned up as I could, given that I still had yesterday's clothes on. I cranked up the Mustang and headed back toward Abbott Martin Road. If you stay on Abbott Martin long enough, you wind around through Belle Meade, through the curving streets bordered by mansions on either side, until you come to Harding Road. I turned left on Harding at the light, then drove one more light to Belle Meade Boulevard.

I turned off the Boulevard and wandered through the sidestreets, enjoying the day, until I got to the Jamesons' gate. I reached over and hit the button on the security console, and in a few moments, Emily's voice came through the speaker.

"Yes?"

"Emily?"

"Yes, this is Emily."

"This is Harry Denton. I'd like to talk to you if I could."

"I'm sorry, Mr. Denton. Miss Betty's not at home."

"I know, Emily. I want to talk to you. Can I come in?"

The speaker went silent and the imposing iron gates spread slowly apart before me. I pulled onto the drive-

way and coasted around to the front. Emily had the
door open by the time I'd hit the first step.

"Morning, Emily," I said. "Thanks for letting me
through."

She eyed me suspiciously, but stood aside as I entered the house. "So Miss Betty's out for a while," I
said.

"Yessir, until sometime this afternoon."

I turned to face her as she pushed the door. She was
heavy, wide through the beam, but still in proportion.
As she turned, I saw strain in her face. This can't have
been an easy few days for her, either; perhaps a lot
longer than that.

"Actually, Emily, I knew that. She left a message on
my machine. Her mother's with her, right?"

Emily nodded.

"Where's the General?"

She motioned toward the back of the house. "In the
garden. He sits out there and watches Jack work."

"Is there some place where we can talk. Privately?"

"Come on back to the kitchen," she said. "I've got
work to do anyway."

She passed me in the foyer and led the way down a
hallway. We turned right into a large dining room
painted a dark clay red, with ceilings that had to be
fifteen-feet high, crown molding, plaster ceiling medal-
lions, and a long mahogany table that could seat about
twenty people. Framed portraits dotted the wall and
there were two large china cabinets, one at each end of
the room.

Emily walked around the table and through a white
swinging door. I followed her into a kitchen that was
about as large as my apartment. A Garland stove took
up one corner, and a stainless-steel walk-in refrigerator
took up the better part of one wall. A large restaurant
sink filled the wall beneath a bank of windows, and to

the left of the sink, a door led out back. The delivery entrance, I supposed.

All in all, it was a lot of equipment to feed four people. And I guessed that with the onset of age and disease, the General and Mrs. Jameson didn't do a lot of entertaining these days.

There was a pile of fresh produce on an expansive country kitchen table in the center of the room. Emily sat at a chair in front of the vegetables, and motioned for me to take a chair on the other side of the table. She picked up a kitchen knife and began expertly chopping the greens off the tops of carrots.

"You got an extra knife," I said, trying to sound bright and cheery, "I'll help you with those."

"You don't have to patronize me, Mr. Denton," she said without looking up from the carrots. Her hands moved in a switching rhythm: chop the greens off with one motion, then roll a few degrees to the side and slice the carrots in a stainless-steel pan with expert back-and-forth movements. She performed the action unconsciously, her hands never stopping, never missing a beat.

"I'm not patronizing you," I said. "I'm just a hired hand myself."

Her hands paused a moment and she looked at me. "Sorry." Then back to the carrots.

"I need your help," I said. "To tell you the truth, I'm trying to figure out what makes these people tick."

She dropped the last slice of one carrot into the pan, then reached for another and began again.

"I've worked for the General and Mrs. Breckenridge for thirty-five years," she said. "And I haven't figured it out yet."

"The thing that bugs me most is why Stacey seems so bent on destroying herself. Man, I just don't get it."

Click, click, click. She moved like a machine, silently and smoothly.

"Can you help me here?" I asked.

Nothing.

"Well, let's try this. Did she say anything to you before she disappeared yesterday morning?"

"She didn't feel none too good," Emily said. "She was hungry, wanted breakfast. She had a bad headache. Or so she said."

"Did she want you to get her anything for it?"

"Coffee and aspirin."

"So you made her breakfast and took it up there. She eat much of it?"

Emily moved swiftly to the pile of carrots and pulled a half dozen more toward her.

"Not much. She drank the coffee, though."

"And you heard her get in the shower?"

"Not exactly," she replied. "You can't hear Miss Stacey's shower from down here. It was only when I went upstairs to get her breakfast dishes that I heard the shower running."

"Was the door locked then?"

"I didn't check it," she said. "I figured I'd come back later."

"How much later?"

"I went downstairs and got my cleaning supplies out of the butler's pantry. Then I dusted the dining room. When I came out in the hall, I heard the shower still going."

"How much time had passed?"

"Maybe ten, fifteen minutes."

"And you thought that was odd," I offered.

"Seemed like she'd been in there a long time. So I went upstairs and tried her door. That's when I found it was locked."

"Did you yell for her or anything?"

"I knocked, but I didn't want to start yelling. Mrs. Jameson was asleep down the hall."

"Yeah, I think I know where her room is. So what'd you do?"

"I came down and got the master key, then went back upstairs. Miss Stacey was gone."

"Just like that," I said.

She nodded her head.

Emily brushed the pile of greens into a plastic waste-basket next to her.

"So tell me, Emily, did Stacey have the key to her bedroom? As much trouble as she gets into, seems like you'd want to be careful she couldn't lock herself in anywhere."

She stared at me blankly, her face stone ebony, quiet, dignified, strong.

"You care about this kid, don't you, Emily?"

"Mr. Denton—"

"Call me Harry," I interrupted. "Like I said, we're both just employees."

"Harry," she began, "I helped bring those two girls into the world. They was like my own babies. I changed their diapers and I held their heads when they threw up in the commode. I bathed them and watched them and took care of them. I love 'em just like they was my own."

"Well, I don't want to hurt your feelings, Emily, but you didn't watch Stacey too close yesterday."

Her bloodshot eyes went right through me. She glared, unblinking, until I got uncomfortable enough to crank my mouth into gear again.

"In fact," I said, "it occurs to me that maybe you helped her. Is that possible, Emily? With a seventeen-year-old girl who's bent on killing herself, that you would help her run away again?"

"Has it occurred to you," she asked, "that maybe Miss Stacey's not trying to kill herself? Maybe she's trying to save herself."

Chapter 11

After that, it was like a door had slammed shut between us. "Save herself from what?" I asked.

Emily looked down at the pile of work before her. Then, silently, she turned back to it. I watched her fingers as they worked quickly, nimbly, without thought.

"Maybe you're even hiding her," I prodded. "Wonder what would happen if I dropped by your house about midnight tonight."

She turned to me. "In my neighborhood at midnight," she said, "I expect you'd get your skinny white butt shot off."

"Have you got her, Emily?" I demanded. "Do you know where she is?"

"No. I don't have her. But I'm glad she's out of this house. There's death in this house."

That was the last I got out of her. Nothing I said or asked after that got me anywhere.

Now I knew that Emily had helped Stacey run away again, and one option would be to use that knowledge as leverage. But I'm a great believer in instinct, and my instincts were not to push too hard. At least not yet.

I left the kitchen through the swinging door, traversed the dining room, then down the hall to the entrance foyer. I stopped in front of the General's office, the room where I'd first met Betty Jameson. The door was pushed open, the lights off inside. On impulse, I stepped in and shut the door behind me.

There was enough early afternoon sun filtering through the sheers to enable me to see without turning on the lights. I walked quickly over to the antique desk, a brass banker's lamp in one corner and a telephone on the other. A leather-bordered blotter filled the center, with a large gilded leather cup holding pens and pencils.

I opened the center drawer to find a legal pad, a calculator, some of the General's personalized stationery, and a large checkbook, the kind that comes in a binder. I opened the checkbook. There were check stubs still mounted in the binder rings, with notations that indicated this must have been the account for household expenses. There were also checks written to pharmacies, doctors, insurance companies, medical-testing labs, hospitals. No surprises here, but I wished the check stubs told me who the money'd been spent on.

There was a part of me that felt guilty for nosing around in a client's private affairs like this. It was not something I made a usual practice. But neither was it my usual practice to find rich runaways passed out naked one room over from a corpse in a bathtub and bring them home, only to have the maid help them run away again.

Other than a lack of the kind of clutter I'd expect to find in a desk, there was nothing unusual about this one. The drawers contained bank statements and stacks of investment reports, business correspondence, mutual fund statements and the like.

I finished digging around and shut the drawers, hoping that I hadn't disturbed anything noticeably. A quick glance around the room gave me no insights. A leather easy chair sat in the corner, where the wall bookcases came together, with a small table next to it.

I checked my watch. I'd been in the room less than two minutes, but my anxiety levels were climbing fast. Stacey was certainly gone, as were Betty and her mother. The General gazed off into the distance in the gardens in back of the house, while Emily toiled away in the kitchen. Until I'd been gone long enough for Emily to wonder where I was, there probably wasn't much risk of getting caught. But still . . .

The house was dead quiet. What must it be like, I wondered, to roam the halls of this huge place in the middle of a sleepless night? Does wealth provide any comfort, any solace? Does it make you sleep better?

Okay, I admit it; I wouldn't mind finding out.

Set in the bookcase on the opposite side of the room was a closed cabinet door. I crossed over to it and pulled the doors open. An inner glass door was locked over a rack of hunting rifles, with a drawer in the bottom that was also locked.

I gently pushed on the doors to the General's gun cabinet. I remembered seeing pictures of him in the local papers when I was a boy, photographs of his return from an African safari in the days when it was still acceptable to herd exotic animals into a trap and shoot them. General Jameson was renowned as a hunter and sportsman. He was a vital, energetic man. The thought of that magnificent mind and vigorous body in decline was not a pleasant one.

Frustrated, I stepped quickly over to the office door and cracked it open. There was no one outside, so I slid the door open and took the stairs to the second floor two at a time. I'd taken a chance for nothing.

Down the hall, Stacey's bedroom had already been cleaned up. The first time I saw this room, I was amazed that an American teenager would live in a room so neat and so utterly lacking in the things with which adolescents mark their territory. No rock or movie posters, no teen magazines, no piles of dirty clothes in the corner with a life of their own. Just stuffed animals, and these were more childlike than anything else. It was almost as if Stacey Jameson was only a temporary occupant of the room, or an apparition like her mother.

I opened Stacey's center desk drawer. There were several spiral-bound notebooks inside and more clutter than I expected. The notebooks were emblazoned with the Harpeth Hall seal. The first couple were filled with class notes and scribbles, nonsensical doodles and snatches of what must have been some kind of communication. Her sketches were compact, dark, even frenzied, but clear and accomplished.

Then I opened the other spiral notebooks. In them, Stacey had written poetry and scraps of longer pieces, some just jumbled thoughts in a diary-like fashion. Her poems were dark, almost hallucinatory, obsessed with suffering and death. She had gone beyond adolescent melodrama, though, and into an angst-ridden frontier that was all too common in the young these days.

Stuffed in another drawer was a photographic portfolio and stacks of contact sheets. Stacey preferred black-and-white images of statues in cemeteries, gargoyles, barren trees, and photograph after photograph of homeless people, street bums, handicapped beggars. The photos were shot on high-contrast film, then pushed to the max in development so the photos came out grainy and surreal. She had an eye for the visual, I thought; a real gift for capturing the dark side of life.

Her bookcase was equally revealing. Stacked neatly between the obligatory textbooks were copies of the doomed poets she idolized, the photographers who saw with an eye she imitated, the writers who described their own torment in words she could understand.

I waded through the detritus, finding nothing that would give me a clue as to where she'd gone. I wanted an address book, letters—anything that could give me some insight into the girl. Who was she? What made her tick? What was inside Stacey besides pharmaceutical soup and agony?

Her closet contained the usual wardrobe of a teenage girl with a large clothing allowance: stone-washed jeans, custom torn, probably costing a hundred bucks a pair; hand-embroidered Indian blouses; T-shirts that probably did not come from the Kmart over on Charlotte Avenue. Expensive running shoes, dress shoes, and sandals lined the floor of the closet.

None of it looked like it had been worn in a long time. The last time I'd seen her, she was naked and filthy. Her underwear was torn and gray, and her jeans looked like they'd been left in an alley overnight.

I sat down on the edge of her bed and stared. What in the hell had gone on here?

One thing was certain: I wasn't going to find Stacey Jameson under the bed. I'd done all I could here. This house wasn't giving up any more secrets. Not today, anyway.

By the time I got back to the office, the sun had warmed the streets almost back to summer temperatures. As I turned onto Seventh Avenue off of Broadway, I could see heat waves shimmering off the pavement.

Inside my office, the answering machine blinked away. I jogged my mail into a neat stack and thumbed through it. No checks, nothing pressing, a couple of bills. The usual. I pressed the button on the answering machine.

"Hey, man, call me." Lonnie's taped voice had a tinge of his Brooklyn accent in it, which usually indicated tension. "If you're not going to Kentucky with me, I got to round up somebody else."

Then, Marsha's voice, a bit tense, uncertain: "Hi, just wanted to check in, see if you were still you and I was still me. I mean, what we talked about last night. Anyway, just checking ..."

I called her back, but Kay Delacorte gave me an ex-

tended, graphic description of what was preoccupying
Marsha at the moment. Something about advanced
states of decomposition requiring flash freezing before
autopsy so you could pick the critters out.

"After all," she joked, "you can't autopsy someone
when they won't sit still."

I left a message, then dialed Lonnie's number. He
picked up on the third ring. "Yeah?"

"Lon-man," I said, "what it is?"

"You going with me tonight?"

"Can't, dude. I'm going back to a show bar tonight."

"Well," he said, chuckling. "At least you have your
priorities straight."

"Nothing like that," I said. "That girl I was looking
for . . ."

"Yeah, the one you found?"

"She rabbited again."

"So it's back in the sewer for you."

"That's what it is, too. A sewer."

"Sure you won't change your mind? I got a 450SL
I'm picking up in Hop-town. I'll let you drive it back.
You can even put the top down."

Driving a convertible Mercedes back from Hopkins-
ville, Kentucky on a clear moonlit night was ordinarily
something I'd have jumped at.

"Not tonight, guy. I really got to find this girl. She's
pretty deep in it."

"How deep are you in it?"

"Depends," I answered.

"On what?"

"On whether I get caught."

He snorted into the phone. "That's damn comforting,
Harry."

"How late you going to be out?" I asked.

"Should be in around four in the A.M.."

"Want me to look in on Shadow?"

There was silence on the phone for a few heartbeats.

"If you want to," he said. "She ought to be okay. If you get a chance."

"Okay, if I get a chance."

"Know where the key is?"

"Under the rusty DeSoto hubcap, right?"

"Yeah, by the northeast corner of the trailer."

"Gotcha."

We hung up, both knowing I'd check in on the old girl before bedtime.

I grabbed a quick lunch at a greasy spoon on Union Street called the Cork & Fork, which could have been more aptly named the Snarf & Barf. Then I called Betty Jameson. She wanted to know why I didn't wait until two to come by. I told her I needed to search Stacey's room and then get busy. I didn't have time to wait until two. Neither did she. We hung up and I realized I'd forgotten to ask about the retainer check.

Damn.

I spent the rest of the morning and early afternoon buried in the stack of printouts from the tax assessor's office and the secretary of state. By the time I'd finished, I'd mapped out a pretty good schematic of the corporate connections between the clubs and the properties they occupied.

The three companies listed as owning the properties—K & K Enterprises, Ltd., Camerotica Inc., and Bluenote Corporation—had only one name in common: M. L. Klinkenstein, which was the name Corey mentioned the night I met her. Klinkenstein was the president and CEO of K & K, and a director of the other two companies.

There were three major corporate players in Nashville's show bar/massage parlor/adult bookstore biz, with only one person having a finger in all three rice bowls. And Red Dog Turner worked for him. Was he a bag man, a roving troubleshooter, or just a flunky? I figured that Red Dog probably worked all the clubs

Klinkenstein was involved in, and it was only blind
luck and persistence that led me to encounter one
person on the phone dumb enough to tell me where
he'd be.

It was equally blind luck that I'd found Corey at the
Club Exotique and that she'd been willing to help me.
And I wouldn't exactly call it luck, but it had just been
a roll of the dice that the night we picked to trail Red
Dog was the same night someone else decided to mur-
der him.

This was all very interesting, but it didn't help me
find Stacey. I needed something; some key, some secret
handshake, and the only thing I knew was that it was
out there somewhere and I didn't have it yet. From
what I'd seen, most of the other girls who worked the
show bars were hardened and cautious. They weren't
going to help me unless there was something substantial
in it for them. It had taken a special blend of inexperi-
ence and naïveté for someone like Corey to want to
help me just for the thrill of it.

Truth was, I hated to involve her again. There was,
after all, a murderer out there running loose. On the
other hand, Stacey was at even more risk. She had seen
the killer, presumably could identify him. She was ill
and she wasn't thinking clearly. My job was to find her
and get her somewhere safe, wherever that might be. I'd
keep all my options open, but for now it seemed the
best bet was to find Corey, keep my eyes open, and
hope something would lead me to this lost girl.

First, of course, I'd have to stop by the cash machine.

If the doorman at the Club Exotique recognized me,
he didn't let on. I got the same automatic rap about the
cover charge: the two-drink minimum, BYOB, we don't
serve alcohol, don't touch the babes, blah, blah, blah.

I nodded my head like a good little voyeur and
stepped into the noise. Clouds of cigarette smoke re-

flected back the flashing blues, reds, and purples of the
strobe lights. The B-52's' "Hot Pants Explosion"
pounded in my ears, my head, almost as if in time to my
heartbeat, loud enough to shake the mirrors. The place
was half-empty, with a few men occupying the chairs
right against the center stage, the rest at the smaller tables dotted throughout the room.

On the stage, a muscular, nude twenty-something
with albino white hair was facedown on the floor, her
head pointed toward the center and her legs spread wide
in front of the men behind her. Then she stretched like
a cat and pushed off the floor with her arms, her back
bending into a curve of spine, rump, and legs. She
pulled herself up, spread her legs wide enough to do a
complete split, then brought her torso forward until she
was sitting up. She dropped her face to the floor again
and pushed with her legs to raise her hips off the floor,
her back arching again, her bottom in the air.

I gazed across the room at her. She had an exquisite
body, and as she rolled her head to the side and looked
across the stage directly into my eyes, she smiled. Her
teeth shimmered like white diamonds in the black light.
Her lips glowed with the fluorescent lipstick she wore.
She had a thin, aquiline nose and high cheekbones. There
was a sweet smell in the air: perfume and cheap cologne,
cigarettes, musk, the warmth of bodies.

She shifted smoothly into a sitting position, then spun
around the slick floor on her pelvis, her legs splayed
out, a moving, circular display of anatomy.

I sucked in a deep breath as a waitress in a tight
black skirt, white ruffled tuxedo shirt, and bow tie sauntered up to me.

"Can I get you anything?" she shouted over the music, the singer declaring at the end of the song that those
hot pants were so hot he might have to take 'em off.

Dumb question, I thought, given the two-drink minimum. "Sure. Club soda with a slice of lime."

The disc jockey was in a B-52's mood; he segued straight into "Good Stuff," and the singers wailed "Take me down, where the love honey flows. . . ."

To my right, a huge bearded logger type with a bucket of beers in front of him that he'd brought in himself handed a twenty to each of two women. The first, a redhead in a baby-doll nightgown, pulled two tables together. The second, a thin, deeply bronzed blonde in a neon orange bikini that seemed to shine under the lights, dropped the two piece suit in one smooth, practiced motion. She hopped up on the tables and twisted into a crab position, gyrating her hips, her legs spread painfully wide, inches from the logger's face.

The redhead stood next to her, slowly pulled the nightie off and squeezed her breasts together. She pulled them up toward her chin, then bent her head and began licking her own nipples.

The DJ cranked the music even louder. Thought became impossible. Lights flashed, bodies squirmed, the senses became overwhelmed by the onslaught. I found myself dizzy, the blood in my head pounding. The woman on the stage leaned down, caught my eye again, then jiggled back and forth with a broad grin.

Someone tapped me on the shoulder; I jumped about a foot and the waitress nearly lost her tray full of drinks. She recovered her balance without ever dropping the smile from her face.

That was one thing you couldn't help but notice; they never lost the smile.

The song wound down, and in the brief, blessed silence before the DJ started yelling into the mike, the waitress said: "Where ya' sitting?"

For a moment, I didn't understand the question. The blonde on the stage collected her stack of dollar-bill tips and bent over to pick up the costume she'd so cavalierly shed a few minutes earlier. I felt a shiver, and wondered if the air-conditioning had been cranked up.

I turned again. The waitress was staring at me. "You okay?"

I fought to think. *What was the question?* Oh, yeah, tables. . . .

"Anywhere," I said, pointing to the nearest table in front of me. "Here's fine."

She set the drink down and said, "Five dollars," but by that time the DJ had cranked up another one and I was lip reading.

I sat down and sipped at the drink as another dancer took the stage and began trying to take us where we'd never been before. The first night I'd come to this place, it was like being in a state of fascinated shock.

Tonight was different. I felt blood and heat tonight, and suddenly had a sense of how one could become addicted. The assault on the senses was overwhelming, every avenue for sensation flooded with stimuli. The perfect, whole bodies became a collection of body parts, and in so doing, the objectification was complete. Sexuality was reduced to a commodity, a drug that could be prescribed, bought and sold, ingested, and enjoyed until it became just another jones, with ever-increasing doses required to overcome the numbing effects. No emotion, no intimacy required or even wanted. Only the rush.

I felt simultaneously aroused and revolted. I wanted out. I needed out, before this went any further.

I wanted to stay. I had to stay. Damn.

I searched the room, scanning the girls for Corey, but she was nowhere to be seen. Had she called in sick, taken the night off? Was she in the dressing room, on break?

The two girls off to the right finished their table dance with the bearded guy, who by now had turned his attention to another pair. The blonde in the neon orange

bikini tripped off away from my table, but the redhead
in the baby-doll nightie put me in her sights.

She sauntered over. "Hi," she said, raising both hands
high over her head, stretching, then running her hands
through the mass of long red curls. "I'm Tawny."

Her skin was pale white, dotted with freckles, and
she was larger on top than most of the other girls. When
she raised her arms, her breasts followed, the nipples
raising shiny points in the sheer cloth.

"Hi, Tawny," I said. Then it hit me. Tawny was the
girl who'd told Corey about Red Dog's having the hots
for the blonde dancer.

"Like a dance?" she asked. "I saw you watching us
over at the other table."

I pulled a twenty out of my pocket. "No dance,
Tawny. Just some conversation."

She smiled, sat down. "Great. I could stand to get off
my feet."

Tawny pulled her chair in closer to me, until we were
shoulder-to-shoulder around the tiny table. She took the
twenty, folded it in her hand, and made it disappear.

"Drink?" I asked.

"Sure. Apple juice."

I raised my hand to the waitress. "I met another girl
who worked here, liked apple juice, too. Maybe you
know her. Let's see, what was her name? Ginger, I
think."

"Oh, yeah," she said brightly. "I know Ginger. Not
real well, though."

"She working tonight? She was a nice girl."

"I don't know," Tawny said. "Haven't seen her."

The waitress strolled over and set the tiny glass of
apple juice on the table. I peeled off another five and let
it go. Then I figured if I couldn't find Corey, maybe
Tawny could help me.

"Tawny, I'm a private investigator working on a
missing person's case."

Okay, so that was a little blunt. I felt her harden next to me. "Young girl," I continued, raising my voice to be heard over the music. "She may have worked here, may not have. But she used to run around with Red Dog Turner."

Her eyes went as cold as a bill collector's heart.

"Yeah," I said. "Red Dog."

She swallowed the rest of the drink in one gulp, then stood up wordlessly.

"At least look at her picture," I said. "She's only seventeen."

She stopped and her eyes, for a moment, seemed to soften. I pulled the picture out of my jacket pocket, palmed it, and held it discreetly next to the candle in the red glass on the center of the table.

Tawny bent down almost imperceptibly, stared for a moment, then shook her head, the long red ringlets bouncing across her shoulders. "Never seen her," she mouthed.

"If you had, would you tell me?"

Then the hardness was back. "I said I'd never seen her. Thanks for the drink."

Then she was gone, melting into the crowd like rush hour at Grand Central Station. I didn't think it was going to work anyway, but it was worth a shot.

The woman who'd been onstage when I came in was circling the room now, working the tables, looking for a dance. She caught my eye as one fellow in a dark suit and tie shook his head, refusing her offer.

The smile deepened as she walked past two other tables straight to me. I felt my heart beating about a foot and a half lower in my body than it normally would. Her stride was long and she was tall, with a blonde mane that fell to her shoulders. She wore an American flag bikini, like something Captain America would have designed in *Easy Rider*.

She came to my table and bent low toward me, her head next to my ear, her breasts in my face.

"Buy a dance, sweetie?"

I turned my head so she could hear me over the gangsta rap that blared away behind us. "What's your name?" I asked.

Her breath was hot in my ear; I felt it in my toes. "Tyler, what's yours?"

"Riley," I said. "D. H. Riley. Listen, Tyler, I don't want a dance, but I would like you to sit here and talk to me for a bit."

She stood up and looked down at me, slyly teasing. "The boss likes us to keep moving—"

Before she could finish, I held a folded twenty out to her from between my thumb and forefinger. She bent over, put a hand on each breast, squeezed them together around the bill, and pulled it gently out of my hand. She sat down next to me.

"Buy me a drink?"

I nodded. She turned and made a motion to the waitress.

"You know," she said, turning back to me, "you can sit closer to the stage. We don't bite."

My arm was on the table. She brushed her fingertips on the back of my hand and let the long straight hair drape over my forearm.

"I appreciate that," I said. "But, Tyler, I came in here looking for someone. You can help me."

"Me?" she asked. For the first time, I sensed, this was not part of her script.

"Yeah, I'm looking for Corey."

The smile disappeared for a moment. "You know," I said. "Ginger. She dances here."

Tyler, or whatever the hell her name was, backed off in the chair a fraction of an inch. "You a cop?"

"No," I said. "I'm not a cop. I'm just a friend of hers."

"Well, D. H. Riley, we've got lots of girls in here. It's real bad to get attached to one."

"I'm not attached to her like that," I said, yelling over the music. Damn, it was hard to have an earnest conversation with anyone when you had to scream in their direction.

"I'm afraid I can't help you," she said as the waitress brought over a glass full of red liquid, then took five more dollars from me. Tyler looked away from me, toward the stage.

"I really am a friend of hers," I insisted. "Otherwise, how would I know her real name was Corey? And that she's from Boston, and she dropped out of college last year."

The pasted-on smile disappeared at that. Tyler moved closer to me, looked to her right and left nervously, then bent toward me.

"She's not in any trouble, is she?"

"I hope not," I answered. "That's why I need to find her."

"Has this got anything to do with Red Dog getting killed?"

I watched her for a moment, trying to read past the surface. "No," I lied. "But I've got to find her. There's somebody else involved, a young girl."

"They're all young girls," she said, a hardness to her voice that had not been there before.

I pulled out Stacey's picture and palmed it. "Recognize her?" I asked. "I'll make it worth your while."

She pursed her lips, like she was trying to figure out whether or not to take the chance. Then she studied the picture for a few moments.

"No, never seen her. I think I'd know her if I had."

"The girl's name is Stacey. She's seventeen and she's very sick. Corey was helping me."

Tyler picked up the drink and sipped it. A few drops

of cold water dripped onto her cleavage and disappeared.

"She called in this morning and quit," Tyler said.

"Quit?" Something in me fell heavily. Corey might not have been my last hope, but she was damn near the end of the line.

"Just up and quit," she added.

"She say anything else? Is she leaving town?"

"I don't know," Tyler answered. "Look, I got to go. I can't sit here forever, and this is making me really nervous. Whatever you two are into, I don't want to get involved."

She stood up. I broke every rule in the house by reaching out and taking her arm. No one saw in the chaos of light and noise, though, and I stood up next to her.

"Can you at least give me an idea where Corey might be? Please."

Tyler tucked her chin down toward her chest and coyly pulled her hair down over the side of her head, hiding her face. "Girls come and go," she said, real low. "It's like a revolving door around here," she said. "Try the other clubs."

Chapter 12

There was just a trace of dusk left by the time I retreated into the Club Exotique parking lot. I was dazed, unfocused, defeated. Corey was gone now, as well as Stacey. I tried the direct approach with one dancer, begging with another, and struck out twice. I'd hit a brick wall, and the mortar had held.

All in all, not a good day.

My office was only about five minutes away from the Club Exotique. The streets had bled themselves clean of the rush-hour gridlock, and I found a place on the street right outside the building. As was usual this time of night, the place was deserted. Even Ray and Slim, the two struggling songwriters who had an office down the hall from me, would be off at happy hour somewhere.

I locked my door behind me, then settled into my office chair. I stared at the wall until I realized it didn't have any answers either, then picked up the phone and dialed the morgue.

Marsha picked up on the fourth ring. "Simpkins Center," she said in her professional voice.

"So we're both working late."

Her voice softened. "Yeah," she said, "but I didn't get in till nearly lunchtime."

"How's it going?"

She giggled. "I've been in a fog all day."

I couldn't help but smile. "Yeah, me, too. You take any guff from anybody?"

"No, I've only got about six months of comp time built up. Who's going to say anything? How's your day going?"

"Well, I've lost my teenage runaway for sure this time. The one person who I thought might be able to help has disappeared as well."

"You sound kind of down," she said.

"Yeah, maybe. Maybe just tired." I sighed into the phone, a noise that sounded like despair, although I really didn't mean it that way.

"You are down," she said. "Any of it got anything to do with . . . what we talked about last night?"

"No, it's just that . . . Well, how do I say this?" I scrambled to find the words. "Let's put it this way. If I ever start to get weird on you, you call me on it, okay?"

I could almost see her brow furrow through the phone. "What do you mean?"

"Hanging around these clubs can have a bad effect on a person," I said.

"I can imagine. You think it's starting to get to you?"

"I don't know. Something's getting to me, but I don't know that I can put a name to it. But I can imagine how someone could get hooked on this stuff."

"You mean the show bars? Naked bodies?"

"You know how it was when you were a kid and one of the other kids on the block managed to lay his hands on a *Playboy* and you got to see one for the first time?"

"Not really, Harry," she said, "you see, I—"

"Of course you don't," I interrupted, "girls don't work that way. But the first time I saw a naked female body, there were two levels at work. There was sexual arousal, sure, but there was also a certain thrill at seeing something you weren't supposed to see. There's a kind of kick out of the naughtiness of it, understand? The tickle exists on two levels."

"Well, yeah, it works that way for girls, too."

"So the sexual arousal part of it is, all things being

relative, pretty healthy. A normal part of growing up. But the way you keep it healthy is by developing the emotional side of it as well, right?"

"Like in relationships," she said, "with intimacy and communication and some level of commitment."

"Yeah, all that stuff that scares the hell out of people. But we work at it. We try, anyway. But when you get caught up in the thrill of the naughty, you don't go on to that part. You see those perfect bodies in the magazines and they're not people; they're things and nothing else. And pretty soon, you see enough of them and the thrill's not there anymore. But it's not the healthy sex thrill you're jonesing on, it's the naughty. So you have to move up a level, like a junkie increasing his hit 'cause the same old level of street junk doesn't cut it anymore."

"Where's this going, Harry?"

"Just hang with me a minute. I'm trying to work through this stuff."

"So what's the next level?"

"I don't know. Maybe pornography, erotica. One-handed reads. Then it's on to X-rated movies and the like. Then even that's not enough, you need to see it live. The real thing. So you go to show bars, where for the price of admission and a two-drink minimum, you get your own personal obstetrics and gynecology lecture."

"Harry, that's disgusting," she said.

"And after that, it's sex clubs where you get to watch people doing it live."

"This is getting pretty weird, darling."

"Where does it all end? Rape? Serial killing? I read somewhere a lot of serial killers and rapists are sex addicts."

"So you think the logical conclusion to a teenage boy's sneaking a gander at *Playboy* while locked in the bathroom is Ted Bundy," she said. "My God, Harry, you're becoming a Republican."

"No, please," I implored. "Not that. I'm just fascinated by the dark side of this."

"You think maybe this is hitting your dark side, babe?"

"I don't know," I said. "I didn't even know I had a dark side. At least not *this* dark side."

"Everybody's got a dark side," she said. "What makes you think you're any different?"

"It's depressing to be in these places," I said.

"Good, that means you're healthy."

"But I go into them and I can't help but stare. I can't help but be, on some level, aroused. And I hate that."

"Look, it's just human. You go into a room full of naked bodies, you're going to stare. It's nothing to be ashamed of.

"But," she added, "if you finish your case and find this girl and still keep hanging out in a room full of naked women, then we're going to have a little talk."

"Hey, listen, after this is over the only naked woman I want in a room with me is you."

She laughed. "From your mouth to God's ear."

"The woman that was helping me," I said. "She seems to have changed jobs. I'm going to look for her, give it one more night. If I can't find her, then it's time to switch directions."

"One more night won't hurt anything, I guess."

"If I get in early, I'll call you."

"Make it tomorrow. I'm going to bed early," she said. "I'm exhausted."

I think this would have been easier if I hadn't been alone. There's something about walking into a room full of men ogling naked women that makes you feel almost naked yourself. It's not like you can hide why you're there; it's not like you could have wandered into the place inadvertently and then decided to stick around because the atmosphere seemed cordial.

The first place I hit was off Division Street, down near Music Row in the neighborhood of brick homes that had gone commercial and now housed independent record labels, studios, and office space. I pulled to a stop in front of a two-story brick building painted glowing purple except for the windows, which were painted over in flat black.

I parked by a meter and crossed over to the sidewalk leading up to the place. Flashing on the front of the building was a sign in shimmering pink neon, with four-foot-high letters that spelled out: LIVE NUDE GIRLS.

Oh, good, I thought, *as opposed to dead nude girls.*

"Jesus," I whispered as I approached the door, "just don't let anybody I know see me walking in here."

I pulled the heavy glass door open and stepped in. The music at this place was booming from upstairs, a thumping, unrecognizable beat that shook the floor joists above us. The downstairs was, for lack of a better description, a supermarket. Only instead of picking up bread, milk, butter, and eggs, you could walk out with any sexual device, toy, gadget, tool, or contraption imaginable. I'd heard of plastic inflatable love dolls, but I never knew they came in every conceivable size, gender, race, creed, and place of national origin. And if you didn't want the whole doll, you could just buy the anatomical parts that appealed to you the most.

I shook my head in wonder. There were three or four guys walking around among the display shelves, perusing the videos, the magazines, and the racks of pornographic CD-ROMs for the more technologically minded. Behind a glass counter filled with everything from condoms to adult playing cards, sat an older, fat bald man smoking a disgusting green cigar. He eyed me as I walked in, then returned to the paperback he was reading. I flashed on showing him Stacey's picture or asking about Red Dog, but I figured that'd get me tossed out in a heartbeat.

I walked around for a minute or two, trying to get my bearings. One section of the first floor was devoted to gay porno, another to whips and chains, and a third large one to what I gathered were amateur videos. There were hundreds of those, anthologies and collections of things people had filmed in their own bedrooms, thanks to the marvel of video cameras.

Too much, just freaking too much.

Around the corner, past a wall display of dildoes, vibrators, butt plugs, and a variety of other multicolored battery-powered devices was a doorway. Through the doorway, a narrow set of stairs ran up to the second floor. A sign read: PRIVATE DANCERS UPSTAIRS.

I took a deep breath and started up. The light dimmed, with only the ambient light from the downstairs room and the red of an Exit sign illuminating the way. I came to a landing, with a closed door in front of me. Another sign declared: IF NUDITY OFFENDS YOU, DON'T COME IN!

Too late for that, I thought as I pushed the door open. The room was large and took up most of the second floor. Bare, scuffed wooden floors betrayed the building's origins as a warehouse of some kind. Around the edges, little cubicles had been thrown up haphazardly. They were constructed of badly finished drywall and ran up to within a foot of the ceiling. Paint peeled off a couple of them. The entrance to each cubicle had a curtain pulled across.

The music blared, an urban gangsta-rap kind of ditty, something about one man having sex with another man's sister and mother at the same time in order to get revenge over a business transaction that had soured.

At least I think that's an accurate transliteration. Kind of hard to tell.

Four sofas were lined up facing each other in a

square in the center of the room. Two men sat on adjoining couches, each with a nominally dressed woman.

A tall redhead wearing a black patent-leather bra, garter belt, and dog collar walked up to me and got right in my face.

"Hi, I'm Candy," she yelled over the music.

"Hi, Candy," I answered.

"You ever been here before?" she asked brightly.

"First time."

"Well, here's how we do things up here," she said. "You're welcome to sit around and meet a few of the girls, and when you see one you like, you go into one of our booths for a private dance. If you want topless only, that's twenty. Bottomless only is thirty-five. Totally nude is fifty. Dances last about twenty minutes or so and are totally private. It's just you and your favorite fantasy, all alone.

"How does that sound?" She smiled and gave me a coquettish turn of the head.

"Great," I answered. "Okay, if I hang out a bit?"

"Sure. Can I get you a drink? We don't serve any alcohol here, but you're welcome to a soft drink."

"How about some ginger ale?"

"Coming right up."

She walked away, heading into the shadows across the room. My eyes adjusted to the dim light and I saw a small bar in the corner. Several women wearing next to nothing were leaning in, talking to the bartender, who apparently doubled as the disc jockey. There were also a couple of real big guys in suits just lingering around.

The two gents on the sofa looked up from their girls as I stood there. I felt nervous, awkward, like the nerdy guy who got invited to a party where he didn't know anybody and came alone.

I walked around the sofas, over to a corner where two other vinyl couches were lined against the wall. I slid onto one of them, then stopped suddenly. Something sticky was on the material. I winced, stood up, then gingerly sat down on the other sofa.

One of the women at the bar spotted me and moved in for the kill. She had dark hair, so black it had to be dyed, circles under her eyes, and was so rail thin the outline of her ribs showed through her pale skin. She wore a navy blue string bikini and patent-leather hooker heels.

"Hi," she said, landing on the sofa next to me. I was against the heavily padded arm of the sofa, my left arm resting on the side. She wedged herself in so tight next to me she pushed me even farther into the cushions. In the dim light, I could see bruises on her arm, and perhaps some scarring.

"Hi, I'm Rio."

"Hi, Rio," I said.

"Wanta buy a private dance?"

"Maybe in a bit."

"Great. While you make up your mind, I could sure use a drink."

"Okay," I said. "She knows what you want, right?"

Rio nodded her head.

"Go ahead then."

Rio made a quick motion with her head, an almost imperceptible nod, and Candy—who was headed toward us with my drink—reversed course and walked back to the bar.

I turned to Rio. She was early thirties at least, much older than the girls I'd seen working the Club Exotique. And the two women on the sofas right by the entrance were older as well, with a hell of a lot more mileage on them. They weren't in as good shape either; the woman in the see-through nightie needed to lose about thirty pounds.

"How long you been working here, Rio?" I asked.

"About six months," she said.

"Where'd you come from?"

"Oh, Detroit, by way of Gary and Indianapolis."

"How long you been in Nashville?"

"About six months."

"What, you got transferred down here or what?"

Candy approached with a tray and handed me a ginger ale and Rio a Coke. "Five dollars, baby," she said.

That was about half the cost of the drinks at the other place I'd been, which I took as further evidence of this joint being way down on the feeding chain.

I handed Candy a twenty and watched as she carefully counted out five ones and then a ten. I handed her back one of the singles and stuffed the rest in my pocket.

"So," I said, "where were we?"

Rio sipped the drink. "You were asking a lot of questions."

"Just making conversation," I said. "Not trying to be nosy."

She pressed her thin arm into my right shoulder and rubbed the toe of her shoe into my calf. "Be nosy. We might get to know each other real well," she said.

The music changed to a driving metal beat, the shrieking of guitars exceeded only by the shrieking of the talentless idiots who brayed that crap.

This place was a miasma, a pit that couldn't have been too far from the last stop on the ride from high-paid dancer to Dickerson Road street whore. Corey might wind up in a place like this someday, but she wasn't here tonight. I'd have bet the rent money on it.

"What's in those cubicles?" I yelled over the noise.

"A couch. The walls have mirrors. We go in there and have a little privacy and a lot of fun."

"How much fun?" I asked.

"You got to go in to find out, baby," she said. She grinned at me, flirting, teasing, coaxing. Her teeth were crooked and there was a large gap between two uppers. She laid her arm across my lap. I looked down at it, studied it, tried to focus on the lines that formed in the crook of her elbow. Her skin was loose, flaccid.

"Listen, Rio, you're a real sweet lady, but I think I've got to run," I said.

"Oh, c'mon, don't be a stick in the mud," she said, pressing down on my lap with her arm. My heart started to beat a little faster and I felt a tightness in my chest.

"Thanks," I said, "but no thanks."

She opened her palm and ran it between my thighs, up my legs to my crotch. When she found what she was looking for, she began squeezing rhythmically.

There was no table in front of us, so I leaned over her arm and set my glass on the floor. Then I sat back up, took her arm out of my lap, and pushed it over. I stood up and looked down at her.

"See ya 'round, Rio," I said.

Her eyes turned dark and the smile was gone. "Not if I see you first, jerkoff," she hissed.

The evening went downhill from there. No new leads and no Corey. At the Otra Vez Club, a stoned junkie in a leopard-skin bikini spilled a drink in my lap. When I wouldn't let her take my pants off to dry them, she tried to mop up the mess with her tongue.

At the XXX A-Go-Go, two frat boys who'd brought in just a bit too much Maker's Mark got into a tangle with one of the girls and got tossed out into the parking lot. The bigger of the two went for a baseball bat he kept under the front seat of his Chevy S-10 pickup, which caused him to receive one of the more severe stompings I'd seen anyone get in a while. I coasted out of the parking lot just as the cops peeled in.

The doorman at the Odyssey informed me that the club wasn't a show bar anymore; it was under new management and was now a swing club. He was explaining the rules to me when I walked away from him back to my car.

In front of the Classic Cat on Eighth Avenue, one of the older, more established clubs in the city, I got accosted by a drunk transvestite in a red evening gown who needed a shave and five bucks for a taxi. He'd had someone lift his purse at Victor/Victoria's, the drag bar across the street from the Cat. The guy was crying so hard I felt sorry for him, but truth was I was fast running out of cash myself.

At the Double Platinum Club, I might have found Corey. It was nearly as elegant as the Classic Cat and Deja Vu. I hung around for over an hour, spent twenty bucks on the cover and drinks, and slipped a dancer twenty and my card and told her there'd be a hundred more in it if Corey came to work there and she called me. On impulse, I pulled out Stacey's picture again and asked if she'd ever seen her. No luck.

By this time, I was losing track of the time and the amount of cash I'd spent. I emptied my wallet into the seat next to me while waiting at a red light and realized I had less than twenty-five dollars left. That wouldn't get me very far, but the truth was I was running out of places to look anyway.

The light on Church Street turned green and I pulled across the intersection, over I-40, and drove toward Elliston Place. There was one other place I could think of—a place over near Baptist Hospital—that back in the Seventies used to be a gay bar called The Cabaret. I'd been in it one time back then, with a bunch of people from a party who thought it was too early to go home. It was such an amiable, fun place that straights were welcome to come in and gawk as long as they behaved themselves.

It had closed down for a while and reopened a couple of years ago as a show bar. I'd seen their ads in the *Scene*, but couldn't remember the exact address. I wandered through the maze of streets around the hospital, then finally caught a glimpse of a purple-and-green flashing neon sign that read FANTASY ISLAND.

Well, I mused, *de plane . . . de plane.*

The dude with hair down to his shoulders in the mandatory ill-fitting tuxedo explained the rules to me, which were pretty similar to everybody else's. It cost me ten bucks to get in, and ten bucks more on the drink minimum, which meant I wouldn't have anything left over to encourage the girls to talk to me. No big deal; it was after midnight and I was discouraged and exhausted. I was going to last just long enough to have a look around.

The music here was Seventies rock, hard-driving Bob Seger, Huey Lewis, stuff that moved but lacked the hard death's-head edge of the gangstas and the metalheads. Okay, I thought, good way to wind down the evening. A cute blonde in a French maid outfit, complete with fishnet stockings, took my order and brought me a Coke. The girls paraded around, relaxed and casual. It was the kind of place where nobody's going to "accidentally" spill a drink on you so they could pat your crotch dry.

The one center stage jutted out into the audience, with a Victorian fainting couch at the upstage end, complete with wall-to-wall mirrors behind it. There was only one brass pole here for the girls to climb on.

The DJ shouted into the mike that Debbie was up next, and a tall brunette with straight hair that hung below her waist, Crystal Gayle-style, paraded onto the polished wood and went into her routine. I scanned the crowd and occasionally turned my eyes to the stage, but by this time, it was more of a "been there, done that" proposition than anything else.

Debbie finished her routine with a flourish and wild applause from the thirty or so guys that were still there this late. The other girls applauded and yelled for their colleague as well. I had to hand it to them: this place had more esprit de corps than any other place I'd been to.

"Now gentlemen," the obnoxious idiot yelled, "let's hear it for Fantasy Island's next bodacious beauty! Put your hands together and give it up for Ventana!"

I looked up from my drink and slapped my hands together with as little enthusiasm as I could muster. The curtain to stage left parted with a flash of calf and thigh.

And then Corey sauntered onstage wearing the same purple lace bra and panties she'd had on the day I met her.

Chapter 13

While the spotlight was still in her eyes, I switched tables, moving to one in the back corner that was shrouded in the shadow of a large planter filled with ferns.

I couldn't watch her dance. My eyes scanned the crowd.

The men hooted and hollered and stomped their feet and shoved dollar bills at her. I stared into a watered-down Coke as the music pounded rhythmically like the jungle drums in some ancient black-and-white racist Tarzan epic. The strobes flashed and the colored lights slipped in and out of the edge of my vision like liquid.

It was over in what seemed to me a painfully long time, but was probably less than five minutes. That's the way they do it in these places; keep things moving so the suckers don't get bored. Let them get numb, get hard, get stoned, get stupid. But never let them get bored.

I looked up as she collected her lingerie and the dollar bills off the slick wooden stage floor. The disc jockey's voice became a loud fuzzy blur. Off stage left, Corey walked down a few steps and disappeared to the side, clutching her clothes and the bills.

A few minutes later, she appeared once again, this time dressed, as far as it went, and with her hair combed neatly. I settled back in the chair as she worked the floor, hustling for a couch dance. The men weren't

154

buying; it was late and, besides, the babe now shaking her stuff on the stage was a real looker.

She came around from my right, polling each table, smiling demurely, flirting in an innocent, light way that she wouldn't be able to invoke in another year or two.

Two tables over, a depressed-looking guy in a white Polo golf shirt and green polyester pants looked like he was going to take the offer. She bent down, practically spilling herself into his face, and chatted amiably for a few seconds. He smiled, reached into his back pocket and took out his wallet. He held it open, discreetly checked the cash situation, then folded it closed and stuffed it back in his pants.

Corey smiled at him. She may have been disappointed, but she certainly didn't bust his chops. Then she stood straight, chest out, and strutted over to the table where I held my head down to my drink, my eyes rolled up, barely looking at her.

"Hi," she said, bending over to make herself heard over the music. "I'm Ventana. Would you like a—"

The smile disappeared from her face like a window closing as I lifted my head.

"I thought you didn't hang around in places like this."

"Sit down," I said. "Please."

"I'm new here," she said. "They expect me to hustle."

"I know," I said. "I've been looking for you all night and I'm out of cash. Can't you sit for a minute?"

She pulled out the black chrome-and-vinyl chair and slid in next to me. "What do you think you're doing, Harry?"

"Trying to find a very sick girl," I said.

That caught her off guard. Her face froze for a few moments. "You mean, she's—?"

"Yeah. She took off again."

"Boy, you'd think they'd watch her," Corey said.

"You've got to help me find her."

She shook her head, the mane of fine brown hair swishing back and forth across her bare shoulders.

"Oh, no brother. Not me."

"Corey, please." I reached out and took her hand.

She settled into the chair next to me. "Why do you care?" she asked. "You got hired to find her, you found her. What they do with her after that is their problem."

I shook my head. "You saw her. You know what kind of shape she's in."

"So let the police handle it."

I hung my head, stared into the blackness beneath the table. "Maybe I should. But I've just got a feeling that's all it'll take to push her over the edge."

She touched my chin with her free hand and pushed gently upward until my face was level with hers. "You're a sweet guy, Harry. But these guys have killed somebody. They're serious."

"That's another reason I'm worried for her. The way I figure it, Stacey must be hiding out with somebody she met through Red Dog. I hesitate to use the word 'friends,' but did you ever see Red Dog hang with anybody?"

"No, he was always alone at the club."

"I got one of Red Dog's neighbors to talk. An old lady who said a short-haired guy hung around the apartment occasionally. Said he talked like a Yankee. Ring a bell?"

She shook her head. "No. Nothing."

"Look, I know I've got no right to drag you back into this, but you're the only one who'll even talk to me. I've shown Stacey's picture around all night. Everybody clams up."

She stood up, putting her navel at roughly my eye level. "You're serious, aren't you?" she asked. "You really mean to find this little girl."

I bit my lower lip and nodded.

"What time is it?" she asked.

I checked my watch. "One-fifteen."

"I get off at two. You can give me a ride home. Park across and down the street. We're not allowed to leave with the customers."

"All the money you're making here and you don't have a car?"

She put her hands on her hips and cocked them slightly. "I'd been getting a ride with one of the other girls at the Exotique. Now that I'm not working there, I've been taking taxis until I could find what I want."

Corey turned to walk away, the curve of her hips melding into the hollow of her spine in lines that were young and firm, and seductive enough to make a dead man ache.

"Hey, Corey, I just realized something," I called after her.

She stopped and turned. "What?"

"I don't even know your last name."

"It's Kerr," she said. "Corey Kerr." Then she circled around and smoothly walked away.

"Did you quit the Exotique because of the other night?" I called after her again, this time louder.

She looked over her shoulder at me and curled her lips. "No," she teased. "I was afraid I'd run into you again."

Outside, the night air was cool and damp. The streets were mostly quiet, but I'd spent enough time downtown in the middle of the night to know that didn't mean they were safe.

I turned on the radio to an AM station and listened to the announcer's voice as it scratched and hissed in the night. I roamed the dial, picking up the late-night call-in hate shows, whacked-out preachers screaming about the apocalypse, the endless parade of commercials.

Hunger and fatigue gnawed at me. I almost wished I

smoked so I'd have something to do with my hands, something to keep me company. I checked my watch by the dim light of a nearby streetlight: ten more minutes of waiting.

Ten minutes felt like an hour. Finally, the door to the club opened and Corey walked out, dressed in a pair of jeans and a blue denim work shirt. Her hair was pulled behind in a ponytail. She looked like a coed on her way home after a night in the library.

She stood talking to a bouncer for a moment, then looked across the street and saw me in the Mustang. The bouncer said something to her and she shook her head, reassuring him. Then she clutched her shoulder bag tightly and trotted across the street.

I reached over, unlocked the door, pulled the latch up and pushed the door open a crack. By the time she climbed into the passenger's seat, the car was idling along at a purr.

"Where to?" I asked.

"I'm renting a duplex up in Madison," she said.

"Great, I live in East Nashville. Same direction."

I headed for the light at Broadway. "Your fiancé won't mind my bringing you home this late?"

"My what?"

"You know, the college boy. The one you're going to marry."

She gazed out the window, away from me as shadows flicked by.

"There isn't a fiancé," she said.

"What about the ring?" The light at Broadway switched to green. I sat there for a moment while three oncoming cars ran the red light, then turned onto Broadway and headed toward the river.

She held her hand up in front of her. "It's fake. CZ. All the girls wear them so we don't get hassled."

I shifted through the gears, the car winding up and

down in a smooth rhythm. "I'll bet you're not from Boston either."

Corey put her hand back into her lap. "You can be a real SOB, Harry. Anybody ever tell you that?"

"Twice a day. So where are you from?"

We got caught at the Second Avenue light. I braked to a stop as a line of drunk tourists crossed in front of us, headed back to their cars from the Wildhorse Saloon and the Hard Rock Cafe.

"I was born in Franklin, Kentucky," she said after a moment. "We kind of traveled around a lot, though."

"So you didn't drop out of Simmons College. . . ."

"I was in college," she said defiantly. "Only not there. I was a sophomore at UT-Chattanooga. I started dancing in the clubs down there."

"Chattanooga's a pretty rough town," I commented.

"Why do you think I got out of it?"

The light changed and I eased us through a hole in the passing parade. I turned on First and drove up the hill toward the bridge. "How'd you lose the Southern accent?" I asked.

"I was a theater major. Lots of speech classes. Mimicking movies when I was a kid."

I turned to her. "Good job."

We were silent as we crossed the river into East Nashville. The traffic was almost nonexistent as we made the turn at Main Street and headed up Gallatin Road.

"So what do you want me to do?" she asked.

"Somebody at one of the clubs has to know something," I said. "Just ask around. You know, 'Red Dog had a girlfriend. She was living with him when he was killed. Whatever became of her?' That sort of thing."

She shifted uncomfortably and sighed. "The problem is I really don't know anybody at Fantasy Island. I know the girls at the Exotique best."

"We don't have a lot of time here, Corey."

"I guess I could go back to the Exotique. That might be the best place to start."

I braked at a red light, then turned to her. "You can do that? Just quit and go back?"

She smiled. "Bobby's cool. He likes me. I'll tell him I tried it a night at Fantasy Island and we just didn't mesh."

"If you think that's best. Don't go out on a limb, though. Just keep it real casual."

The light changed. I put the car in gear and eased through the intersection. "You're slick. You can do it."

"Gee, thanks."

"You mind if I make one stop?" I asked.

"Sure. What?"

"I got to check in on a sick friend," I answered. "Won't take a minute."

She shrugged. "What do I care? I'm not sleepy anyway."

"Where's your family now, Corey?"

"Don't you think we've had enough questions for one evening?"

All the lights on Gallatin Road flashed yellow as we made our way toward Inglewood. I turned left onto the side road that runs behind the old Inglewood Theatre, made the curve, then coasted to a quiet stop in front of the chain-link fence that bounded Lonnie's junkyard.

Corey looked out nervously over the dashboard. "Where are we?" she whispered. I opened the door, the interior lights of the car bathing us in weak yellow light. This seemed to frighten her.

"Don't worry," I said. "It's okay."

"It's creepy as shit," she said.

"You want to stay here? I'll be back in a minute."

"You're crazy if you think I'm sitting here in *this* car in *this* neighborhood by myself."

I stepped out and let the door fall closed. "Okay, then. Let's go."

She climbed out behind me and jumped over to me, grabbing my arm with both hands.

"You mind telling me where we are?" she asked as we walked up to the chain-link fence. I reached into my pocket and pulled out a second keyring, then fumbled with the smaller keys in the harsh blue-white light of the security lamp mounted on a telephone pole above us. I found the small brass key I was searching for and unlocked the padlock that held the chain together. I unthreaded it from the gate and pulled the latch up, then pushed the chain link open.

"It belongs to a friend of mine. He's out of town."

"If he's out of town, what are we doing here?" she asked, pulling closer to me as we wound our way through the discarded auto parts and bodies toward the trailer.

"Checking on a friend," I said. I knelt down in front by the corner of the trailer and lifted the DeSoto hubcap. Just as I stuck the key in the doorknob, a deep-throated rumble from within started real low, rolled around for a little bit, then erupted as a powerful, full-fledged bark from hell.

"Holy shit!" she gasped. "You're not going in there, are you?"

"Ssshh. It's okay."

Then I opened the door a crack. "Shadow," I said in baby talk. "Hi, girl. Hello, baby."

She let loose with another fearsome roar, and I heard her shuffling as she struggled to get off the couch. I didn't want her jumping down too quickly, so reached inside the door and flicked the light on fast. The sudden flash shocked my eyes and made her go silent, which I knew was when it was really freaking dangerous.

"Shadow," I cooed again. "C'mon, baby."

Corey had stepped behind me and grabbed my shirt-tail, holding on as if she could jerk me out of danger. I didn't have time to tell her that if Shadow decided to

take us out, a battalion of show girls couldn't yank me
back in time.

I made a low cooing noise back in my throat, then almost a gurgling sound. I called her name again. There
was a second of silence, followed by whimpering.

"C'mon, we're okay," I said.

Corey grabbed my shirt and pulled.

"No, it's okay," I repeated.

I opened the door and stepped up onto the floor.
Shadow was spread out on the couch, her tail thumping
against the fabric like an airplane propeller gone wild. I
stepped over quickly and dropped down on my knees in
front of her, then wrapped my arms around her massive
neck.

"Hi, baby," I whispered. I scratched her fur, between
her ears and around her back, then on her belly. She
lifted her immense head and covered me in slobber. I
laughed, pulled back, then tucked my head and rubbed
against her neck.

I turned and looked behind me. Corey stood in the
doorway, a bit more relaxed, with her arms crossed
watching us.

"So this is your sick friend?" she said. "What's he
got?"

"She," I corrected, "and she's got something you
wouldn't understand."

"What?" Corey demanded as I stood back up. My
knees creaked with stiffness.

"Old age," I said.

I looked around. There was a pile on the newspaper
Lonnie'd laid down for her. I wrapped it up in a ball
and carried it to the garbage can outside the door, then
set out more for her. I filled her water bowl and poured
some of the special diet, expensive-out-the-ya-ya dry
food into her food bowl.

Shadow was tired, though. She climbed down from
the couch and scooted over to the food bowl, but her

haunches started to sag after only a few seconds or so. Then she shuffled back over to the low couch, set herself against it on the side, and kind of rolled onto it.

"Bless her heart," Corey said. "What's the matter with her legs?"

I sat down on the edge of the sofa next to Shadow and rubbed behind her ears some more.

"She's a timber shepherd, half German shepherd and half timber wolf. The shep half carries a genetic hip problem. They get old, the joints deteriorate, they slowly lose it. I don't know exactly how it works, but I think it's kind of like degenerative arthritis in humans."

Corey got up from the folding metal chair she'd taken and walked over to the couch.

"Poor baby," she cooed. She held out her hand to pet her.

"Go slow," I said. "Let her smell you first. Get used to you a little."

Shadow's great black nose lifted off the couch and skittered across the back of Corey's hand. Then her thick pink and black-dotted tongue ran across it.

"You're okay," I said. "She knows you now."

Corey sat down and petted Shadow as I walked into the kitchen, sealed up the dog-food bag and got everything else squared away.

"Who does she belong to?"

"My friend Lonnie," I said from the kitchen. "He's up in your neck of the woods, picking up a Mercedes, I think it was."

"Picking up?"

I stuck my head around the corner. "He's a repo man," I said. "That is, when he's not skip tracing or bounty hunting."

Corey looked around the living room of the trailer. Old green filing cabinets were against one wall, a desk made out of a door backed against another, with greasy auto parts and tools scattered haphazardly around the floor.

"And he lives here?" she asked.

"Mostly works here," I said. "He's got an apartment somewhere, but he's been staying here a lot since Shadow got sick. She ran this place in her day."

Corey looked down at Shadow again and ran her hand across the thick brown and black fur on her belly. Shadow's tail weakly bobbed up and down.

"Must be awful," she said.

"Lonnie told me the vet says she's not in a whole lot of pain. Not yet anyway."

"Will she be? I mean, one day?" Corey raised her head to me; her eyes shimmered.

I nodded my head. "Yeah, one day. Soon probably."

"Then you'll have to?"

"I won't have to," I said. "I don't think I could. But Lonnie will. He won't let her suffer."

She stood up, crossed the room and stood in front of me. "I don't think you could put anything to sleep, Harry. You really care about her, don't you?"

I shrugged. "She's good people."

The light behind her filtered through the strands of her hair, diffusing, unfocusing her. I felt her hand reach out and touch me, on my collarbone, just below my shoulder. She touched me gently, let her hand linger there.

"You're good people, too," she said. "I don't meet many good people these days."

Her brown eyes were large, warm, and there seemed to come off her a heat that sent waves through me. Thoughts flashed through what was left of my exhausted brain, and most of them began with: *What in the hell do you think you're doing, boy?*

And then she moved in closer to me, lifting her chin as her upturned face moved to mine. Her right arm came around my waist, her left over my right shoulder.

I discovered, to my unending confusion and surprise, that my arms were around her as well, pulling her to me. I felt her breath, warm and sweet, unsullied with all the things that come with age, against my neck. Then she stretched to reach my face and I felt my lips touch hers, just grazing at first, hesitating. But then harder, pressing, her lips parting, searing hot and wet inside.

I pulled her tighter, squeezing her, her weight against mine. We wrapped around each other silently, with Corey up on tiptoes, her arms around my neck.

We kissed until there was no air left anywhere, and our eyes opened, and our heads came apart, and we each took a deep, sharp breath.

Then reality hit.

She stared at me like she'd never seen me before. "What?" she asked.

My knees had gone watery and I felt light-headed, inebriated, out-of-control. She'd called me good people; if she only knew. Arousal mixed with guilt, anticipation mixed with desire and reproach, made a thick, fiery soup that threatened to drown me. One woman who's the best thing that ever happened to me is lying in bed right now trusting me, and I'm standing in front of another woman young enough to be my daughter and I want her so badly I'm about to have a coronary.

Well, I thought, *that's one way out.*

"Harry," she said, "what's the matter?"

My voice locked up in my throat and I couldn't answer her. I took a step back away from her. "Corey, I'm sorry," I said after a moment.

"Why?" she asked.

Slowly, my heartbeat returned to what could pass for less than a medical emergency. My thoughts came a little clearer, although not much. Maybe blood was returning to my brain from wherever else it had been.

She inched herself closer to me and held out her hands. "What's wrong? I mean—" Then her brow furrowed and her voice dropped. "Oh, I get it. There's somebody else."

I nodded my head.

"She real special to you?"

I nodded again.

She sighed—a long, drawn-out release of resignation—and looked away from me. "Oh well, shit happens."

Corey started to turn away, but I reached out and took her hands. They were soft, tiny in mine. I looked at them, and in the glow of the fluorescent tubes above us, I saw the lines and wrinkles and the blue of the veins and the outline of the bone on the tops of my hands. And in hers, only the soft, unbroken skin of a girl.

We faced off for a second, neither of us having an answer.

"C'mon," I said, "I better get you home."

Chapter 14

Driving home through East Nashville at three o'clock in the morning, I felt lower than snail snot. The streets at that time of the night are nearly deserted, with only the roving cars of restless ghouls and outlaws cruising for trouble.

I've heard women speculate that men's brains were in their crotches, but this was the first time in a while that mine had migrated in that direction. I tried to figure out what was going on. Where was this coming from? Around and around in my head the thoughts buzzed like the crazed seagulls in a scene out of Hitchcock's *The Birds*. Was it fear? Had Marsha's crisis of body and heart—the desire for a baby and my perhaps too-quick agreement to go along with the program—somehow put fear and doubt into a level I couldn't comprehend? Or was I just a dirty, middle-aged, neurotic man?

One thing I knew for sure, though, it wasn't just sex. There was something about Corey that had touched me beyond that region. We were in a different place now, in a deeper running passion, in something that was dangerous. Really dangerous.

And the guilt. Oh, hell, the guilt. I tried to settle down by repeating like a mantra that I'd only kissed her, not bedded her. I hadn't really been unfaithful to Marsha. It was shallow comfort though, for like Jimmy Carter had once done with a different woman, I'd lusted after her in my heart.

* * *

I was so far gone into the bottomless well of sleep that the ringing phone sounded muffled, filtered through distance and time. I was deep enough in that I wasn't even dreaming, a sleep more like death than rest.

Subconsciously, I counted the rings. As the fourth ring began, I grabbed the phone before the answering machine could take the call.

"Yeah . . . ," I muttered.

"So who's the babe?" The voice sounded familiar.

"What?"

"The babe, dude. Kinda robbing the cradle, aren't you?"

"Oh." I pulled the blanket the rest of the way off my head and fluttered my eyelids, trying to get used to light. "Lonnie, what's happening?"

"You must have had a rough night last night," he commented. "It's nearly noon."

"Yeah," I agreed. "Bad one."

"So, have I caught you at a bad time?"

"No." I sat up in bed and held the phone to my ear with my shoulder as I stretched my arms out. "I've got to get up anyway."

"She already gone, huh?"

My forehead wrinkled. "What?"

"The cutie," he said. "The babe."

"How did you know about—"

"C'mon, Ace. Wake up."

Slowly, thoughts began to form an interconnecting web in my head and make a little sense. I'd forgotten about the motion-activated video cameras that covered every part of Lonnie's junkyard.

"Yeah," I said. "How much did you get?"

He laughed. "How much was there to get?"

"Don't pick on me, man. I haven't had my coffee yet."

"I just saw the tapes from the two cameras in the front. Hey, thanks for checking on my girl."

"She okay?"

"Yeah," he answered. "She's asleep on the couch right now. And by the way, you never answered my question."

I rubbed my eyes, stretching the skin of my eyelids back and forth, then massaging my forehead. "She's a show girl," I answered sleepily.

"What are you doing running around with a show girl?"

"Still looking for the runaway," I said. "Hold on, I've got to switch phones."

I set the phone down, then walked into the kitchen, grabbed the cordless phone, and headed into the bathroom.

"You there?" I asked.

"Yeah. What's that noise?"

"I'm taking a whiz, if that's okay with you."

He laughed. "So you spent last night making your way through a throng of naked girls, looking for just the right one." He broke into a loud guffaw that made me want to smack him through the phone. "It's a dirty job, dude, but somebody's got to do it."

"Would you come anywhere near believing me if I told you the whole experience was depressing as hell?"

I twisted the faucet and started the water running. It took about ninety seconds to get hot water into my apartment from Mrs. Hawkins's basement water heater.

"You know something, Harry? You're the only guy I know who can get totally bummed by a room full of naked women."

"Thank you, I think. C'mon, man, get serious. I've got to find this girl before she walks straight into the white light."

The chuckling died down. "Where do you think she is?"

"The only thing I can think of is that she went back to somebody she met through Red Dog, who was the guy I told you about who worked in the show bars."

"And who got his name in the papers by getting his little self murdered," Lonnie said.

"Yeah, but we're not going to talk about that. Anyway, I found the girl and got her home, like I told you, and she ran off again. Corey's going to dig around, see what she can come up with. In the meantime, I'm open to suggestions."

I turned the cold water faucet and began mixing the two spouts.

"Let me introduce you to a friend of mine," he said. "Guy might be able to help."

I fumbled with the leaky stopper, trying to pool enough water to get a decent shave. "Who?"

"Tell you what," Lonnie said. "Meet us at Mama Lee's in forty-five minutes. We'll get lunch. Or in your case, breakfast."

Mrs. Lee had an even deeper scowl on her face than usual. I walked through the thick spicy aroma of Szechuan cooking and up to the counter. She looked up at me from behind the cash register, cocked her ballpoint, and poised her hand over the green-lined pad, all business.

"Take you ohdah?" she asked.

I stood there silently for a moment. "Okay, what's the matter?" I asked.

"What?" she said irritably. "Something got to be da maddah?"

"C'mon, there's something eating at you. What's going on?"

"You gonna ohdah or what, Harry? I don't got time for this." There was a thin bead of sweat above her upper lip and a sheen on her forehead. Something told me this was not a good time to push her.

"Sorry," I said. "Didn't mean to intrude. Let me try the ginger chicken and a sweet tea."

She scribbled Chinese characters on the notepad. "Four-seventy-five," she said.

I pulled the remaining five-dollar bill out of my wallet and handed it to her. "A man's down to his last fiver," I said, "this's the place to spend it."

She handed me back a quarter. "T'ings dat bad, Harry?"

I grinned back at her. "No, just kidding. Didn't have time to run by the bank."

"You can run a tab," she said, "as long as you don't tell nobody else."

I shook my head. "Not necessary. But thanks for the offer. I'll remember it."

I stood back while she clipped my order to the circular steel wheel that hung over the window into the kitchen. There were only three other tables taken in the place; unusually quiet for lunch hour.

"Lonnie's meeting me here," I said.

"Gweat," she answered. "Now da place go down da tubes for sure."

I folded my arms and watched her. She rubbed the counter with a folded, damp white towel, a wisp of board-straight salt-and-pepper hair falling down on her forehead.

"Hear from Mary?" I asked.

The pressure increased on the towel, like she was trying to turn the stainless steel into a mirror. She bowed her head and bent to her work with an intensity that bordered on fury.

"When's she getting into town?" I asked. Hell, I was just making small talk. Mrs. Lee continued polishing, this time with the tail of the white cloth snapping in time to her efforts.

I sighed. Obviously, I'd caught her at a bad time. "Oh, well," I said, "you hear from her, tell her I said hi."

She slapped the towel on the counter so hard it rang. "You want to shut up about Mary?" she snapped.

Shocked, I stepped back. "Sorry."

"Mary says she not coming home," Mrs. Lee said, her eyes glistening.

"What?"

"She going to place in Cape Cod for break. She say her and girls in dorm. But I know she going wit' that boy. We have fight ovah phone.

"Hah," she spat. "Cape Cod!"

"Aw, Mrs. Lee," I said. "I'm really sorry."

"I don't know what I going to do wit' her." A single tear ran down the side of her face from her left eye. It was the strongest display of emotion I'd ever seen in her.

"It's none of my business," I said, then held up a finger to silence her before she could agree with me, "but I just can't see Mary doing anything wrong. She's a good girl, Mrs. Lee."

"She brings disgrace on her family," Mrs. Lee said.

"Only if you let it be on you," I said.

"My daughter's lies bring disgrace," she insisted.

"Would it not be better to know they are lies before you accept the disgrace?"

Christ, I thought, this is starting to sound like *Kung Fu*. If one of us calls the other one "Grasshopper," I'm going to heave.

Thank heavens, the counter bell behind her rang and got me out of this mess. She turned and took my tray from her husband through the access window, hiding her expression from him in a mask of business. Behind us, Lonnie walked in with a thin, dark-haired man in a black pair of jeans and black T-shirt. I motioned back to a table, then took my tray from Mrs. Lee.

The mask was on now for me as well. As she turned toward Lonnie and his friend, I whispered: "Don't worry. It'll be all right," and received no response.

I went to work on the ginger chicken, biting into the chunks of ginger and getting that sensation you get when the dentist puts your jaw to sleep right before he goes to work on you with the drill. Lonnie led the thin man up to the table. I looked up at them with a chunk of dark chicken dripping from my chopsticks.

"Thank God you showed up when you did," I said, my voice low. "I was getting into a really weird conversation with her."

"What's going on?" Lonnie asked.

"Let's just say Mary's time at Harvard has not been an easy one for the Lee family."

Lonnie arranged his Styrofoam dishes on the table, then took his tray and the other guy's and set them on the table next to us.

"Harry," he said as he sat down, "when the hell did you become friggin' Ann Landers for every parent who's having trouble with a teenage daughter?"

"Maybe I ought to hang out a shingle, go into business."

"Can't do any worse than you are now," Lonnie speculated.

I stuck my hand across the table and held it out for the stranger. "Hi, name's Denton. Harry Denton. You a friend of this rascal's, too?"

The fellow reached out with a thin arm and took my hand. His grip was dry, tight, and his hands were so lean the knuckles stuck out like knobs.

"Oh, sorry, man," Lonnie said. "Forgot my manners. Phil, Harry Denton, private investigator. Harry, Detective Phillip Cheek, Metro Police Department."

My hand froze in midair. "Metro *police*?"

Lonnie scooped in a load of stir-fried vegetables and

spoke with his mouth full. "Yeah, this's the guy I's telling you about."

I stood up, glaring at Lonnie. "Gentlemen, I don't mean to be rude, but if I had known you were going to bring the police here, I wouldn't have even shown up."

Lonnie sucked in a bamboo shoot. "Don't get your panties in a wad. He's in vice."

"What difference does that make in terms of my client's confidentiality issues?" I asked.

"He owes me a favor," Lonnie said.

"Is there anybody in this town who doesn't?" I asked, with the voice inside my head wondering just how much snottier I could get.

"Harry," Detective Cheek said. It was the first time he'd spoken. His voice was lightweight, kind of high, without that induced authority stuff they teach you at the academy. "Lonnie didn't tell me anything about the case you're working on. He just asked me to give you whatever background I had available. I won't ask you any questions and you certainly don't have to violate any client considerations."

You say that now, I thought. *Wait until you find out I was in Red Dog Turner's apartment the night he was murdered.*

"C'mon," Lonnie said. "Finish your chicken."

I sat back down, although my appetite was shot. I stared at him, wondering just how much I could say, and how to get started.

"My client hired me to find and recover a seventeen, almost eighteen-year-old runaway. There are indications that she may be involved with someone who works in the—"

I thought for a moment. No need to give away too much.

"—sex industry here in Nashville."

Lonnie looked up from his fried rice, grinning.

"What? There's a sex industry? In Nashville? Get outta here. . . ."

The cop smirked back at him. "So you think this girl—"

"I never said it was a girl."

Detective Cheek dug into his sesame noodles and speared a forkful. "Well, Harry, we don't get a lot of underage boys in the sex industry, unless you're talking about male prostitution, which is. a different game."

"Okay," I said. "Girl."

"So you think this girl is, what? Working in a massage parlor?"

"I can't go into that much detail," I insisted. "But I want to check out whoever owns these adult bookstores, massage parlors, escort services, show bars, the whole nine yards. Then I want to start digging into the employees, because I think that's who the girl's involved with. I don't think she's working in one of these places. Not yet, anyway."

"You think she's playing hide the salami with one of the boys that works in the joints."

"That's an indelicate way to put it," I said, "but yeah, that's about it."

"Well, I can tell you one thing," Detective Cheek said, lowering his voice, "unless she's got a twat that lays golden eggs, he'll have her working soon. That's how they recruit these girls."

I didn't bother to tell him that this was, metaphorically speaking, precisely the case. "You mean prostitution?"

"Hell, anything. Massage parlors, the show bars. All of it. I mean, the show bars are a little different."

"Like how?" I asked.

"For one thing, girls come in off the street to apply for those jobs. There's so damn much money to be made."

"Yeah," I said. "I've heard that."

"But eventually it all boils down to the same thing. They start out in the show bars," Cheek said, "and they work them while they're young and in good shape. But along the way, they smoke a little weed, maybe pick up a coke habit. Next thing you know, they're desperate. And the show bars are like casinos; desperate money never wins.

"So they lose their jobs and they work their way down the ladder of the show bars. Then they either go for the escort services, if they're lucky, or the massage parlors."

"Where they start real prostitution," I said.

"Usually," he said. "Technically, a massage at a place like the Havana Sauna out on Twelfth Avenue or the Garden of Delight on Nolensville Road just gets you a hand job. But you can always negotiate more."

Detective Cheek filled his mouth with a mass of dripping vegetables and beef, then continued talking.

"They work that for a few years. By this time, they're in their thirties. Maybe older. They might have a real good drug habit by then and are starting to look kind of skanky. Either that or they get knocked up and have a couple of kids, which means stretch marks and about forty pounds. When they lose their last job in the parlors, they bottom out."

"And quit?" I asked. I thought of Corey, and what she'd look like in another ten years.

He grinned. "Quit? No, nobody ever quits. Not until they box 'em up and plant 'em. They hit Murfreesboro Road or Dickerson Pike. Now they're street whores, and there ain't nothing worse or more dangerous."

"I would think they'd be kind of pitiful at that point," I said.

"Oh, you would, would you? Well, you can start by assuming every one of them's HIV positive. Most have hepatitis as well. You got any idea how many people they're infecting? They'll turn enough tricks to pay

their way into a crack house, then get laced out the
wazoo, then back on the streets when they come down.
The worst of 'em never eat, never bathe. And most of
'em get a real charge out of ripping you off without giving sex. They conk you on the head, grab your wallet,
jump out of the car. Man, that shit makes their day."

I fingered my plastic cup full of iced tea. The cold
sweat on the side trickled onto my fingers. "Jeez," I
said. "Great life, ain't it?"

Lonnie stared at me for a second. "I get the feeling
you're losing your professional detachment, hot shot."

"I've seen the girl," I said. "She's just a kid."

Detective Cheek stopped his fork halfway to his
mouth. "Thought you said she was a runaway."

"She is. I found her, got her home, and damn if she
didn't run off again. I want to get her back before she
winds up in your bailiwick, or worse."

Cheek swallowed a mouthful of food, chewed slowly,
then scraped his plate with the plastic fork.

"I can tell you what I know," he said, "for whatever
good it'll do you. For starters, virtually every sex-
related business in this state, from show bars to adult
bookstores to the escort services and massage parlors,
is owned by a small number of people. Maybe three or
four guys, and there are definite organized-crime
connections."

My eyes met Lonnie's. "Great," I said, "so I'm dealing with the Mafia here."

Cheek shrugged. "We think so. That's what our intel-
ligence says. And we know that of all the vice operations
out there—numbers, drugs, sex, whatever—that this is
one of the most profitable. Right up there with drugs,
and way the hell ahead of anything else."

"You're kidding?" I asked. "I mean, I knew there
was money involved. . . ."

"It would stagger you," he said. "And most of it's
protected. It's either legal, like the show bars, or the

right grease is laid down. Or it's like the massage parlors, that have been around so long they know the law inside out and can beat you on entrapment.

"In the massage parlors now," he continued, "you gotta get totally naked before the girl even comes in the room. Makes it kind of hard to wear a wire."

"I don't know," Lonnie said, grinning, "you could always hide one somewhere."

Cheek smiled back at him. "You know, one of the guys tried that once. The little wire dangling out of his ass gave him away."

Both broke into laughter. I rubbed my eyes. "You guys think you could get serious for a minute?"

Lonnie scowled at me. "You know, Harry, you're getting more humorless all the time."

I let that one go. "If I wanted to talk to the guy who runs the operations around here—especially say, the show bars—who would I go to?"

"Oh, that's easy," Cheek said. "Go see Big Moe."

"Who?" I asked.

Cheek slammed another ball of chicken and bamboo shoots into his mouth. "Big Moe," he mumbled, sauce dripping out of the corner. "Maurice Klinkenstein. They call him Big Moe."

Chapter 15

So that was the *M* in M. L. Klinkenstein.

"Big Moe?" I asked incredulously. "Please. Tell me you're kidding."

Detective Cheek grinned. "If you were an organized-crime big shot named Maurice, wouldn't you use a nickname?"

I opened my notepad. "And how would I find Big Moe?"

"He's got an office behind one of his bookstores, a place called The Purple Firefly out on Nolensville Road. I don't know the address, but it's down near the Fairgrounds."

"A triple-X-rated bookstore called The Purple Firefly?" Lonnie asked. "Sounds more like a gay bar."

"A lot of adult bookstores are gay pick-up places," Cheek said. "Surprised the shit out of me when one of the other guys told me that, but it's true. Swear to God."

I looked up from my notepad. "I checked out a couple of bookstores while looking for the girl," I said. "I'd say a good half of each was devoted to gay porno."

"Big market for it," Cheek said. "The City Council's been trying to pull the doors off the peep-show booths for years, but it never gets anywhere. Big Moe's got good lawyers."

"I'll bet he greases a few palms," Lonnie said.

"That's not all he greases," Cheek said. "Big Moe's one himself."

"One what?" I asked.

"One of *them*," Cheek whispered. "You know . . ." He held his hand out in front of him and shook it back and forth in a limp-wristed motion.

"Oh, brother," I said, "the king of all adult-oriented vice in Music City is a gay guy—"

"Jewish guy," Cheek interrupted.

"I stand corrected. A gay, Jewish guy named Maurice," I continued.

"Sure you don't mean the queen of vice?" Lonnie commented.

"Gentlemen," I said, "this conversation has descended to a new low in the history of human discourse."

"Big Moe sounds comical," Cheek said, "and he looks that way, too. He's a fat tub of lard in brown polyester pants. He wears glasses as thick as the windows at the White House. And he usually smells bad."

"Charming guy," I said.

"And dangerous. We know of at least three hits he's personally ordered. That's 'hit,' as in 'resulting in a dead person.' A few of his girls who didn't behave themselves wound up butchered as well. Not killed, mind you, but messed up enough to where they couldn't work anymore. We think he may have ordered the whack on one of his own employees just a few days ago, a real scumbag who went by the name of Red Dog."

"One of his own employees," I said, shaking my head. "Damn, man, that's cold."

"He's got a bodyguard, guy name of Caramello. Angelo Caramello, but they call him Mousy. A New Jersey import. Weighs about one-forty, buzz cut, skinhead-militia type, swastika tattoos. Dyes his hair blond. Weird look in his eyes, like he could've blown up a federal building full of kids, too, if only he'd thought of it first. An extremely dangerous punk. Watch your ass."

New Jersey import, I thought. The Yankee the old lady in Red Dog's building saw ...

"Where does Klinkenstein live?" I asked. "Where's Mousy live? What kind of cars they drive? Give me a place I can go sit in front of."

"Sure," he said. "I can do that. As long as you promise to hold off on the John Wayne shit. You find the girl and you can't get her out easy, you call me."

"You got it," I said.

Phil got up and went over to Mrs. Lee's pay phone. He nestled the phone in the crook of his neck and pulled a small notepad out of his back pocket. Lonnie and I watched as he dialed, spoke softly, then made a few notes. He was back in less than two minutes.

He ripped off a page and handed it to me. "Mousy and Klinkenstein have the same address."

"My, oh my," Lonnie commented. "Just one big happy family."

"Yeah, maybe," I said, "and maybe it's Klinkenstein's paranoia. How many guys you know need a full-time bodyguard?"

"Their cars and tag numbers are down there, too," Cheek said. "Mousy drives a Lexus, Klinkenstein a BFC."

"BFC?" I looked up.

"Yeah." Cheek grinned. "Big Fuckin' Cadillac."

"Phil, I really appreciate this."

He shook my hand. "You get in a jam, you call us, okay?" He reached into his jacket pocket and pulled out a business card. "Here's my pager number. Just key in the number you want me to call, then wait for the three beeps."

"Got it."

Cheek shook Lonnie's hand. "I got to run. Thanks for the chow. You guys be careful, right?"

"Hey," I said, "is Mousy Caramello Big Moe's boyfriend?"

Phil Cheek smiled from ear to ear. "I don't know. Why don'cha ask him?"

I didn't know if any of this was even worth pursuing, but I had nowhere else to go. Nowhere else to go, and no cash to pay the fare. The gas tank on the Mustang was pushing empty. At least I guessed it was. Truth was, the gauge didn't exactly work anyway. My expenses while looking for Stacey Jameson were mounting fast, and so far I'd fronted all of them. It was time for Betty Jameson to pony up.

She wasn't home when I called from my office, but Emily told me she'd be back by three or four. I called Marsha at the morgue and talked for a while, but it was awkward, uncomfortable small talk mostly. I told her I'd be working late again tonight, but could we do dinner the night after? She agreed, but there was distance in her voice.

There was the usual mail to go through: bills, junk mail, a once-in-a-lifetime chance to subscribe to a professional security magazine at half-price. No checks, though. I canned the junk mail and filed away the rest, then cleaned my office up a bit and typed another invoice for Betty. I tried not to think about Corey and what had happened the night before, which in the relentless light of the afternoon sun was beginning to take on more and more of an unreal air. Maybe it hadn't really happened.

But if it hadn't, then I was spending entirely too much time daydreaming.

I coasted the Mustang out of the parking garage and drove up Broadway past the newspaper building I used to call home and got onto Interstate 40. This time of day, I'd save a little time by taking the freeway even if it was longer.

I got off I-40 at White Bridge Road and crossed Charlotte Avenue, past The Carousel, an adult book-

store that had been there for about a jillion years. I'd always noticed it without really noticing it, had certainly
never been inside it. Now it stuck out prominently in
my consciousness, like never realizing how many blue
Volkswagens there are on the road until you buy one.
Then it seems like they're everywhere.

I made my way down the thickening traffic on White
Bridge Road, then turned right on Harding Place and
drove into Belle Meade. Once I hit the Boulevard, the
traffic thinned and I made it to the Jamesons' without
hassle.

Emily pulled the door open and stepped aside for me.

"Hi," I offered. "How are you, Emily?"

"Fine, sir. Miss Betty's waiting for you in the General's study."

She pointed the way and I stepped toward the door,
then turned. "By the way, hear anything from Stacey?"

Emily gave me a heavy-lidded, blank look. "Why
would I hear from Miss Stacey?"

I hooked a thumb in my pants pocket. "I think you'd
be the only one she would call."

She pushed the door and walked toward the kitchen.
"Well, I ain't heard nothing from nobody," she said as
she passed me.

I gave it a mental shrug. Maybe she had, maybe she
hadn't.

Betty Jameson was behind her father's desk. "Would
you mind shutting the door, please?" she asked as I
came in.

I closed the door and took a seat in front of the General's desk. The shades were pulled and the lights were
down low, with only a pair of table lamps providing
most of the light. The air-conditioning was cranked up
enough to put a chill in the air.

Betty Jameson wore a pair of pleated khaki pants and
a white blouse with military-style epaulets. Her hair was
pulled back and she wore little makeup, as if she'd been

outside tending to the garden, riding horses, or something equally patrician and highborn. "What have you found out?" she asked.

"Not much, but there's some progress. The way I figure it, Stacey's got to have run off with somebody she met through Red Dog. She hasn't got a car, probably hasn't got much in the way of cash—"

"We'd already taken away her credit cards," Betty interjected. "And her checking account was nearly always empty."

"So she hasn't got much in the way of resources, and the shape she's in, nobody in this neighborhood's going to take her in. It's got to be somebody she got involved with through him."

"So how does that help us?" she asked. "What makes you think any of these people will help us?"

"That's why I wanted to talk to you," I said, pausing, forming my words carefully. "Listen, Betty, you want your sister back, right?"

"Of course."

"And you want it done the quickest, easiest way possible."

"All that matters is getting Stacey back." The anger at her sister that had been in her voice when I first met Betty Jameson was now replaced by genuine concern, even desperation.

"Okay," I said. "I think I've got an angle. I can't imagine whoever's with Stacey is helping her stay hidden out of love and affection. These guys just don't work that way. I'm willing to bet that Red Dog Turner found out about the trust fund, and that he told whoever's helping her now. They're after her money, and they figure if they can keep her hidden until she's eighteen, then it's easy pickings."

"If you're right," she said, "they've got us over a barrel."

"Not really," I answered. "If they think you'll go to

court to have Stacey declared incompetent, then two things'll happen. First, Stacey stands a chance of losing control of the money and her appeal to these scumbags. Second, there's a pretty good chance a judge will order that she be produced for an examination. Then the police will go after them for real."

Betty frowned and wove her fingers into a knot in front of her. "But we can't do that. I've told you. That will never happen. My parents will never stand for it."

"The sleazeball who's hiding Stacey doesn't have to know that," I said. "If they buy that you might, then what's the percentage for them? On the other hand, if whoever's got her can make a quick score and get out, that's better than nothing."

She thought for a moment. "So what are you proposing?"

I leaned forward on the desk and stared straight down at Betty. "Buy her back."

She opened her mouth, shocked. "You mean pay a ransom?"

"What ransom? She hasn't been kidnapped. You're just offering a finder's fee."

"But that—that's wrong."

"There's something to be said for expediency," I said. "Look, you won't let me bring the cops in. I can't go in there shooting the place up and playing Dirty Harry. Stacey might get hurt. In the heat of the moment, one can lose control of events very quickly."

Boy, I thought, *did I know that one. . . .*

Betty leaned back in her father's high-backed leather chair. The hinges and springs squeaked in a drawn-out chirping. "How much would it cost?" she asked, her voice tentative.

"How much is it worth to you? Say, a hundred grand? That's chump change compared to the value of Stacey's trust fund."

She blanched. "I don't think I could lay my hands on

that much cash. Certainly not without the General knowing."

"Well, how much could you raise?"

She bit her lower lip and stared off into space, thinking. "I don't know. Maybe twenty-five thousand."

I whistled. "That's all? Not much in the great scheme of things."

"I know," she said. "But so much is tied up in stocks, trusts, real estate. We're not very liquid. It's hard to come up with quick cash sometimes."

I shook my head. "Problems, problems, problems . . ."

"That's cruel of you," she said.

I gestured around the room full of antiques. "It's hard to feel sorry for you."

"Believe it or not, Harry, wealth is not all it's cracked up to be."

I stifled a laugh. "Speaking of wealth, mine's down the toilet," I said, pulling the invoice out of my coat pocket. "I've run up a lot of expenses and I haven't received anything from you yet."

"I told the accountants to send you a check," she said.

"Well, I don't have it yet. And I could use some reimbursement here."

She took the invoice out of my hand and studied it under the desk lamp. "Good God, Harry, what have you been doing? Buying drinks for the whole house?"

"Information costs money," I said. "I've had to buy almost everything I've gotten."

"How much of it's going to that girl who was with you the other night?"

I fought the urge to say something very harsh to her.

"Not much," I said coldly. "But she's nosing around for me right now, as we speak, and she deserves something."

"I don't know if I'm happy about that," she said.

"I'm not here to make you happy," I answered. "I'm

here to find your sister. If you want happiness, my rates are much higher."

"Yes, of course," she said crisply, then pulled open a side drawer in the desk and took out the same large, bound checkbook I'd been nosing through yesterday.

She wrote out a check and handed it to me across the desk. "I can cover your expenses out of the household account," she said. "The rest will have to come from the accountant. I'll check on it. It should be in the mail."

Jeez, I thought, *even the rich use that line.*

I folded the check and stuck it in my shirt pocket. "Okay, so I can go to these guys and offer up to twenty-five grand for the safe return of Stacey. If she's not returned before her eighteenth birthday, you're going to get a court injunction to stop the transfer of money to her and to request a commitment hearing."

"You can tell them that." She sniffed. "Nothing else."

"Great," I said, standing up. "It'll probably take me a day or two to track down the right people. I've got a line on Red Dog's boss, but that may not lead anywhere."

She raised her face to me, worry lines on her forehead, around her eyes. "Speaking of that man," she said. "Has there been any . . . any fallout from the other night?"

"I'm walking a thin line," I said. "So far, I've managed to keep it under control."

"I hope you can continue that." She put an elbow on the armrest of the chair and rested her cheek in the palm of her hand. "I don't know what I'd do if—"

Suddenly, the door behind me opened with a whoosh of wood sliding on carpet. Betty Jameson went instantly silent. I turned.

A large man with a great shock of white hair stood in the doorway, thick arms held precisely at his sides. He wore a pair of tan trousers and a white silk shirt that looked custom-made to fit his trim frame. His blue eyes shone in the dim light.

"Dad," she said tentatively.

"Who is this man?" he asked, fixing his gaze on me.

Betty got up out of the General's chair and came around to the side of the desk. "This is Mr. Denton, Dad," she said, steadying herself. "He's—"

She paused. I saw the momentary flash of panic in her eyes and realized that not only did the General not know who I was, Betty probably hadn't even told him Stacey was gone.

I stuck a hand out and stepped toward him. "General Jameson, I'm Harry Denton, sir. It's an honor to meet you."

He took my offered hand and shook it with a tight, firm grip. He seemed to me to be a man in near-perfect condition, especially given his age. His stance was solid and straight, his eyes sharp and focused.

"I'm a security consultant, sir," I said, winging it big-time. "I asked for an appointment to see Ms. Jameson about a new line of wireless motion detectors that the company is offering. I was just explaining to her that—"

"Betty," he interrupted with the air of a man who had something to say and wasn't in the habit of waiting to do so. "I've spoken with your mother's doctor. He feels we need to make a change in her medication. See me upstairs when you get a moment."

He turned to me. "We're quite happy with the security system that's in place now, Mr. Denton. But thank you for stopping by."

"Certainly, sir," I said, my voice a blend of fawning sycophancy, "and again, General, it's a great honor and pleasure to meet a man such as yourself, sir."

General Breckenridge Jameson turned and walked off before I got the last half of it out. I turned to Betty; she wavered, as if she might fall over. I stepped over to her, took her arm and guided her to the chair where I'd been sitting. The door to the office was still open, but I'd heard the General's footsteps up the staircase.

"Why didn't you tell him?" I said, my voice low.

She held her hand to her eyes and rubbed her face, then dropped her hand back in her lap. "In his condition," she said, "I just didn't want to worry him."

"His condition?" I demanded. "He looks as healthy as a Clydesdale."

She shook her head. "He's not like that very often."

"Why are you so afraid of him?"

She smiled weakly. "You were doing a pretty good job of sucking up yourself."

"Never assume that what you see on the surface is reality. Besides, you haven't answered my question," I said, leaning in close to her, my face inches from hers.

Her head rolled from side to side. "You don't understand," she said. "You just don't understand."

I stood up straight. "Yeah," I said, "but I'd sure like to try."

Chapter 16

Once again, I drove through the front gates of the Jameson estate with the undeniable sense that I was leaving a well-appointed asylum. So far, I had a rich war hero with Alzheimer's disease who's sharp as a tack; a strong, independent take-charge woman who buckles in her father's presence; a teenage daughter hell-bent-for-leather on killing herself; a mother who haunts the second floor like a ghoul; and hovering over them all, a Sphinx-like, wise, old maid who probably knows everything but is damnably good at keeping secrets.

If Tennessee Williams were still alive, he'd have a field day with these people. . . .

If I hurried, there'd be just enough time to get Betty's check into the bank before closing. The drive-in window at my bank was only open until five-thirty. I cut across two lanes of oncoming traffic on Twenty-first Avenue and got in the line of five cars at precisely five-twenty-three. A few seconds after I pulled in behind a smoking Lincoln Continental with a Vanderbilt Commodore Club sticker in the back window, somebody from inside the bank came out and put a sawhorse in the lane.

I breathed a little easier knowing I'd made it. After ten minutes of waiting, I finally rolled up in front of the glass enclosure that was the drive-in teller's cage.

Betty'd written me a five-hundred-dollar check, and I'd filled out the deposit slip to get a hundred in cash.

The teller punched some numbers on a computer terminal, then studied the deposit slip.

"I'm sorry, Mr. Denton," she said through the cheap speakers. "Your balance is less than the deposit, so we can't give you any cash out of this check."

"But it's drawn on a local bank," I protested. My blood pressure rose and I felt my skin flush.

"Yessir, but it's not drawn on this bank," she said.

"But, but—" I stammered.

"I'm sorry, sir. This check will have to clear before we can give you any cash out of it."

"How long will that take?"

"Three to five days."

Bloody goddamn sodding hell, I thought. "Well, how much have I got in my account?"

The pretty young girl behind the glass typed in some more numbers. "You have available for use, thirty-eight dollars and forty-seven cents."

Jeez, I'd cut it kind of close. "Okay," I said. "Let me have thirty-five of it."

She looked at me with pity, then cleared her throat into the microphones. "It's none of my business, Mr. Denton, but the statements are getting processed tomorrow. Wouldn't you like to leave enough in your account to cover the monthly service charge?"

I hate banks.

I sank lower in the driver's seat. If she'd been snotty or condescending, I could have reared back on my hind legs and bitten her. But like most Southerners delivering bad news, she was so goddamn nice about it that it was hard to scream at her.

"Okay," I said, averting my eyes, "let's try thirty." At least I could get dinner and put gas in the car.

She smiled, chipper once again. "Great." She counted out six five-dollar bills—to make it look like more, I guess—and put the cash in the drawer along with my deposit receipt.

"Thanks for stopping by, Mr. Denton," she chirped. "Have a nice day."

"Have a nice day, my ass," I muttered as I pulled back into the traffic.

A tractor-trailer rig had overturned in the westbound lane of I-440, which meant the eastbound traffic had slowed to a fast walk so the rubberneckers could take a good, long look. I suffered through the parkway traffic until I got to Nolensville Road, thinking that once I took the exit ramp, things would start moving again. Only problem was, everybody else had the same idea.

We crawled around the curved exit ramp, with a few cars at a time getting through the light into a continuous stream of nearly gridlocked traffic on Nolensville Road. This was a part of town I didn't get to often, but in many ways it resembled East Nashville. Nolensville Road down near the Fairgrounds is a collection of older retail storefronts, gas stations, convenience markets, palm readers and fortune tellers, and odd little places like converted houses turned into stores that sell concrete animals, yard ornaments, and lawn jockeys.

Being older and basically a borderline poor to blue-collar part of town, it was also filling up with immigrants. The best Thai restaurant in town was around the corner on Thompson Lane. A combination grocery store and restaurant that was rumored to have the only real Mexican, non-TexMex food in town was near I-440. A strange fusion of funky, redneck, and ethnic . . .

And there were, of course, the compulsory adult bookstores, massage parlors, and private-dancer joints.

The Purple Firefly was down Nolensville Road near the entrance to the Fairgrounds, next door to a guitar-picker honky-tonk that had a great view of the Nashville Raceway behind its parking lot. I'd driven by it many times, but as before, had never really paid much attention to it.

The building was one story, red brick, with the windows painted over in purple and a few parking spaces in front. A sign read ADDITIONAL PARKING IN REAR. I drove around behind the building, figuring it was always better to be out of sight at places like this.

There were a few spaces taken in the back, mostly older sedans, a couple of pickup trucks, and a muscle car or two. I parked as far away from the others as possible, then stopped the engine and sat there for a few moments.

I looked back over the few notes I'd made. Big Moe Klinkenstein's office was in there, along with Mousy Caramello and God knew what else. I suddenly realized I was at that point in a case when one begins to ask oneself what in the hell one is doing.

Finally, there was no putting it off, and truth is, hanging around in the parking lot of a porno bookstore is likely to get you in as much, or more, trouble than actually going in.

There was a rear entrance, a single purple door set in the windowless red brick. Painted on the door in black cursive letters were the words:

THE PURPLE FIREFLY
ENTRANCE
IF NUDITY OR SEX OFFENDS YOU,
DON'T COME IN

I pushed the door open and a blast of heavy, icy airconditioned air billowed out onto me. The smell of disinfectant and smoke hung like a pall. The store was one fairly small room with walls made out of cheap paneling, and unpainted, unstained pine bookshelves nailed crudely throughout the store. Industrial-type fluorescent lights hung in white fixtures by chains from the ceiling.

I walked in and looked around. Two muscular guys in T-shirts were over in one corner, huddled over a bin full of magazines. A well-groomed young man wearing a polyester shirt straight out of the disco Seventies, with three earrings in one ear, two in the other, and one through a nostril stood to my right behind a cash register. He smiled at me as I came in, revealing a row of straight white teeth below a sharply trimmed brown mustache.

A couple of guys in coat and tie milled around self-consciously, clearly business types who'd stopped by to do something adventurous before they went home for an evening of television and microwaved dinners with their wives. One scrawny-looking teenager with terrible skin and greasy peroxided hair stood furtively next to a rack of videos featuring men loving men in a catalogue of positions.

My stomach knotted up and I had this sharp pain in my gut. I realized I was standing there looking like a doofus,. so decided to mosey around a bit, scoping out the place and trying to figure where Big Moe Klinkenstein's office might be. There was a counter set to the right of the back entrance, with eight-foot-high racks of adult videos in row upon row behind the counter. The boxes of videos in the shelves were empty, for display only. You wanted to buy a dirty movie, you brought the box up to the counter and paid for it, then the clerk got the videocassette off the rack.

Pretty well takes care of the shoplifting problem, I thought. And then I noticed, hanging in discreet mounts from the ceiling in all four corners of the store, small video cameras. Given that he had a full-time bodyguard and security cameras everywhere, I drew the inference that perhaps Big Moe was a little paranoid.

I never saw a door inside the place, at least not one that might lead to an office. Only the front and back entrances could be seen.

Finally, I screwed up my courage and sauntered over to the counter. The natty cashier with the Seventies fixation had just finished checking out another customer.

"May I help you?" he asked, smiling at me. His voice was high, prim and proper.

"Yeah, I hope so," I said. "My name's Denton, Harry James Denton, and I'm a private investigator."

"Oh my goodness," he said. "A private dick."

I cleared my throat and took out my license. "Uh, yeah. I'm trying to find Mr. Klinkenstein."

"Who?" he asked coyly.

"Mr. Klinkenstein. You know, the guy that owns this place."

"Oh, that Mr. Klinkenstein." He sniffed. "Mr. Klinkenstein doesn't usually see anyone without an appointment."

I thought back to the movies I'd seen where hardboiled private eye Mike Hammer/Sam Spade types would have, at this plot point, hooked a finger in the guy's nose ring and yanked him over the counter. Alan Ladd or Robert Mitchum would have had this guy squealing in a heartbeat.

Somehow, though, I didn't think this would work in real life, especially since for all I knew, there was a guy the size of Hulk Hogan monitoring those security cameras.

I lifted one of my business cards out of my license holder and handed it across the counter. "Would you mind at least asking him if he'd see me? And tell him, please, that I'm here on behalf of the Jameson family."

He perused my card, then looked at me and lifted an eyebrow. "Who are the Jamesons?"

"You know, the Dysfunctional Belle Meade Jamesons."

He grinned, then shrugged like that was supposed to mean something to him. "Oh, *those* Jamesons. All right, I'll talk to him. Wait here."

He turned and disappeared into the stacks of book-

cases behind the counter. At the end of a row, he turned
right. I moved to the right myself to try and see where
he was going, but that end of the room was heavily
shadowed.

I turned and leaned against the counter with my back
to the stacks. Over in the corner, the two guys I'd seen
when I first came in were giggling over a magazine one
of them held. As they laughed, one put his arm around
the other's shoulder, then ran his hand down his back
and patted him affectionately on the bottom.

The back door opened, letting a shaft of afternoon
sun, like a pillar of gold dust, into the room. I folded
my arms self-consciously and wished the counter person would either come back and take me to Klinkenstein's office or run me off. One or the other, but don't
leave me hanging here.

A tall guy walked in through the back door, mirrored
aviator shades reflecting the harsh overhead light. He
wore a cowboy shirt and tight jeans, and the sharp-toed
cowboy boots known around here as "cockroach killers" for their ability to get into corners so well. He gave
me a look, the skin on his acne-scarred cheeks lifting in
a smile. He passed the counter, barely brushing my arm
as he went by, then turned down one of the aisles and
stopped in front of a bin filled with magazines in glass-
ine envelopes. The aroma of cheap after-shave floated
lazily in his wake. He flipped through the magazines
one at a time, then glanced up at me and smiled again.

Behind me, I heard footsteps as the clerk returned.
"Mr. Klinkenstein says he'll see you. This way."

I walked around the end of the counter and followed
the clerk as he led me between the shelves of tapes. We
got to the end of one row, turned right, walked another
ten feet or so, and stopped in front of a stained wooden
door. The clerk rapped a couple of times on the wood,
then opened it for me.

I stepped through the door into a rectangular, carpeted office with a massive wooden desk just off center. A couch was against one wall facing the desk, with a table and lamp next to it. A credenza with a fax machine and a bookshelf stereo system on top was against the other wall. An open door to my right led into a bathroom.

A short but obscenely fat man behind the desk looked up from a stack of papers. "Yeah," he barked, squinting at me through thick glasses, "sit down." His voice was high, almost a squeal.

In the corner, below a window unit air conditioner that had been mounted in a hole in the wall, a young man stood. He leaned into the paneling with one ankle crossed over the other. He wore combat boots and camouflage fatigues topped by a sleeveless white T-shirt. Though small, his arms were thick and well developed, with large tattoos on each bicep and shoulder. His hair was close-cropped in a dyed-blond buzz cut and his face was hairless. He stared at me intently as I crossed over and sat down.

"Mr. Klinkenstein," I began, "I appreciate your taking the time to—"

"Yeah, yeah, yeah," he interrupted. "Right." He swung the chair around and popped up from behind the desk with a speed astonishing for a man his size. He crossed over in front of me and stood for a second.

His brown pants were dotted with food stains and spilled drink. He wore a thick, wide belt, with an enormous bronze buckle that had a large hamburger on it, with HOME OF THE WHOPPER stamped below.

"Cut to the chase." He grinned. "What do you want from me?"

He plopped down on the couch next to me so hard the floor shook. As I'd been warned, Big Moe Klinkenstein smelled like he hadn't had a shower in a few days. The dark stains in the armpits of his checked shirt looked permanent.

"Well, I—" Then I stopped cold as he laid his enormous hand, dirty fingernails and all, on my thigh and began kneading it through my pants. Over in the corner, the militia guy with the strange look in his eyes grinned meanly. He shifted and turned to his right, exposing a tattoo on his left arm that depicted a Nazi swastika entwined about an American flag.

I cleared my throat and fought the urge to run. "Mr. Klinkenstein, I represent a woman who's very concerned about the welfare of her younger sister."

"Younger sister, huh?" Klinkenstein said, staring at my leg as he rubbed my thigh. Then he leaned into me and kind of fell against my shoulder. "What's that got to do with me?"

"Nothing directly, sir. But we have some indication that the younger sister—who by the way, Mr. Klinkenstein, is underage—may have been involved with one of your employees. A Mr. Turner, I believe."

Klinkenstein's head shot up and he made eye contact with the guy across the room. Something passed between them, but I'm damned if I can figure out what it was.

"I had a Turner who worked for me," he said. "But not anymore."

The guy in the corner grinned again. I'd be willing to bet there are a lot of wingless butterflies around thanks to this fellow.

"I see," I said. "But the family is still concerned about the safety of the girl. In fact, they've authorized me to offer a substantial reward for her safe return."

Klinkenstein turned to me and kind of scrunched up his face, sort of a squint and a grimace all blended together. His hair was long but thinning, black and greasy, and hanging down over his forehead. He was close enough for me to get a big whiff of sour-milk breath.

"Substantial reward, huh?" he asked. "Define substantial."

He moved his hand down to my knee and massaged it. This was getting weirder by the moment, but if I slapped his hand, chances are I wouldn't get much in the way of cooperation. Not to mention getting my head bashed in by Mousy. "The Jamesons have offered up to twenty-five-thousand-dollars cash, no questions asked, for the safe return of their daughter, Stacey Jameson."

"Oooh, twenty-five large," the guy in the corner taunted. "Big fookin' deal . . ."

Klinkenstein shot a look across the room. "Shut up, Mousy," he ordered.

Mousy Caramello took four quick steps across the room and stood right in front of the sofa, glowering down at us. "C'mon, Moe, what the fuck you doing talking to this pussy? Let me boot his ass outta here."

"Will you cool your jets, goddamn it?"

"And look at you," Mousy complained, "pawing at him like that. Why don't you just lean over and suck his dick. . . ."

A wave of nausea swept over me.

"Shut up!" Big Moe barked. "Or you're going to be very sorry."

Mousy stepped over in front of me and bent down. His eyes were dark, huge, full of hate. "What do you care about this little cunt? You been putting it to her or what? Maybe you'd rather have it from the Klinkster, huh? They don't call him Big Moe for nothing."

I could feel my blood pressure rising with each heartbeat. This kid was sick, a stone psycho, and as much as I wanted to punch his lights out, I knew if I wanted out of here with minimal damage, I'd better stay cool. I took a shallow breath and turned slightly to face Klinkenstein.

"As I was saying, Mr. Klinkenstein," I began. Then, out of the left side of my vision, I saw the kid shift toward me, his head moving like lightning. I jerked but it was too late, there was nowhere to go.

Mousy Caramello had his tongue out like a cat. He ran it up the side of my face from my lower jawline to a point just next to my eye. I stiffened, locked my jaw solid, but held still. His tongue was hot, but dry, almost scratchy against my skin.

I sat there in shock more than anything else. Then he twisted slightly, flicked out his tongue again, and caught the bottom of my earlobe. This time, I snapped back and glared at him.

"Try it," he whispered. "Go for it."

Klinkenstein reached over and put a hand on Mousy's chest and pushed. "Damn it, Mousy. Quit playing games."

Mousy stood up and backed off a couple of feet. I stared at him, trying not to blink, but the kid was cold, cold and good. In a few seconds, I blinked and looked down at the floor.

"You'll have to excuse my friend here," Klinkenstein said. "He doesn't know when a joke stops being funny."

"Yeah," I said. "Guess not."

"Now, as to this token reward you're offering. I, of course, don't know what you're talking about. But say I did. Twenty-five grand won't even buy you a decent car. So don't insult me, baby."

"Right now, it's the best they can offer up front in cash. There's always the possibility of more," I said.

"And what if they don't find the girl?"

"That's where things get a little sticky," I said. Above us, Mousy snorted derisively. I raised my head slightly; he still glared down at me like a snake trying to hypnotize dinner.

"You see, this young girl comes into some money on her eighteenth birthday. Only problem is, her behavior has convinced the family she's incapable of handling her own affairs. So if the girl isn't returned to the safety of her family, they're going to court to have her declared incompetent."

"That'd be tough if they couldn't find the little bitch," Mousy said.

"Maybe," I answered. "But if one of your employees, Mr. Klinkenstein, is say, 'helping' the girl out by hiding her in hopes of the girl being able to repay the favor . . . well, that's just not going to happen."

Klinkenstein's hand, which had been just resting on my knee during our conversation, suddenly came to life again and ran up the inside of my thigh.

"Since none of my employees have any interest whatsoever in helping a runaway teenager, this is a useless discussion," he said.

I moved my knees together in hopes he'd take the hint. He didn't.

"I understand that," I said. "I'm just delivering a public offer. Anyone who returns the girl is entitled to the reward. It's a stand-up offer."

"Well," he said brightly, pulling his hand out of my crotch and patting my knee, "fair enough."

I eased away from him and slowly stood up, with Mousy behind me now. I felt his eyes on my back like a heat lamp.

"I appreciate your time," I said. Klinkenstein reached out and grabbed my hand. His grip was weak, his palms nearly dripping. He held my hand as he pulled himself up off the couch.

"It's been a pleasure," he said. "Come back any time. I mean that."

Behind us, Mousy said, "I'll bet you do."

As I stepped toward the door, I felt my mouth starting to open and the words coming out before I could stop them. I tried to put on the brakes, but it was too late.

Damn, I hate when I do that.

"Oh, there is one other thing, Mr. Klinkenstein," I said, stopping at the open door and turning back to him.

"Yeah?" he said.

I tilted my head toward him and gave him an earnest smile.

"Tell that little, sawed-off psycho son of a bitch who works for you that if he ever touches me again, I'll kill him."

Behind Klinkenstein, Mousy Caramello's hands doubled into fists. Klinkenstein held up a hand, palm toward Mousy, and stopped him.

"Can you do that for me?" I asked.

"Yeah," he said. "I can do that."

"Thank you. Have a good day, sir."

Chapter 17

I slammed the door of the Mustang so hard the glass rattled, then pounded the steering wheel blindly until my hands rebelled in pain.

"Damn!" I yelled, punctuating each curse with another hit to the wheel. "Damn, damn, damn, damn, damn! How could I be so stupid!"

One thing was certain: the next time I saw Mousy Caramello, I'd better have a few really big guys with me.

I sat with my eyes closed, trying to slow my breathing. My mouth had written checks my ass couldn't cash before, but I'd never bounced one like this. In my mind's eye, I saw the swastika tattoo on his arm, the crazed glint in his eye. Klinkenstein could control him up to a point, but beyond that it was anyone's guess.

I regained what little was left of my composure, then started the car and pulled out of the parking lot, around the building, and back into the Nolensville Road traffic. Inside the glovebox I had a small box of tissues. I yanked a half-dozen out of the box and scrubbed the side of my jaw until pieces of white fuzz clung to my stubble.

I hit the ramp onto I-440 with a squeal and laid on the accelerator until I was hitting seventy. For some reason or other, the Friday-evening rush hour had abated sooner than usual. I pulled into the parking lot of Marsha's condo inside of twenty minutes and coasted into a space across the lot from the Porsche.

She opened the door on the third knock, still dressed in her professional doctor duds. "Hi," she said cheerily. "I was wondering if—"

I brushed by her into the hallway. Behind me, she pushed the door closed.

"What's the matter?" she asked.

I turned. "I've had a really bad day. I need a drink and a shower."

"There's some white wine in the fridge."

"Got anything stronger?"

She walked by me into the kitchen. "You *have* had a bad day. What's that white fuzz on your cheek?"

I brushed the side of my jaw. "Never mind. I'll explain later."

"Jack and water okay?"

"Sure, thanks. Do me a favor, okay? Bring it into the bathroom."

She turned and looked at me, concerned. "Yeah. Have it right in there."

I had my jacket and shirt off by the time I made it down the hallway into her bedroom. I kicked my shoes off and peeled off my pants and socks. The bathroom filled with steam as I stepped into the hottest shower I could stand. Marsha had a loofah sponge hanging on the wall. I grabbed it and proceeded to rid myself of any remaining traces of The Purple Firefly.

The door opened as I scrubbed away, my skin turning as raw and red as a bad sunburn. I pulled the shower curtain back as Marsha held out a tumbler full of amber and ice cubes.

"Hey, be careful with that thing," she said. "You'll wear the hide off yourself."

I swallowed the drink in two gulps, the alcohol hitting my stomach in a burst of fire that jolted me all the way down to the balls of my feet.

I handed her the glass and returned to soaping myself

up. The shower curtain was open just enough for me to watch her in the bathroom mirror.

Marsha set the glass down on the bathroom counter and leaned against the tile, folding her arms in front of her. "You want to tell me what's going on?"

I put both my arms out and leaned against the back wall of the shower and lowered my head. The spray from the nozzle hit my raw skin like needles.

"I met the man who owns most of the sleaze joints in the whole county, maybe the whole state," I said, my voice low, barely discernible over the shower. "He put his hands on my thighs, and his bodyguard licked me."

She shook her head. "I'm sorry, I missed that. Did you say . . ."

I turned my head and looked at her. "Yeah. Licked me."

She grimaced and squeezed her eyes shut. "Oh, God, Harry. What have you gotten yourself into this time?"

I rinsed off the last of the soap and twisted the faucet handles until the water stopped.

"I don't know," I said wearily, taking the thick towel she offered. "But I want out. This is way too much. A real overdose . . ."

"Then get out."

I ran the towel through my hair, knocking off most of the water, then wrapped it around my waist.

"Problem is, there's still the girl."

"Let the police handle it."

"The cops come into this, I think the girl's dead."

"You think they'll kill her?"

I stepped out of the shower. "I think she'll kill herself."

"People kill themselves, Harry. Sometimes nobody can stop them."

I pulled the towel off my waist and started patting myself dry. "That's cold, Marsh. You been around too many dead bodies."

Her lower lip trembled.

"I'm sorry," I said quietly. "That was real shitty. I didn't mean it."

She gazed off into the fogged-up mirror for what seemed like a long time without talking.

"What do you have to do to get this out of your system?" she finally asked.

I closed my eyes and buried my face in the towel, furiously rubbing as if there were still something left of Mousy Caramello on me.

"Find the girl," I said. "Get her home."

"Then do it, Harry," she said. "Do it or get out of my life. I won't have you like this."

She turned and walked out of the bathroom. I followed her, right on her heels. Next to the bed, I reached out and stopped her.

"Wait. I'm sorry. I don't know what's gotten into me. But I know I don't want the other."

"The other?"

"Out of your life." I put my arms around her and pulled her in close.

"I don't want you out of my life either. But this is the pits, babe."

I ran my fingers through her hair. "I've been thinking about what we talked about the other night."

"Yeah?"

"I think we should get married."

She pulled away from me, just a bit, but still away. "Oh."

"Yeah."

"Harry, I don't think it's such a good idea to get married just because you're going through a real bad time. Marriage creates more problems than it solves."

"Okay," I agreed. "You're direct, but you're right. Let me get through the bad time. Then we'll do it."

She looked away. "I'm not sure I'm ready for marriage."

I felt my brow furrow. "But the other night, we talked about—"

She turned back, her eyes dark. "*You* talked about getting married. I talked about having a child. They're two entirely different issues."

I felt like she'd hit me in the chest with a two-by-four. "Oh," I said.

She held out her hands. "Yeah, someday maybe. Time's not a factor there. We can get married any time the time's right. This is different."

"Yeah," I said. "I understand. You just need breeding stock right now."

"Oh, Christ, Harry!" she snapped. "Why'd you have to put it like that?"

"How would you like me to put it?"

She turned and started out of the room. "I think you should get dressed. Get dressed and go."

"No, wait." I reached out and grabbed her arm. "You can't just walk away in the middle of this! This isn't right, Marsh. You're telling me you don't want me, you just want the part of me that gets you what you really want."

"How can you say that?" Her eyes glistened and her face softened. I pulled her to me. She held back for a moment, but then let herself slide over. "That's not what I mean at all. Doesn't it count for anything that I didn't even want this until I met you? I didn't even know I had a biological clock until you came along."

I held her close, her arms around me, mine tightly around her shoulders. "I'm sorry," I said.

She pulled away from me, her cheeks wet. The towel slipped off and fell to the floor between us. She stared at me as I stood there, naked, defenseless.

"I'm sorry, too," she said. "I wish I had some snappy comeback to all this, but I don't. What do you want, Harry? What do you really want?"

I held out my arms and she took my hands. I pulled her gently back toward me, finding her lips with mine when our faces met. I kissed her wet cheeks, her face, hair. And her arms came around me and pulled me tight. I ran my hand up under her blouse, to the bare skin of her back, to the heat between her shoulder blades just behind her heart.

"You," I whispered. "You."

I felt her nuzzle close to my ear as I drifted in and out of a half sleep. Exhaustion and relief had finally caught up with me. We'd made love with a passion that bordered on desperation, and afterward, I'd told her everything. I'd told her of finding Stacey in the bedroom next to where Red Dog Turner lay murdered, of spiriting her out of there, and I told her about Corey.

Everything.

"I wish you'd told me sooner," she whispered. "I'd have understood."

"I felt so guilty," I muttered. But I'd said it past tense. The guilt was gone now, confessed and absolved.

"Because you're involved with me doesn't mean you're never going to be attracted to anyone else again. It's not a matter of that part of you going away. It's what you choose to do with it."

"I think I was scared," I said. "Suddenly I felt old. For the first time in my life, old. This whole business of having a kid, and being exhausted and stressed out. And seeing that sick, desperate girl ... Jesus."

She moved in closer to me, on her side, and slowly moved her left leg across me.

"Hmmm," she moaned. "I don't think so."

"Think what?"

"That you're old yet."

I chuckled. "Thank you for the compliment, but it doesn't solve my problem."

"I know. You've still got to find the girl."

I turned to her. "What about the rest of it?"

"What?"

"Well, my dear, I've just confessed to the city assistant medical examiner that I was at a murder scene, tampered with evidence, bodily removed a material witness, and probably conspired to obstruct justice."

She propped up on an elbow and looked down at me. In the near total darkness of the room, I saw only the outline of her face framed in wisps of hair.

"Boy, you're in a boatload of trouble," she teased.

"C'mon, I'm serious. The last thing I'd ever want to do is cause you problems."

She giggled. "It's a little late for that."

"Get serious."

"Hmmm, I guess the right thing for me to do would be to call Lieutenant Spellman over in Homicide and turn your butt in. Only thing is, I've grown rather fond of you and I don't have time for jail visits."

"So I guess it's curtains for us, right baby?" I said in an abominably bad Edward G. Robinson imitation.

"I'll bake you a cake with a file in it, how's that?"

"I think the sticks are on to that one now," I said. "Seriously darling, what do we do?"

"Well," she said, settling back down and staring at the ceiling, "as far as I'm concerned, the bedroom is the same as the confessional. If somebody asks me under oath, I'm not going to lie. Until then, I'll just keep my mouth shut and hope you stay out of any more trouble."

I laid my hand on her stomach and rubbed gently. "Something else's been on my mind as well. I don't know who she's with now, but that sleazy little psycho that works for Klinkenstein was grinning too much not to know something. He's either got her or he knows who has."

"You're not going to do anything about him, are

you?" Her voice was somber now. "If he's in this, then you will get the cops involved, right?"

I said nothing.

"Right?" she demanded.

"I'll be careful."

"That's not the answer I wanted."

"It'll have to do," I said.

We were quiet for a while after that. I lay back down and nuzzled close to Marsha, her warm breath on my neck.

"Listen," I said, "I want you to know that what went on with her that night was just a fluke. One of those weird, unexplainable things that's never happened before and won't ever happen again."

"Jeez, Harry, you just kissed her," Marsha said. Then, after a second: "Right?"

"Yes, that's all. But for a moment there, just for a heartbeat, I wanted to do more."

"But you didn't."

I smiled in the darkness. "That's right," I said. "I didn't. But I've been a real jerk. I never should have gotten Corey involved in this. It's too dangerous on about a half-a-dozen different levels. As soon as I find her, I'm pulling her out of this mess. Tonight. Before she gets into any more trouble."

Marsha twisted next to me. "My stomach just growled. You hungry?"

"Sure," I answered. "And then after that, love . . ."

She ground in close to me and pulled me tightly into the Y of her outstretched legs. Then she rolled with her arms around me and pulled me on top.

"Yeah," she said. "You've got to go."

Leaving Marsha alone on a Friday night after the evening we'd had was about as hard as anything I'd ever done. We'd found a place of resolution, though, some peace between us. This had been the most frustrating, maddening week I'd ever had, and I was relieved that at least as far as Corey was concerned, it was almost over.

The parking lot of Club Exotique was packed, with a beefy weightlifter in jeans and a white T-shirt at the entrance to the lot waving people off with a flashlight. I turned left and drove past him, around the corner, and found a slot on the street.

I parked the Mustang, then walked around the corner and halfway down that block to the club entrance. This being such a busy night, two guys out front were collecting the cover charge and explaining the rules, rather than the solitary bored dude in the cheap tux.

I handed the first guy a pair of fives. He looked at me oddly.

"Sorry, pal," he said. "Friday night. Cover charge's twenty bucks."

"Didn't know that." I pulled my wallet out and plucked out two more. "Why the crowd? Is it like this every Friday night?"

"Special guest artist tonight," he explained. "Chesty Del Rive."

"Who in the hell is Chesty Del Rive?" I asked as I eased past him toward the door.

"Famous fuck film star," he called over his shoulder as he held out his hand for the next guy.

Great, I thought as I joined the line waiting to get in. I hope I can even find Corey. I had no inclination to spend even a minute longer than I had to inside the Club Exotique.

The obligatory sensual assault hit me as soon as I entered the building. Sweaty guys packed in like Alabama fans at the Auburn game, music thundering from every direction, lights flashing, nearly naked girls swarming around like bees in a field of wildflowers.

I stopped just inside the door and tried to get my bearings. A clearly smashed frat boy slammed into me from the side, turned and offered a boozy pardon, then stumbled off. Another guy bumped into me from behind and I instinctively checked to make sure my wallet was still where it was supposed to be. I knew there wasn't any percentage in picking my pocket, but how would anybody else know that?

I scanned the room, as much of it as I could see anyway. Onstage, three naked women danced and cavorted at the same time. Their movements were more frenetic than I'd seen on any other night, more electric. There was an energy in the air that hadn't been there during the week. It seemed almost explosive.

The torrent of testosterone carried me farther into the room, with the traffic pattern finally dissipating as the crowd found seats. Corey was nowhere to be seen; I didn't recognize anyone else.

I searched for an empty table, a hiding place, really. Nothing. Every available spot was taken, with throngs of men hovering in the spaces between the tables. I backed off into a corner. Behind me, on an elevated platform, a small woman with a tangle of blonde curly hair lay on her back on a coffee table, her head bent over backward so far she was eyeing me upside down. Her legs made the victory sign in midair. Two men sat on the couch blankly studying her.

I turned away, then thought maybe Corey was off giving one of these little private displays. I began easing around the room slowly, dodging between crowds of men, the women in see-through whatevers gliding past me with the obligatory smiles.

I worked my way around the room, across the back, then down the long side that led toward the stage. In the din of voices, banging music, yells, cheers, claps, I heard the DJ announce that the special guest dancer of the evening was about to take the stage.

"Gentlemen, let's hear it for Chesty Del Rive!" he screamed.

A roar went up like a New York ticker-tape parade. I turned as a huge woman with the most apt name I'd ever seen sauntered onto the stage wearing a white satin bikini and heels that had to be at least eight inches. She wore around her neck a silk flyer's scarf that was almost hidden by the haystack of platinum blonde hair that fell below her shoulders. As the music boomed, she began dancing. No, dancing's not the right word. She prowled the stage. She hunted. She pillaged. The audience was fresh meat, and she was a hungry Amazon.

I turned away as the top of the bikini came off. Bedlam erupted. Two guys jumped up from a table screaming and fell backward over their chairs, sprawling into the crowd, creating a human chain of falling dominoes.

Where the hell was she? She said she'd be here, damn it!

I snaked my way back around the room. I'd checked out every private booth, and if Corey was in any of them, she was buried so far you'd never find her. In the back of the room, there was a little space that was rapidly filling up with more men coming in from outside. Somebody let loose with a rebel yell right in my ear and nearly shattered my eardrum, then let fly with a drink that splattered all over me. I'd have given him a severe dirty look, but truth was he hadn't even seen me. His rapt gaze was fixed on the stage, where Chesty Del Rive was down to her last article of clothing. Only the scarf remained.

I had to get out of here, but not without seeing Corey first.

Then, out of the corner of my eye, I spotted a pile of white hair on a tall frame. I pushed around two guys in matching T-shirts and bright maroon parachute-cloth pants to get a better look.

She wore an American-flag bikini.

What was her name? *Her name, damn it!*

I'd pulled it up before I was halfway over to her.

She'd just come out of the dressing room, was standing with several other dancers in front of the DJ's platform.

"Tyler," I called over the music as I pushed through the crowd toward her. If she heard me, she'd hid it well. She looked bored, tired.

We made eye contact about three feet away from each other. She looked at me, confused, and then it hit her. She turned quickly, said something to one of the other girls, then headed back to the dressing room.

I caught up with her right in front of the curtain beyond which I could not go.

"Tyler, wait!" I reached out and grabbed her right arm at the tricep.

She whipped around, angry. "Don't grab me like that, man! I'll get your ass tossed out of here!"

I jerked my hand back, but held my ground. "I've got to find her. Where is she?"

"Where's who?" She put her hands on her hips, just above the Stars and Stripes, and cocked her head back defiantly.

"Corey," I said. "She's supposed to be here."

"I told you, man, she don't work here no more."

"I found her at another place. She said she was coming back here tonight."

"Well she lied to you, bud, 'cause she ain't here," she yelled over the music. "Get over it, man!"

"Tyler, she didn't lie to me—"

"Listen, Ace, you are not welcome in this club," she said in a lull in the noise. She pointed at my chest with a brightly painted, sharply nailed index finger. "We do not want your sorry ass here. And if you don't split, you're going to get stomped in places you didn't even know you had. Now beat it."

I felt a hand the size of a dinner plate on my shoulder. I turned to find the hand was connected to an arm about as big around as my thigh.

"This guy bothering you, Tyler?"

"Yeah, Tommy, he's getting on my nerves. Toss his ass outta here."

I looked at the guy and held up my hands, palm outward, in supplication. "I was just leaving."

"Yep, that's right," he agreed. He jerked my shirt up off my shoulder and led me through the crowd like a dog on a leash. The throng of men separated like the Red Sea parting, and in a matter of seconds, I was thrust into the fresh air like a fish tossed back because he wasn't worth keeping.

The Mustang coughed, spit back at me a couple of times, then died. I'd flooded it, and now it was a matter of sitting here a couple of minutes before taking another crack at it. I glanced down at my watch; it was still early by show-bar standards, but the middle of the night for a man beyond exhaustion.

Where was she? She wouldn't have lied to me. Or maybe she would have.

There was only one way to find out.

I cranked the car until the motor caught, then tickled the accelerator gently until it ran steady. I turned around and made my way over to Broadway, then away from downtown.

The parking lot at Fantasy Island, the sleazier club where I'd found Corey working, was nowhere near as packed as the Club Exotique. The block was darker as well, the streetlights barely illuminating the asphalt and concrete in front of the silent brick buildings.

Once again, I wished I hadn't come alone. I didn't want to be here, didn't want any part of this, was trying to get out. One thing I knew for certain, I was sure as hell tired of throwing cash at these people by the handful.

A nondescript guy in yet another ill-fitting tuxedo stood at the door. I had my license holder out of my pocket by the time I got to him. I flashed it at him and started talking before he had a chance to open his mouth.

"Name's Denton. I'm a private investigator on a case involving a runaway girl who may be working in one of the show bars. She's underage, so there'll be some heat when we find her."

"Hey, we ain't got no—" he sputtered.

"Shut up and listen," I said, holding up a finger. "I'm not trying to cause any trouble, but I can get the cops here with one phone call, understand? That's all it takes. But I don't want that. You got another girl working here who we think's maybe a friend of hers. She was dancing here last night. I saw her. Her name's Corey Kerr, but her stage name's Ventana."

I studied his face, figuring he'd either bought the macho rap hook, line, and sinker, or I was about to become airborne. One or the other.

"Let me get the manager for you," he said. "C'mon in."

I followed him into Fantasy Island, my heart beating double time in relief. Jeez, he bought it. Maybe I ought to pull this tough-guy stuff more often.

Then again, maybe I got lucky just this once.

Fantasy Island had about half the men in it as the other club, but they made up for it by having the volume cranked even louder. The doorman got a guy inside to cover for him and led me through the club, past the bar, and through the door into a long hallway. Two women—baby-doll costume on one, leather and dog collar on the other—stepped out of a door with a cardboard cutout star pasted on it. They giggled as they walked past.

"Dressing room," the doorman explained. He led me to the end of the hall, opened another door, and shuttled me in. A guy with a goatee and thinning hair sat behind a cheap, surplus green desk, with a stack of paper and a large calculator in front of him. He motioned me to a chair and dismissed the doorman.

I showed him my badge and ran the rap by him. He listened closely, looked like he wanted to cooperate. And when I was finished, he shrugged his shoulders and smiled.

"Yeah, she worked here, but she called in this afternoon and quit. We got a helluva turnover here, you know?"

"She tell you where she was going?"

"She didn't say; I didn't ask. Like I said—"

"Yeah, yeah," I interrupted as I got up from the chair, "you got a helluva turnover."

Assuming Tyler wasn't lying to me, which was a big assumption, and that the manager at Fantasy Island wasn't either—an equally large assumption, I realize—there was only one conclusion to draw from the evening's search.

She'd run out on me.

Oh hell, I thought, maybe it's better this way. Now I could start all over, start trying to figure out where Stacey Jameson was rather than juggling so many things at once. Like I said, I'm a lousy juggler and the older I get, the more that comes home to me. I'm much better off tackling one thing at a time.

I thought of driving back to Green Hills, but chances were Marsha was long off to sleep. No point in waking her up. I'd give her a call in the morning, let her know what was going on, then regroup.

I hit the freeway through town, then took the ramp to I-65 north. A couple of exits up, I took the Trinity Lane ramp and headed toward East Nashville and the comfort and safety of my own little apartment.

But something nagged at me, and it wouldn't let go no matter how hard I tried not to listen. Corey and I'd wound up going through a lot together in a very short and intense amount of time. Like two soldiers sharing a foxhole, I felt I'd come to know her.

And I just didn't think she'd take off like that. I've been wrong about people before, more times than I care to remember. This felt different. No matter how tired I was, this wasn't going to go away, and sleep wasn't going to come until I knew.

I crossed over the Ellington Parkway on Trinity Lane, then on impulse took the ramp onto the parkway northbound. In the heat of the other night, I'd foolishly forgotten to write down Corey's address. I didn't even have a phone number, but I thought I could find the place again. She'd guided me through Madison, past where the parkway ended and became a residential street. When I let the Zen take over, I'm pretty good with directions.

I followed my instincts, turning right off one street, following another through a neighborhood of brick ranch-style homes built back in the late Fifties, early Sixties. The road snaked off to the left, then abruptly curved back to the right. Past that right, I thought I remembered there was a dead-end street, kind of a cul-de-sac.

There it was! I slowed, made the turn and strained to see the houses on the unlit street. Corey lived near the end of the road, on the left, in one side of a small brick duplex that was unoccupied on the other side.

A small sign staked in a front yard read DUPLEX FOR RENT with a phone number after it. I parked the car and killed the lights.

The place was dark, no lights inside or out. The house next door had a security floodlight mounted on the soffit that partially illuminated Corey's driveway.

I stepped warily out of the car, careful not to make too much noise. I didn't want my visit interrupted by a wandering pit bull or an overly cautious neighbor with a shotgun.

The gravel crunched under my feet as I walked the level driveway to Corey's front porch on the left side of the house. Dark shadows in acute angles and sharp edges jutted out from the brick. I stepped onto a cracked concrete walk and up to the porch. An aluminum storm door was locked, but sprung open with a sharp tug. I knocked three times as softly as I could.

Nothing.

"Damn it, Corey," I whispered. "Be here. Wake up. C'mon."

I knocked again, louder. Still nothing.

I tried this strategy a few more times, then gave up. The storm door slid shut with a hiss as I backtracked down the walk, and around the house to the backyard. A chain-link fence surrounded the yard, with an open, unlocked gate at the end of the driveway. I stepped through and into the shadows behind the house.

Two concrete steps led up to a back door into what I guessed was the kitchen. I hadn't gotten the tour, had only let her off at the front porch with a promise that I'd find her tonight. It was a promise that I apparently intended to keep.

The back of the house was equally dark. I knocked once. The door eased open about two inches.

My heart banged in my chest.

I stepped aside just in case anyone was inside, like I'd seen in the movies, and with one hand gave the door a shove. It opened farther. Only silence escaped.

Frightened for real now, I crept around low and stared into the darkness. Nothing was there, nothing moving, at least not anything I could see.

I stood up in the doorway, reached inside and swept the wall looking for a light switch. My hand caught hard plastic and flicked upward lightly.

The room exploded in white light from an overhead fixture. My eyes squinted in pain and shock. I forced them open and looked inside, struggling to focus. Then my heart caught in my chest again, like a side stitch twenty miles into a marathon.

Corey Kerr's apartment looked like a bad day in Bosnia.

Chapter 18

Drawers yanked out, plates smashed, garbage strewn everywhere, a basketball-sized hole in the drywall next to a pantry door that had been ripped loose from its top hinge . . .

I stared dumbfounded for a few moments before my brain kicked into gear. I jumped over a pile in the middle of the floor, shoved a table out of the way, and ran through the hallway and into the living room.

"Oh my God," I whispered. The sofa had been ripped open across the cushions, stuffing thrown everywhere. An expensive component stereo system had been tossed off a bookcase and stomped into useless metal, glass, and circuit boards. A coffee table in the center of the room would barely pass for kindling.

Panic drove caution out. Whoever'd done this could have been waiting in the next room with a meat cleaver. No matter, I had to find her if she was here. I muttered curses under my breath and rushed back into the hallway.

There were two bedrooms on either side of the hall at the end of the duplex. I dashed down the hall, swiping at a light switch as I scurried by. The room on the left was empty except for a few packing boxes that had been upended. Old record albums, clothes, the packed salvage of life had been cast around the bare wooden floor like so much useless junk.

Opposite that was Corey's sparsely furnished bed-

room. I flicked on the overhead. Glass from a second
shattered television littered the floor. Drawers had been
pulled out of a cheap bureau, with clothes torn and
shredded all over the place. The sheets were ripped
from the bed and crumpled. A few small, coppery
brown blobs dotted the mattress.

I reached over and ran an index finger across one of
the stains. I'm no expert, but it looked like blood. It was
thick, sticky, nearly dry.

"Okay," I said out loud. "Think this through. Don't
get hysterical here."

The trashed bedroom indicated nothing but blind
chaos, a hurricane of destruction. I backed out into the
hallway, turned, and scooted down to the living room.
Cushions slashed, drawers snatched. Yeah, somebody
could have been tearing the place apart, looking for
God knew what.

But the shattered stereo and booted television belied
that. You can't hide anything inside a picture tube. No,
there was a fierceness to this that had nothing to do
with robbery or burglary.

This was vengeance, stone-cold revenge, passion,
fury.

I leaned against the wall, drained, and berated myself
for ever getting her involved. I should have thrown her
out of the car the moment she invited herself in. It was
bad enough that I'd gotten her involved in the first
place, but to have gone out and recruited her again was
unforgivable.

Decisions, choices, had to be made. The police?

Yes. No.

Maybe.

That would complicate things even further, and my
gut feeling was that I didn't have time.

Time for what, though? An hour ago, I didn't have a
clue as to how to find one missing girl. Now I didn't
have a clue as to how to find two.

It was just past midnight, and my options were shrinking fast. In the stampede of confused and panicked thoughts, one thing stood out. I couldn't go this alone anymore.

Lonnie.

He was maneuvering the tow truck through the chain-link fence as I pulled up in front, a dark green Mitsubishi GT3000 on the hook. I followed him through, then stopped, got out, and locked the gate after us.

Lonnie climbed down from the cab and slammed the door behind him.

"Nice car, huh?" he said. "Whaddaya think?"

He must have seen the look in my eyes in the harsh floodlights of the junkyard. "Man," he said. "What's wrong?"

"You remember the girl on the videotape?" I could hear my own voice wavering.

"Yeah, cute lady." `

"She's gone. Missing."

"Listen," he said quickly. "Let's get inside."

I followed him to the trailer door. He whistled as he opened it to let Shadow know we were coming in. I followed him, pulling the door to behind me.

Shadow's tail thumped against the sofa. Lonnie gave her a quick scratch behind the ears, then headed into the kitchen.

"What am I going to do?" I asked, desperation in my voice. "She might be, God—"

I sat on the edge of the couch next to Shadow. I leaned over, absentmindedly scratched her head between her ears, then nuzzled her neck. Her fur felt warm, thick, comforting. Jesus, I thought, what have I done?

He turned the corner and cocked his arm. A beer can sailed through the air; I caught it right in front of my forehead, then set it down on the table.

"Not now."

"Missing," he said. "Where'd she go?"

"If I knew that, butthole," I shouted, "she wouldn't be missing!"

"Screaming ain't gonna get her back, Harry. Just chill and tell me what happened."

"I was supposed to meet her tonight at the Club Exotique," I explained. "Only she wasn't there. I asked a few too many questions and was politely escorted out. I went to another dive. No luck there either. I'd decided to cut her out of this. It was getting a little too creepy. Finally, I decided to check her apartment."

"And?"

"The place'd been trashed. Big time." I gave Lonnie the quick, down-and-dirty version of the entire week, including finding the murdered Red Dog.

He thought for a second. "Man, you're in it this time for sure."

"I met that guy your vice-squad buddy was telling us about, Big Moe Klinkenstein. And his psycho body-guard as well. It's too much of a coincidence that I meet those two the same day Corey disappears."

"So you think Klinkenstein and Mousy wrecked this broad's place?" Lonnie asked.

"If they didn't, who did?"

I stood up, pacing nervously around the tight con-fines of Lonnie's living room. "I'm through reacting, damn it. This whole thing has been watching the dance go one way and trying to keep up. I think it's time we started leading."

"We?" he asked.

"You up for it?" I asked.

He stepped toward me and raised his can in salute. "Question is, are you?"

"Whatever Corey's into, it's my fault. I owe it to her to get her out. I'm responsible, man. As for Stacey

Jameson, I got a feeling one thing's going to lead to another."

"If these people are like Phil Cheek says," Lonnie said, "it might mean getting down to their level."

"I've already been down to their level," I answered. "The only way back to fresh air is to find those two girls, then bail."

"It might mean getting serious, old sport. If you're not going to bring the law in, then you got to play it by the Marquess of Sleazeberry rules."

I thought for a moment. Maybe it wouldn't come down to that. But then again, maybe it would.

"If that's the way it has to be . . ." I said.

He polished off the beer and flipped the can into an overflowing wastebasket. "Okay," he said, "let's get started."

Lonnie changed out of his greasy jeans and into a black nylon running suit. "You sure you don't want me to go to Klinkenstein's?" Lonnie asked, tying a pair of black athletic shoes.

"No, it's my call. You go to The Purple Firefly, see if either car is still there. I'll check out Klinkenstein's house."

I unfolded the scrap of paper Cheek had given me and studied his scrawl.

"Jesus," I said. "Kingston Springs. Webb Hollow Road. Ever hear of it?"

"Yeah," he said. "Take the Kingston Springs exit off I-40, go left at the top of the ramp. Go back over the freeway and past the truck stop. It's back up in the hills somewhere. County road, I think. Just gravel and tar."

"Great," I said. "Wouldn't you know Big Moe Klinkenstein'd live out in the middle of fuckknuckle nowhere. I hope that truck stop's got some decent coffee."

"Here," Lonnie said, tossing me a keyring as we

walked out the door, "don't take the Mustang. It's too easy to spot. Take the Jesus truck."

The Jesus truck—so known because of its large front license plate that read HONK IF YOU LOVE JESUS!—was a rusted-out 1978 Ford F100 pickup. Beneath the orange-and-brown streaks was a rebuilt eight-cylinder that'd been turbocharged, bored, and stroked, and all that other stock car lingo I don't understand. I only know that Lonnie and I took it on a repo run one night and it hit one hundred and forty before I diplomatically asked him to back off.

"Use the cell phone to keep in touch," he instructed. "I'll have the handheld in the other truck."

I started for the truck, but Lonnie reached out and grabbed my arm.

"C'mon, before we split up," he said. I followed him over to the Chevy. He opened the door and unlocked the glovebox, then reached inside.

"I believe you know how to use this," he said as he handed me a small, short-barreled revolver.

I took the gun from him and held it gingerly. "Damn, I don't want this," I said.

"Damn, you'd better take it. It's the Airweight .38. I've loaned it to you before." He reached back inside the glovebox and extracted a small cardboard box.

"Extra cartridges," he said. "Take 'em. One of these days, I'm going to check you out on a speed loader."

"We don't have time for that now."

"You going to take the damn thing or what?"

"Yeah," I said, shaking my head and sliding the pistol into my jacket pocket. "Yeah, I guess I'd better."

"Good boy. Don't get caught with it, okay?"

"Listen, one more thing," I said. "Should we call the cops about Corey's apartment?"

He shrugged. "Your call, dude. But if you get involved with the cops, you sure as hell ain't going to be able to go after her yourself."

I thought for a moment. "How about an anonymous call?"

Lonnie grinned. "You got her address."

I pulled out my notepad. "Yeah, this time I wrote it down."

"Give it to me," he directed. "I'll stop at a pay phone. Untraceable, anonymous tip. Happens all the time."

"Yeah," I said gratefully. "And if you find those two dipsticks, call me."

He nodded his head. "The same for you if you find them at the house, okay? Call me first. Don't go busting in there like John Goddamn Wayne."

Lonnie laughed and climbed into the Chevy. "Stay in touch. And," he called out the window, "bring my pistol back in one piece."

Even this time of night, it was a hard forty-five minute drive to Kingston Springs, a small town west of Nashville that had become a popular bedroom community for folks looking to get out of the city. I coasted to a stop at the top of the exit ramp and sat there for a second with the engine idling. My eyelids were heavy; it was nearly two in the morning and I felt like I hadn't had a decent night's sleep in a decade. To my left, a busy truck stop blazed golden light over the dark hills farther behind.

I slipped the truck into gear and crossed back over the interstate, then glided to a stop in a lot near a long line of parked tractor-trailer rigs. Even outside, the place smelled of deep-fat-fried whatever and cigarette smoke, all mixed in with diesel fumes and sweat.

The restaurant was about half-filled with truckers in jeans, flannel shirts, some with leather vests and cowboy hats, all being attended to by one harried waitress in an ill-fitting white uniform. I walked in, feeling a little out of place, and took a seat at the counter. The waitress scurried around delivering plates to the drivers, then danced behind the counter and had her pencil out from behind her ear by the time she got to me.

"What'll it be, baby?"

"I'll make it easy on you tonight," I said, smiling at her. "Large coffee, milk and sugar, and some directions."

She scribbled. "Where you headed, baby?"

"Looking for Webb Hollow Road. S'around here someplace. Ever hear of it?"

She thought for a second or two. "Naw, but I'll ask Leroy."

She disappeared through a double swinging door into the kitchen, yelling as she went: "Hey, Leroy baby, you ever hear of a Webb Holler Road?"

A beat later, she was back through the doors and over at the coffee machine. "Could you make that to go, please?" I asked.

"Sure, baby, you got it."

A guy in a T-shirt and apron pushed the door open and crossed over to the counter.

"Yeah," he said, "go out of the parking lot and turn left. I don't know the name of the road, but you just follow it for about three or four miles. It curves around, gets real dark out there. It'll take you up Webb Ridge. When you cross the ridge, start looking on your left. There's a road takes you down into the hollow. That's it."

"Thanks," I said as the waitress put a large plastic cup down in front of me.

Outside, the air seemed cooler, heavier in this part of town, away from the city and the concrete and the asphalt. Outside of the freeway whine and the trucks in the lot, it was quieter as well. I climbed back into the Ford and pulled out onto the two-lane road that passed the truck stop, and in a minute or so, was so deep into the country that Nashville was just a memory.

There were streetlights for perhaps a mile, but as the

road started curving up the ridge, the lights were left behind. The road turned and banked, climbing higher, the houses becoming progressively older and more like farmhouses the farther you went.

I geared down, slowed, because of the darkness and my unfamiliarity with the countryside. Occasionally, I'd see a light shining dimly from within a house, and here and there a security flood lamp. Mostly, the world was as dark as lampblack.

A few miles along, I topped the ridge and started back down on the other side. I slowed even further, searching for a road off to the left. A sign came up: WEBB HOLLOW ROAD. I eased through the turn and onto a gravel-and-tar county road. A road sign depicted the universal graphic for crossing deer.

Gravel crunched under tires and the road narrowed until hay brushed the side of the truck. The headlights flicked back and forth, doing only a fair job. I reached into my pocket and pulled out the scrap of paper with Klinkenstein's address on it.

A mailbox came into view. I crept past it, reading the number on the side: 8463 WEBB HOLLOW ROAD. Klinkenstein lived at 8825—still a ways to go.

The road curved off to the left, and the headlights swept around as the truck turned. Ahead of me, a large pipe several inches in diameter lay across the road. I pressed the brake.

Then the pipe moved.

I locked the brakes up and scattered gravel as I stopped. I backed up, peering over the front of the truck.

The pipe moved again. This time, it raised its head and two glistening eyes stared at me in the reflection of the headlights.

Snake. Damn, I hate snakes.

His head moved toward the truck, pulling the body behind into a curve. He had to be five feet long at least,

and about as big around as my forearm. He was shades
of brown and gray, as far as I could tell in the artificial
light, with a pattern of interwoven diamonds on his
back. As he slithered into the center of the road and
coiled, the tail flicked into the vertical, vibrating on the
end.

I'd heard you could find eastern diamondbacks
around here, and that some of these suckers get to be
six- or seven-feet long. I just never thought I'd see one.

Without thinking, my hand moved over and rolled the
window up. Then I realized what I'd done.

"Dumb ass," I said out loud, "he ain't coming in the
freaking window at you."

We sat there for about thirty seconds in a standoff. I
didn't figure it was right for me to run over him; hell,
I was on his turf. On the other hand, I wasn't going to
sit there looking at him all night.

I wondered what the rattle sounded like.

Then on the seat next to me, something buzzed, loud
and abrupt.

"Jeez!" I yelled, bouncing about a foot off the seat
and smacking my head sharply on the metal roof. My
hand went to the door handle, my heart went to my
throat, the coffee cup became airborne, and my ass
slammed shut like a sprung trap.

It went off again, right next to me.

"Aw, geez," I spewed, letting loose with a sigh of release that made me crumple against the steering wheel.
I looked down on the black console next to me; a
blinking green light stared back at me.

The cell phone.

"Yeah," I said into the handset as I rubbed the top of
my head.

"Where ya at, dude?"

"Parked in the middle of Webb Hollow Road," I said,
"looking out at the mother of all rattlesnakes."

"You serious?" Lonnie's voice went up a notch, excited.

"Can't even get by him. He's blocking the road."

"Get by him, hell! Get out there and grab him, boy! There's a crate in the bed of the truck. Gather his ass up and bring him home."

My jaw dropped. "*You* gather his ass up and bring him home. I ain't getting out of this truck."

"You wussy. Just grab him behind the neck. He can't get to you then."

"Neither can you, so you won't mind my suggesting that you and the snake get together and perform an anatomical impossibility."

"And here I am trying to help you. . . ."

"Right. And where might you be?"

"Out behind The Purple Firefly. Hey, this place cooks in the middle of the night. I've already had two guys walk up and invite me home."

I laughed, grabbed a rag off the seat, and threw it onto the puddle of coffee on the floorboard.

"You going to take 'em up on it?"

"No, I'm saving myself for marriage."

"Good luck. Any sign of that Lexus or Klinkenstein's Cadillac?"

"Nothing. I'll stick around for a while, then check back with you."

"Yeah, okay. I'm nearly to Klinkenstein's house, if this pit viper from hell will get out of the way. If there's nothing there, I'll call you."

"I'm getting kind of crisp around the edges," Lonnie said.

"Me, too. Stay in touch."

Outside the truck, the snake was gone. I'd looked down for just a moment, then back up. I looked around, as far as the headlights would allow me to see.

He must have slid off into the high grass.

I pressed the accelerator and the truck eased forward.

I didn't feel any bumps, hear any snake screams, so must not have hit anything.

My heart was almost back to a normal beat when I spotted a black mailbox on the right that had only a number on it. I slowed again.

I'd found Klinkenstein's house, or at least his mailbox. Truth was, the driveway went down a slope and into the trees with no sign of a house anywhere.

Here, I thought, was a man who didn't want people casually dropping by.

I drove past his house perhaps half a mile, found a driveway to turn around in, then switched off the headlights and made my way down the road by the dim glow of the running lights. I pulled to a stop in front of Klinkenstein's property and killed the engine and the last of the lights.

It was a moonless night, but the spray of stars in the sky above bathed the area in enough ambient light to discern shapes. I'd forgotten what the sky looked like, how beautiful it was, away from the city.

How quiet things were. . . .

Behind me, the rhythmic *barrumph* of a bullfrog looking for love was the only break in the silence. I sat there for a couple of minutes thinking. I'd pulled far enough off the side of the road that if I ducked down, the truck would just look like it was broken down and abandoned. At the first sight of oncoming traffic, I intended to be under the dashboard.

Still, it wasn't doing me much good to just sit here. I couldn't see down the driveway or to the house. As long as it was so dark and quiet, I might as well work my way down the driveway and scope out the place.

I opened the door of the truck carefully, afraid it would creak with age. Lonnie'd done a good job, though, and the door glided open as smoothly and silently as if it had just come off the showroom floor. I stepped out onto the gravel-and-tar road and instantly realized why the snake had taken up residence. A residual warmth radiated, almost glowed from the surface after being stored there all day by the sun.

Then my stomach did a somersault: the snake.

I looked around, my eyes straining in the dim blue light. If there was one, there were bound to be others. I gritted my teeth. Maybe I'd jump back in the truck, drive down the driveway, lay on the horn and dare anybody to do anything about it.

If Stacey and Corey happened to be down there, though . . .

Okay, that's it. I'm going home, going to bed. I've had enough. I resign.

I stood there, my head swimming in fatigue and fear. "Snakes," I whispered. "Rattlesnakes . . ."

I swallowed hard, then put my left foot in front of my right foot, then my right foot in front of my left. I did that again and lived. One more time, I thought.

Listen for the rattle.

But isn't that like incoming artillery? If you hear it, it's too late?

"Stop it," I said out loud. "Just walk down the damn driveway."

I tried to empty my mind, sort of a *Zen and the Art of Being Scared Shitless* approach to life.

The driveway was aggregate concrete, classy and expensive, and ran down from the high shoulder of the road into a thicket of trees. I paced down the driveway quickly, noiselessly, with my hand inside my coat pocket wrapped loosely around Lonnie's pistol.

To my right, in the trees, the hoot of an owl, followed by a rustle in the bushes beyond . . .

Off in the distance, toward the ridge, the baying of a coyote . . .

Sound carried far in the heavy night air. If I listened carefully, I could hear to the east the whine of truck tires on the freeway racing by at eighty.

I got to the grove of trees and continued on. The leaves made an arch overhead, blocking out what little light was available, throwing deep black formless shadows over everything.

I was moving by feel and instinct alone now. Perhaps twenty yards into the grove of trees, I saw the light of stars again as the driveway came into an open space. The clear lines of a house shot into the sky, black and angular. I was maybe thirty-, forty-feet off. I stood there in the middle of the drive, out in the open, studying the house for a few minutes. My eyes picked out a covered gallery that ran the length of the front of the house, which was built into the side of a hill. The side porch was supported by stilts. The driveway curved around in front, then back on itself, with no sign of a garage.

I strained to see. No cars, no light, no movement, no noise. Either nobody was home, or the whole house was off in dreamland.

A little more boldly this time, I walked toward the house. I stepped carefully along the pebbled concrete, watching for movement, light, any sign of danger.

Suddenly, there was a click and the front of the house was bathed in the harsh glare of a row of security lights. I hadn't counted on motion detectors.

I jumped off the driveway and hopped into the trees, oblivious to what reptiles might be sleeping there. I dove behind a small bush, then pulled the gun out of my pocket and crouched as low as I could get. Sweat poured off of me, and once again, my heart pounded in my chest. Despite the sweat, I shivered in the cold night air.

Nothing.

I'd expected a light from within, a face at the window. Something, anything. But no one came to check for intruders.

I stood up after about five minutes. Maybe this sort of thing happened a lot, stray deer perhaps. I stepped back onto the driveway. The house was made of rough-hewn logs, and nicely dressed out. I walked quickly over and crouched down behind a row of bushes that ran along the front.

Listening carefully, I was poised to take off like a jackrabbit at the first rack of a shotgun shell. Still, though, I heard nothing. I stood up, walked around the right side of the house and paused, ready to run.

Silence. Behind me, the security lights clicked off, the timer reset, and the whole area was once again dark.

So Klinkenstein had sensors on the front. I guessed he'd installed them so he could find his way to the house when he pulled in at night.

I walked around to the back, up the slope of grass that was slick with dew. A patio had been dug out of the side of the hill, made out of carefully placed flagstones and concrete, with a latticework trellis around it. It made a kind of hidden arbor in the back looking out on the trees. On the patio, a covered hot tub sat.

Real nice setup, I thought. Lot of money in perversion.

I stepped onto the patio. A sliding glass door was closed, with drapes pulled behind it blocking any view. No matter, the light was too dim to see inside anyway. I stepped around the patio, only to discover that the edge of the woods came right up to the other side of the house. I could make it if I tried, but then I thought of the snakes again.

To hell with it, I thought, nobody's here. I'll make my way back to the truck, call Lonnie on the car phone, figure out what to do next.

I hadn't heard a thing, had seen no indication of people. Still, I wondered what the inside of the house looked like. Maybe there was a basement, and maybe Stacey and Corey were tied up, safe and together. I could cut them loose, get them out of here, be the hero.

Why not? What's a little B&E after everything else that had gone down this week?

I stepped over to the sliding glass door, pressed against the wall off to the side, and slowly put my hand on the chrome handle.

It gave slightly at my touch. I pushed harder; it slipped maybe half an inch.

It wasn't locked.

I cracked the door wide enough to hear if anything was inside, a guard dog or a large man with a long shotgun.

Air blew gently through the crack, and with it came a slight aroma of ripeness, of fecundity. No sound, though.

I pushed the door wider, maybe a foot now, and reached in. My hand hit drapery fabric. I pulled back, reached into my pocket and took out the revolver, then slid the door open another foot or so.

With the gun in my right hand, I pushed the drapery fabric out of the way and stuck my head in. No light, no sound, only total, pitch-black darkness and the odd, yet not quite offensive, smell. With my left hand, I felt gently around the wall, feeling for a light switch.

I felt the hard plastic, sucked in a deep breath and held it, then flicked the switch upward. The room was instantly aglow in white light.

Instinctively, the breath shot out of my lungs and I let loose with a yell.

Big Moe Klinkenstein was spread-eagled on the bed, laid out and gutted like a field-dressed deer.

Chapter 19

I sat in on an autopsy once back in my early days as a reporter. From time to time, I'd mentioned to Marsha that I thought it might be interesting to see one again.

Now there was no point.

Maurice Klinkenstein's arms and legs were tied with thick rope to the four corners of the bed. He was slit open from throat to pubis, his intestines protruding halfway out of the incision in shiny great brown and blue loops, the skin on his sternum peeled back and curling. There was a great dark scarlet gash where his genitalia should have been. Beneath that horrible wound, a large plastic vibrator was half-visible.

Torrents of blood had run down his torso, onto the bed, then the floor. I stepped closer to the bed, in shock, around the side, avoiding the thick coagulating puddles. A coppery smell filled the air now, along with the ripeness of new decay.

There was a red bandanna stuffed in his mouth, forcing his cheeks out like a trumpet player's. His eyes were open, sightless in death. His chest was peppered with the red ticks of stab wounds. The level of savagery was beyond all thought, all sense.

Suddenly, the room started to go dark, little purple and gray sparkles dancing into the edges of my vision. The sides of my head tingled and my legs felt as if they'd gone to sleep.

Vertigo swept over me in waves. The truck-stop

coffee roared up in the back of my throat. I fought to keep it down. My chest locked up. I couldn't breathe. Everything went darker; the green aura of panic set in.

I staggered backward, nearly tripping over a stool, and backed into the sliding glass door. I yanked the drapery aside, pulled a handkerchief out of my pocket and held it to my face, then closed the sliding door behind me quickly.

The cool air wasn't enough. I stumbled across the patio, into the clearing, and ran to the bushes. Doubled over, I retched and heaved until all I could come up with were dry spasms.

My ribs ached, my head pounded. I stared into the darkness, terrified. Whoever had done that could still be out there, watching me, stalking.

I'd never felt such fear and revulsion and anger, all at the same time. Sustained logical thought left me; my impulses were reduced to rabbitlike hysteria. Adrenaline went through me like the Johnstown Flood and I ran down the slippery grass, lurching across the dew, barely in control. Disassociation set in, and I found myself outside myself watching me run as if I were someone else.

Once I hit the driveway and found traction, I really lit a fire under it. Behind me, the motion sensor threw the security lights on like a photographer's flash and the area before me lit up in ghostly whites and greens and purples. My shadow on the driveway was twenty feet long and I pounded after it, up the grade, around a curve and into the even deeper shadows thrown by the grove of trees. Past that, I found myself plunged into darkness again, straining to catch the outline of black forms in the night.

Then it hit me. I had to go back.

I stopped under the canopy of an enormous oak, bent over, put my hands on my knees, panting.

What if Mousy were in the next room? What if Corey and Stacey were in there? What if they were still alive, or worse yet, barely alive and in need of immediate help? I couldn't leave, couldn't abandon them.

Then Klinkenstein, or what was left of him, was back in my mind again. I gagged.

"Oh hell," I said out loud.

The pistol felt warm in my hand. I walked back down the outside edge of the driveway, skirting the middle in hopes of not setting off the motion detector. I stumbled once over a large branch, but managed to make it to the side of the house in darkness.

I crept up the hill along the side porch, then mashed against the rough logs. I slid against the timbers the rest of the way up the hill to the patio, then stood outside the sliding glass door into Klinkenstein's bedroom. I'd foolishly left the light on, but could hear no one inside. I pushed aside the drape and stepped in, focusing on the artwork on the walls, the ceiling fixtures, anything to keep from looking at the bed. I pulled the door behind me, then folded my handkerchief in half and held it to my face with my free hand. I tiptoed carefully around the bed and into the hallway, swallowing panic and terror as hard as I could.

Darkness lay ahead of me. I paced quietly, carefully down the hall, the Airweight .38 held out in front of me. Everything was silent, not even the hum of an air conditioner or a refrigerator. I came to an open door, reached in, and flicked the light on.

I entered a meagerly furnished spare bedroom. I walked quickly over and opened up the closet. A few cartons, some clothes on hangers. Back in the hall, I checked the other bedroom opposite. Nothing appeared to have been disturbed.

Nothing in the bathroom, either, except for a variety of prescription-medicine bottles and a half-empty bottle of Stoli. At the end of the hall, I found a large room with exposed logs and ceiling beams. A huge fireplace with a stone hearth dominated one end of the room, with a large-screen television next to it.

Piles of videotapes were stacked on the floor next to the television. I picked one up: *Pretty Boys in the Hood* the title read.

The boys were pretty, and quite undressed. Guess Big Moe liked to sample his own inventory. . . .

Fear heightened my senses. I felt my own heartbeat, the muscles in my arm pulsing as I scanned the room with the pistol held out. I hurriedly checked the rest of the house. Nothing. No sign of anyone or anything. Relieved and anxious at the same time, I decided to leave by the front door. No sense in bothering Big Moe again.

Once I hit darkness, shock wore off and dread took hold again. I sprinted up the driveway, came to the road, and dashed across it to the pickup truck, panting like a racehorse. Sweat poured off me, my rib cage heaved and pumped madly. I yanked the door open and jumped in, slamming it shut behind me. I dug through my pockets searching for the keys, then dropped them twice before I could get the ignition key in the slot.

I grabbed the cell phone and punched 911. My hands shook beyond control. My guts felt full of water.

"Jesusohjesusohjesus," I stammered. "Answer the phone."

The phone rang nine times before a female voice answered: "Emergency."

"I want to—" Then it hit me. Cell phones were traceable.

I pulled the handset away from my head and hit the disconnect button. I'd have to call the police, but not this way.

The cell phone back in its cradle, I twisted the key. The truck came to life. I threw it into gear, yanked the headlight switch, and stomped on the gas pedal. The tires spun like crazy, throwing gravel and tar everywhere, and finally caught.

The curve in front of me came up too quickly and I had one tire off on the shoulder before I knew it. I twisted the wheel, came up off the accelerator, countersteered and danced, then finally got back on the road without going off in a ditch. I slowed, trying to pace my breathing, gather my thoughts, and not have that heart attack I was clearly overdue for.

I made the turn off the county road onto the asphalt and raced to the truck stop. It seemed to take forever, but I made myself slow down. Now was not a good time to be pulled over. I was too close to the slaughter-house.

I coasted into the truck-stop parking lot and pulled up to a phone booth.

"Emergency," the same female voice answered.

"Listen carefully," I said. "There's been a murder committed. 8825 Webb Hollow Road."

"Wait, sir—" the voice said. But by the time she got the second word out, I'd slammed the phone down.

I hit I-40 headed back into Nashville, matching my speed with the rest of the traffic and melding into a line of tractor-trailer rigs a half-mile long. Once settled into the anonymous line, I reached for the cell phone again.

"Where you been?" Lonnie's voice was crackly and filled with static. "I been trying to get you."

"Where are you?"

"Outside the Firefly, half-asleep, ready to go—"

"Go home," I said. "Quick. I'll meet you."

"Meet me? Why don't we call it a night?"

"I'll be there in half an hour. Maybe less."

"Harry, you got any idea what time—"

"Do it, damn it!" I yelled into the phone. Then I hit the disconnect button and turned the phone off.

As the traffic droned, tires whining in the night, I tried to come up with a prayer for Maurice Klinkenstein's soul, but the words wouldn't come.

All I could see was the evil in Mousy Caramello's eyes.

Even Lonnie was shaken by this one.

"Holy Mother of God," he whispered. "What kind of animal could do that?"

"Who do you think it was?" I snapped. "It had to be that sick little fuck who works for him."

"Animal's not even the right word." Lonnie sat on the edge of the couch, his arm draped across Shadow, his fingers buried in her fur. "Animals don't do that to each other."

I paced the floor in front of him, restless to the point of manic. "Something happened," I said, thoughts in a direct connection with mouth. "Something happened, but what? What drove him over the edge?"

I ran my fingers across my scalp, then grabbed a fistful of my own hair and pulled until it hurt. The pain seemed to sharpen my thoughts, focus my energies.

"He's got Stacey," I said. "And Corey, if she's still alive."

I thought of Corey and of what Mousy Caramello could do to her, would do to her. I had enough sense left to know that it was probably too late, that the best I could hope for was that whatever had happened to Corey had happened quickly, and that her last moments passed in the blessed numbness of shock.

"You think there's much chance either of them's alive?" Lonnie asked.

I pulled the hank of hair even tighter, until it threatened to rip loose. Finally, I let go and turned to Lonnie. "If Mousy's really gone psycho as a shithouse rat, then he'd have set her out on display the same way he did Klinkenstein."

"Maybe he did and we just ain't found her yet."

"Maybe. And maybe we've still got time."

"For what?" Lonnie gasped. "Look, dude, it's time to call in the cavalry here."

"The cops?"

"You know any other guys in blue uniforms?"

I tottered over and flopped into a chair, defeated. Lonnie was right; events had run their course, and the course had been out of my control from the beginning. It was time to turn this over, way past time.

"Who should we call?"

"Start with Phil Cheek," Lonnie said. "You still got his card?"

I fished around in my jacket and pulled out Detective Cheek's card. "Yeah, here it is. You want to call him or should I?"

Lonnie pulled the cordless phone out of its console and tossed it to me. "It'll look better if you do it."

I punched in the vice-squad detective's pager number, then dialed in Lonnie's number after the three beeps. Then I rang off and settled back into the chair with a resigned sigh.

"Now we wait," he said. "Want a beer?"

I shook my head. "Don't think I could keep one down. Wonder how long it'll take him to call us back?"

He shrugged just as the phone rang.

"Not long I guess."

I picked up the phone and pressed the connect button. "Yeah?"

"Lonnie?"

"No, Phil, this is Harry."

"Make it quick, Harry, I'm up to my ankles in it tonight."

"Shit's hit the fan, buddy. Moe Klinkenstein's dead."

There was a moment of silence, punctuated by the static of a cell phone at the other end. "How'd you know?" Cheek asked, his voice serious.

"How'd *you* know?"

"Don't get smart with me, not unless you want the

entire murder squad up your ass with a magnifying glass. I asked you a question."

"I found him. I went to his house tonight, looking for the two girls. The sliding glass door to his bedroom was open and the lights were off. I went in and there he was."

"He was dead when you got there?"

"Very. I guess I went a little loopy. I got sick in the yard, then hauled ass to the truck stop and called 911."

"Okay, so that was you. Listen, the Cheatham County Sheriff's Department called us. The murder squad's on its way down there with the mobile crime lab and the medical examiner. Howard Spellman called Vice when he heard it was Klinkenstein."

"Guess this probably blew those folks away out there," I said.

"Let's put it this way: the sheriff's deputy was so upset he took his bullet out of his shirt pocket and put it in his gun."

"Don't laugh. When you get out there," I said, "you'll understand why. It was real ritual stuff. Looked to me like he was tortured, then set out on display like a trophy."

"Great, and I had to eat spaghetti for dinner," he quipped.

"What should I do?" I asked.

"Stay close to home," he said. "I'll tell Howard Spellman what you told me. It's a pretty good guess he's going to want to talk to you. I suggest you arrange your effluent in an organized fashion."

"Gotcha."

I clicked the phone off and set it down. Lonnie stuck his head in from the kitchen. "What'd he say?"

"He told me to get my shit together," I answered, wearily rubbing my eyes. "The next few days are going to be real interesting."

Lonnie popped the top on a can of Budweiser. "That's the understatement of the decade."

I stood up. "I got to get some sleep. I can't think straight anymore."

"You're not going home, are you?"

I stared at him. "Where should I go?"

"That guy could be waiting in your driveway for you."

That did my gut a lot of good. I grimaced at the pain spike, then rubbed my side. "Thanks, Lonnie. I needed that."

"I'm serious. What if he's there?"

"Then I should get home because of Mrs. Hawkins. Look, I'll keep the pistol if you don't mind."

He shrugged. "Under the circumstances, I insist."

It was nearly four in the morning by the time I finally pulled into the driveway. I was beyond fatigue, beyond shock. I climbed out of the Mustang with the pistol in my hand, poised and ready to fire. If Mousy Caramello was waiting for me, I wondered if I'd be able to do it.

Phil Cheek had said the medical examiner's office in Nashville had been called. Some of the outlying counties didn't have fully staffed medical examiner's offices and depended on the state ME or one of the larger cities for help. There was a pretty good chance Marsha was out in Kingston Springs right now, zipping Klinkenstein up in a body bag and shipping him downtown to finish the butchering.

I wondered if I could really let this go. I wondered if Corey was still alive. Exhaustion had set in, dulling the senses, fuzzying the thinking. But sleep was probably not on the agenda.

Chapter 20

Sleep came, finally, but there was damn little of it, and what there was was anything but restful. I'd expected nightmares; I got anesthesia.

When the ringing phone pulled me out of it, it was like waking up in a six-foot-deep bowl of pudding. Every movement was slow, every thought torturous. I kept thinking my eyes wouldn't open, then I realized it was still dark outside.

"Hello," I said, somewhere in the direction of the phone in my hand.

"Harry Denton?"

I mumbled a yeah.

"Spellman," the voice said. "Three words, Denton—get your butt down here."

"I think that's five, Howard." I yawned into the phone.

"Now," he said, not in the mood.

"That's six," I said, but he'd hung up by then.

Klinkenstein seemed like a dream now, his bloated, desecrated body only a surreal image. What was more real to me now, as I slugged down one quick cup of instant before heading downtown, was the prospect of having to deal with the police, not to mention the consequences of my failure.

My whole reluctance to bring in the police had been based on my client's wishes that nothing become publicly known about the family and the problems Stacey

Jameson was having. They could kiss that one goodbye. I hadn't even found the morning paper, but I'd be shocked if Maurice Klinkenstein's gruesome murder wasn't plastered all over the front page. One thing would surely lead to another.

I sleepily finished my coffee and pondered how I'd tell Betty. I could begin by proposing that a scandalously troubled teenage daughter wasn't the worst thing that could happen. The world was full of screwed-up kids. Most of them managed to grow out of it and become reasonably functional. Five years from now, nobody'd give a damn if they even remembered.

One thing I did owe Betty Jameson was a face-to-face. News like I had shouldn't be delivered over the phone. But first, there was Howard Spellman and the Metro Nashville Murder Squad.

Lieutenant Howard Spellman wore a pair of jeans and a trendy sport shirt, which was about as casual as I'd ever seen him. His sandy blond, thinning hair was brushed back over his scalp, and his weary eyes were appropriately bloodshot for a man who'd been up all night too many times in his life.

Next to him at the table was E. D. Fouch, a middle-aged, overweight detective in a wrinkled suit whose most remarkable feature was a red network of spidery veins overlaid on a bulbous nose. His whole face, in fact, looked like a 3-D road map. They'd been kind enough to invite me into a conference room down the hall from Spellman's office rather than one of the usual bare interrogation rooms. I appreciated that. They'd set a cup of hot, thick police-station coffee in front of me and watched as I stirred enough powdered creamer in it to shift from black to a disgusting shade of gray.

Spellman shuffled the first edition of the morning newspaper and folded it with a slapping motion, then set it down on the table in between us, front page out.

I didn't read the copy, but the lead headline shouted:
BRUTAL KILLING SHOCKS KINGSTON SPRINGS.

"Hear you had a rough one last night."

I stared across the room, past the two men across from me. "Yeah, it sucked actually."

"Want to tell me what you were doing out there?"

"Looking for a girl, and no snappy comebacks, okay?"

"Harry, I've got two murders on my hands that I think you know something about. Not to mention the seven other killings that have gone down in the last three days. So I'm a little past snappy comebacks. How about it?"

I figured by now there was nothing left to lose by being straight with them, and a great deal of damage that could be done by not telling the truth. So I told them everything: Stacey Jameson, Red Dog, Corey, everything. It only took about three minutes; a short amount of time, I thought, for such a long series of disastrous choices on my part.

"I wish you'd come to me earlier," he said when I finished.

"If I'd known how this was going to play out, I would have. I honestly thought I could get the girl back with a minimum of fuss," I said. Then after a moment: "I'd appreciate it if you'd tell me how much trouble I'm in."

Spellman rubbed his cheeks, pulling them up toward his hairline, then down almost to his neck. "That's not my call, Harry."

Fouch made a couple of notes, then shifted uncomfortably in his chair. "What about the hooker?"

I bristled. "She's not a hooker."

"Stripper, show girl, whatever . . ."

"I haven't heard a word from her since before I found her apartment trashed."

"We'll send a couple of guys over there," Spellman

said. "Look around, see what they can come up with. Detective Fouch is handling the Turner murder. Technically, Klinkenstein's murder is in Cheatham County's rice bowl, but Fouch is working with them as liaison."

"I pulled the NCIC printout on this kid Caramello," Fouch said. "He's got a string of arrests, but only a couple of assault convictions. One rape charge, but the girl disappeared before trial. He was a suspect in several murders in New Jersey, but nobody ever made anything stick. No outstanding wants or warrants."

"Great. So when did we start taking New Jersey's garbage?"

Spellman shook his head. "I don't know. I wish we could send them some of ours." Then he got serious.

"I was talking to a Newark detective last week about another case. He said that some of these kids who are coming up in the ranks now are so crazy even the old-line Mustache Petes are scared of them. Bunch of fucking animals . . ."

Spellman turned to me. "He said a lot of times, they'll send these kids somewhere, down south or out west, just to get them out of their hair."

"Great," I said. "Mousy Caramello wound up in Nashville because the Mafia couldn't handle him. Where does that leave us?"

"It sounds like Caramello's a stone psycho freak. A real sick puppy. Jesus." He sighed. "Skinheads and gangbangers. I only got two more years till retirement. Maybe I'll take it, move to Florida. What do you think, Ed?"

Fouch grinned meanly. "What makes you think Florida's any better?"

I thought again of Corey, and of where she might be, of what might have happened to her, and it made me feel like I weighed a ton.

"Howard, Corey's a nice girl, really. I hate to think anything bad might've happened to her."

"We'll find her, or what's left of her anyway. In the meantime, we've got all we need from you right now. This means, Harry, that you are finished. Understand? You're out of this."

I nodded and held my hands out, palms front. "Right. You guys won't have Harry James Denton to kick around anymore."

Fouch stood and hitched his pants up. "You know," he said, his voice drifting, "my old man served under Jameson in World War II. Thought a lot of him, too. I kind of hate to see the old guy wind up like this."

Spellman rose from his chair, pulled his arms behind him and stretched. "What the hell, nobody gets out of this alive anyway."

Emily stood at the door, almost at attention as I walked in.

"It's Saturday, Emily," I said. "Don't you ever get a day off?"

Her face was still, with only the yellow of her eyes moving back and forth. "I'm off Sundays and every third Saturday," she said stonily.

"Pretty liberal," I said, thinking that there was no reason for me to be such a smartass but here I was, anyway. "Where is she?"

"Miss Betty asked that you wait in the General's office. She'll be down directly."

I clenched my jaw. "Good for her."

I walked into the darkened office as Emily disappeared down the hallway. The house was silent, no sound of a radio or television, no footsteps, no chatter of friends or neighbors or family. Upstairs, Betty Jameson's mother sat in a tortured prison of her own making. Somewhere else on the grounds or in this overpriced dungeon, the General wandered around inside his own head, gradually losing his hold on himself and the world around him.

This place is a damn morgue, I thought. I was glad this would be my last visit. The rich could have it.

After I'd been waiting ten minutes, I started to get restless. Sitting still was not something I was particularly good at under the best of circumstances. I got up from the plush leather chair and paced the room nervously. I went to the window and looked out the slats of the blinds. Outside, in a corner of the yard closest to the street, General Breckenridge walked slowly along the ivy-covered brick wall. I watched as he pulled his coat tighter around him in the autumn wind, the brown leaves crunching underfoot. He held his head high, his eyes sharply focused, his cadence precise and regular. There was no shuffle, no fuzzy stare to his presence.

He did not look like a man in the grip of Alzheimer's.

I unconsciously chewed on my lower lip as my gaze followed him. He walked to the driveway, then up the bricks to my car. He stopped, looked inside the car, then up at the house. He scanned the front of the house, then stopped at the office window. We made eye contact. He frowned, then started up the steps to the front of the house.

Outside the office, in the hallway, the front doors squeaked as he pushed them open. His footsteps were heavy.

I turned to the door as he entered. He stared at me as if I were one of his errant noncoms from decades long past.

"General," I said.

"Who are you?"

I crossed my arms and leaned against the windowsill. He stepped into the room and came closer to me, studying me. Somewhere inside, he remembered.

"I'm Harry Denton, sir. We met the other day."

"Oh, yes. The security—"

"Actually, General, I'm a private investigator."

"Investigator?" He stared hard at me.

"Yes sir. I've been hired to find Stacey."

His face reddened slightly. "By whom?"

"By Betty."

"Why would she hire someone to find Stacey without telling me?"

"You'll have to take that up with her. I think she didn't want to worry you."

His eyes softened, as if a momentary, small wave of confusion had layered itself over his thoughts. "Besides, Stacey's not missing."

I stepped toward him, uncrossed my arms, and uncomfortably stuck my hands in my pants pockets. "I'm afraid she is, sir. She's run away. I found her, brought her back. Then she ran off again."

"How could Stacey run away? She's just a baby."

His eyes drifted off to somewhere besides this room. I wondered what effects stress had on the progress of the disease. Was I doing him harm by telling him this?

"She's a very troubled young lady. She needs help."

"Well, then we'll get her help. We'll get her help."

"Yes sir, I know you will. Just as soon as we can get her back here."

Betty Jameson stepped into the room behind her father. She wore tight jeans, a cowl-necked cashmere sweater, and her hair was tied loosely behind her.

"Dad," she said. "What's going on?"

The General turned to face his daughter. "This man says Stacey's missing," he said, almost pleading. "Where is she?"

Betty glared at me, hatred in her eyes. Her fists were clenched at her side. Her lips pulled back, baring her teeth at me.

"Pay no attention to him. He doesn't know what he's talking about. Stacey's fine. She's just off seeing some friends."

"Betty, he needs to know," I said.

"Shut up!" she barked. "I'll deal with you later." She turned back to her father and softened. "Dad, I think you should go back outside. Let me handle this and I'll talk to you about it later. Okay?"

"I don't know," he said. "If Stacey's missing, I need to—"

"Don't worry. Everything will be just fine. Why don't you get Emily to fix you lunch?"

"Okay," he said, his voice thinner, older. Betty took his arm and pushed him gently back toward the door. His military bearing had fallen, and his footsteps became smaller, more shuffled. She led him out, called for Emily, then lingered in the hallway until her father was safely gone.

She came back in and pushed the office door closed, then walked over to me and before I could stop her, hauled off and slapped the stew out of me. Her right hand hit the left side of my face in a stinging smack. My eyes teared up and my head jerked back. I was stunned, shocked.

Let me tell you; no matter what it looks like in the movies, it hurts like bloody freaking hell to have somebody do that to you. There's about a half second of numb shock, and then it feels like your face is on fire.

She raised her arm again and this time I grabbed her by the wrist before she could get one off.

"Don't do that again," I said. Something in my voice must have told her I was serious.

"How dare you!"

"He needs to know, damn it."

"Who the hell gave you the right to decide that?"

"There's been another murder," I said, plainly and straightforwardly.

Her arm relaxed and I let go of her wrist.

"And maybe a third," I said. "I can't find Corey and her apartment's been torn apart."

"Corey? The girl who—"

I nodded. "Red Dog Turner's boss was killed last night. I was scouting around his house, hoping to find Stacey and Corey. I found his body instead."

Her eyes filled. "Oh my God," she whispered. "Stacey ..."

"She wasn't there. And there's more," I said. "The police know everything. There's too much going down now to keep them out of it. It's out of my hands."

At that, she let loose with a sigh that came from somewhere so deep inside that she probably didn't know it was in there. Her shoulders bent forward, and her spine seemed to curve down. She walked backward and almost fell into a chair, then brought her hands up and covered her face.

"That's why they have to know," I said. "You've got to prepare them. The police are involved and it's going to become public. There've been two murders, a kidnapping, and possibly—"

Betty looked up from behind her hands, her eyes wet and brimming. "Possibly what?"

I gritted my teeth and looked away from her. "I think you need to prepare yourself as well," I said. "There's a chance that we won't find Stacey. At least not alive."

She stiffened. "Who's got her? And where?"

"Turner's boss was a man named Klinkenstein, and he was a major player in the smut business. He had a bodyguard, a skinhead psycho named Mousy. I think Mousy and Red Dog were helping hide Stacey because they knew about the trust fund. Something went wrong. They got in a fight, or Red Dog pissed off Klinkenstein. Hell, I don't know. But Red Dog Turner wound up dead, and Mousy got to keep Stacey for himself. Then Klinkenstein and Mousy got into it over something. Maybe Klinkenstein knew the potential for trouble and figured Stacey wasn't worth it.

"Anyway," I continued, "Klinkenstein wound up dead, and now with two murders that can probably be hung on him, Mousy's got nothing to lose. That's the way I figure it. I could be wrong, but I don't think I'm too far off."

"God, poor Stacey," Betty murmured. "She never had a chance."

"You've got to prepare yourself for whatever happens," I said. "And you've got to get your parents ready."

"There has to be some way to stop this," she implored. "You have no idea what this is going to do to this family. If this goes far enough, it will destroy us."

That was it; I'd had enough. Before I could even put the lid on it, disassociation set in once again, and I stepped outside myself and watched as I exploded at her.

"You and your blasted reputation!" I yelled. "You supercilious, arrogant, spoiled brat! Don't you realize Stacey's life is more important than your goddamned membership in the goddamned Belle Meade Country Club? What do you care what people say about you? You've got everything in the world, and none of it means anything if Stacey doesn't come out of this in one piece!"

She jumped up out of the chair and was in my face in a heartbeat. "Don't lecture me, you patronizing son of a bitch! You don't have any idea what's at stake here!"

"The bloody hell I don't! I know precisely what's at stake here—the life of a sick, screwed-up rich girl and another girl who stupidly tried to help me help her."

"That is your problem, mister. You are the one who got the other girl involved in this. You're the one who has to live with it!"

My face reddened and I felt like my head was about to burst. "You think I don't know that! If anything happens to Corey, I'll carry that with me the rest of my life."

"And the same goes for me with Stacey!"

"Then start acting like it," I yelled. "I'm out here busting my hump trying to find your sister and you won't even tell me why she ran away! From the very beginning, you've not been straight with me. I just don't understand this!"

"There's no way you could," she said. "No way you could."

"How do you know that? If I knew what was really going on around here, then maybe I could figure out . . . well, hell, I could figure out what was really going on around here."

I knew emotion had the better of me. I wasn't making much sense. But I didn't have anything to hang on to.

"The money really doesn't mean anything," she said. "All anyone's really got is their good name. To lose that now, after all we've been through."

I scratched my head. "Will you please make some kind of sense before I become completely disoriented?"

She crossed the room, over to the bookshelves, as far away from me as she could get. She wrapped her arms around herself, turned her back to me and hugged herself tightly, as if fending off a cold so deep no amount of heat could help.

"Look, Betty, I don't know how many times I have to say this. The world is full of messed-up kids." I crossed the room, stood behind her, and without thinking put my hands on her shoulders and kneaded gently. She was tight, every muscle in her body locked in a knot.

"There's no shame in it," I said. "Your family's reputation is not going to be damaged because you have a screwed-up sister."

She raised her head slightly and stared straight into

the row of leather-bound books in front of her. And when she spoke, her voice was a dead monotone.

"That's just it, Harry. There is shame, more than you'll ever know. Stacey is my sister," she said slowly. "But she's also my daughter."

Chapter 21

Holy freaking Chinatown. I hadn't even slapped her.

Why is it that every time I think things can't get any worse, circumstances prove me wrong? I mean, I'd heard all the requisite jokes about Southern inbreeding, even laughed at some of them.

If your wife divorces you down South, is she still your sister?

"Pa, I just found out Jolene's a virgin!" "Well, send her home, son. She ain't good enough fer her own kin, she ain't good enough fer us. . . ."

Suddenly, those old jokes weren't very funny.

My hands dropped from Betty Jameson's shoulders and I stared at the back of her head, stunned. I struggled with words and nothing came out for a long time. Finally, I put together a pretty good shot at a coherent sentence.

"How can you—" I stuttered. "How can you even stay here in the same house?"

She turned, her arms folded across her chest. "You mean with him?"

"Of course. How can you even look at him?"

She sighed. "He's my father, Harry. I love him."

I spun on my heels and walked across the room, half out of agitation, half from revulsion.

"How? How can you love someone who did that to you?"

She dropped her arms. "It wasn't like that. Not like

258

you think. It was a stupid, horrible mistake that we've both always regretted. But we've somehow managed to stay together, to keep the family together. Until now, anyway."

I stared at her, silent and uncomprehending.

"I was seventeen," she continued. "The spring before I went off to college. Mother was losing it by then. She'd been depressed for a long time. The drinking had gotten worse. She was just about helpless. There was a terrible power struggle going on at the company as well. My father was under the worst business pressures he'd ever seen. He stood to lose everything."

She shook her head. "I was an only child, and I adored my father. But things were pretty bad around here."

I put my hands on the back of a wingback chair and squeezed hard. I wasn't sure if I really wanted to hear this, but at the same time had almost a compulsion to understand.

"It was over spring break. The heat had come early that year. I'd come in late one night from a pool party. I'd been drinking. I wasn't drunk, but I was pretty close to it. I partied a lot that year. I'd gotten early admission into college and I just decided . . ."

She paused for a moment. "Well, I just decided to have a good time. I even lost my virginity that fall, but the boy and I broke up right after."

"So," I said, "you came home from a pool party on a hot night, and you'd been drinking."

Betty nodded, her expression fixed, her voice still flat. "I was still in my swimsuit, soaking wet. I came in the front door and noticed my father in here. I assumed he was working late, but when I stuck my head in, I saw he was sitting on this couch, drinking as well. I stepped in and he offered me a drink, said that now I was going off to college, it was time we had a drink together.

"I was delighted," she went on. "To be treated like an

adult, like a grown woman, by someone older and so important and powerful was something I'd always dreamed of. He started in about his marriage, telling me all the troubles he'd had with mother. Mother was—is—a cold and demanding woman. She'd stopped sleeping with him after I was born. She'd cut herself off emotionally and physically from the rest of the world. He was lonely, had been lonely, for almost two decades. He refused to consider divorce. For him, it was a matter of honor."

"Honor?" I asked, appalled. "Honor? Betty, there are lonely men all over the world. Not all of them impregnate their daughters."

She winced, took a deep breath and held it for a moment. When she spoke again, her eyes were full and her voice almost choked.

"It was late. We had a lot to drink. One thing led to another."

She turned away again. "It was a horrible mistake. We both knew it immediately. A few weeks later, I learned I was pregnant. My mother, of course, went completely off the deep end when she found out."

"Your mother knew who—?"

Betty nodded. "I fell apart myself when I found out. I told her. Big mistake. She literally went crazy. She would have divorced my father, ruined him, ruined all of us, except that she was so far gone he hospitalized her. A place down in Florida."

She sat down on the couch, crossed her legs, and leaned wearily against the arm. "I graduated high school before I began to show, then skipped my freshman year of college and went to Europe alone. Stacey was born in Greece. I'd intended to give her up for adoption, but when it came down to it, I just couldn't."

"So you brought her home."

"My father lived here alone for almost a year. He'd won his power struggles. My mother came out of the hospital about the same time, and was well enough to go through the motions. She agreed to take care of Stacey as her own and to keep the secret."

"And you?"

She gazed off behind me, almost absentmindedly. "You have no concept of the level of shame involved with something like this."

"You're right. I don't."

Betty looked back up and her eyes met mine again. "It was a different time then, Harry. People didn't talk about these things like they do now. There were no support groups, no political lobbies, no television movies. Incest simply wasn't discussed. So I kept silent and went off to college, but something had changed. I shut down. I went through my whole four years in college buried in work, depressed, angry, and not knowing why."

"You didn't know why?"

"I thought I'd worked through it all," she insisted. "Put it behind me. I thought it would be okay, that I could get on with my life. And then, my senior year I met this boy. He was kind, gentle, very patient. Extremely patient. We began dating and he asked me to marry him after graduation. I finally said yes."

"So you got married," I said.

"It was a disaster. At that point in my life, I couldn't stand being touched, not by him, not by anyone. I'm sorry to say—ashamed to say—that I did everything to that boy but kill him."

"Did you ever tell him?"

She shook her head. "Never. I couldn't. It was still too raw then, too soon. We were married two years before I finally broke him and he filed for divorce."

"And what about Stacey?"

"For the next dozen years or so, things were quiet. I lived in Chicago for a while, then New York City. My parents raised Stacey as their own. Physically, she

seemed fine. A very bright, active girl, full of energy
and not much time for anything that didn't interest her."

"A normal little girl," I commented.

"Yes, if perhaps a bit overindulged. Then, about five
years ago, things started to fall apart again."

I did a quick mental tote. "Let's see, about the time
Stacey started to, I think the euphemism is, 'blossom.' "

Betty nodded. "My mother became paranoid, depressed, and the serious drinking started again. I began
getting frantic, drunken phone calls in the middle of the
night. My father was abusing Stacey, according to her."

"Sexually, she meant."

"Yes. At first, I didn't know what to believe. I flew
home, confronted my father. He, of course, denied everything. But when I talked to Stacey, and saw no evidence, I began to believe him. Which only sent my
mother over the edge even further."

"How did Stacey handle it?"

"Like any kid whose family is falling apart. She pre-
tended to be tough and understanding at the same time,
and never let on that she was upset. But you could
tell. . . ."

"So you decided to move home."

"No, not then. Not until last year. As Stacey grew to
be a beautiful young woman, my mother continued to
deteriorate. The home situation was beginning to have a
bad effect, and Stacey started having problems at
school. Disciplinary problems, academic problems.
Running around with the wrong crowd. Drinking. Later,
I suppose, drugs. Things just got worse and worse, until
finally . . ." Betty stopped talking now. I waited as pa-
tiently as I knew how, wondering what awful things
were going through her mind.

"On Stacey's sixteenth birthday, Mother got incredibly drunk and abusive. A bad imitation of an Edward
Albee play. She and Stacey got into a fight, and in the
middle of it, mother blurted it out."

"My God," I said. "That must have been hellish."

"You can't imagine. Dad called me in New York and I caught a plane down immediately. He met me at the airport and on the way home, we decided to tell her the truth."

"Why in heaven's name did you do that?"

Betty looked up at me, tears in her eyes, pain in her face. "How could we hide it forever?" she cried. "As soon as Stacey saw me, she knew. And she hated me. Hated me with every cell, every breath. And hated herself as well."

"Jesus, Mary, and Joseph," I muttered.

"At the same time, my father was just beginning to lose it. He was pretty well forced into retirement. We finally talked him into a series of tests about six months ago. You know the diagnosis."

"Is that when you moved home?"

"I had to," she said. "Mother was medicated all the time, if not by the doctors then by herself. Dad couldn't control Stacey anymore, and she'd gone completely wild. She'd been kicked out of private school and run off at least four or five times. This last time, we found out from one of her girlfriends about this horrible man she'd run off with."

"And that's when you called me," I said.

"You know the rest," she said. She turned away from me, stared out the window again, and we were silent until she spoke.

"It's odd, Harry. I thought of aborting her when I found out I was pregnant, and then I thought of giving her up. If I'd done either of those things, none of this would have ever happened. But I'm glad I didn't. As ashamed as I am of how this all happened, I'm not ashamed of her."

I swallowed hard.

"My parents won't last long," she continued. "We're

the last of the line, Stacey and I. When Mother and Dad are gone, she's all I'll have left."

"Betty," I said cautiously, "these things happen, probably more than we realize. Even in your social circle. There's no reason to assume this will become public. But there's still the problem of finding her."

Her face dropped, her chin practically on her sternum. "I don't care about it becoming public anymore. I just want her back safe."

Then she looked back at me. "Are you quitting?"

I put my hands on my hips and paced back and forth in front of her. "I don't know. I mean, I—well, the police and all. I just don't know what else I could do. I don't know where else to look."

"Can't I help?" she implored. "Isn't there anything I can do?"

I shrugged and spewed out a long, weary sigh. "If I knew the answer to that one, I'd tell you. But I don't. The only thing I can do is go back to the beginning. Try to find someone or something that will give me some idea of where Mousy Caramello could be hiding them. And then hope to God I can get there before he does anything that can't be undone."

"He sounds like an awful man," she said.

"He's not a man. He's a savage."

She got up from the couch and walked across the room to the windows overlooking the wide expanse of front lawn. She stared out for a few seconds, then spoke.

"Harry, you're the only one I've ever told, except for a few therapists up north who probably can't even remember my name."

"Don't worry," I said. "The Jameson family secret is safe. You know, Betty, she's going to have to go away somewhere. Someplace safe where she can get some intensive help."

"I know that."

"Maybe your parents, too. Your mother needs all the help she can get, and pretty soon the General's going to need more care than you can give him."

She nodded.

"You could wind up in this house alone for a while."

She smiled weakly. "That's a chilling thought. Maybe I'll sell it when all this is over."

"That strikes me as not a bad idea. Get Stacey well, then take her someplace where the two of you can start over. You're both still young. You could have a life."

Her eyes filled once again. "You think so?"

I nodded. "Sometimes just surviving can be as big a bond as blood and love."

At that, Betty brought her hands to her face and sobbed. Her whole body was wracked and contorted with torment. I crossed over to her, unable to help myself, and gathered her in my arms. I held her as she wept and shook. And when it was over, I let her go. I pulled myself together and told her—despite my pledge to the police—that I'd do what I could.

Emily held the door open for me as I walked out of the Jamesons' opulent digs and down the steps to my car. And as I pulled down the driveway, off to my left in front of the garage, General Breckenridge Jameson stood ramrod stiff in the autumn wind, his eyes focused sharply, intently, watching me like a bird of prey spotting a field mouse from above.

I'd been warned off by Howard Spellman. I'd run completely into a dead end. There was nowhere else to look, nowhere else to go. It seemed that my search for Stacey Jameson and Corey Kerr had come to an end no matter what I wanted.

I felt numb. The drive back to my office went unnoticed. I trudged upstairs, dejected, tired. The red light on my answering machine blinked rapidly. I punched the button and heard Marsha's voice.

"Harry, are you okay? I haven't heard from you today and I know all about Kingston Springs. They called me out in the middle of the night. Listen, I'm in the office until lunchtime and then I'm going home. Call me, okay love?"

Then Lonnie: "Jesus, man, you read the paper? Talk about fireworks! Listen, I was running down to Manchester tonight to pick up a couple repos, but I can hold off if you need me for anything."

"Thanks, pal," I said. "Only problem is, there's nothing you can do either."

I sat down at my desk and propped my feet up. Where the hell could he be? I'd been told Mousy Caramello lived with Klinkenstein, but it wouldn't hurt to check otherwise. I pulled down the phone book and turned to the Cs. Nothing. No Caramello of any initials. I'd scraped together the money to buy a new city directory last month, and now put it to use for the first time.

Nothing.

I picked up the phone and called information, just in case he didn't have his number in the book. No Caramello in Nashville, Kingston Springs, Hendersonville, Mount Juliet, Franklin, or any of the other small towns that surround the county.

I pulled out the folder that I'd started on the Jameson case, made some handwritten notes more as exercise than anything else, then slipped them into the folder. I set it down in front of me and stared at the wall for a while, then picked up the phone and dialed Marsha's number. She answered at home on the second ring.

"Hello, love," I said.

"You sound tired."

"So do you. What'd they call you out in the middle of the night for?" The city had two forensics investigators who usually covered crime scenes.

"I gather you haven't seen any news today," she said.

"Why? What's going on?"

"There was a triple murder in North Nashville last night. Drug deal gone sour, corner of Twelfth and Clay Street. Then there was a domestic case out in the Hickory Hollow area. Guy shot his wife, blew his brains out. After that, there was the three-car pileup—"

"Enough already," I interrupted. "Please. So you were shorthanded last night."

"Yeah. But it must have been pretty awful for you, babe. I mean, seeing somebody like that."

I rubbed my eyes, stretched my neck to get the kinks out. "It was about as bad as I've ever seen. Funny, though, it seems kind of otherworldly now. Not quite real."

"That's trauma for you. Kind of a blessing, when you get right down to it. Makes for unreliable witnesses, though."

"I won't be much of a witness, anyway. I found the body. That's it. Have you done him yet?"

"No," she said. "Too busy. I'll have to go in tomorrow, get a head start on the week."

"Tomorrow's Sunday," I protested. "I was hoping we could hide out together."

"I like that idea. Maybe I'll just go in for a couple of hours."

"How about tonight? I'd really like to see you."

"Let's stay in. I'll cook."

"You're on. I'm going to hang around the office and brood for a while. See you around seven, okay?"

"Sure, love," she said, her voice soothing, comforting.

The comfort of Marsha's voice only lasted a few seconds after we hung up. I dropped my feet off my desk, stood up, and paced back and forth in my tiny office like a caged animal. There had to be something I'd missed, something I hadn't seen. Virtually everyone, with the exception of Betty Jameson, had waved me off

the search for Stacey, and now for Corey. But I couldn't
let it go.

Wouldn't let it go . . .

There had to be something. I sat back down at my
desk, pulled all my notes out of the Jameson folder,
jogged the stacks of paper into neat piles, and prepared
to start all over.

When I was hired to find Stacey, my first drill was
the usual tracking of paperwork. I wanted to know who
owned the Club Exotique, and once I found that out, I
wanted to know what else they owned.

The corporate trail wasn't going to get me anywhere,
I figured. With Big Moe Klinkenstein dead, it didn't
matter how many dummy corporations and umbrella
companies were out there hiding his sleaze. So I
thumbed through my notes and the list of corporations
and made a mental note that if worse came to worst, I
could still track down the other people involved in
Klinkenstein's companies. That could wait for now,
though.

What I was after was the list of properties.

Klinkenstein's house in Kingston Springs wasn't
listed, of course, being in another county. But his
corporations—K & K Enterprises, Ltd., Camerotica
Inc., and Bluenote—owned properties all over the city,
and I'd pulled printouts on all of them.

I recognized the address of the first property; it was
the Club Exotique. I grabbed the phone book and
started cross-checking the other properties, and quickly
crossed off the Otra Vez Club, Autumn Dancers, the
XXX A-Go-Go, The Purple Firefly, and a club down on
Charlotte Avenue called the Modern Times Lounge. The
Modern Times, I recalled from my newspaper days, was
more of a jazz club than a strip bar, although one could
find an occasional naked body there as well.

I didn't figure that would lead me anywhere. Unless
there was a much wider conspiracy afoot here than I'd

ever imagined, Mousy Caramello wasn't likely to hide Stacey and Corey in a building full of other people. I had no proof that Mousy had killed Klinkenstein, but his pronounced absence sure made him look guilty. If I thought he was guilty, it was pretty easy to figure Klinkenstein's associates, partners, friends, and employees would as well.

Mousy Caramello was likely to be a man of few friends right about now.

There were six other properties belonging to corporations owned or managed by Moe Klinkenstein. One address was down West End Avenue, in a block near where West End changed names and became Harding Road. I mentally drove down the wide avenue, then remembered a drugstore in a small strip of buildings past St. Thomas Hospital. I cross-checked the phone books and matched the addresses. Yeah, that's it, the drugstore.

Okay, scratch that one off.

The next printout was the record for a building on Second Avenue South, which would be on the side of Broadway away from the overdeveloped touristy part of Second. That area was mostly garages, auto-repair places, more industrial than the other parts of downtown. I tried to visualize Second Avenue three or four blocks south of Broadway.

Then it hit me. That's right, there's another club down there. What the hell's the name of it?

Punk Aeschylus, that's it. The alternative, pierced-nipples-and-black-lipstick club. Okay, I thought, a black, windowless building. There's probably a basement, perhaps some rooms set off from the main part of the club. You could tie up a couple of women and hide them pretty well there.

"Maybe," I whispered. "But he'd still have to have someone's cooperation who works there."

I thumbed through the business listings of the white

pages until I found the number for Punk Aeschylus. I dialed it and a recording came on that said the club would be open from nine that night until four the next morning.

That one's a possible. I made a tick mark on that printout and set it aside. The next property was off Trinity Lane, in an industrial park near the new East Sector police station. There were warehouses over there, a couple factories, some rental storage places.

"Maybe," I whispered. I put another mark on that page and set it aside. I could drive by these places, discreetly check them out. If I found any evidence that Mousy was around, I'd call the cops and get them in there to do the Rambo thing.

As the afternoon went on, the shadows cast by the buildings across Seventh Avenue deepened. I stood at my window, looking down Seventh toward Broadway, wondering if Corey and Stacey were even alive.

I tried hard to stop thinking that way. The only thing I could do was turn back to the work. There were two printouts left from the assessor's office. The first was an address down on Division Street near the university. I closed my eyes, trying to picture the building. I know that area pretty well; I ought to be able to figure this one out.

I seemed to remember a doctor's office down near the Chinese restaurant. Wait, was it a doctor or a dentist? I grabbed the yellow pages and looked up dentists. There was a locality guide; I scanned the listings in the university area.

Got him! Guy even had a display ad. I wondered if Dr. Michael Fields, D.D.S., "No Down Payment on Braces," knew who really owned the building he rented.

Scratch that one. Just one more left, an address down Church Street, which was the cross street for my office building. I couldn't place the number, but it had to be somewhere between Seventh Avenue and I-40. That was a pretty good stretch, of course, and took in the Church Street Viaduct, which was the bridge across that area known as "The Gulch" where I used to park my car as a newspaperman.

Damn, why can't I place it? Okay, there's the theatrical supply house, then that place that I think is a gay dance club and bar. Could that be it? I remembered the name, Groucho's, then looked it up in the phone book.

No, that's not it, although from the number, the property I'm looking for is closer to downtown. I continued my mental travelogue, passing the Downtown Y, some restaurant on Eighth, a sports bar, then that place that's been empty for so long that—

"Yeah," I said out loud, "that place. What is that place?"

I studied the printout from the tax assessor's office. The property was only carrying an assessment of $110,000, which struck me as more of a residential than a commercial value, especially downtown. Only there were no houses on that stretch of Church Street. It was all business.

So what are the alternatives? A building carrying that low an assessment must be practically falling down. I studied the printout some more, and there it was. The breakdown on the assessment was eighty grand for the land, thirty for the building. A $30,000 building on Church Street ought to be a dump; in fact, ought to be an eyesore.

That had to be it. The building had been empty for years, at least fifteen, maybe twenty. In fact, there'd been an incident where a piece of the building fell off several years ago. I tried to remember the story from the paper, and then it came back to me. It had been a small movie theatre, one of the last in the downtown area until it closed in the Seventies. It was the marquee that had collapsed on the sidewalk. No one had been injured, but it made a hell of a story.

I smiled at the memory, one of those odd, funny stories that are harmless and gratifying because no one suffers.

Then the smile went away. I remembered what kind of theatre it was and why it had been closed for so long. The marquee, when it was still attached to the building, once read DOWNTOWN CINEMA. For a brief period in the Sixties and Seventies, it was a landmark, an infamous landmark. It had been picketed, threatened, sued, padlocked, and cursed from every pulpit in the county. It was a relic now, an abandoned and decaying artifact of a culture that seems strangely young and innocent compared to the dark, sinister sexual climate of today.

God, I hadn't thought of the place in years—Downtown Cinema, Nashville's most famous porno theatre.

Chapter 22

With the invention of the modern videocassette recorder, the traditional downtown porn palace largely went the way of the eight-track tape and pet rocks. Why sit on some crusty movie-house seat surrounded by people you should probably be afraid of when you could be getting really kinky in the privacy of your own bedroom?

In the late Sixties, however, during those early halcyon days of the sexual revolution, adult theatres were the rage. White-collar types drove in from the suburbs on Saturday night and brought their wives. Respectable people went to adult movies, then analyzed them critically at cocktail parties afterward.

Those days are long gone. The peep shows and adult bookstores still thrive, but there aren't many full-size theatres left that offer triple-X-rated fare, at least not around here.

I glanced at my watch and realized I still had a couple of hours left before I had to go home for a shower and change of clothes. The building had been locked and boarded up for years. It probably should be condemned. A person would have to be crazy to go into it.

"Yeah," I said. "Crazy."

No harm in checking it out, I reasoned, and besides it was a pleasant Saturday afternoon. Good day for a walk.

273

It occurred to me that it might not be a bad idea to call Howard Spellman, let him know what I'd found. Maybe even see if I could get him interested. I thumbed through my card file and dialed his office number.

Nothing. It rang ten times with no answer. I looked up the number of the Murder Squad and dialed that number. It rang twenty times before I hung up.

Frustrated, I remembered that we had the same problem back in my reporter days. Maybe police departments everywhere are like this, but here in Music City, if there's no one in the office, the phones just don't get answered. There's no central switchboard, and I guess nobody ever heard of answering machines.

I threw on my jacket and locked the office door behind me. Outside, on Seventh Avenue, the wind cascaded down the concrete and asphalt ravine in dry gusts. A swirl of dust and litter whirlpooled in the gutter on my left. Up the hill thirty feet or so was Church Street.

I started up Seventh, but then stopped midblock. The chances of my finding anything weren't good, but it wouldn't be a bad idea to go prepared anyway.

I reversed my footsteps and walked back down the street to the parking garage. Inside the garage, locked in the trunk of the Mustang, was a small portable flashlight I kept around for emergencies, along with the Bodyguard Airweight Lonnie'd lent me.

The flashlight went into my left jacket pocket. I held the revolver uneasily in my hand. Its small rubber grip and tiny size weren't much comfort, not to mention the fact that I'd never even fired it. I pushed the cylinder release forward and dropped the cylinder. The flat ends of five shiny .38 cartridges glinted in the bare overhead lights of the garage. I pushed the cylinder home again. I could almost cover the entire gun with my outstretched hand. I wondered what good it would do if there was trouble, and what use I would be in the heat of it.

"Stop that," I whispered, looking around to make sure no one caught me in the middle of one of my increasingly frequent conversations with myself. "Useless dead end anyway . . ."

I slipped the gun into my right-hand jacket pocket and locked the car back up. Out in the open air again, I felt conspicuous, self-conscious. There was little pedestrian traffic, and no reason to think that anyone would guess I was walking around illegally carrying a concealed weapon.

Rounding the corner onto Church Street, I searched for the Downtown Cinema. If memory served me, it wasn't too far down, a few blocks at most. I came to the crossing at Eighth Avenue, waited a moment for the light to turn, and then when it didn't, jaywalked the intersection.

There it was, two storefronts down from Eighth. As I'd remembered, the marquee wasn't there anymore, but the glass ticket-seller's cage was, with the double plate-glass doors next to it all boarded up. A length of chain ran between the handles of the doors, bound together with a rusting padlock that looked as if it hadn't been opened in years. The entrance to the theatre was inlaid tile set in an alcove a couple of feet off the sidewalk. A pile of discarded bottles and trash littered the tile, which smelled faintly of sweat, bad wine, and urine.

I stepped up to the glass and tried to see inside through a crack between two sheets of plywood. All I got was dim shapes and grays. Stepping back, I looked right and left. The buildings butted up against each other. Three storefronts down to the right, though, an alley intersected Church Street.

"This is nuts," I muttered as I pressed on down the street. I came to the alley and peered around the side. Strewn with garbage and with an overflowing Dempster

Dumpster at the end, it looked like just the kind of place you'd want to spend your Saturday afternoons.

My feet crunched gravel and broken glass as I sauntered down the alley alongside the building as casually as possible. At the end, another alley intersected and ran behind the buildings. I turned left, mentally replaying which buildings were which. I counted until I came to what I figured was the rear of the abandoned theatre.

A steel door painted in chipped gray, with fat black Magic Marker taggings from the graffiti artists, was centered in the building. But unlike the front door, with its rusty chain and corroded padlock, this door had a shiny new, industrial-strength cylinder lock, with a metal protection plate over it to guard against burglar tools. It was as secure as a New York City apartment, and there was no way I was getting in.

Strange, I thought.

I didn't have my picks with me; besides, I'm really just an amateur locksmith. There was too much open space around anyway. The last thing I needed was to get popped for breaking and entering with an unlicensed gun in my pocket.

The building next to the theatre had a fire escape, a rusty red iron cage and steps that ran up the backside. I stepped over and saw that the ladder to the fire escape was about three-feet higher than my head. I needed something to use as a boost or a step. There was plenty of garbage, but nothing that would help.

Around the corner, I thought, the dumpster. I trotted back down the alley and over to the stinking green metal box. Some kind of slimy goo ran down the side. Rotting vegetables covered in flies lay on top of a heap of boxes and crates.

Holding my breath, I gingerly pushed the lid on the dumpster all the way open. I pushed aside the top layer of rubbish and dug around. My hand hit something wet and I jerked back with a start.

Okay, so now I'll really need the shower.

In the far corner of the bin was a wooden packing crate that looked more wood than cardboard. I yanked it forward through the refuse and pulled it over the side of the dumpster onto the alley. Whatever this thing was, it couldn't have been here too long; otherwise someone would have pulled it out and converted it into an apartment by now.

It was maybe five feet long and two or three feet around, a rectangular cube. I dragged it behind me up the gravel-and-tar alley to the building and propped it against the bricks under the fire escape. I tooled around with it until it felt pretty solid, then planted a foot on one of the side boards and climbed up. It held my weight without too much protest, so I climbed a step higher, holding onto one edge of the lumber in a death grip.

The bottom step of the fire-escape ladder was just above me now. I reached out, and by pushing out with the balls of my feet, grabbed the bottom rail and hung suspended in midair about ten feet off the ground.

Great, I thought, what do I do now?

I hadn't done hand-over-hand work since gym class in high school. I'd put on a few pounds since then as well. I grunted as my right arm contracted, pulling me up to where my left hand could grab the next rung above. I got a grip there, then decided to try it again. This time, I slipped and had to scramble to keep from letting go.

I gave another heave and this time made it. Time was a factor, though. I didn't know how long I could hold on. I jerked myself up another rung, then quickly got the one above that. That got me far enough up the ladder to set a knee on the bottom rung and give my arms a break.

I rested there a few moments until my knees started to ache, then pulled myself up another notch and got my feet on the ladder. Now I could climb up in the traditional fashion.

I got to the landing on the fire escape and started up the stairs. The building was four stories high, same as the theatre. I made it to the roof quickly and stepped over a block-and-concrete parapet onto the roof. Around me were vents and air-conditioning units, huge fans with metal grates on top and wires crisscrossing the area. I started to crouch low and sneak across the roof, but then realized there were a dozen buildings around that were higher than this one. The best thing would be to act like I was right where I belonged.

As I strode intentionally across the roof, I kept my hand in my right pocket resting carefully on the .38. I was beginning to see the appeal of these things; it's a terrible thing to have to admit, but I felt safer carrying one.

The roof of the theatre building was about four feet below the building I was on. As I looked over the edge, I saw what terrible shape the place was in. Over in the far corner, an air-conditioning condenser unit the size of a trailer had collapsed and fallen, punching a hole in the roof. Garbage was strewn everywhere and the tar on the flat roof was dry, cracked, and broken. Wires had snapped and draped themselves haphazardly over the area. There was another section of the roof that was collapsing little by little on the street side.

I climbed up on the wall overlooking the theatre roof and sat there on my haunches for a few moments. It was only a few feet; not a terribly dangerous jump. But what if the roof didn't hold? I'd hate to go through and find myself fifty feet below before anything caught me.

It finally came to a simple go or no go. I rolled over on my stomach, lowered my legs toward the tar, and held on until the last second before dropping.

Something creaked and made a tearing noise, but the ceiling held. I looked around again at all the garbage, broken machinery, pipes, wires, and collapsing roof and wondered how the hell I was going to get out of here.

What it may come down to was getting into the building from up here, then going downstairs and letting myself out the back door. That is, of course, if the lock on that door didn't require a key to get out as well as in.

I couldn't worry about that now. I stepped carefully through the debris, past a gaping two-foot hole that revealed exposed, rusting beams, over to a door that led onto a stairway down into the building. This door was padlocked as well, but the hasp looked so corroded that I might be able to pop it.

Again, though, what if someone above was watching? I looked around, didn't see anyone in the windows of the higher buildings, and decided to hell with it. A chunk of iron pipe protruded from the collapsed air-conditioning unit. I gingerly stepped over and grabbed the pipe, twisting and turning until it snapped loose from its fitting. It was about two feet long, a drain for moisture sucked out of the air.

Back at the door, the pipe wouldn't fit in between the hasp and the door. I twisted the doorknob and yanked as hard as I could. Dust sprayed out of the hinges and on me from the door frame above. The door jerked and the hinge pulled out from the frame maybe a sixteenth of an inch. I pushed the door back in, hard, and got the edge of the pipe just into the space. I jimmied it until it went in a few inches.

Then I planted my foot against the door frame, grabbed the pipe with both hands, and gave a sudden tug with all the strength I could muster.

The rusty hasp snapped in two and I went sailing backward. I dropped the pipe, spun my arms like propellers, and stopped only when my left foot hit a soft spot in the roof and I went in up to my knee.

I yowled despite myself and eased back onto my butt.

I'd hurt my wrist when I went down and my leg was scratched all to hell and back. Visions of tetanus danced in front of me as I carefully untangled my leg and pulled it out of the hole. Nothing serious, but it was going to be sore tomorrow.

The door in front of me was open, though. I'd come this far. No point in going back now.

I limped over and stared down into the darkness. The flashlight cast its thin beam down the concrete-and-iron stairwell, with an array of cobwebs as evidence of how long it had been since anyone had entered.

"What the hell am I doing?" I whispered, then started down the steps.

Down one flight, then another, until I came to a door with a sign on it that read AUTHORIZED PERSONNEL ONLY. I cracked the door and shone the flashlight in.

A room full of ancient motion-picture projectors, equipment tables, huge reels, and control panels opened before me. Fascinated, I pushed the door ajar and walked in. I had an inkling of what Howard Carter must have felt like in 1922 when he pried open the door to Tutankhamen's tomb. Cobwebs hung from the ceiling, the equipment, around the tables. A thick layer of dust covered everything. I made my way carefully across the room and stared out the projection window.

I couldn't see much, but it looked like the theatre seats were still in the auditorium, and what was probably the tattered remains of a movie screen hung in front. There was no sign of movement, of any human activity in years. The place was a crypt.

Something danced inside me as I approached the door on the other side of the projection room. I opened it carefully. Garbage, coils of wire, a few empty discarded moldy beer bottles filled the staircase. I stepped carefully out onto the landing, and warily made my way down the flight of stairs to the lobby.

A dank smell filled the air; something scurried by

low and fast in the corner opposite from where I stood. The flashlight beam flickered around the lobby. I could see pretty well because the cracks between the sheets of plywood let in a fair amount of light from the outside.

It was a small lobby, just a room with a staircase off to the left as you entered, which was the staircase I'd just come down from the projection booth. Another stairway on the other side led up to somewhere else. Two doors in the center obviously led into the auditorium. There were restrooms off to the right, and next to that, a snack bar. Behind me was the cashier's booth.

I pushed the double doors open and entered the auditorium. Looking around, my eyes adjusting to the available light, I was surprised at how shoddy it was. Thirty years ago, this place was supposed to have been quite chic, even hip. The floor, though, was uncarpeted concrete with cheap seats bolted directly into it. The air was filled with the smell of mildew and rot.

"Well, hot shot, what do you do now?" I whispered.

I walked down the center aisle, all the way to the slightly elevated stage. The screen was still there, only it was ripped down the middle in a jagged tear and hung loose from one side. I checked out the backstage area quickly, finding no other doors that led anywhere. Then I walked back into the lobby. I remembered a thirty-year-old rumor we passed around as teenage boys. We were, of course, unduly fascinated by this place and convinced it was a real treasure trove of sin. The most prevalent rumor, though, was that the theatre was also a cathouse, a house of ill repute. One of the guys used to say you could watch a porn flick upstairs, then go downstairs to a private place where you could find even more naughty wickedness. We joked nervously that it was one-stop shopping.

I wandered around the lobby and up the other set of stairs. That staircase led up to a small office, the manager's, I guess. Nothing there.

Back downstairs, I checked the tiny bathrooms. In the men's room, a urinal had been yanked off the wall and broken into several huge hunks of dirty gray porcelain. The women's room was even smaller, a reflection of the customer ratio, I supposed.

I was beginning to panic. I guess if I had to, I could get out by crossing back across the roof. But that meant somehow climbing the wall to the next building's roof, then scaling the fire escape and risk being caught. I'd rather find that back door into the alley.

A ratty, torn curtain hung next to the edge of the snack bar, behind it and at an angle to the bathroom doors. I stepped behind the glass display case and popcorn bin and pulled the curtain aside.

There was a closed door.

"Well," I said, "I'll take door number three."

I bunched the curtain up out of my way and gently turned the doorknob. The door opened easily, exposing another stairwell that led down at a steep angle.

The flashlight beam focused downward, illuminating a staircase that was surprisingly uncluttered. The stairs led down so far I couldn't see to the end. Slowly, cautiously, I took one step, then another, being careful to test each step for squeaks.

Everything was dark, silent, all the way down the stairs. Two-thirds of the way down, the walls stopped being sheetrock and became rock and mortar. A few feet farther down and I was in the basement of the building, with the silent, dead boiler to my left and a narrow passageway leading past it. The floor was rough, hard concrete. The air was musty, cold, with the dank aroma of mold and mildew. I walked past the boiler room, turning sideways so as not to touch anything, and into another drywalled hallway that dead ended at a wall. I ran the flashlight down the wall and saw nothing. Two steps farther, though, exposed an alcove on the right.

I padded over quietly, holding the flashlight down as low as I could and still see, to the end of the hall. The walls were painted a bright shade of hot pink that was muted only by decades worth of thick gray dust. A black-and-white checked door off to the right was set in the hot pink.

I smiled. So the rumors had been right. I had discovered the long-lost, underground brothel.

I gently draped my hand across the doorknob and squeezed. It turned easily in my hand. I carefully pulled the door open just a crack.

From behind the door, light . . .

I switched the flashlight off and stepped aside, straining with all my might to hear the slightest sound. I stood there for what felt like hours.

Slowly, I pushed the door open and saw a square room with partitioned booths and curtains spaced around the walls. A faded, torn black vinyl sofa and chairs were pushed against one wall. A single gas lantern turned down low illuminated the room, aided by the series of floor-to-ceiling mirrors that covered every blank wall. The colors again were hot pink, with black-and-white checked linoleum covering the floor.

My hand wrapped around the .38 Airweight and brought it slowly out of my pocket. I wrapped both hands around the grip, like Lonnie'd shown me, and held the revolver out front. My head swiveled, scanning, searching.

Nothing. Well, I thought, then who the hell lit that lantern? I relaxed a bit and lowered the gun.

Then, to my left, from inside one of the booths, a sob erupted.

Chapter 23

I stood silent, stone still, until my legs started to ache. Had I imagined the noise?

No, that wasn't possible. But where did it come from? I cocked my head, listening hard, hoping to get a fix. And then the silence was broken again, this time by a soft drawn-out moan.

The sound clearly came from the far corner of the room, diagonally to my left. I was still in the doorway, partially hidden. Stepping farther in would mean exposure if anyone were watching.

I took a careful step forward and looked around. The room was empty, although there was no way to tell who might be in the partitioned booths. I stepped quickly across the open space to against the wall, then skulked past the curtains until I came to the entrance of the last booth. The flickering lantern cast crazy shadows and sparkles of light that jitterbugged off the mirrors. I looked up to see dozens of Harry James Dentons lurking in the glass; they all looked terrified.

I eased over and stood right outside the curtain. I was close enough now to hear strained breathing from inside, and then another moan. A foul stink drifted out of the room. I turned and, still holding the gun in a two-handed stance, pulled the curtain aside with the barrel.

Corey was naked, tied spread-eagled to the metal frame of a single bed on a bare, putrid mattress.

"Oh, my God," I muttered and jammed the revolver

back in my pocket. I rushed over and in the dim light, fell to her side. She was filthy, her hair stiff and splayed out in all directions.

She rolled her head over, barely conscious, and I could see she was trying to focus on me.

"Harry?" Her voice was thin, weak. I brushed her cheek with the tips of my fingers. Her eyes welled with tears.

"Harry," she squeaked, her voice cracking. And then she began weeping, sobbing, her body shaking.

"What's he done to you?" I whispered, my own voice tight and strained.

"Please," she croaked, "untie me." But I was already at her right hand, which was pulled tight to the frame by a length of coarse, thick rope. Her wrists were red, scraped, swollen, and it looked in the shadows like her hands were becoming discolored.

I fumbled with the knot and couldn't untie it. I pulled at the rope and Corey whimpered in pain.

"I'm going to have to cut it, baby," I said. "Just hold on."

I pulled out my short pocketknife, a small two-inch knife that's not good for much besides cleaning fingernails. And as I bent over her, I saw where the stench was coming from.

A bucket on the floor, next to the bed frame, had served as toilet, obviously for quite some time. I held my breath and fought off a gag as I lifted the bucket and moved it carefully out of the way.

Corey sobbed the whole time. I sawed like crazy and finally cut through the rope in a minute or so. When her arm came loose, she pulled it down to her side and cried out in pain from the movement.

"I know, I know," I said, trying to comfort her. "It hurts, but it's over now."

I went to work on the other arm, and managed to rip through the rope a little quicker this time. When her left arm sprang free, she pulled it down to her side and doubled over in pain. I reached behind her, pulled her into a sitting position, and scooted her down the bed to relieve some of the tension on her legs. She shivered uncontrollably, whimpering and moaning as I held her in my arms, rocking her back and forth. She was filthy, smelled horribly. I pulled away from her, and my mouth dropped open as the reflected light shone full on her for the first time.

Her face was a mass of bruises, deep purple and green and red, a nauseating alloy of blood and damaged tissue. Above her left eye, a cut ran from her eyebrow out the side of her face a couple of inches. Her lips were swollen, cracked, and caked with dried blood.

"What in God's name has he done?"

She turned her face away, ashamed. I stood up and shifted so the light would fall on her.

I felt ill and fought back the compulsion to retch. Her breasts were dotted with hideous red marks and bruises. A horrid black patch was on her left nipple, covering part of the aureole. On her right side, more welts and discolored patches. Her knees were abraded, the skin raw and bleeding.

She looked down at herself. "Cigarettes," she sobbed. "He burned me."

I didn't need to ask any more. She'd been tortured, beaten, almost assuredly raped. A million thoughts ran through at once: regret, sorrow, pity, but most of all, fury. Hatred as raw and naked as he'd left her. I'd never felt anything like it before, the power and focus and passion of pure, unadulterated hate.

Corey covered her face with her arms and bunched into a tight ball, pulling her legs up toward her torso as far as they would go. "Please," she begged, "give me something to cover up with."

I yanked off my jacket and wrapped it around her.

"Can you work on your wrists while I get your legs free?"

She nodded. I turned and sawed away at the leg ropes like a maniac. The left one gave way in a few seconds. I looked at the right one and thought perhaps I could untie it without cutting. I fumbled with the knot and got it loose just as Corey threw the last piece of rope on her wrists across the room.

I massaged her ankle, but too hard. She yelped and pulled it away.

"Sorry."

"It's okay, I just—" Her voice failed her.

I turned back to her and wrapped my arms around her once again. Her hair smelled of filth, sweat, mildew, and rot. I kissed the top of her head, smoothed her hair down as best I could, then quickly pulled away and looked into her face.

"Can you stand up? We've got to get you out of here."

She nodded. I reached into the side pocket of the jacket, pulled out the revolver, and slipped it into my pants pocket. She saw it, closed her eyes, and nodded again weakly.

"Yes," she whispered. "Please. Let's go." She pulled the jacket off her shoulders and then put it back on with arms through the sleeves. She pulled it tightly around her and swung her feet over the edge of the bed.

I helped her up, but her legs were still tingling and unsteady. She wavered back and forth, dizzy, as I held her upright and tried to stabilize her. She pulled the jacket to cover herself as much as possible.

"Okay?"

She nodded. "Harry," she said, choking again.

"What?"

She let her head fall against my chest. "I'm really sorry." Her voice broke and the tears rolled again.

I hugged her tightly. "I'm the one that's sorry. It's all my fault."

She started to say something. "Not now," I interrupted. "We've got to get you to a doctor."

I made a movement toward the curtain, pulling her along with me.

"No." She gulped. "It's Stacey. She's here, too."

I stopped. "Where?"

"In one of the other booths." Her breath was rapid now, shallow and panicked. "He's got her doped up on something."

I thought for a second. Maybe the best thing would be to get Corey out and come back with the Marines. Yeah, this was a no-brainer. Corey came first; she'd suffered enough. I'd be back for Stacey.

"We're going to get you out of here first," I said firmly. "Stacey'll be okay."

I held her up for a few seconds until it felt like she could walk, then I pulled her over to the curtain and we slid through it together.

Corey stiffened and a scream came up into her throat, but didn't make it any farther.

Mousy Caramello stood near the entrance of the hot pink room. In front of him, trapped in the crook of his left arm, was a frail, brittle, heavily drugged Stacey Jameson.

She had her hands on his right forearm, more to hold herself up than to attempt to fight. She wore a torn T-shirt and a pair of jeans with no shoes. Around her left wrist, a pair of handcuffs hung. He wore a pair of camouflage hunting pants and an olive drab T-shirt. His buzz-cut haircut looked like a bristle brush in the dim light.

In his right fist, Caramello held a bone-handled knife with a glistening silver blade at least a foot long. It was the size of a bayonet, and looked like a collector's knife, expensive and deadly.

The knife blade was at Stacey's throat.

"Oh, no." Corey whimpered. "Oh shit, no . . ."

I slipped my right hand into my pants pocket and pulled out the Airweight. It felt heavier in my hand now, but solid. I gently pushed Corey away from me; she leaned against one of the mirrors and fought to stay on her feet. I held the gun out in front of me, both arms straight, both hands on the grip. I sighted down the barrel and put Mousy Caramello's face just above the sights.

"Well, he's got a gun," Caramello said. His eyes were wild, with great dark circles under them, and his cheeks were sunken. The swastika tattoo on his left arm shifted up and down as his arm flexed.

I gritted my teeth until my jaw ached, then somehow managed to relax and take a deep breath. I let the breath out easily and spoke calmly. Don't ask me where it came from, but somehow I managed to pull it off.

"Let her go," I said firmly, "and step away from the door."

He grinned and tightened his grip around her. He ran the blade along Stacey's pale neck. I shifted my line of sight to look into her eyes. There was no fear, only a dull stare coming back at me.

"How'd you find this place?" he asked.

I didn't know if I felt like engaging in discussion with this animal or not, but thought that as long as we were all still talking, nobody was getting hurt.

"Property tax records," I said. "Even Klinkenstein had to pay his taxes."

He stared at me a moment, like he was trying to figure out whether or not to believe me.

"Speaking of Klinkenstein," I continued, "why'd you kill him? And Red Dog, too?"

He laughed, a thin, mean laugh that made something cold come up in me. "That fag kike bastard had it coming," he said. "He wanted me to give up my little girl here. Said it wasn't worth the risk. 'Course he hadn't had any of it, so what'd he know what it was worth?"

"Okay, how about Turner? Why'd he have to go?"

His arm relaxed around Stacey's throat and he shook his head. "I didn't do the Dog, did I, baby?"

Stacey coughed and sniffled. Mousy nuzzled in close to her and buried his face in her hair.

"Tell him, baby, tell him who killed Red Dog."

Stacey shrugged and shifted nervously in his arms.

"Go on," Mousy ordered. "Tell him."

He tightened his grip and shoved her in the lower back with his hip. She grunted and strained against him, then relaxed and let him carry her weight.

"Daddy," she slurred, so low it was almost inaudible.

"Jesus, Caramello," I barked. "You can do better than that."

He made some kind of a motion, something that hurt Stacey. She groaned and jerked in his arms.

"No," she said. "Daddy'd been following him. We didn't know. Billy came home that night and we were—"

She hesitated. "Tell him, baby." Mousy hissed.

"Billy was on me," she said. "And Daddy walked in."

Mousy grinned. "Now was it really Daddy? Or was it *Granddaddy*? Let's see now, who can keep it straight? I'll say this much; the old man's still got balls."

"I don't believe you," I said.

"I didn't kill Red Dog," he said. "But I'm going to enjoy killing you. Real slow, just like Klink."

My arms were getting heavy now, cramping up on me. I was having trouble holding the gun steady. The sights wavered back and forth, first on Mousy, then on Stacey. I felt dizzy myself, as if shock were wearing off and reality setting in.

"You're not killing anybody today," I said. "Let go of Stacey and get out of the way."

"I have a better idea," he said. "You kick that gun over here and maybe I'll let the girl live."

Behind me, Corey sucked in a gulp of air.

"You won't kill her," I said. "You want what she's got, and if you kill her, you'll never get it."

"You got it all wrong," he said. "My little girl wants to die, don't you, baby? She's a mutant, a defective."

"Stacey, you don't want to die," I said. "No matter how bad it gets, that's a one-way solution. You take that way, then that's it. No options left."

Her gaze was far-off, completely without fear, without energy. In her own mind, she was dead now, had been dead for a long time.

"Corey and Stacey and I are leaving this building right now," I said. "If you try to stop us, I will shoot you."

I turned to Corey. "C'mon, let's go."

"*Harry,*" she said, strained.

"Let's go," I said, louder. I took two steps toward Mousy and Stacey, with the gun in my left hand pulled back to my hip, and my right arm extended toward them, hand held out.

"Give me your hand, Stacey. I won't take you home if you don't want to go, but I'm getting you out of here."

"Why?" she asked, her voice plaintive, almost mournful.

"Because, babe," I said. "I don't want you to die."

Mousy yanked her backward, to my right, shifting the two of them toward the row of booths and out of the way of the door frame.

"Corey, come around behind me and start up the steps," I said. Her bare feet on the floor were silent, but I caught a glimpse of her reflection in the mirror as she moved behind me.

"You'd better tell her to be still," Mousy warned. His eyes flickered back and forth and his voice was waver-

ing. I took another step toward him, my hand still outstretched.

"No, this is over," I said calmly. "Let's go, Stacey."

Her eyes jumped up to meet mine with an energy and
a life I hadn't seen before. I nodded yes to her and held
my hand out barely two feet from her now.

Mousy jerked her backward, his arm around her
throat like a vise now, her head tilted back, her eyes
pleading.

"Stop it," I said. "Let her go."

Her right hand flinched, and she slowly raised her
arm toward me, reaching for my hand. Mousy's eyes
went cold for just a moment, then erupted in fury, as hot
and as intense as the hatred I'd felt for him when I first
saw Corey. But in his rage, he'd lost control.

The muscles in his right arm flexed.

"No!" I screamed, bringing the revolver up.

The knife quivered for a part of a second.

Tension under my finger.

Stacey's eyes widened as the knife leapt.

I stepped to the side, trying to sight.

His elbow flashed, a dull flesh-colored streak.

Behind me, Corey screamed.

Stacey's mouth flew open. Nothing came out.

I roared.

Metal flashed, then red, bright, flowing, spurting, red.

He shoved her toward me and charged. Stacey
dropped. I squeezed until something jerked and
snapped, then there was a puff of gray smoke, a red
flash out the side of the gun.

No noise. I heard no noise.

Where was the fucking noise?

Mousy Caramello sprang like a tiger. His mouth was
open in a silent scream, his eyes on fire, the arm with
the knife raised, still coming at me, a red splotch
spreading on the front of the T-shirt.

I stepped back, unconsciously.

Pulled again. A quick, sharp burst of gray smoke and more red flash. Then again.

And again.

Again.

He stopped. There was a moment where he looked directly into my eyes, and I saw him as he was; the connection made, perfect intimacy. No moment like it would ever exist again for either of us. It lasted no more than a second, but for that second we were brothers. The fury and the passion, the fire and hate, went out of Mousy Caramello's eyes. His right arm dropped; the knife fell from his hand, appearing to flutter to the floor in slow motion like an autumn leaf from an oak, dead in its beauty.

He fell.

Corey dashed across the room to where Stacey'd fallen. I dropped the revolver, jumped over Caramello, right behind her.

Stacey was on her back, trying to scream, her eyes flitting side to side in panic, her arms flailing at her neck, her body bouncing off the floor.

Her throat was torn from ear to ear.

Great spurts of red rhythmically splashed over Corey. I shoved her aside, knelt down, did the only thing I knew to do; shoved my hand flat palmed against the side of her neck, against the stream of thick, bright red.

Stacey bounced from side to side. I tried to hold her down, keep her still. To my right, Corey, blood dripping off her face in torrents, in her hair, fell on top of Stacey, her weight forcing the younger girl's arms down.

With my free right hand, I ripped my shirt open and pulled it off my arm, then around me and down my left arm, using it as a bandage, a bundle to press against the neat, nearly surgical slice across her throat.

Still, no noise. The gun, the screaming. Where was the noise? All I heard was a distant roar, like being under a waterfall.

A jolt of pain hit my throat, and I knew where the roar had come from.

Me.

As I knelt next to her, my shirt pressed against her, trying to stop the bleeding without strangling her, her flailing slowed gradually and her eyes dimmed. And I felt the pressure against my hand lessen.

The roaring stopped and there was only silence. Corey pushed herself up off Stacey and I sat down on the floor, cross-legged, and scooped the child into my arms and held her there. We were drenched, soaked. I stared into her eyes and took her hand, the silver handcuff dangling like jewelry.

Her mouth opened, closed, trying in vain to speak. She squeezed my hand. Faint, barely detectable.

A tear welled up in her left eye, then only blankness. I held her as she died.

Corey's hand was on my shoulder.

I bent my head and pulled Stacey to me, then kissed her forehead, my lips wet with her blood.

Chapter 24

When Stacey Jameson died, something inside me died as well. When the light went out of Mousy Caramello's eyes, my light was altered.

Killing someone changes you forever.

The Jamesons entombed Stacey three days later, in a private service at the family crypt in a fashionably old section of Mount Olivet Cemetery. I wasn't invited. A week or so afterward, I carried flowers out and laid them at the door of the vault.

The police held me for questioning, but only for a few hours. It was clear what had gone down. They couldn't even bring me up for the unlicensed handgun. The legislature had added a codicil to the state's wild west law that basically said if you shoot somebody in self-defense, it doesn't matter whether or not you have a carry permit.

Howard Spellman looked like he was going to eat me alive during questioning, but after hearing all the details, he backed off. Guess he figured it'd been a bad enough day already.

Corey went straight to General Hospital but was only kept overnight. Mousy Caramello had indeed raped her, repeatedly and brutally. She would have the shadow of AIDS hanging over her for the next year, until four quarterly test results came back in her favor. But for the time being, none of her injuries were considered life threatening. No broken bones, no injured internal organs; not exactly minor but not deserving of an extended hospital stay either in this new era of managed care.

She'd move slowly for quite some time, though.

As for the emotional scars, the counselor from the victim-assistance program visited Corey in the hospital. She wanted to set up a series of appointments with the volunteer therapists at the local women's center. Corey explained, though, that the only thing she wanted to do was get the hell out of Dodge.

There was no way she was going back to her apartment. Corey took a motel room for a couple of days until we could clean the place out, which mainly consisted of salvaging what little was salvageable and trashing the rest. Caramello had been very efficient.

"I've got cousins in California," she said. "They're good people. They said I could stay with them until I get back on my feet. I'll get a job, establish state residency, maybe go back to school."

"Through with the show bars, huh?"

"For good, Harry," she said, snapping the lid shut on a suitcase. "Never again."

"What about the shrink stuff?" I asked. "You're probably going to need some help getting through this."

"I don't know," she said. "I don't want to think about that now."

"Need any money?"

"I saved a lot of cash while I was dancing."

Good, I thought, 'cause I don't have a freaking nickel to my name.

I borrowed one of Lonnie's pickups and carted her boxes over to the bus station to ship them off. Passing through downtown, I cut right on one of the sidestreets, past the Union Rescue Mission, and saw an enormous hunter green billboard with a scantily clad woman lounging on a couch.

CLUB EXOTIQUE! it read. WHERE THE PARTY NEVER
ENDS!

The next day, I drove her to the Nashville International Airport. She wore a lot of makeup and big dark sunglasses to hide the bruises. We were both strangely quiet, almost awkward, as I drove down Briley Parkway.

At the airport, I helped get her bags squared away, then walked her to the gate. She checked in and got her boarding pass just as the gate attendant started calling rows.

"I guess I'd better go," she said.

"Yeah. Listen, take care of yourself."

She started to go, then turned back. "Harry," she said, hesitating, "I just wanted to thank you for getting me out of that awful place."

"Jesus, Corey," I spewed, loud enough to turn heads. "I nearly got you killed!"

"It was my choice to get involved. You weren't responsible for that."

I couldn't look at her. "Go on. They're going to leave without you."

She touched my chin and turned my head back toward hers, then pulled me down and forward so our noses were almost touching.

"I love you," she whispered. "And I don't ever want to see you again."

There was a lump in my throat the size of Montana. I cleared it and tried to talk. "You ever need anything—"

She raised her finger to her lips, shushed me, then stood on tiptoe and kissed the side of my cheek. A moment later, she turned and was gone.

The day after Stacey's funeral, Detective Fouch got a warrant and searched the Jamesons' house. Locked inside the General's gun case was a German Walther P38, a 9mm souvenir he'd taken off a captured Panzer corps commander somewhere in North Africa. Ballistics took about an hour to confirm that the bullets that killed Red Dog Turner came from that weapon. Stacey had told the truth after all.

General Jameson took Stacey's death hard, and by the time the grand jury got around to deciding whether or not to indict him, there was enough medical evidence to conclude he was too far gone to stand trial. Within a matter of days, he was in a nursing home. I suspect he'll soon be with Stacey.

I learned all this from newspapers, for Betty Jameson wouldn't take my calls. I only tried a few times, then it became clear that I was the last person she wanted to hear from. Emily sounded like she was dealing with her own demons for having helped Stacey run the second time. I don't know what will become of her, her mother, or Emily.

A check arrived from the Jamesons' accountants a week after Stacey's death. They'd paid my invoice, but it was hard money to take.

The story got a lot of play in the news media. I disconnected both my home and office answering machines and took all phones off the hook. I wasn't in the mood to talk to anybody.

I thought I was going to be all right. Just give me a few days off and I'd be back in the game. As time went on, though, I found myself less and less willing to get back in. As journalists will do, they forgot about the Jameson story quickly. But my phones stayed off the hook, and I holed up in my apartment.

Sleep was what I seemed to need more than anything else. I'd wake up at noon, wander around in a fog for a few hours, and then crawl back into bed for an afternoon nap that would last until dinnertime. Then it was either out for a quick bite or open a can of soup, followed by some hours of TV and back to bed. I couldn't even focus enough to read a book.

I'd never experienced anything like it. It wasn't particularly painful, and I wasn't terribly disturbed by it. In fact, it was quite comforting. I'd go days at a time without speaking to anyone, even Mrs. Hawkins downstairs. After trying to reach me for over a week, Marsha finally called Mrs. Hawkins and had her deliver a message, which I dutifully filed away to deal with later. Lonnie had Mrs. Hawkins deliver a howdy-how-the-hell-are-you as well, and I appreciated that.

One night I did sort of feel the need for human company, but without entanglement. So I dressed and shaved, then drove over to Lee's Szechuan Palace for dinner. Mrs. Lee was behind the counter. She looked at me strangely, as if I somehow had grown horns or something.

"Hi," I said. "How are you?"

"I fine, Harry. How ah you?"

"Okay," I replied. "Just thought I'd stop in for a bite and a visit."

She took the pad and scribbled down my order. Then, suddenly, she reached across the stainless-steel counter and patted my hand.

"I read about you bad time in papahs, Harry. We all real sorry foah you."

"It's okay," I said. "Really."

"How you doing?"

"Okay. Just fine. Taking a little time off. Haven't had much vacation in a while. Just thought I'd lie low for a bit, let some of the rough edges grind down."

"Good. Dat real good."

"What do you hear from Mary?"

Mrs. Lee's eyes darkened. "She came home foah break after all," she said. "She bwoke up wit' dat boy. He dump her, I mean. She said he got mad she wouldn't—well, you know."

"Oh, yeah, well. See, things worked out after all."

"I don't know, Harry. Dat's da first time she break up

wit' anybody. I never see her cry like dat before. I not like see my liddle girl suffer."

I stared at her blankly for a moment. "She'll get over it," I said.

Then I took my dinner, ate it silently, went home, and climbed back into bed.

Some days later, I was well into my afternoon nap when I heard a pounding at the kitchen door. I hadn't been dreaming; my sleep lately had been so deep and solid and comforting that all dreams had stopped. I closed my eyelids and it was like drawing down a black screen.

At first, I thought the pounding was a dream, a dream in sound with no video. But then I opened my eyes and the pounding continued.

I was flat out on the bed, in a pair of jeans and an oxford-cloth, button-down-collar shirt. Lately, I'd taken to sleeping in my clothes, at least during the day.

I stirred slowly, sitting up on the edge of the bed.

"Okay, coming," I called.

A couple of shakes of my head and a quick eye rub brought me back to semiconsciousness. I walked into the kitchen barefooted, pushing my hair back across my head.

Marsha was at the kitchen door. I opened it. "Hi."

"Hi," she answered.

"C'mon in. Let me go wash my face off. I was asleep."

She stepped in, passed me as I turned, and walked into the bathroom. I ran the water until I got some heat in it, then doused a washcloth and planted it on my face, tilted my head back, and let it lie there. I hadn't shaved in a couple of days and the cloth felt scratchy. The warmth soaking into my skin, though, felt good. I stood there for a while, just feeling the glow on my face. Finally, I dried off and opened the bathroom door.

Marsha stood by the kitchen sink, leaning against the counter, her arms folded in front of her and one ankle crossed over the other. Something about her seemed different.

"Hi," I said.

"Hello."

"How've you been?"

"Okay," she said. Then after a moment: "Missing you, though."

I shrugged my shoulders. "Yeah, me, too. I just needed a little time. You want some coffee or something? Tea?"

"Got any herbal?"

"Thought you were a coffee drinker."

"Gave it up," she said.

I filled the teakettle, then popped it on the stove and lit a flame under it.

"What have you been up to?" she asked.

"Nothing much," I answered, fumbling through the cabinet looking for the boxes of tea. "Resting mostly."

"I've tried to call, but your phones are always busy. Office and home both."

"Yeah. I took 'em off the hook."

"Hmm, pretty serious," she said.

"Not really. I just needed a break."

She pulled out one of my kitchen chairs and sat down at the table. I put a cup in front of her with the boxes of tea and a jar of honey, then one for me on the other side of the table. I got out a couple of napkins and spoons as well.

"I'm out of milk," I said.

"S'okay. I don't use it."

The teakettle began to burble.

"So when are you going back to work?"

"I don't know. Haven't given it much thought, really." I fiddled with a kitchen towel, folding it and refolding it. "Maybe never. I may retire."

She chuckled. "Harry, you're only forty years old. You sure you're ready for retirement?"

I turned to her. "Oh, I'm very sure of that. Whether I can pull it off or not is a different question."

The teakettle whistled. I took it off and carefully poured water into the two cups, then set it back on the stove.

We stirred tea bags and honey for a few awkward moments. She pulled her bag out and twisted it around the spoon to get the water out, then placed it carefully on a napkin.

"I'm worried about you, love," she said.

"Don't," I said, smiling. "I'm fine. Like I said, just need a little time off."

"I wonder. I had lunch with Howard Spellman last week."

"Yeah? How's the lieutenant?"

"He's fine, Harry, but he's a little worried about you, too."

I laughed. "I didn't know the old bastard even gave a damn."

"He told me what it was like in the basement of that building. He told me everything."

"Yeah, well, he shouldn't have done that."

"Why?" she asked. "Don't think I can take it?"

I glanced at her over the top of my cup as I raised it to my lips. "You cut open dead bodies for a living," I said. "I know you can handle it. It's just that it's, well, it's not something we really ought to talk about anymore, that's all."

"Harry," she said, frustrated, "Howard said the only reason you and Corey are alive is because of what you did. He said there was no way that guy was going to let you go."

"Marsha, can we not—"

"Caramello set in motion a chain of events that you

could not control. You could not have stopped him from killing that girl. No one could have."

I slammed the cup down on the table, hot water splashing on my hands. "I know that," I said. "I know all that."

"Then why have you completely cut yourself off from the rest of the world? It's been over a month, love."

I turned my head, stared out the blinds, through the dirty glass and into Mrs. Hawkins's backyard.

"It's not guilt about killing somebody," I said. "Major bummed, yeah, but not guilt. Mousy Caramello was going to kill me or I was going to kill him. He set it up that way. All I could do was play it."

"Yes, so why don't you—"

"None of that matters. The fact remains that I have killed another human being, and that is something I never thought I would do. Could do. He was coming at me, Marsha, and he had that big fucking bayonet aimed right at my heart and I had to kill him or he was going to kill me. But right at the moment he died, at that split second when the last bit of life went out of him, he looked into my eyes and there was a . . . a *thing* between us. I can't explain it, I can't describe it. But it's real, and it ain't going away.

"And there's Corey," I continued. "I used her, and she got hurt so badly she may never get over it. She's never going to be the same, and it's my fault. And if I hadn't screwed up, Stacey might still be alive."

"That's not true," Marsha insisted. "Stacey Jameson took her own path. Nobody made her run off with those people."

"You don't understand," I said weakly.

"I don't understand it," she said. "I can't possibly understand it because I haven't been there. I just know I want you back in the world."

"I am back in the world. It's just that ever since all

that went down, it's like everything's flat. All voices sound like monotones. Again, I can't describe it. I look outside and see brown trees and green grass and a black asphalt driveway and a blue sky and it's all the same color. Weird, very weird."

She looked down at her cup. "Sweetheart, I think you need some help."

I turned back to her. "Yeah, maybe."

"I'm serious," she said. "You're not dealing with this in a very healthy way."

"I just need a break, Marsh. If this doesn't lift in a little while, then yeah, I'll go put in some couch time."

She reached across the table and took my left hand in both of hers. "Okay," she said. "Deal. But in the meantime—"

"Yeah?"

"I'm not saying this because I'm hovering or trying to be overprotective or because I think you're going to do anything stupid. I just miss you, that's all."

"What are you talking about, love?"

"Will you come spend a few days with me? I'll go in to work during the day, you've got the place all to yourself. I'll leave you the car if you want it. Watch movies, lay around in the Jacuzzi. I don't care. Just get some different surroundings, that's all."

I thought for a few moments, my eyes tracing the outline of her face, her hair. "Yeah, sure, okay. Why not?"

So I packed a bag, threw my bathroom stuff together, and climbed into her Porsche. My eye caught the DEDFLKS vanity plate and it was all I could do to keep from breaking into hysterics.

We drove across town and stopped at the grocery store to pick up provisions. She wasn't in the mood for wine, and I certainly didn't feel like any, so we rented a movie and sat next to each other on the couch until the movie was over and it was time for bed. All evening long, I had the feeling that she wanted to make love, but I had about as much sex drive as a slug. After a while it seemed that she just needed company.

We crawled into bed, exhausted, and within seconds I was back in the empty theatre with a silent black screen in front of me. It seemed as if I were falling, but it was a comforting fall, as if into clouds that would hold me up, keep me off the hard ground forever. Time lost its own sense, and the night passed by without notice. There is consolation and serenity in unconsciousness.

Then there was shaking.

I opened my eyes, cracks of light filtering piecemeal through my gunked-up eyelashes. My mouth was dry, foul, and my head ached as if I had a hangover, although I hadn't touched alcohol for weeks.

Marsha was on the side of the bed, in a satin robe, shaking me by the shoulders. "What?" I muttered, shifting in the bed.

"Wake up, love. C'mon, wake up."

I pushed myself up on my elbow. "What?" I said, still half-asleep.

"I want to show you something."

I shook my head, trying to waggle the cobwebs out. "What? What is it?"

"You awake?"

"Yeah, mostly. What's going on?"

Her left hand came up from her side, holding a white piece of plastic, about the length and width of a Popsicle stick.

"Look." She held the plastic out to me. I reached for it.

"Don't touch that part," she scolded. "It's got pee on it."

I looked up at her. "Pee on it? What the hell are you—"

Then I saw the light in her eyes, and I looked back

down at her hand. In the middle of the white plastic, there were two little windows. Whatever was in the window was a slightly different shade of white than the rest of the stick.

And inside the windows, tiny horizontal lines of blue.

My mouth fell open and I stared at her hand for a moment, then back up to her face.

"You're—?"

She grinned, bit her lower lip, and her eyes filled. Her head bobbed up and down, nodding.

"Well, I'll be—" I muttered.

And then suddenly, my head was in her lap, my arms locked tight around her waist, and I was weeping.

Life.

Printed in the United States
22467LVS00007BB/176